Published by Jason M. Vallery 2021
Copyright © 2021 by Jason M. Vallery

All rights reserved.

Editing by Erin Young and Laura Kinkaid
Cover and illustrations by Casey Gerber

ISBN 978-1-7347479-0-4 (hardback)
ISBN 978-1-7347479-1-1 (paperback)
ISBN 978-1-7347479-2-8 (ebook)

First Edition

Content Warning
People with sensitivities to the following subjects may find some sections of Arboreal Path difficult to read:

Death of an unborn child
Loss of life partner
Combat involving animals

In your naming is existence acknowledged, importance confirmed, and impact actualized.

In your naming you are not forgotten.

You are Leo, and your mark on the world lives on through all who know your name.

CONTENT

Map	vi–vii
Arboreal Path	1–400
Glossary	401–403
Acknowledgements	404
About the Author	405

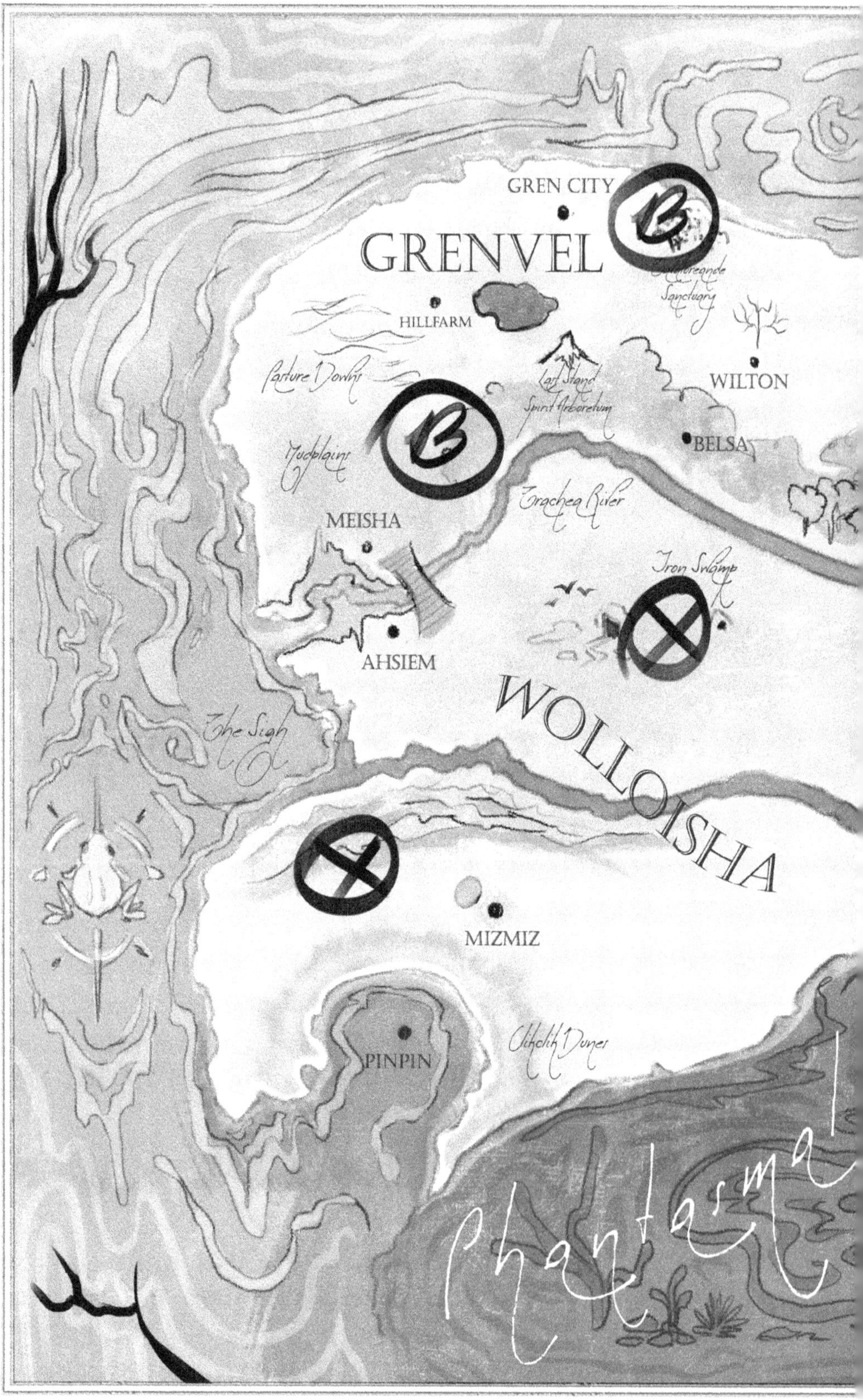
GREN CITY
GRENVEL
Sanctuary
HILLFARM
Pasture Downs
Last Stand
Spirit Arboretum
WILTON
BELSA
Mudplains
Trachea River
MEISHA
Iron Swamp
AHSIEM
WOLLOISHA
The Sigh
MIZMIZ
PINPIN
Clikclik Dunes
Phantasmal

COVETED SOUTH

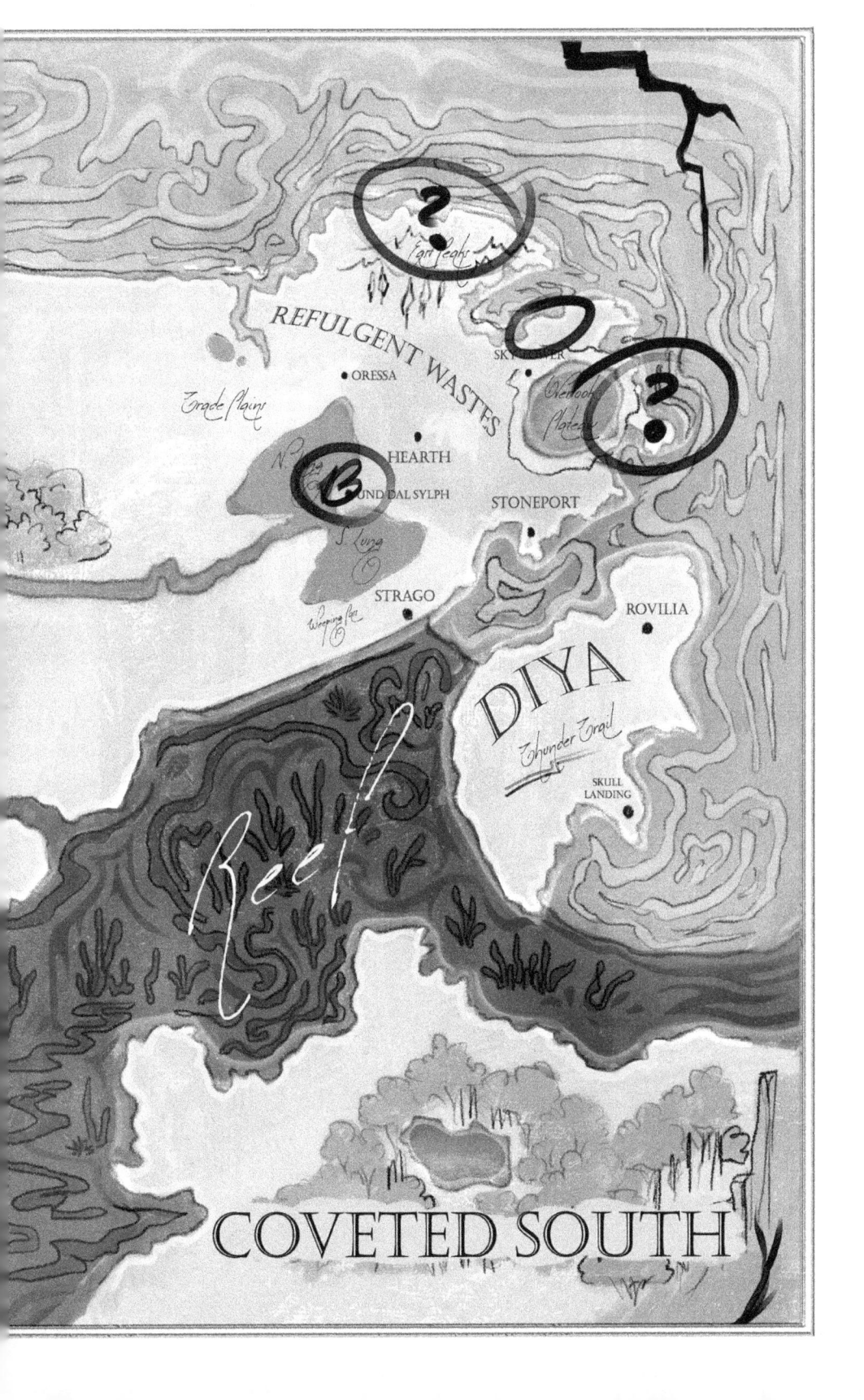

REFULGENT WASTES

- Oressa
- Jade Plains
- Hearth
- Stoneport
- Strago
- Rovilia
- Skull Landing

DIYA

Thunder Trail

Reef

JASON M. VALLERY

ARBOREAL PATH

CHAPTER 1

The shadow donned three faces. One for each life trapped within. Sunken features rippled across a vaguely human-shaped head before giving way to a feminine silhouette. Then masculine. It cycled between each face like a spinning roulette wheel. For the shadow to take form of its own volition... such a thing hadn't occurred in a lifetime.

Hali stared at the tattoo on the underside of her left forearm. A circle with two lines inside, forming a bottomless triangle. The ink changed from white to black like dye spreading through water on her brown skin. As it spread, the two colors swirled and floated along the rune, never settling on one color for long. A cord of black mist connected her tattoo with the shadow spirit.

Face mid-transition, the shadow slithered up the knotted oak tree behind Hali. She scrambled away, letting the book and ragged black coat in her lap fall to the grass. Patting herself in search of her daggers, she found only morning-dew-soaked leaves coating her black tunic and pants.

Any onlookers would assume he was a shadow puppet created by the morning sun and clever use of fire magic, but nobody came to the unkempt, forested park behind Wilton's town library. She was alone. Without weapons or any useful spells prepared. Did it even matter? For all the good they'd do, Hali may as well defend herself with the acorns littering the dirt road.

The shadow's upside-down head peeled itself off the branches and stretched down to stare at her. Hollowed-out eyes with purple grape-like flesh stretched over them. Her stomach churned as the sour stench of oranges wriggled through the air.

With an outstretched boot, Hali attempted to drag her book closer. There weren't any spells inside capable of fighting Kthon, but this cursed spirit couldn't be allowed to reclaim Hali's family.

Hundreds of tiny hands burst from the shadow's stomach and grabbed the book before Hali, passing it up to Kthon's long, spindly-fingered grasp. The spirit scraped a finger along its cover, only to pass right through it. Every hand lining Kthon scratched and tore at his body, and shadow gave way to a pulsating orange underbelly. Kthon's mist rejuvenated, not quite keeping pace with the rebellious hands. Exaggerated, monstrous proportions shrank into that of a human man. His empty eye sockets caved in on themselves, and the shadow's face shifted again. To that of Hali's son—Rasal.

Rasal and Rev—Hali's partner—had won. Or at least their intertwined existence within Kthon had. When Rev had been added to Kthon's collection, she'd somehow fought back, and instead of becoming masks for Kthon to wear, Rasal and Rev had merged separately. A combination of the two, yet neither. Hali had named this new existence Ikazu. It was thanks to Ikazu that Kthon had been trapped deep within his own body—until now.

Hali crashed between the tree's roots, clutching her book as if dropping it again would trigger an earthquake. "How about a warning next time?"

Ikazu's hands latched together into the sign for "Sorry." Although Ikazu couldn't speak, Hali had taught him to use hand signs. Even if Ikazu wasn't truly her family, being able to talk to a facsimile of them still brought its own twisted joy.

"Don't be. This is my fault for getting complacent. There's not much you can do from inside the rune. I promised to set you free from Kthon, but it seems we're running out of time." Hali sighed. "At least you're okay."

Despite lacking facial detail, Ikazu's mouth twitched and contorted into something resembling a smile. No voice, yet Hali could hear his laugh. Like a distant memory of how Rasal might have sounded if he had been given a chance to live.

A recurring thought crossed her mind. *Would Rasal look like me without those shadows obscuring him?* She imagined a man with the same bouncy, dark auburn curls as her. Observing the world through green eyes.

Or would he have taken after Rev more? The man in her head changed. Pink hair with peacock feathers sticking out from the back, extending down past his shoulders.

He couldn't inherit Rev's hair color and feathers, but it was cute to imagine Rasal that way regardless. Rev's feathers were Hali's favorite part of her, so Hali would have been grateful if Rasal had inherited them by some miracle. Hali even had the same purple and green feathers knit into the black cashmere cowl wound tight around her neck.

"Memory please," Ikazu signed. Despite learning many words to express himself, Ikazu rarely said more than this phrase. Sometimes it made her regret teaching him.

"No—wait until I sleep."

Ikazu—and Kthon before him—siphoned energy from Hali's memories while she slept. The ones with Rev were most effective. Whether because Rev liked to reminisce or Rasal found joy in watching his moms interact, Hali wasn't sure. The process gave her vivid, almost lucid dreams. Forced her to live out an approximation of her past.

Sometimes Hali wished he would erase her memories so she could live in ignorance. Pleasant or depressing, they were all painful. But the recollection-fueled nightmares were what motivated her to shun sleep altogether. Even if Ikazu had become better at avoiding nightmares, he slipped up from time to time, and skipping sleep was preferable to experiencing such paralyzing fear.

While Hali wanted Ikazu to recharge, letting him do so in a public park—even if nobody came here—was too risky.

Ikazu drizzled onto the dirt in ribbons.

Pouting? Please don't let that become a trend. "Stop being dramatic. We'll memory hop later, got it?"

His head undulated as if a swarm of insects might burst through until a feminine face sprouted in the back. Rev. Was she going to scold Hali for being mean to their son? Hali smirked, wishing they had such ordinary family moments.

Hali traced the rune on the book's white velvet cover with her finger. It matched the binding rune on her arm. Except the color was a static, faded black. She pried the book open and flipped to her rune reference page in the back. A dozen or so of her favorite runes were listed on the page. Each set of symbols represented a spell written in the language of spirits. Though the effects weren't easy to predict, Hali had become adept at determining a rune's spell based on the symbols. To the point where she'd learned to create her own spells from scratch. No mixture of runes had ever managed to release her family from Kthon, nor destroy him, but Hali tried every day. She'd read every book in Grenvel to glean any new information she could, and most of her life had been spent crafting new spells in the pursuit of her family's freedom. She was close to a breakthrough, but every design she came up with required an immense power source.

Ikazu's hand grasped Hali's wrist.

"I'm trying to read." Her attempt to swat him away only resulted in her hand passing through chilling air. If anyone else had interrupted her like that, she might have thrown a dagger instead. Reading time was sacred, even if this wasn't a for-fun read like a novel.

Chapter 1 Hali

"Memory please," Ikazu's hands repeated. Only this time, Hali swore she heard a voice in her head croak the phrase in conjunction.

"I said later." *Time to return you to the rune.* Hali raised her hand into the air. Blood burned in her body, her veins swelling as light emanated from her binding rune.

Ikazu's gentle features peeled back, revealing Kthon's eyes as shadow tendrils squirmed into Hali's skull. As they burrowed, Hali's world darkened. With a moist click, countless sets of judging eyes creaked open around her. Something Hali hadn't witnessed since a time she'd gone by a different name.

The air within Sky Tower's expansive stone stairwell tingled Sereia's throat like inhaling a cloud of pepper. It was strange seeing the bustling center of research and education abandoned. Every workstation had been left in immaculate condition—beakers and flasks tucked neatly into one corner and stacks of books in the other. As if the tower's alchemists and mages had to follow strict organization guidelines. How did they have time to put everything away so neatly after receiving Rev's evacuation notice? The quarantine zone was so far from here, Sereia would have left a mess to get there in time. Just looking at the workstations made her want to knock everything over.

Two voices spoke at once within Sereia's head. *My celestial, you must focus or this spell will kill you.*

Please don't read my mind, Malakine, Sereia said with her thoughts.

I cannot help that any more than you can help breathing.

Being linked to the celestial spirit was the worst. Sereia had spent years as a celestial without having a spirit take residence in her body. While Malakine's presence greatly expanded Sereia's power… the sooner Malakine was gone, the better. *When this is over, I'm never linking with a spirit again.*

Without my power, what hope do you have of curing the ethereal plague?

Sereia reached the top of Sky Tower and peered over the edge. *The spell may have been your idea, but I'm doing all the work.*

It had taken months to perfect, but Sereia had cured ten people. The method required celestial magic—which only Sereia could perform. She had to absorb the plague into her own body, then use a special binding rune painted on her forearm to keep herself safe while cleansing it. But tens of thousands were infected, and anybody cured ran the risk of becoming reinfected. Somehow, Sereia needed to get every drop of the plague at once. Including the bits lingering in the air.

Clasping her hands together in a vain attempt to appear ready, Sereia said, *You're only here so I can afford the blood toll for a spell of this magnitude.*

Runes had been painted along the tower's base and up the walls. The result of several days' worth of labor on Sereia's part. Being the highest point in Thauma, this was the only spot where the spell could properly cascade through the entire country.

She walked to a massive telescope at the tower's edge and glanced into it, adjusting until the tiny tents of Rev's quarantine zone came into view. People the size of ants wandered about as doctors tended to the infected.

Studying the plague had been enough to convince Sereia to take this job. Instantaneous loss of magic always came first. Even the best mages succumbed. Which element of magic sparked within their blood didn't matter either. So long as somebody was born with magic, this plague could take hold.

The second symptom was far worse in Sereia's mind. Fading memories. Witnessing children become strangers to their parents in days was by far the worst. The thought of forgetting Rev and Rasal drove her the whole way through developing runes to amplify her celestial magic's reach.

Chapter 1 Hali

Malakine's deep voice drowned out the softer as they said, *Use my power to open the Lunar Vault. With it, you can power your runes safely.*

A jagged, shimmering green scar lingered in the sky. The Lunar Vault. A reminder of when it threatened to rain destruction onto the world beneath it. Even with years more experience and Malakine's help, Sereia knew harnessing the Vault's power would cause more harm than good. Sealing the Vault was the first thing she'd done as a celestial. The whole reason she became one to begin with. And now everybody expected her to repeat that success here with the plague.

Great idea. End one disaster by causing another. Opening the Vault would kill hundreds of thousands of people in every country, not just Thauma. Grenvel, Wolloisha, Diya... Sereia said, tugging on one of her curls. *I sealed it for a reason. Our power is enough. And should I die from the blood toll... exchanging my life to save those countries is an easy choice.*

And your son? Malakine asked.

As if on cue, Rasal kicked Sereia's ribs from the inside.

Sereia patted her protruding belly in gentle reassurance. *This would've been easier in a month, but the plague won't wait for Rasal to be born. Make sure we survive. And if I hit etheric drought, you can escape with my son.*

My celestial cannot die. Do you realize how long I waited for a new one?

Anyone can become one. I'm expendable.

Rasal will be protected. Malakine's presence sputtered as they receded, hiding somewhere within her veins. The unpleasant feeling of being stretched over Malakine like a couple-sizes-too-small dress remained, but at least there was quiet. Putting up with this was worth it for the cure and Rasal's safety.

Kneeling at the tower's center, Sereia painted a diamond and connected its corners to the runes on the tower's sides, then placed her hand in the

Arboreal Path

diamond's center. Each rune took its toll, boiling Sereia's blood. Light filled the lines, tracing a path along the runes until Sky Tower became a blinding beacon. Pink, green, and purple vapor wafted off the runes and poured over the tower's edges, stretching across Thauma and beyond.

The blood toll was a mere tingle as the spell connected her to the plague lingering throughout Thauma's air and within the country's people. Sereia hadn't imagined Malakine's help would trivialize such an expensive spell. There wasn't even a hint of lightheadedness, much less the intense boiling she had experienced while curing a single person.

The vapor crawled back up the tower, changing from its bright ethereal colors to white as it surrounded Sereia with a lovely citric scent. Every muscle in her body tensed as she pulled the plague-infused vapor towards herself.

Standing with her arms towards the sky, Sereia's skin might as well have been melting off her bones as the plague seeped in through her binding rune. Its black ink quivered as little white dots speckled the rune, and she coughed a cloud of white and black fog onto the stone floor. The fog writhed. Something about it was different than she had seen previously. It was alive. A spirit, much like Malakine and the ones from Sereia's celestial trials. Had her spell somehow pulled in a spirit?

Before she could ask Malakine for help, the fog shaped itself into a jagged claw and latched onto Sereia. It dragged her in as a gaunt face with eyeless sockets formed.

A second claw crept from within and pierced Sereia with an unnaturally long, crooked finger. She recoiled as a crushing headache took hold. Each time it prodded, it merely passed through her as harmless as a cloud—except for the worsening scraping in her skull. Her own heartbeat blasted in her ears in step with each pump of blood threatening to burst her veins.

Everything became muted as the claw ripped Malakine from Sereia, forcibly unlinking her from the spirit. Obscured by the deepening fog, only their glowing white half was visible until they vanished into a circle of glittering stars.

Chapter 1 Hali

Gray mist dripped from the fog's fingers into its embedded face, and Sereia's insides twisted. She screamed, but no sound came. Crying cut through the silence as the fog coalesced into the appearance of a human baby.

The shadow released Hali, face-changing from Kthon to Rev. The mist faded as the binding rune reined the now-feminine Ikazu in and trapped her within Hali's forearm tattoo.

Twice in a day you've saved me, Ikazu. Keep weakening Kthon for me until I figure out these new runes.

Memory hopping like that was worse than the dreams. Something about the way Kthon used the ability increased every painful sensation a thousandfold, and he obsessed over reminding her of every mistake. Every flaw.

Reaching for her book again, Hali stared at the runes she'd used for the ethereal plague cure. *If I was still a celestial, it would be simple to power a rune and free my family.*

Was that the solution? Hali may not have had celestial magic anymore, but she knew how to unlock it. It might not be possible for anybody to become a full-fledged celestial again, but only basic celestial magic would be necessary. All she needed was somebody to teach.

CHAPTER 2

Books and games of both the board and card variety lined little shelves on the bark walls of Tio's tree home. Flicking the leaf-shaped charms dangling from the silver bracelet on his left wrist, he checked each for its sharpness until he found one that still had its edge. Blood trickled down golden-brown skin as he pricked a finger. Placing the hand against the wall, pressure built in his veins and the tree wriggled in response. The blood evaporated, consumed for his flourish's magic. The tree accepted his guidance and its bark stretched into a new shelf.

Homes like Tio's were a dying style. Not enough druids to tend to them. Newer districts in Belsa resorted to building homes by molding dirt and stone with the earth flourish. Not preferred, but at least they weren't built with dead wood like most of Grenvel. Seventeen people had been born with the nature flourish in the past seventy years, and only fourteen were still alive.

Tio placed his newest card game, *Volatile Lemurs*, by itself on the pristine shelf. It looked lonely. *Guess I need to add to my collection to fill this space out.*

Chapter 2 Tio

Playing seemed unlikely since it required at least three participants, but the cute cartoon lemur on the box was irresistible. It was asking a bit much of him to gather people. Belsa was a sparse city to begin with, and Tio didn't go out of his way to make friends. Plenty of his other games could be played solo, so he had options when nobody was around. Which was always.

Purring came from below. A fuzzy black cat hopped off one of many cushions thrown about his floor and rubbed against Tio's legs. He petted Sir Fluffyboi—the name she'd chosen for herself—in return.

"Feed me, kitten," Sir Fluffyboi said, following with a meandering meow.

His own familiar referred to him as a child, despite him being twenty-six. All because speaking to animals didn't come naturally to Tio. Other druids had deep bonds of respect with their animal familiars. Practicing seemed the obvious choice, but the cat slept through her days. Talking to other animals was more interesting than talking to people, but it scared him in equal measure. What kind of druid was he if holding simple conversations with animals was a struggle? People would laugh. Besides, leaving home was too much trouble. Tio always kept that excuse in his repertoire, so it would be ready at a moment's notice.

Tio tried his best to say, "You ate already." But, "I ate all your food," came out instead.

Sir Fluffyboi clawed at his leg in response. "I'll go hunt for myself then, kitten." She hopped out of the tree's open circular window.

Hunt? Go begging on the streets, you mean.

Brushing a cat's worth of fur off his ill-fitting pants and oversized brown tunic, Tio grabbed some tangled green vines with yellow leaves to cinch his clothes. He didn't care to maintain his appearance under ordinary circumstances, but a meeting with Belsa's druid Conclave was more than a little important. Even with the makeshift vine belt, Tio's tunic was more like a robe, with sleeves drooping off his elbows and the bottom almost touching his knees. Shopping for clothes for this meeting hadn't occurred to him before, so this would have to do.

Tio wrapped his new green cloak, embroidered with the Conclave's golden fig-leaf insignia, around his shoulders and clasped the matching metal leaf. Combing back his short, grassy-green hair with his fingers, he slipped into his woolen shoes as he walked through the drapes that served as his front door.

A steep drop to his right led to the twig-and-grass-covered ground level, where people tended to sheep and blackberry brambles. Air-flourished mages guided animals with gentle gusts. A water mage misted the plants. Soil churned under the power of earth mages, and fire mages checked on nearby lanterns.

Some outsiders had trouble adjusting to Belsa's way of life, but Tio had felt at home right away. Learning to treat flora and fauna as equals made sense to him. Other parts of the country harmed animals for food, supplies, territory, and even sport. Belsans—whether druids, mages, or pallids—only used renewable goods created by plants or animals, such as vegetables, fruit, milk, wool, silk, leaves, or other non-vitals. In exchange, druids gave food, shelter, or protection. No harm came to anything here except in self-defense, and even then, the defender was likely to become a pariah. A dedicated druid once struck a deal with a wolf pack to act as their servant. He did anything the wolves wanted as long as they agreed to protect Belsa's wildlife from other predators and hunters. Nature magic was key to this way of life. Mediating trades was impossible otherwise.

A series of cypress-tree homes stretched ahead of Tio. Belsa's old residential district. The sun-blocking canopy was his favorite part. Afternoons got hot in Belsa, even in fall. It was also the least crowded area, and Tio had built his home on the edge of this district with isolation in mind. Each tree connected to the next with thick branches that could pass for trunks, wide enough for five people to walk side-by-side.

Chapter 2 Tio

Jumping off and breaking his legs seemed more appealing to Tio than walking past those homes. As few people as there were, somehow somebody tried to talk to him every time he took this route.

Suppressing his desire to go the long way, Tio forced his obstinate legs to carry him through the residential district. Red, yellow, and brown leaves sprinkled the walkways as he moved, careful not to step on them to preserve the pretty aesthetic. Fall had only just started, so plenty of gaps were within reach of his long legs.

He reached the residential district's end and rushed down the stairs, skipping every other step. At the bottom, he nearly crashed into a man carrying an enormous watermelon. Tio squeaked out a barely audible apology before the man spoke up.

"Hey, Tio, how's it going?"

Hoping to dissuade further discussion, Tio stammered out a short response. "H-Hi. I'm fine." He stopped in his tracks when the conversation didn't end on the spot. *You know better, Tio. Be more assertive. Say you don't have time.*

"Great, great. Me too! What was your subject in school again? Eth… ether—"

A former classmate? Can't remember his name, so let's call him Melonlord.

"Transmutational etheric alchemy." Ether studies sufficed, but Tio found the nonsensical descriptive title way more fun to say. People's eyes always bugged out of their head like it was either the most impressive or ridiculous thing they'd ever heard. Generally followed by judgemental questioning, arguing he might as well have been mastering acting or religion for all the good studying ether accomplished.

"Yeah, that," Melonlord said. "There was a rumor the Conclave hired you because of it. Your cloak confirms it! Who would've thought?"

Being a druid and having strange schooling granted him more than enough fame, but when the Conclave hired him seven months ago… Now the city itself knew his name.

Okay, now's the time to excuse myself. "It's true. Actually, I have a meeting—"

"Are you part of the winter solstice celebration? I heard all the druids are growing a new great tree. I'm hoping it's for a tavern. A modern place to hang out would be great."

A tavern? Tio finally remembered Melonlord from school. He spent more time planning parties than paying attention in class and had the air flourish but might as well have been a baker with no flour. Not that flexing skill with magic was the purpose of attending school. It wasn't one of Grenvel's academies after all, which were less schools and more mage training centers.

Druids weren't accepted into the academies. Most magic was about exerting control over an element, but nature could never control—only communicate and influence. Given how rare it was and how different it was to teach, none of the academies believed it was worth employing druid teachers, so people born with the nature flourish had to come to Belsa if they wanted to learn how to use it. Tio was one such outsider, born in Ahsiem on the Wolloisha's side of the Trachea. If it weren't for his mom convincing him to learn to use his flourish, Tio would be working the mines in Iron Swamp.

Without giving Tio a chance to respond, Melonlord continued, "Are you going to be the next Conclave elder? There hasn't been a new one in thirty years. Guy like you, bet you could grow the new tavern tree by yourself, am I right?" He nudged Tio with his elbow, grinning as if the two were the best of friends.

Dying inside, Tio snatched his arm away and rubbed it as if wiping away filth. *Would it be rude to tell him not to touch me?* With an exasperated sigh, he said, "Look, the Conclave is waiting for me. I have to go." Tio walked away without waiting for a response.

"Oh, okay! Didn't mean to be a bother—"

Whatever else Melonlord had to say was somebody else's problem now. Brown cypress trees shifted to white ash trees, marking his arrival

Chapter 2 Tio

in the education district. Belsa's library and school looped around the district in a large wooden circle consisting of sixteen large sideways trees. At the back, a redwood tree overshadowed Belsa. That was the Conclave's meeting tree.

Hordes of people wandered the plaza with an assortment of birds, wolves, and deer roaming amongst them. Students hauled their books to class in grass satchels, mages headed to the library to hone their craft, and various Belsans climbed the redwood's bark stairs to take their concerns to the Conclave. Tio's hands shook until he clasped them tightly together.

Deep breaths, he chanted in his head as he squeezed through the crowds, trying his best not to touch anybody.

Controlling his breathing calmed his nerves all the way to the redwood. Stairs molded from the skyscraping tree's bark led from the bottom of its trunk to the top. About three quarters of the way up, a big hole guided Tio to the waiting room.

It seemed as if more people were stuffed inside the small room than he'd passed to get here. Of course, that was impossible, but his brain didn't listen to reason. Perched on a stone, a small, shiny yellow warble acted as a receptionist for druids. Tio scanned the stone up and down until he found his name.

Malakday | Twelfth bell | Mona, pastry chef
Sylday | Third bell | Tio, Conclave druid

Third bell? That was later than Bel had mentioned. Unless he'd misheard her? All the names above him were from yesterday, so they weren't busy.

The bird chirped at him. "Tio, you're early. Please take a seat. We'll be with you in a moment."

With slow and deliberate words, he tried to respond with, "Can you ask the Conclave if they can meet now? I was told first bell." Instead, it came out more like, "I'm number one—tell the old people I'm here." He fiddled with his bracelet, cursing himself for butchering the words.

15

It gave a condescending song in return. "Just sit, Tio. They're preparing for your meeting as we speak."

Green floor cushions and rugs covered the floor, and most were occupied. He looked for one without people next to it, so he could sit alone. A series of scoffing whistles urged him to hurry up. Either that bird disliked Tio or its job. Probably both.

Rushing across the room, Tio sat squished between two people and only then realized how exhausted he was. *I need to exercise more.*

People chattered all around him, nearly shoulder to shoulder. It felt like every word of every conversation floated through the air, smothering him. Was it just him or were there thousands of people in the room? Tio tugged on his cloak as the racket threatened to drown him in a sea of words. He closed his eyes.

"Was that Tio? He had a hard time with the receptionist," a shrill voice said.

"I know, right? The Conclave must be desperate for druids at this point," a burly voice said.

Everything sounded more and more warped, as if they were speaking through a glass bottle.

A third voice whispered, "Shameful, truly."

His breaths echoed. Walls inched closer. Closer. Tio was trapped. His hands jittered. *Deep breaths.* Hoping to snap out of it, he poked his fingers into the dull-edged leaves of his bracelet, but nothing happened. *Deep breaths.*

A beak pecked him on the forehead, and aggressive tweets raided his ears. "Pay attention, chick. I said the Conclave is ready to see you."

Tio gave the bird a blank stare. "Sorry."

He glanced at the sea of people with black, red, brown, and blonde hair. Nobody was talking about him at all. Even if they were, none had the nature flourish necessary to have overheard the bird. His anxiety was playing tricks on him. Again.

Chapter 2 Tio

An acolyte approached the bird's stone wearing flowy white robes with green triangles along the bottom and on the sleeves. The outfit was associated with healers, though druids couldn't heal anymore. One of many powers they'd lost over the last few centuries. Seeing the robes in person made him appreciative of his cloak. It was fashionable by comparison.

From the top of the stone's list down to Tio's name, all the engravings filled in until there was no evidence they had existed. The acolyte carved several new names and times on it before giving Tio a smile that screamed, "I'm just here to do my job." *I can relate.*

"Please follow me," she said.

Relieved to get away from the crowd, Tio exhaled once more for good measure.

After traveling one more story up and passing through an extravagant green curtain, all three Conclave elders stared at him like something straight out of a nightmare. They were seated at a square table, with one empty chair waiting for him. The furniture grew from the redwood itself and remained attached to the floor—an older, inconvenient style of seating nobody used anymore.

That's going to get annoying. What if I need to adjust my chair? Tio turned to thank the acolyte, but she was already gone.

"She won't be joining us," Ren said as she brushed her green fishtail braid from her shoulder. Her tone always made Tio think she hated him, at least compared to the other elders. She was even taller than Tio, which was a feat considering he was accustomed to always being the tallest in the room.

"Your first meeting as an official member of the Conclave. I look forward to seeing what you've brought for us today," said the soft-spoken Pai. His name always reminded Tio of food. *Maybe I should bake a blueberry pie when I get home?*

Pai's hair and long beard had grayed with age, but flecks of teal were still sprinkled throughout. Tio wasn't looking forward to the inevitable religious debate Pai would drag this meeting into.

A notebook and pencil waited for Tio at the empty seat across from Ren. He looked to his left at Bel.

Bel gave a warm smile, sans a few teeth. "I know how you like to draw while we bicker amongst each other."

Her name was the most common in Belsa for all genders—which made it difficult to know if people were referring to Archdruid Bel or some random person. Tio couldn't understand why anybody would voluntarily name their kid after a city.

At 113, Bel was the oldest living druid. She was also the shortest of the elders, even without being hunched over. Her short curly hair looked like ocean waves the way the white and blue mixed together. Given her age, it was surprising any blue remained. Pai would have people believe it was a sign Bel had a strong connection to the spirit tree, like their ancestors.

When Tio sat, he found a mural dominated his view. Splotches of haphazard paint on the wall depicted the spirit tree as branching pure light atop a yellow whale's back—back when people believed the Corporeal Realm resided on a frog's head with its three eyes as moons. Cosmic whales and frogs didn't strike Tio as the answer to life's big questions, but the imaginative nature of the past never disappointed.

Pai smacked his lips as he prepared to speak. A sign he was about to put on his Conclave elder voice. "Tio, you've had months to verify your claim that the spirit tree is dying. Did you find anything at Spirit Arboretum?"

Tio made a conscious effort to sound knowledgeable. "The arboretum's haze barrier had no outward signs of weakness, but I detected some abnormalities." As he spoke, he drew lines on the notebook, connecting them into triangles or squares. "How ether surges form barriers is unknown, but the relationship between surges and magic is clear from Thaumic texts and Diyan enchanting books."

Ren stood and slammed her hands on the table. "Get on with it! And stop drawing. Show a little respect."

Chapter 2 Tio

All the words in Tio's head fell out through his ears. How was he supposed to respond to that?

Pai's words soothed the sting. "Ren, let the young druid speak. This is his meeting, after all. We're here to listen."

"And have my time wasted?" Her chair, still attached to the floor, scooted forward and forced her back into it.

Bel tapped her fingers against the table. "Sit down. You're an embarrassment to your namesake."

She always knew where to hit somebody. Ren was named after Drassil Ren, the first known druid. Something Ren was proud of and quick to remind people of, despite it just being a name.

"Tio, please continue. Skip to what you discovered. We have enough background," Bel said, rubbing her temples.

With regained composure, Tio resumed. "Ether leaks from surges regularly, by all accounts giving us magic. I determined ether has five components. Upon close examination, four shared several similarities with blood-test results from mages of each flourish. Since nobody has performed similar analysis on nature-flourished blood, I believe the fifth component to be nature."

Combined triangles formed a circle on Tio's notebook as he juggled talking and drawing. "The nature component was smaller than the others. About one thousandth the size. I believe this is linked to why druids have become so rare."

Pai stroked his beard. "The disparity between these 'components' is eerily close to last year's Grenvel census results."

Adding antlers to the circle on his notebook, Tio said, "In addition, ether has had a drastic reduction in overall output even in my brief time investigating. The nature flourish will be gone by this time next year. The other flourishes will share the same fate within three generations."

"As dire as that sounds, what does your discovery have to do with the spirit tree?" Ren asked.

"Tio, could you elaborate for our dear Ren?" Bel's words had a sweetness to them, but a venomous tang coated Ren's name.

Putting down his pencil, Tio glanced at each elder as he spoke. "Surges, particularly those with haze barriers, once facilitated long-distance communication for the Conclave. Our historical archives describe it as 'speaking through the roots of Empyrea.' If Empyrea's roots are inside surges, then I propose the reduced ether output reflects Empyrea's health."

Ren slouched in her chair. The look on her face said she was taking in everything he'd stated while searching for a flaw. "Bel, you're the one forcing us to give this theory credence. Suppose it's true. What are we supposed to do with this information?"

Bel set a jewelry box on the table and removed thirteen rotted seeds from it one by one. Each of the first seven were more decomposed than the last. "Since the time of Drassil Ren, these have been passed down from archdruid to archdruid. Empyrea's seeds. The first rotted long before any among us were born. Three more have done the same in the last two years."

If Bel hadn't already mentioned what they were, Tio would've sworn the six healthy seeds were white ether lights meant to be strung up as winter solstice decorations.

"These are all we have left," Bel said.

Pai gasped so hard he choked and coughed spit into his beard.

"When were you planning to share the news with the rest of us?" Ren asked as she leaned over to get a good look.

Tio couldn't take his eyes off the seeds. A subtle mist surrounded them—they really were made of ether. White was an unusual color for ether, which usually came in shades of pink, purple, and green. What made it stranger was ether only became visible in high concentrations or when stimulated by magic.

Bel returned the seeds and closed the box. "Previous archdruids assumed they were simply expiring as all seeds do when not returned to soil. I did not believe it cause for alarm until now."

Gears turned rapidly in Tio's head as he tried to place this new puzzle piece into the equation. "Why not plant them before they rot?" *It could be valuable to at least see what would happen.*

Pai said, "Plant Empyrea's seeds in the Corporeal Realm? Blasphemous."

After druids first noticed their numbers dwindling, a new subsect had formed that treated Empyrea as a deity of sorts. Tio contributed it to loss of knowledge... or desperation. The rest of Grenvel treated the spirit tree as a druid religion too. This played a big part in druids losing their place in Grenvelian society, since the country had grown wary of religion after casting out the previous Old Faith regime. But how could one prove the existence of Empyrea when the only evidence was old text, same as any religion?

Pai continued, "What right do we have to plant them without asking first?"

No argument there. Pai had a point. Druids always asked permission before using their flourish on any flora. Connecting with magic was enough to allow a quick exchange of thoughts, but how did one ask permission of Empyrea when it couldn't be seen or touched?

"Each archdruid tells the next not to plant them unless the need is dire, but I don't think blasphemy has anything to do with it, Pai. Drassil Ren and other archdruids planted plenty. Two failed attempts can be found in Spirit Arboretum. I fear the reason for failure was lost to time, but they meant to renew our flourish," Bel said.

It's a shame nobody ever taught archdruids to write things down.

Tio shaded in the triangles on his notebook. "Maybe no locations left are capable of supporting one?" It may be a leap, but a seed from Empyrea could require ether to grow. In that case, the issue likely involved finding a place with sufficient ether to facilitate the seed's growth. Like a surge.

"Enough of this. If the spirit tree is dying then the need is 'dire,' but what is it you expect us to do about it, Tio?" Ren asked.

"You don't have to do anything. I believe I can find a way inside ether surges, with enough time. Just give me an official blessing to do so, and your part is done."

"To step inside would surely lead you to the Ethereal Realm! Mortals cannot—should not be on the same plane of existence as Empyrea. It would be against our teachings. The spirit tree sits above all things." Pai was even more dedicated than Tio thought.

It seemed he was taking a literal interpretation of an old proverb. *Empyrea is to be aspired to but never attained. Leave it to Pai to twist a life lesson about working hard without seeking perfection into dogma.*

Ren smirked. "Young Tio thinks himself Empyrea's equal." She never passed on opportunities to rile Pai up.

Before Pai could respond, Tio said, "The other side of a haze barrier is not the Ethereal Realm. Surges are points where ether leaks through the Ethereal Realm to ours. Haze barriers form when too much ether sits in one location, and acts as a dam, controlling how much ether gets to us. It isn't as simple as walking into the Ethereal Realm—"

He stopped himself before he got even more technical and lost his audience. Diyans theorized the Corporeal and Ethereal Realms sat on top of each other, occupying the same space somehow, but it wasn't a vacation destination to pick out on a map.

Bel brought the conversation back on topic. "You have my blessing."

"Breaching the haze barriers could be dangerous. Both for the boy and for us. I can't approve of this course of action." Ren sounded concerned. Almost. She was either trying to suppress it to save face or didn't really believe what she said. Tio couldn't decide which was more plausible.

Pai stroked his beard harder this time, as if he were trying to remove crumbs before anybody noticed. "If surges don't lead to the Ethereal Realm… I feel better about allowing a druid through. What is your plan? Should we rally the other druids to go with you?"

Chapter 2 Tio

Tio had no clue what to expect. For all he knew, the inside of a surge was identical to the outside. One thing he knew for sure was that he didn't want other druids involved. Ideally, he would work alone. The only people worth bringing would be fellow ether experts.

For once, Tio was happy to hear Ren speak. "Between winter preparation, Spirit Arboretum maintenance, fauna trade routes, city renovations... we have no druids to spare."

No longer in need of the distraction, Tio put his pencil down. "Don't worry, help is unnecessary. I'll start with the two known haze barriers at Spirit Arboretum and Tovaloreande Sanctuary. All I'm going to do is investigate. Finding Empyrea's roots and checking for damage is my priority. With luck, a way to heal it will be revealed."

White teeth shone through Pai's beard. "Healing the spirit tree... what a noble goal. A righteous goal. You have my blessing."

Bel looked to her left. "Ren?"

Ren straightened her posture. "I still believe we don't know enough to put a druid's life at risk. We are too few." She paused and looked Tio dead in the eyes. "Do what you want, but if you get a single hint what you're doing will cause yourself or our people harm... abandon this quest for Belsa's sake. You have my blessing."

Bel handed the jewelry box to Tio. "Take the seeds. Better with you than sitting in my stuffy house. Learn what you can from them."

Ren took a pen and paper from a bag hanging on her chair, writing as she talked. "Tovaloreande Sanctuary has been closed off from the public for a couple years. You're going to need a letter of introduction to get entry permission from Gren Consortium. Don't expect them to do you any favors. Our word isn't worth much these days, I'm afraid."

With druids out of favor, Gren Consortium had taken over as Grenvel's sole governing force. Every major group of people had representation except druids. Mages had the headmasters of Grenvel's mage academies. Scholars had the head librarian. Merchants had the president of Sipherra,

Arboreal Path

a mining and engineering company. Even farmers had somebody, though he was more well known as the leader of the Dreamer mercenaries than for farming.

"Thank you. I'll prepare to leave tonight."

Breaching Spirit Arboretum's haze barrier alone was unlikely. His first destination was Wilton to discuss his discovery with Barbaroli Pensa. None of Tio's findings would have been possible without Barbaroli, since he'd written one of the few modern books on ether.

At this time of year, he set up shop at Wilton's makeshift marketplace, Tent Town. Last year, Barbaroli had visited Belsa to meet Tio and discuss ether, showing him a special map of Our Stranded Lands. Ether surge locations all around Grenvel, Wolloisha, and Refulgent Wastes had been marked on it. He'd even included whether the surge had formed a haze barrier.

If all goes well with Barbaroli, we can recruit his protégé, Rachel. No doubt about it. The three of them could solve the Empyrea dilemma.

Tio arrived home to find Sir Fluffyboi slapping his new game off the shelf. *Never change, jerk.*

Hugging the black cat, Tio clasped his hands and poked a finger into the sharp leaf charm to draw a drop of blood. Talking may prove difficult for Tio, but he couldn't mess up words in a communion—a direct connection between the minds of both parties. Unlike speaking, communing required a blood toll. The cost was lower the higher the druid's bond with the animal was, so it was often reserved for familiars like Sir Fluffyboi.

Sir Fluffyboi's thoughts indicated more of the same. *That was fun. I'm hungry, Tio.*

Emotions slid between them, intermingling until distinguishing druid from cat proved difficult. Relief. Love. Happiness. Anxiety.

Tio sent his own thoughts in return. *I'm leaving Belsa, probably for a long time. Take care of yourself, okay? Don't leave our home in shambles either. You won't like me when I'm angry.*

Purrs joined the linked thoughts. *You don't get angry. Everybody knows that, kitten.* Sir Fluffyboi rubbed the top of her head against Tio's. *Don't worry, I'll keep the place warm for you. My fur will be everywhere.*

The mental connection ended when the hug was released, sending waves of relief through Tio's veins like air being released from a balloon. Tio hadn't traveled for more than a week at a time since coming to Belsa. It was unclear how long his investigation would take, so it was good Sir Fluffyboi was home to say goodbye.

Given how tired he'd been after climbing the Conclave's meeting tree, Tio thought it wise to bring an okapi to ride and carry his things. Besides Sir Fluffyboi, the long-necked horses with black-and-white striped legs were the only animals that treated him with respect despite his speech impediment.

After gathering veggies, fruit, bread, and pastries into his grass satchel and strapping a sleeping bag to his back, Tio entered Belsa's uninhabited forest to find an okapi.

CHAPTER 3

Late again. By this point, Alim knew they hadn't left a good impression. But who schedules a lecture at first bell? Either the library hated sleep or ancient magic wasn't a popular subject. Of course, Alim chose to believe the former. *Librarians are a cranky bunch. Knock over a bookcase one time…*

"No running in the plaza," a guard said as she stepped in front of Alim. "Headed off to war with that armor and fancy helmet?"

Being outsized was normal for Alim, but this person made them feel tiny. Positive it would annoy the guard, they drummed a finger against their worn-down steel helmet on one of many small dents. Each repetition soothed Alim's nerves.

"I'm late for a lecture is all." Alim pointed towards the three-story-tall library with its glass walls and roof.

"Armor doesn't seem necessary for that." The guard gave Alim a suspicious once-over, as if examining their sun-engraved steel cuirass for vulnerable points.

"You haven't seen the size of the books in there. Now, if you'll excuse me..." Alim walked around the guard, but she grabbed their bare arm and stopped them.

"Keep your visor up, kid. It's rude to hide your face," she said.

With their helmet's twin crescent moon visor down, only Alim's pale chin and mouth were visible. Orange and yellow paint, on the left and right moons respectively, had chipped and faded from frequent exposure to the unending harsh sunlight in Refulgent Wastes. Their dad always said the visor's eye slits made Alim's gray eyes appear like roaming storm clouds. Even lifting the visor didn't reveal any distinguishing facial features, which they preferred.

Kid? I'm twenty-four. "Nobody else in Wilton minds my helmet." Based on the fire-breathing mole—a pyre dredger—on the guard's gambeson, she was from the city of Oressa. "But I'm sure you'll recognize this." Alim dug a long yellow cloth out from under the bracer on their left wrist and dangled it.

The guard's eyes widened, and she released Alim. "Sorry, didn't know Dreamers were posted in this backwater. Forgive me."

Former Dreamer, but she doesn't need to know that. Alim shrugged as they tucked the cloth back into their bracer. "I'm not 'posted' anywhere. Move aside."

With no further delays, Alim pushed past the guard and continued through the brick plaza. The library's large open interior was bombarded by sunlight from all directions, cooking Alim within their armor. All three floors were visible from the bottom due to glass floors and walls. A neat effect, but they'd lost count of how many times it had made them trip. The concept was an extension of the glass ceilings libraries had across Grenvel due to being converted from abandoned Old Faith churches, where the glass allowed gods to witness the worship—or something along those lines.

The first two floors were packed with people and shelves, but the top was still barren. This was where Hali's classroom was. Alim climbed the bookshelf-lined spiral staircase in the center of the library, fighting the falling sensation accompanying each step. At the top, they found the classroom and nudged the door open.

"Lecture's canceled. What's the use in a sign if nobody reads it," Hali sighed, looking up from a white velvet book. The binding style reminded them of old tomes found in Refulgent Wastes. With only slightly yellowed paper and frayed edges, it didn't appear hundreds of years old. Like somebody had taken impossibly good care of it.

"Oh, Alim!" She stood and straightened her asymmetrical, jagged coat. Her tunic's collar and belt straps poked through where the coat opened above its tied sash. All black, as was her usual style. "Have you considered paying attention to time?"

"Hey, I have a good excuse this time. Some monster of a guard stopped me! I could climb on your shoulders and we'd still be shorter."

"Let me guess, you used your golden distraction? That'll backfire someday." Her unusual accent always sounded like an elegant song to Alim.

"Are those runes? Planning the next lesson?"

"A side project."

"You wanted to talk to me after class today, right? Is that canceled too?" Alim asked.

Hali closed her book and tossed it onto a stack. "Today's lesson would've been about Thauma's techniques for analyzing blood before machines existed."

They braced themself for the worst news since finding out they were pallid and had to retire all notions of becoming a mage. "What, did you discover some new disease tucked away in my sample? How long do I have?"

With a serious tone barely stifling her laugh, Hali said, "Seventy or eighty years, tops. You're healthy, so relax." She looked away and straightened the bookstacks and pens across her desk. "What if I told you there's a type of magic you can learn as a pallid?"

"Like runes? That's ten kinds of illegal—not gonna invite that kind of trouble into my life."

"Oh, please. As if anybody in today's world can recognize runic magic. I don't intend for you to use runes." Hali walked to the board behind her desk and scribbled dots on it with chalk. A night sky? "Celestial magic. It's what Thauma's founder used."

"Really? Wasn't the founder the first born with magic? Able to use four gifts at once—air, water, earth, and fire."

"First to use modern magic is more accurate. To have magic come from within rather than deriving it from runes. Though its source was a bond with spirits, not birth."

"Spirits? Like what druids believe in?" Alim had never thought Hali to be the religious type.

"Not exactly." Hali drew a stick figure wearing a helmet, arms held up towards the stars she'd drawn earlier. Above the stars she added a tree and squiggles flowing from it, down through the sky and around the stick figure. "Celestial magic connects you to the source of the world's ether—don't make that face."

Is my confusion that obvious? Alim covered their mouth with a hand. "I can't help it. You're throwing a lot of information at me. Are you a celestial?"

Alim had decided to attend Hali's lectures when they'd heard she could teach people magic despite being pallid herself. Having attended for some time now, it was clear Hali knew more about magic than any mage Alim had ever met. Maybe this celestial magic was the reason?

Hali tugged on the peacock-feather cowl around her neck. "Not anymore."

Anymore? Is the power temporary?

She slapped the books on her desk. "Let me wrap up my research for the day. If you're interested in becoming a celestial, meet me at The Amethyst Snag. You know the place?"

"Best food in town—of course I know it!" Alim salivated at the mere mention of the inn. A tad pricy for their wallet right now though…

"For somebody who hides their face behind a helmet, you emote far too much. Put away that frown." Hali drew a chalk smiley face inside the sun on Alim's breastplate. "Food's on me."

Alim left the library and followed the dirt path acting as Wilton's main street, curving between plain wooden structures that looked like the town architect had stacked a pile of logs and called it a day. As they arrived in the newer part of town, steel buildings with dome tops littered the town square, a brick road connecting them. In the absence of the usual glowing twin moons, a giant festival wheel illuminated the darkening sky with pink, purple, and green lights.

It's never too early to celebrate winter solstice! In two or three months, when celebrations began, the wheel would be the centerpiece of Grenvel's biggest winter solstice festival ever. Alim had planned their whole year to ensure they'd be in Wilton for it.

A glass-tube sign shaped into a dead tree flickered with neon purple mist, marking the entrance to The Amethyst Snag. The last time they were here, they'd spent half their night weighing the merits of each item on the menu until deciding to resolve the dilemma by ordering one of everything. One among many reasons their wallet was on strike.

Rain pitter-pattered against their helmet as they finagled the inn's janky front door. It never opened on the first try, requiring more of a shove than any business owner should be comfortable with. Every visit, Alim braced themself to plow over some poor patron on the other side by accident.

With a bang and a slight stumble, Alim made it into the jam-packed dining room. Raucous visitors chowed down at communal tables covered in blue cloth and speckled with silver snowflakes. Matching banners hung from the walls among dangling lanterns, shining light through pink, purple, and green tinted glass. Even the cushions on the bar stools had been reupholstered with the same pattern. The bartenders and waitstaff

Chapter 3 Alim

dressed in variances of the same colors, and a bard strummed peaceful winter melodies on the stage.

Most places didn't appreciate somebody waltzing up like a human-sized living frying pan ready for war. Alim removed their cuirass, bracers, and shin guards, leaving everything with the innkeeper. A loose-fitting sleeveless yellow shirt, dark pants, and brown boots with gray metal on the toes were all that remained in the absence of protective gear. At least the helmet stayed on.

Alim sat at one of the few tables with two empty seats.

"If it isn't the helmeted runner," an off-duty guard seated at a nearby table shouted across, barely audible over the music and adjacent conversations.

Great. Her again. "That's me."

"Where'd you get that helmet? Never seen a Dreamer wear something like that."

"Custom-made."

Allister—leader of the Dreamers—had commissioned it for Alim as a reward for finding a cache of enchanted artifacts. He'd based the design on the company's insignia with meticulous accuracy. Right down to the order of the moons and the way they mirrored the horizon at a new month's beginning, with clouds in the center to represent the collective dreams and aspirations of the Dreamers. Allister was a pretentious poet and it showed in the company's branding.

The guard said, "Surprised you're not on duty here. Pay is great, and this year's solstice will be huge with Gren Consortium finally acknowledging it as a national holiday in remembrance of kicking Diya out of Oressa!"

"Solstice time is about fun. I'm in it for parties and pretty lights. Not to work or be patriotic."

The ethereal lights were the best part of the solstice—no, the whole year. Every city in Grenvel took to the streets at night, not wanting to miss them. Alim often took shifts going without sleep to scout for the lights. Skipping sleep was otherwise not an Alim-sanctioned activity.

The natural light show started at the Lunar Vault. Looking like an angry god had left a wicked green scar in the sky by smashing a moon, the Vault would unleash an array of purple, pink, and green waves. Each color twirled and frolicked in the air, like a group of artists were smearing paint on the sky but couldn't agree on a color. The whole event lasted ten to eighteen minutes before the lights blasted southeast, towards Refulgent Wastes.

Before the guard could tear into Alim for lacking love for their country, a completely soaked person crashed through the door. His hood fell back as he caught himself with not a drop of poise, revealing shiny green hair. Wrapped around him was a green cloak wrapped with a prominent golden-threaded fig leaf embroidered on the back.

What's a druid doing in Wilton? Alim hadn't met a druid before. How many were left? Fifty? This could be an opportunity for a new friend!

The innkeeper grimaced from behind the front desk as the druid left a series of puddles in his wake.

"Yo, druid!" the guard called out loud enough to burst an eardrum. "Come join us—we could use an overwatered houseplant."

Everybody laughed except Alim.

The soggy druid didn't say anything for a moment longer than was comfortable before announcing, "No thanks. I hate people."

Now that's funny. Alim wasn't sure whether to think of the druid's remark as a joke or the most honest statement ever made. Either way, he had guts.

Alim tried to calm the stewing guard. "Would you hang out with somebody who greeted you with an insult?" *And, seriously, houseplant? Sounds like a phrase children would sling at each other.*

As if nothing had happened, the druid grabbed a room key from the innkeeper and walked by their table towards the hall of rooms.

Chapter 3 Alim

The guard snatched the druid by the wrist. "Walking in here with a hood… what're you hiding?"

This again?

One of the guard's friends yelled, "Go back to your shrub-husband!"

Another heckler joined in. "And your dog-wife!"

Sweat built under Alim's helmet. Their heart pounded, yelling at them to intervene. *This isn't going to end well.* Confident they were going to regret picking a fight with a woman twice their size, Alim forced the guard off the druid. "Leave him alone."

The druid scrambled behind Alim.

Fire manifested in the guard's palm. "You think you're tough with that bucket on your head, kid? Let's see your gift."

Didn't know I could feel so little empathy towards a person after such little time.

"Hey, magic's not allowed in here!" the innkeeper yelled.

Alim mirrored the guard, extending an open palm and wiggling their fingers. "I've no gift to use. How about we skip the whole fighting thing?"

"They let plagued lung sacs in town now?"

Oh good, now we're comparing pallids to the ethereal plague. This guard truly is the queen of slights. Alim's last drop of empathy flushed down the drain. *I don't want to hurt her, but if it comes down to it…*

Alim wanted to retort with some witty historical fact, but a gust of wind snuffed out the guard's flame. As they searched for the source of the magic, Hali glided into the middle of the feud. Taller than Alim, she still only came up to the opposing mountain of a woman's chest. All the same, Hali approached the guard with a this-fight-is-already-over swagger. Alim had assumed the scars on Hali's chin and cheek would be a mundane story, but now they wondered if she'd taken part in an epic battle.

"We got two druid lovers in our midst?" the guard asked.

"Druids don't concern me," Hali said. "But showing respect for plague victims concerns everybody."

"It's been hundreds of years. Don't be so sensitive."

Patting the guard's back, Hali spoke with a seriousness Alim hadn't heard in her voice before. "You're right. We're well past caring about such things. Sit, relax. Don't blame me if the plague victims' phantoms haunt you."

Hali's palm came away with a dark red stain on it as the guard crumpled like an emergency restroom visit was imminent. *What happened?*

"Watch," Hali whispered to Alim.

With a crash, the guard fell, hitting her head on the table and knocking it over. All the drinks poured onto her face, and the entire dining room guffawed in unison, with mocking applause mixed in for good measure. A crowd circled them.

The innkeeper squeezed through the people and glared at them. "Alim… should've known you were causing trouble."

"Sorry, I'll clean up the mess." Alim whipped the yellow cloth strap from their bracer, tying it around their elbow.

"Oh… a Dreamer. We gotta get outta here." One of the guard's annoying friends untangled her from the festive tablecloth.

As the druid haters left the inn, Alim noticed something red on the guard's gambeson. Between the crumbs caked on it and the parts washed away by drinks, they couldn't tell the exact shape. Was it a rune?

Hali lifted the table back in place and collected the empty cups while Alim dispersed the onlookers, their Dreamer cloth doing all the convincing.

"You okay?" Alim asked the druid, only then realizing he was almost as tall as the guard.

He sputtered and tripped over his words like a kid trying to explain themself to an upset parent. "H-Had better days…" Silver leaves jangled on his wrist as he poked each one in turn. "Thanks."

"Wilton isn't usually like this—promise."

Anti-religious fervor had been part of Grenvel since the Old Faith had been kicked out of power at the beginning of the new calendar, 700 years ago, but it was worse in Oressa. Anybody caught with references to

Chapter 3 Alim

a religion were treated like monsters, whether druids or Solstorans—even if they weren't practicing the belief themselves. It was a surprise the guard hadn't fussed over the sweltering sun of Solstora sitting on Alim's breastplate earlier. Being so close to the druid city of Belsa, Alim had assumed druids wouldn't experience any trouble in Wilton.

Keeping his distance, the druid said, "I know. Not my first time here."

"Can I get some food to make it up to you?" Alim asked.

"You're welcome to eat with us, but Alim here can't pay for squat," Hali said.

"Aw, come on. Don't call me out in front of our new friend," Alim whispered to Hali.

A tinge of nervousness remained in the druid's voice. "Not hungry, uh—Alim, how should I address you? Dame or sir?"

Another person confusing Dreamers with knights. "Just Alim is fine. Dreamers don't deserve titles. We're not knights." *Even if they wish it like children hopped up on fairy tales.* "Secondly, neither title would apply to me." Alim tapped their helmet. "I am my armor. Whatever's under it is of no consequence."

The druid shifted his weight awkwardly as if he were unsure whether he'd offended Alim. "Got it. Not a knight, no title necessary, identifies as a helmet."

"I might identify as an axe on some days too," Alim said, laughing, reassured by the druid's willingness to make a joke. "And you are?"

"Oh, sorry. I'm so bad at introductions… How—I—Tio, my name is Tio."

"My curly-haired friend that moves like she paid big money for walking lessons over there is Hali."

"Don't listen to Alim. 'Rich people walking lessons' aren't a thing," Hali said as she sauntered towards her seat with exaggerated strides.

Hali spun in her barstool and threw her arms wide as if presenting the town to Tio. "Welcome to Wilton, land of the uninteresting and ignorant."

"Don't pretend you aren't in love with this place, Hali."

"I'd much rather be on a beach with a good novel. Or at least holed up in Wilton's dinky excuse for a library." She sniffed and recoiled. "Was somebody drinking orange juice? Alim, you're dead to me if it was you."

"Smells pleasant to me," Alim said.

Tio laughed and, for a moment, almost looked comfortable. "I won't be here long. One visit into Tent Town tomorrow and then I'll be on my way."

"Going shopping?" Hali looked the druid up and down. "Maybe new clothes? I wouldn't normally recommend anything from Grenvel, but Tent Town imports a good selection of Wolloishan fashion."

What a nice way to tell him he's dressed like a homeless person.

"No… I'm recruiting assistance for something important," Tio said.

Hali sighed. "I was joking. Your affiliation with the Conclave is clear from your cloak, so it's obvious you're not here to shop."

"Recruiting? Can we help?" Alim asked.

Hali gave a not-so-subtle glare of disapproval. "The Conclave doesn't need assistance from the likes of us, Alim." She poked their helmet between the eyes. "Can we talk somewhere private, to finish our conversation from this afternoon?"

"Sorry, Tio. Hope you find what you're looking for!"

Hali dragged Alim through the winding hall of rooms, away from the noisy dining area and a relieved-looking Tio. The pair stopped at the dead end, where a metal bench awaited outside the last room.

Grinning from crescent to crescent and body still pounding with excess energy, Alim shook Hali like a bottle of celebratory champagne. "How did you do that wind thing? I thought you were pallid?"

"Would you believe me if I said the inn is haunted?"

"No."

Hali punched Alim on the shoulder with more force than seemed possible for her slight frame. "Are my lectures sticking? Sparks aren't the only way to use magic."

Chapter 3 Alim

"It still throws me off when you use the word spark." Recovered texts from Refulgent Wastes were the only other time Alim had seen the word spark used to describe magic. Besides Hali, only people from Belsa, where flourish was preferred, didn't use the word gift.

"Old family habit. I like it better. Gift sounds too much like somebody gave you magic out of kindness. People are born with their magic, you know? Neither earned nor given."

"Was it runes?"

"If you're asking as a Dreamer, my official answer is that I don't use runes. I merely study them and would never think to call upon such dangerous magic."

Alim laughed. "Former, and they're mercenaries. They don't enforce the law—they do odd jobs."

"For Gren Consortium and Sipherra. The company might as well be Grenvel's military."

"Can't argue there."

It was true that Dreamers had become more and more ingrained in Grenvel's political affairs over the past century. When Alim had joined the company, its focus was less on combat and more on making expeditions into Refulgent Wastes. While side jobs involved a lot of guarding, escorting, and generally being tough and scary, the company's main income had come from filling libraries with discovered texts and magical artifacts, though that had shifted since the Dreamers had been bought by the Sipherra mining company. Being used as a weapon had left a bitter taste in Alim's mouth.

"For real though, did you draw one on your palm?" Alim took Hali's left arm by the sleeve to get a closer look.

Hali yanked her hand back. "Did I mention how great your outfit looks? You should go armorless more often. Casual suits you."

"Don't change the subject, Hali."

"Fine, yes. I used two runes."

"That's amazing." Alim had no idea Hali put her ancient magic expertise to practical use. Since runic magic was considered part of the Old Faith, people using it were condemned and labeled witches. "The sickness was obviously the poison rune you've mentioned in lectures. What was the other?"

"A force rune. Small and focused. Crushes with air pressure. Too much and you'll cave somebody's chest in. Too little and you might as well be tickling them. Requires finesse to tweak runes enough to hit the mark, you know?"

"Must've taken a long time to achieve such skill!"

"Longer than you could imagine," Hali said.

"Don't underestimate my imagination! How old could you be?"

She paused, like she was counting to an impossible number in her head. "Thirty-three."

"Is that old? You're still in your prime! Anyway, I'm ready to hear all about celestials and spirits." Alim tapped their helmet in anticipation. "There's no mention of celestials in any of the Thaumic texts I've read. Where did you learn it?"

"I'm sure there are hints strewn all over Our Stranded Lands. Nobody knew what to call it. Every Thaumic mage city sought to reproduce the founder's power, so we all worked towards that goal."

"You're from Thauma? I thought all the survivors relocated to the Coveted South?" After the Quake had split the southern countries from the northern, there was no way for refugees to return.

"Most did, but Diya and Wolloisha have Thaumic descendants too. Oressa was safe on the Grenvel side of Thauma's Runegate. Every mage city was south of the gate and evacuated for fear the spreading wasteland would reach them. Only Grenvel outright refused to take on refugees—they were convinced the ethereal plague hadn't been cured."

"Your accent isn't Wolloishan or Diyan."

"My family and I lived as isolated as we could, so our Thaumic accent stuck around. I've only been in Grenvel for a few years."

Chapter 3 Alim

"Why'd you come to Grenvel?"

"To create new runes," Hali said.

"And why are you offering to teach me celestial magic?" Alim asked. There had to be a catch.

"My rune research is at an impasse. Everything I create should work in theory but fails to activate with every attempt." Before Alim could ask why, Hali continued, "Ether is the foundation of all magic, you know? Whether spark or runes, it all has ether at its core. Our blood isn't rich with ether—in fact there's precious little there compared even to the surrounding air." Hali twirled her finger like she was wrapping it in invisible strings. "A supply of dense ether is necessary for these new runes. The simplest answer is to draw the rune with blood containing concentrated ether, since a celestial wouldn't be required."

For the first time all night, Hali broke eye contact. If Alim didn't know better, they'd swear she was nervous given the way she kept grabbing at her cowl.

"Does such blood exist?"

"It's preferable to try with a celestial first."

"How does me being a celestial factor into this?" Alim asked.

"Celestials control ether itself. You'd be providing my runes with ether."

"And the goal of these runes is...?"

Pulling her feet up, Hali sat cross-legged. "After losing my celestial powers, runes were all I had left. Only for a celestial to still be required..." She lifted her left sleeve, revealing a simple tattoo. A circle with an upside down "V" inside. "This is a binding rune. Specially made for storing large quantities of ether. See that weird ink?"

How could they not? It was everchanging between black and white as the two colors clashed and retreated in a battle to fill the symbol. "What is it?"

"I wasn't born pallid. There's a spirit trapped inside this tattoo, sapping my magic. Kthon took away my celestial powers and spark alike."

"So we remove Kthon and you get your magic back? I'm all for it." Alim had a hard enough time being pallid in a world of mages and druids, so they could only imagine how difficult it must've been to have had their magic stolen.

"No." Hali slammed her fist onto the bench, cracking one of its wooden slats. "My spark doesn't matter. Neither does celestial magic. Kthon killed my son. Then my partner. They're both a part of the spirit now. Freeing my family and letting their phantoms rest is all I care about."

Here I am whining about being pallid... "Say no more—I'll do everything I can. You mentioned bonding with spirits is how I become a celestial, right? You're sure a pallid can do that?"

Rubbing her eyes, Hali said, "The first celestial became one at a time when sparks didn't exist. Anybody can do it." She rolled her sleeve down and dug through her bag.

Right. The founder. Master of four elemental gifts. "Will I be able to use my water gift? And the others?" Alim stifled their grin but failed miserably. This was a dream come true. Literally. Dreamers had to pick a goal as their "dream" when they joined the company. Alim had chosen "learn magic" as theirs, even knowing the impossibility.

Hali scooted over and set a series of books on the bench between her and Alim. "With years—decades of practice. You'd have to change your blood's elemental affinity. Too dangerous. Stick with ether control. That level of mastery will come with time."

This might be the first time I've wished I was a decade older. "What's the process then? It can't be easy since nobody else has it figured out."

"You're not wrong. First, you need to break through each ether surges' haze barrier using ethereal blood. Find the eidolon inside and eat its spirit fruit. Each fruit attunes you to a spirit and strengthens your connection to the spirit tree."

Alim thumped the bench leg again with their boot. Ethereal blood? *Gross.* Spirit tree? *That's a real thing?* Ether surge? *Sounds like a potent drink.*

"Sorry, Hali. None of those words mean a thing to me. All I heard was 'eat fruit,' and I have no idea how to find an eh-doe-wutzit."

"Then you caught the important bits." Hali took a book from the top of the stack and flipped through its pages. "Give me a few weeks to figure out how to get through haze barriers."

"Figure out? Haven't you done this before?"

"Ethereal blood is something only a druid can get," Hali said.

"Let's ask Tio!"

"He has his own assignment. Not to mention he was dying to stop talking to us the whole time, or did you not notice?"

"But maybe he's got ethereal blood?" Regardless, Alim just wanted an excuse to befriend Tio. He was gutsy when he wasn't looking uncomfortable to exist. A little more time and he would've warmed up to Alim and Hali for sure.

"Not a chance." Hali shut the book with an unceremonious sigh. "The nature spark is too weak to contact eidolons, and that's the only way to get ethereal blood."

"What exactly are eye-dough-loans?"

Hali groaned. "You're doing that on purpose now, aren't you?"

Maybe a little.

"An eidolon is half-tree, half-animal. Think of it as an animal empowered with magic by spirits and the reason surges exist at all."

"I won't have to kill one, will I?" Alim didn't like the idea, but if it was to help Hali's family…

"What? Of course not. As if you could. Best case you'll get on its good side and it'll give you one. Worst, stealing is always an option. Violence isn't recommended."

"So, while you're sorting out the haze barrier puzzle, what should I be doing?"

Hali set the book down and pushed the stack closer to Alim. "You have reading to catch up on."

"Seriously?"

"Do you expect to reshape ether at will when you don't understand it first?" Hali gave a subdued laugh, the way she always did when justifying why ancient magic was an important topic to skeptical students.

"I guess not," Alim said as they grabbed the first book from the stack, *Enchanting & Ether: A History* by Barbaroli Pensa. "What a dry title."

"Right? At least it should give some hints as to where to find the surges." Hali got up from the bench. "Sorry we spent so much time discussing this. Let's get that meal I promised."

Reading wasn't what Alim had expected for their first week of celestial training. How exciting.

CHAPTER 4

Barren branches on a dark purple husk of a trunk marked Wilton's namesake—a dead tree. Although not the first time Tio had seen it, he was as confused now by the strange way people treated it as he had been then. The tree had remained standing for hundreds of years, despite being dead, becoming renowned as the pride of Wilton's people. Where the tree had once been seen as an external manifestation of their own perseverance, it was now a symbol for druidic incompetence. A sign Our Stranded Lands didn't need nature magic anymore.

"It's just a dead tree," Tio whispered to his okapi companion as meandering people trickled into the plaza, going about their morning chores.

"Is a tree without food really a tree?" the okapi asked.

"That's deep, but I'm pretty sure trees without food exist."

"I'd find something edible on them, or my name isn't Stripebutt!" Stripebutt said.

"That isn't your name." *It's worse than the ones I use when I can't remember somebody.*

"You don't get to name me. I chose it."

As his embarrassment ramped and his cheeks flushed, Tio maintained a low voice to keep others from hearing him. "You chose it to get on my nerves."

Tio didn't need a repeat of last night, drawing attention to himself by talking to an animal. Being seen with one so exotic was bad enough. Okapi were only found in a special section of Belsa's forests since they weren't native to Grenvel. As a precaution, Tio wore his hood up and kept his satchel tight against his back to cover the Conclave cloak's fig-leaf insignia. Nothing worried him more than being called out in front of a room of people.

I'm glad those two were there to help me.

"You don't like my stripes? I'll have you know, okapi come from all over for the stripes on my rump."

More information than I ever needed to know. Death was preferable to continuing this conversation. "I'll call you Stripes. That's all you're getting, okay?"

Stripes bumped Tio. "Even better! But you didn't name me. Got it?"

"Got it. Let's go, I want to beat the crowds at Tent Town."

Druids didn't keep pets. If they bonded with an animal enough, they'd be adopted as a familiar. A friend. Animals didn't use names amongst each other, so they named themselves after becoming close with druids on the first step towards becoming a familiar. Maybe the key to Tio's inadequate animal communication skills was that only silly animals could understand him. Sir Fluffyboi's naming process had also been weird. She enjoyed old stories of knights but thought "dame" sounded too much like "dumb." Familiars were more integrated into society than most animals, even having to register with Belsa's town hall, and the druid administrator's eyes had almost popped out of his sockets when Sir Fluffyboi had announced her name. The poor old man had grimaced the whole way through writing the name down on the official city forms.

Chapter 4 Tio

Wilton's dome-topped steel buildings were dollhouses compared to Belsa's towering tree structures. None more than two stories tall, but at least Wilton didn't need dying magic to develop their town.

Counting the bricks on the circular plaza's streets distracted Tio as he walked by teams of mages puppeteering steel golems. The first time Tio had seen a golem, he'd had no idea their hollow insides were stuffed with elements to allow mages to move them around. During his last visit here, he'd watched the golems construct most of the town center. Each golem was twice as tall as Tio, with perfect beady circles for eyes. Their circular heads were stuck on top of a cylindrical body with gangly limbs. Depending on the angle, one might consider them either adorable or frightening.

Could a golem break through a haze barrier? Even if they could, Tio didn't have the right flourish to control one, and it took at least two or three mages per golem. *Hopefully Barbaroli has better ideas.*

A massive wheel dominated the view as Tio left the center of town. He had wanted to see it up close as soon as it had first appeared on the horizon a few days ago. With the night sky lit by the wheel's spinning neon pink, green, and purple lights, it was like witnessing a miniature version of the ethereal lights. In the daytime, however, the colors were muted, barely visible.

"How would you like to talk to that fine animal of yours?" a scruffy man with sopping blue hair asked. Matching dye stained his elaborately gesturing hands.

A fake druid?

"Oh, I can teach you! Free of charge," Druid Trainer said as he closed the crow-like beak on his purple-feather-covered hat. "Shush! Sorry, ol' bird buddy here is such a chatterbox. Can't get her to pipe down!"

It didn't say anything... Is this how people think we dress? Covered in dead animal parts? Hope it wasn't a real bird. Tio pointed to his own authentic grassy hair. "Don't need help in that department. This isn't hair dye." *Unlike somebody here.* "Look, I've got to go."

Arboreal Path

Druid Trainer bopped the road with a two-pronged spear that looked like it was made of cardboard. "A fellow druid!" A dark puddle collected at his feet. "There's always something to learn and time with which to learn it. Watch as I take down a golem single-handedly with my mighty gift."

"You sound agitated, Tio. Should I kick this guy?" Stripes asked.

"No, there's something wrong with him. Let's just go." Tio took the longest strides his legs would allow to somewhere—anywhere but here. The festival wheel was as good a place as any and in the right direction for Tent Town.

Druid Trainer shouted after Tio, "Next time, friend!"

Scuttling even faster, Tio arrived at a neon sign, filled with glowing ether. It flickered in the shape of a pancake stack and a steaming cup of coffee, triggering caffeine withdrawal pangs. As if the sign wasn't enough, the smell of freshly ground coffee sank its hooks into him, dragging him to the sparsely populated outdoor café. Hardly any people and a pleasant chill in the air—perfect for reading a book. He led Stripes through the café's gate and glanced through the prices listed on the menu board.

The sad state of Tio's wallet crushed his morning aspirations. Sifting through the pink, green, and purple paper representing money outside Belsa confirmed Tio couldn't afford the diversion. Even with the Conclave's funding, he'd need to be frugal. Defeated, he sighed.

"Allow me," somebody said with too much enthusiasm. Seated at a table, Alim beckoned him over.

Do they ever take that helmet off? "I can't—"

"I insist. Besides, it's not my money. What're you hungry for?"

Something about Alim drew him in like they were some sort of comfortable magnet. He took a seat across from them. "Not hungry actually, but I could use some coffee after yesterday."

"Order me something," Stripes said.

"You ate your weight in food this morning," Tio said.

Alim tilted their head as if confused. "Not yet, but I'm about to."

Chapter 4 Tio

"Sorry, I was speaking to Stripes." Tio patted the okapi's head.

"That's amazing! Wish I could speak to animals. Bet they have interesting things to say."

Tio shook his head. "Not really. She's as boring as any person."

Stripes headbutted Tio. "I beg to differ. Everything I say is exquisite conversation material."

A waiter dropped off two plates, each with a stack of five pancakes in front of Alim. *Two plates? Is the lady with the lyrical accent here too? What was her name… Hali?*

"Hey, one big ol' cup of coffee for my friend, please?"

"Right away," the waiter said.

"Is Hali joining us?" Tio asked.

Alim laughed and stabbed a fork into their food. "No, she's busy with library stuff. This is all for me, but you can thank her for paying."

"Is that how you're so… muscular?" Tio stared at his own twiggy arms.

"This junk won't build anything but my mood. Maybe if I ate healthier, I'd be stronger."

Stronger? Tio assumed Alim would be more confident considering the sleeveless look they seemed to prefer, as if putting their arms on display. He couldn't blame them. Arms that size warranted showboating. They almost inspired him to lift weights. But not quite.

"It's good to have goals," Tio said. "But you look really strong to me. Like those beefy warriors on romance-novel covers—not that I read those!"

"What about the one you read this morning?" Stripes asked, making Tio blush despite knowing Alim couldn't understand her.

A mouth full of more food than Tio thought possible muffled Alim's response. "Thanks, I think?"

"It's a miracle you're not getting syrup all over your armor." Tio recognized the sun on Alim's breastplate. Prayer walls were plastered with the same symbol where he'd grown up in Ahsiem. "Are you Solstoran?"

"Yes? You won't find me saying 'embrace the sun' or anything, but my parents were big on Solstoran stuff. Dad commissioned the armor for me when I joined the Dreamers. Said, 'Do the sun proud.'" Alim swished water from their glass, gulping loudly enough to elicit a noise complaint from a couple tables over. "Making my parents proud was what mattered. I only joined to get money for them."

That's sweet. I thought mercenaries would be more… jerk-like? "My mom was Solstoran too. Became a priest before I left to study at Belsa."

"Our parents would be fast friends then. Maybe we should set up a play date?"

The waiter slipped a steaming cup on the table.

"Thanks!" Tio let the inviting, nutty fragrance sink in before taking a sip. A bell rang out three times. *Must be later than I thought.* "I can't stay long. Barbaroli is waiting for me at Tent Town."

Alim let their fork drop. "Barbaroli Pensa? The author of… whatever, some ether book?"

For somebody to know Barbaroli wasn't unusual. He was well known for selling magical artifacts and foreign goods no other merchant could find. But to know him for his books on ether studies was new to Tio.

"You're studying ether? That was my main subject in school." This could be a chance to talk to somebody other than Barbaroli. Nobody else in Belsa knew anything substantial on the subject.

"No, no, no. Studying? Me? Not once in my life. Just ask Hali—I'm attending her ancient magic lectures and haven't learned a thing. I've got some questions for Barbaroli. Mind if I tag along?"

Guess I owe Alim that much. "Sure, let's—"

Pancakes disappeared in a frenzy as Alim hacked away like their fork were an axe. Tio had never seen anybody eat with such vigor. It made Tio feel sick, even if it was impressive.

"Ready!" Alim announced with two empty plates and a satisfied grin. "Lead the way."

Chapter 4 Tio

When the three arrived in what was supposed to be Tent Town, there were no tents to be found. Instead, said tents dotted the streets past a grand fountain and the festival wheel. Now that he was closer, Tio could tell how monstrous the wheel was. Taller than anything created by people that he'd ever seen.

"What's this wheel for?" Tio asked Alim. "Stripes and I saw its solstice-colored lights from days away."

"I think you're supposed to sit in the bench and let it take you around the wheel? Hali guessed they put elements inside the steel to let mages spin it around."

"Oh!" *Like golems.* "The view at the top must be beautiful." Tio wondered how far he'd be able to see. Would he see the grass-covered peaks of the mage-made mountain, Last Stand?

A gaudy model of golem was propped against the stone fountain. Not as tall as the construction model from earlier, though still imposing. The only plain part of it was the black dome serving as its head. Matching the city's winter solstice decorations, its cylindrical blue body had irregularly shaped diamonds and black opals embedded in the steel.

"That golem kind of reminds me of the ethereal lights streaking across the night sky," Alim said as if lost in a fanciful dream world.

"Look at the metal though." Tio couldn't take his eyes away from its endless transitions to colors he couldn't name. Its vibrancy put rainbows to shame. "Have you ever seen anything like it?"

"Never. It's not a fancy paint job either." Alim circled the golem. "See how the hues change on their own? This must be a new ore or a weird mixture."

"Wouldn't put it past Sipherra. They're always innovating." Tio had considered working for Sipherra to put his ether studies to use, but solving the dwindling magic problem took precedence. How could he work for them and create new technology if the world ran out of ether or people had no magic to operate Sipherra's devices? "Judging by the arms, it's designed for demolition."

It was more like a rail system than arms, with large sliding half cylinders attached. The hands were folded inside, as if to protect them from impact. The sheer size of the arms made the thin legs look even more ridiculous than those of other golems.

"Not a fan of Sipherra. The day they go bankrupt would be a momentous day for Grenvel—no, Our Stranded Lands as a whole."

How could anybody feel that way about a company advancing technology so rapidly? "Did Sipherra insult your mom or something?" Tio immediately wondered if his joke was in bad taste. "Because you'd be totally… justified? Sorry."

"Near enough. Don't like how they treat people as expendable trash. Simple as that. I stopped working with the Dreamers after Sipherra started influencing our operations."

"So you're not a Dreamer anymore?"

"It's a loose organization of mercenaries—people drop in and out for jobs all the time. Officially I can work for them again any time. Unofficially… Allister didn't appreciate the things I said before I left camp, and he runs the show."

Stripes wandered away and bumped into the golem. "Yeowch! It zapped me!"

"Get away from that—you're going to get us in trouble," Tio said.

"I was bored." Stripes's hooves scraped the ground rapidly like she had an itch.

"Stripes says we have to get moving, Alim."

"I've never said no to an okapi before."

Rows of empty stalls on both sides of the street led to Tent Town's new location. Some had attendants stacking toys or installing kitchen set-ups. More and more people showed up as Tent Town neared. Before long, Tio was lost in the sea. Clusters of people broke off from the pack at the whims of the masses, dragging Tio in random directions as if he was stuck in the Trachea River's currents.

Chapter 4 Tio

Deep breaths.

The mantra did him no good. Trying to breathe only made him feel like something was pulling him underwater. A hundred, no, a thousand gazes fell upon him at once. He stopped in his tracks, crushed under the weight of their judgement.

"Walking fertilizer!" a croaky voice yelled at Tio.

Tio's head pounded with a pressure worse than spending a day using his flourish.

"I'm glad druids are gone. What's the use of them without healing?" a deep, smooth voice said.

"Plagued lung sac—"

"Stop!" Tio yelled.

A hand grasped Tio's shoulder, and he flinched, nearly jumping out of his skin.

"Stop what?" Alim asked. "Hey, you okay?"

Tio fiddled with the leaves of his bracelet. "Of course," he said with a shaky voice.

Alim looked around. "Don't like crowds? Let me be your bulwark. Point me in the right direction and I'll cut a path for you."

Tio squeezed the charms to keep his hands steady. "Barbaroli's tent is over there." He pointed beyond the countless tables, tents, and loud merchants to a large red tent with a wooden sign on it reading "Pensa Emporium of Antiquities."

"The one with the bunny-ear logo with swirly magic bits?"

Tio tried to nod but was sure it appeared more like his head was in the beginning stages of a soon-to-be-messy explosion.

He rushed to keep up as Alim deflected swathes of vendors and shoppers with gentle nudges. Was that mage juggling fireballs? Did any of the colorfully dressed merchants bother them with useless glassware, pottery, clothes, or whatever? How much time passed? Somehow, Tio hadn't paid enough attention to notice.

Barbaroli's oversized tent had a smaller sign out front, carved with the same magic-bunny-ear logo and his slogan, "Tired of expensive fakes? Homemade Diyan artifacts and machines. Power you can smell."

"Is he encouraging people to sniff his artifacts for authenticity?" Alim asked. "Do they have a smell?"

Tio shrugged as he felt relaxation return. "Stay out here, Stripes. We'll be right back."

"Don't get mad if I find my own fun." Stripes plopped down next to the small sign like she were part of the ad.

A looming, stocky old logu turned and spoke his usual greeting with a thunderous voice. "Welcome to my shop! Please take—Tio? Why didn't you send a letter to tell me you were coming? Would've prepared a nicer place to chat."

Tall white furry extensions rose from his head and flopped forward slightly, like rabbit ears covered front and back with fur. Except not really ears—in fact, they acted as fat stores, allowing logu to go weeks without food or water. Barbaroli's royal blue coat, lined with golden buttons, had a new white ascot tucked under his gray neck. It was hard to tell from where Tio stood, but it looked like Barbaroli's shop logo was patterned all over it.

"Sorry, everything got approved so quickly I didn't think to ask any birds to deliver a message," Tio said.

"Who's your friend?" Barbaroli asked.

"Alim," they said.

"Your helmet could use a paint job." The merchant looked Alim up and down with orange eyes. "Or if you're in the market for a new one..."

"I'm not." Alim's tone was as if Barbaroli had asked them to buy new skin. "But if I see anything I'm interested in, I'll let you know." They perused the shop's glass display cases and shelves full of books, enchanted artifacts, and miscellaneous exotic goods from Wolloisha and Diya. "Do these artifacts work?"

Chapter 4 Tio

"Selling functioning artifacts would be highly illegal," Barbaroli said with a chuckle. "But if a friend of Tio needs one, maybe we can work something out."

"Maybe next time."

"Tough customer!" Barbaroli opened his arms wide for Tio. "What brings you here?"

"No touching please." Tio stepped back. "The Conclave approved. I can begin our plan any time."

Applause thundered from Barbaroli's hands, so loud Tio swore the tent was crowded with impressed spectators. "Wonderful news if I've ever heard any!"

"I need your assistance finding surges," Tio said.

"That's why I'm here too!" Alim held out Barbaroli's book. "Was hoping you'd be able to point me in the right direction. If you two are going though, could Hali and I tag along?"

My team needs to be experts. What's a nice way to say no?

"Did you read my book? How about that, another patron of fine literature." Barbaroli's booming laugh was endearing, but it grated on Tio's ears in such small quarters.

Tio twitched as he prepared an answer. "We're going to be doing extensive research, Alim. It could take months to test methods for bypassing the haze barriers. No time to show you around."

Barbaroli's scanning eyes darted between Tio and Alim. "Not so fast, Tio. What do you hope to find, Alim?"

"Spirit fruit from a… hold on. The word was weird." They beat against their visor, making frustrated thinking noises. "Eh-doe—eidolon! Got it. Take that, Hali."

"Never heard of an eidolon, but I take it the fruit isn't for a pie," Barbaroli said.

"It's supposed to give me special magic to control ether. I'm still a bit confused on the details. She's the celestial expert, not me."

Celestial? Did magic capable of manipulating ether exist? If so, that would accelerate the research process. Whatever an eidolon was seemed important too. *Spirit fruit… spirits are born of Empyrea. Maybe studying an eidolon will reveal Empyrea's health? Bit of a stretch, but Alim's goals are more aligned with mine than I assumed.*

"Fine," Tio said. "I could always use more help. Can't promise we'll find what you're looking for, but between the four of us, we've got the ether expertise I'm looking for."

Barbaroli said, "Tio, you'll have my map, but I can't accompany you. My ledger can't afford another long expedition after my recent months in Refulgent Wastes."

"What about Rachel?" *Inexperienced as she is, I can't do this alone.*

"No can do, Tio. Rachel returned to Wolloisha at the request of the priest-king. She'll be tied up longer than me."

"I can wait. We have another year until the next ether cycle," Tio said. "This'll give you time to complete another enchanted artifact too."

"As much as I'd love to give you another artifact to tinker with"—Barbaroli counted on his fingers—"you've miscalculated. My map will be obsolete by the end of the year, and it's not even finished. The surge locations will still be good, but my work in identifying which had haze barriers may change. I ruled out Iron Swamp and Wolloisha. Had some trouble tracking down the surges in Refulgent Wastes and East Peaks, but at least your search is narrowed down."

"Only months to breach the barriers, and I don't even know how?" *No ether experts available either. This is looking impossible.* "How much for the map?"

"Zero should suffice."

"I know you want something." *Barbaroli is nice, but he's still a merchant.*

"Document whatever you discover and give me exclusive book rights. You get thirty percent." Barbaroli extended an open hand to Tio, a grin plastered on his face.

"Deal." Tio and Barbaroli shook hands.

Barbaroli's chortle rattled the nearby displays. "Don't worry, your portion will be placed directly into your bank account. You'd find a way to decline otherwise."

Alim tapped their helmet. "Why do you only have months? How does a map become obsolete?"

You really haven't read that book at all. "Ether gradually shifts over fourteen years through three distinct states. After going through those three states, the barriers change locations," Tio said.

"Meaning this solstice will be the forty-second year and ruin your map?"

They caught on quicker than I thought. Tio smiled. "Exactly! And who knows where in Our Stranded Lands they might be afterwards. Grenvel? Wolloisha? Refulgent Wastes? We'd have to check everywhere."

"Can't we wait for the solstice and redo the map?" Alim asked.

Tio wasn't sure how to explain his mission. He hadn't talked to anybody about it besides Barbaroli and the Conclave. "Nature flourishes will be gone for good by this time next year. If we wait until the solstice, druids will never be born again. Not long after, all magic will be gone. Maybe a couple generations. Three tops."

"Wait, this is why more people are pallid nowadays?"

"It's still a theory, but I think so."

Alim pulled Tio aside and whispered, "Hali said druids open surges' haze barriers by talking to its eidolon. Is there something wrong with your gift?"

"Afraid I've never heard any eidolon speak to me at the barrier back home. I wouldn't be here if I could get in so easily."

"Hali and I will get you through. We're going to be a great team! Team… Barrier Breakers? Well, the name could use some work."

"I don't think we need a name," Tio said.

"Of course we do! Hali's going to love it."

"If you say so." Tio fiddled with his bracelet. He'd expected to need help, but not from strangers.

Still, Alim and Hali had stood up for him. This wasn't the team he'd expected when he set out from Belsa, but there was still a chance this could work.

CHAPTER 5

Lanterns hanging from Hali's cart projected shadows onto the passing shelves and floors. Each sway of the light made the shadows dart into the edge of Hali's peripheral vision like children embarrassed to be seen dancing together. She gathered a slew of discarded books off the ground and put them into organized stacks on her cart. *Is it so much to ask that people clean up after themselves?*

After returning the assorted books where they belonged, Hali stopped by a quiet corner of the library. There was nothing like being alone with a new book. She reached into a box on her cart for a copy of *The Quake: A Spectacular Display of Incompetence*. Plucking out the bookmark stuck three quarters through the pages, Hali hoped to complete the volume during this break.

The cover art depicted the titular Quake. Deep blue dunes with a massive crevasse cutting through, funneling silver holographic foil into the sky. *Using foil to represent phantoms was a nice touch. I need to find out who designed this.*

Hali brought the book close and flipped the pages, taking in the smell of the paper. Her blood tingled as Ikazu pushed against the binding rune on her wrist.

"You can't be here," she whispered.

The lanterns shook and flickered as the exploring shadows fled into the wicks when a familiar voice responded, "Closing already? I just got here."

Alim? "I see you're already back to wearing armor for casual strolls through our treacherous library." Hali wondered if Alim had a helmet-shaped tan-line under there.

"With the dense books you read? I'm going to need to upgrade my gear."

"Might I suggest your first upgrade cover these oversized monstrosities? One good paper cut and you're done for." Hali poked Alim's arm. "Or is it too important the world knows how much time you devote to lifting heavy objects?"

"Oversized?" Alim motioned high above a flexed bicep. "My strength training has a long way to go."

No doubt you train in your sleep too.

A person with hair like short blades of grass stood behind Alim. Close enough to hear the two talk, but far enough to give the illusion of disinterest. Hali saw that technique all the time from introverts. And creeps. She hoped he was the former.

This must be the druid from last night… Tio, was it? Is Alim picking up strays now?

Hali gestured towards Tio. "Alim, is he with you?"

Alim frowned as they looked back, as if the druid were a stubborn puppy refusing to walk. "Tio, don't hang so far back. It's weird."

"Right, sorry. Hi." He gave a wave as awkward and stilted as his smile. "Thanks for helping me with the guard yesterday."

Guess his bravado at the inn was more anxious honesty than narcissism. Looks more a nervous wreck now than after we protected him. "Keep yourself out of trouble next time. What if we weren't there?"

Chapter 5 Hali

Tio's face shriveled like he'd been scolded by his mother.

Alim said, "You and I will be there, Hali, because we're Team Ether Cleavers now!"

Hali pinched the bridge of her nose to prevent her brain from falling out to escape Alim's nonsense. "A what now? I didn't agree to anything, so unless you fill me in and let me decide for myself, you're just Team Stop Bothering Me at Work."

"Told you she wouldn't like the name," Tio whispered.

"We can hash out our team name later."

"There's not going to be a team name." It was times like these Hali doubted Alim was the right choice to train. Lucky for them there were no other candidates. Since pallids were immune to the plague, Hali knew the next celestial needed to be one. To protect them from Kthon.

"Tio here is an expert on ether. He's going to help us locate the surges!" Alim nudged Tio. "Show her the map."

Even with every book in Grenvel it would be impossible to be an ether expert, but the map appeared legit. The cosmic frog compass was a cute touch. She recognized several locations from her own time becoming a celestial.

"That's great, Tio," Hali said. "But unless you've got ethereal blood and can walk us through the haze, we're no further along than yesterday."

"Right, that's why we're here. Alim said you're working on another way. Can you help?" Tio asked.

"If you're asking me, then your spark isn't getting the job done. You'll have to break in with powerful magic."

Tio's puzzled look was one she received all the time from others. "Spark?"

"It means gift. Hali's family is from Thauma," Alim said.

"Why not say 'gift,' so you don't need to explain?" Tio asked.

"Same reason your people use flourish. Keeps my culture alive, if only a little longer."

Arboreal Path

"I can respect that. Give it another generation and I bet Belsa will switch too. Then I'll be an old, graying druid clinging to 'flourish' and telling kids to respect their elders. I'd hope at least one would carry on the tradition for a while."

You're good people, kid.

"What magic can penetrate a haze barrier?" Tio scratched his chin and read the book spines instead of making eye contact.

Celestial magic was the only brute-force method she knew. Runes gave endless possibilities with a little work but were risky, with steep blood tolls and finnicky precision. Any maladjusted line or misplaced curve in their design could alter the result beyond recognition. An enchanted artifact may make it easier. Hali had seen potent artifacts capable of doubling a mage's power, but most were inert now. Diya still had some with functioning enchantments, however the likelihood of finding the exact type required was abysmal.

"Hold that thought. Let me finish this work and end my shift early." *There goes my reading break...* "Meet me at my lecture room? We'll talk through this whole haze barrier 'team' thing."

Alim held up an index finger as if to add an exclamation point to their announcement. "Team Ether C—"

Hali imagined a hundred ways to break that finger. "No name!"

Alim grumbled and Tio's infectious, unrestrained giggling let the whole library know how amusing Alim's disappointment was. She couldn't help but chuckle alongside him.

As the others wandered off, Hali grabbed her cart and rolled it down the hall, restocking the shelves and gathering any books on runes she could find—which wasn't much since the topic was as rare as ether. On the way to her room, Hali poured cups of tea from the batch she kept at the ready during her shifts, stowed away in a hidden part of the break room.

Upon entering, she found Alim looking over Tio's shoulder as he read a novel, *Taming the Coveted South*. A fictional tale of an explorer navigating

Phantasmal Reef and rediscovering the utopian, futuristic cities of the Coveted South.

"You really read this stuff?" Alim asked.

Hali said, "It's not so bad once you get past the romance. Well, if you can suspend your disbelief enough to accept somebody crossing Phantasmal Reef alive." Romance wasn't her subject of choice, but she had set herself the lofty goal of reading every book in Grenvel.

"With an endorsement like that, how could anybody not read it?" Alim said, laughing as they sat next to Tio and kicked their boots up on the table.

"Whatever, this book is really good to me. The ether technology is so inspiring. I'd love to invent something half as amazing. A sassy self-controlling golem? Impossible, sure, but sign me up!" Tio said. "I was rooting for Brad and Sally to couple up since they grew up together, but the author stuck with pairing Brad with Ben. Too obvious if you ask me."

Hali set tea down for everybody. "You're why love triangles exist. You know that, right?"

"I'm not apologizing for that," he said, sipping from his cup.

"Good." Hali thought it was adorable how invested he became, even if playing matchmaker with fictional characters didn't matter to her in the slightest. "Never apologize for who you are."

With an antsy, rushed tone, Alim said, "Hali, please tell me you have the perfect rune lined up for the job?"

"Nothing's turned up yet. My only thought is to draw a rune using ink infused with ethereal blood."

"Draw it with the thing we don't have?" Alim shifted in their seat and played with an empty teacup. *Surprised they didn't swallow the cup with it. They need to learn to savor things.*

"Don't be so sure." Phantoms retained their ether in death, and Rev had borne ethereal blood. Hali had never tried using Ikazu to power a rune before, but the idea had promise. It wouldn't be as seamless as if Rev were

Arboreal Path

doing it, so surely the eidolon would fight against Hali's attempt to open the barrier. *I didn't intend to go with Alim.* Hali's insides twisted into knots. *Facing the eidolons and spirits again is the last thing I want to do.* "I'll figure it out. It's still unclear why you're here, Tio. What does the Conclave want with the surges?"

"Our magic is disappearing." Tio wrote in a notebook with frenetic urgency as he talked, like he was trying to keep track of everything. "There may not be enough ether for any new druid children in a year. This solstice marks the end of an ether cycle. Our map will—"

"You'd have to check each surge all over again for barriers and run out of time." Hali finished her tea. "Noble, but how do you plan to convince Gren Consortium this matters? Are you willing to bend the rules when they deny you?"

"Mages are losing their magic too, Hali! Tio's going to cure pallids. How could they oppose that?"

Tio stammered over his words, clearly caught off guard. "It—don't—I doubt anything we do will help living people, but new generations will benefit hopefully." He flicked the sharp-looking silver leaves on his bracelet. "I'm not afraid to bend rules."

Tugging on her peacock cowl, Hali asked, "When do we leave?"

"Tomorrow morning at the south entrance?" Alim suggested.

"I'll be there."

"Spirit Arboretum is our first surge since it's close and safe," Tio said.

Hali hadn't been there in some time. Rev had collected seeds from around the world for years to build that forest. It contained trees from every country west of the Great Haze—Grenvel, Wolloisha, Diya, Bansil, and Fion were all represented. *And we have to finish by the solstice? Sorry, Rev and Rasal. Our annual solstice trip home will have to wait.*

The three parted ways after briefly assigning duties. Alim volunteered to get food, of course, though their ability to do so responsibly was suspect at best. Hali stayed behind at the library, hoping to glean something useful before morning. It was unlikely she'd design the rune in one evening, so she planned on picking a base and finishing the rest on the road.

Hali sifted through the only two rune books from the library, as well as her own stash of notes about runes, ether, and haze barriers. Her neck ached as the night wore on, and her eyes drifted closed until she face-planted into her pile of stray notes.

Shocks of pain woke her up and shadows leaking from her wrist drew her attention to the corner of the room, where Ikazu clung to the corner with splayed limbs, like a humanoid spider. *Again... druids aren't the only ones running out of time. If my binding is this weak, how much longer until Kthon returns?*

Ikazu scurried along the ceiling until he was above Hali and let his arms dangle as he hung from his feet. His hands morphed between several signs. "Memory please."

"Ikazu, the last time wasn't a pleasant experience for me, and I need to get this work done. I'm doing it for you."

"Memory please," his hands repeated.

"No, you can get some when I sleep."

"Memory please."

Hali activated the binding rune to pull Ikazu back in. "That's enough—"

Ikazu grabbed hold of her head, and the biting chill of each intangible finger ran through her skull. Her vision blackened as Ikazu's face morphed to Kthon and he linked with her.

The bones in Sereia's hand crunched as she punched through the library wall, triggering countless bookshelves to fall over and spill centuries of knowledge across the floor. Regret was immediate when she heaved her entrenched arm out from the wood—for the mess, the throbbing pain, and the immature reaction she'd allowed herself to have.

"If that was supposed to change my answer to yes, I'm afraid it didn't work." Pink hair and colorful peacock feathers shook along with Rev's somber face.

Did Rev not care? How could she choose to do nothing? She had never been so callous before.

Sereia had done what she could to hold back the flood, having not cried since Kthon had taken Rasal, but the tears rolled freely now. "Together we can bring our son back. My celestial magic and your nature spark."

"What's possible isn't the point. The dead should stay dead."

"But then…" *I'll never get to hold him.* Sitting on a fallen bookshelf, Sereia ran her good hand through her tangled auburn curls. "Then what do we do?" She didn't want to give up, but maybe Rev was right. Perhaps resurrection was going too far.

"We'll perform the naming ceremony, grieve for as long as we need, and pick ourselves back up." Rev grabbed Sereia's already-bruising and cut-up hand, letting a soothing warmth caress the wounds, mending them. The healing stopped just before the last bruise disappeared. "Why do you still have this rune on your arm?"

"I—"

Rev squeezed Sereia's hand like she wanted to break it again and pulled back Sereia's jacket sleeve. "You tattooed it on?" Rev must've realized why before needing an answer. "What made you think this was acceptable?"

Sereia's tattoo radiated light from white speckles on black ink. A perfect facsimile of a star-filled sky. "What choice did I have? Let a spirit keep Rasal for the rest of time?" Tattooing over the rune was the only way to keep him safe.

"Imprisoning him is better?" Rev's voice bounced off the library's tall ceiling, ensuring "imprison" was reiterated for Sereia until it sunk in.

She had never heard Rev so upset before. "I'm not—This is only until—"

Chapter 5 Hali

"No, this is too far. Sereia, I can't stand with you on this. Release Rasal's phantom."

"I can't. He's mixed in with the plague and some sort of spirit. It resists cleansing and I don't know how to separate them. What if I make things worse? I could accidentally release the plague again."

"Yesterday you didn't sound so sure a spirit was involved. Did something change?"

"Even from within the rune, I can feel the plague. It's exactly as Malakine feels when they link with me. Like I'm being worn as clothes."

"Then ask Malakine what's going on. As the celestial spirit, they should know what to do."

I haven't seen them since it happened. Not sure I want to. Malakine's failure is the reason Rasal is trapped. "We're not linked anymore. I'll have to go to the Arboreal Path to contact Malakine. Will you wait for me?"

"I'm here on borrowed time. Quarantine zones are still a mess, even with the ethereal plague cured. Whatever's wrong, it's not going to wait for our life to be easy first." Rev's tone was official and cold, like she was giving a report to the Conclave. "Bansil is the first country to accept our refugees, so we're evacuating every city south of Runegate."

It hadn't taken any time at all for one disaster to be replaced by another. The land itself was rotting with a rapidly spreading bleached white wasteland. A quarter of Thauma had already been lost to it.

"Right… I'll starportal to you when I'm done." Wanting to be anywhere but here, Sereia shut out the world and left her body behind to find Malakine.

The world turned into a two-toned void. Black on her left, white on her right. Had something happened to the Arboreal Path? Sereia couldn't see any constellations in the sky. There were no hints of the Corporeal or Ethereal Realms. No road of glowing tree branches. *Is the Path broken?*

The celestial spirit materialized ahead of Sereia, changing from a blurry silhouette to a floating humanoid figure. Malakine's right half had feminine features, smoothed over and pure black. Where their blinding-white left half always reminded Sereia of a puppet, today it was the black half hanging lifeless, waiting for its strings to sway.

"Was your cure a success, my celestial?" Malakine asked.

"Don't speak to me as if everything went according to plan. You didn't uphold your end of the bargain." Sereia would trade the cure for her son without question. "Rasal's dead thanks to you, and now he's trapped with a spirit and the plague."

"Ah, you mean Kthon, the false spirit."

"What do you mean false?" Sereia asked.

Malakine floated through the air and their white half grew a spike where their arm should be. It wavered in and out of existence as the spirit struggled to maintain it long enough to poke it into Sereia's tattoo. "The plague absorbs ether. You saw it with your ethersight, yes? There's no life inside that spirit except for the plague. It took over a dead spirit's body."

"Like you did?" Sereia didn't know which was the original, but Malakine's two halves had once been separate spirits.

"Don't think to compare me to your Kthon. I did what I had to and protected Empyrea from mortals."

"Kthon isn't mine."

"It's thanks to you Kthon has a body. Thanks to your ether that he grows. He's a part of you now."

"Stop. I don't care if Kthon stays and I'm forced to be his prison forever. Tell me how to get my son out of this rune."

"Forget your son. It is the celestial's burden to think only of the Ethereal Realm."

Burden this, burden that. All Malakine cares about is returning Empyrea's stolen ether. "Forgetting will never be my burden. My loyalty is to Rasal and Rev, not you or your spirit tree. You free my son and I'll give you every drop of ether in the Corporeal Realm."

Malakine's feminine half sprang to life and two voices overlapped as they spoke. "Then you're in luck. Kthon will be your key." Their white spike stabbed into Sereia's tattoo again, joined by a black spike. "Bring him to the surges. Let him absorb blood from each eidolon through these runes."

Five symbols Sereia had never seen flashed into her head and burned into her memory.

"Once you have all five, return the ether to Empyrea in the Ethereal Realm. When Empyrea is restored, it will be a simple task for me to bring your son back to life."

The binding rune glowed black on her forearm, and a guttural, static-coated voice spoke directly in her head. *Resurrect. Us.*

CHAPTER 6

Alim, with their golden palomino horse not far behind, found Tio at Wilton's entrance, attending to Stripes.

"Really, Alim? What is all that?" Hali asked, clearly referencing the half-dozen overstuffed bags slung over Alim's horse.

"You put me in charge of food, remember?" Alim said, devouring a chunk of cheese and rubbing their armored belly with closed eyes.

"There's only three of us, or did you forget?"

Alim forced a stubborn wheel of cheese into their bag, desperate to get it to cooperate. "You won't be questioning me once dinner time comes." Wrapping the bag up tight, they climbed onto their horse.

While Alim never traveled without their two-handed battle axe on their back and a throwing axe at their hip, they didn't expect to see Hali decked out for a fight. One dagger was sheathed in her boot and another in the spine of a white book—presumably filled with runes—dangling from her belt. *Two weapons and magic? Way to make me feel inadequate.*

"Do you always hide daggers in your reading material?" Alim asked.

Chapter 6 Alim

"It's much easier to seem threatening with a blade than a book with drawings inside." Hali followed Alim's lead onto their horse.

"Who do you plan on intimidating?" Tio hopped onto his okapi. "Spirits?"

"I've had my fair share of duels with spirits, you know? Weapons aren't effective. Nothing keeps one down for long." Hali rubbed her sleeved forearm. "Learning runes was enlightening though. Each is a word from the language of spirits. To use a rune is akin to calling upon their own magic, and many have special interactions with spirits. Yet there's no rune capable of destroying one."

Has she already tried killing Kthon then? What does Hali plan to do after I become a celestial and we free her family? Keep Kthon trapped in her body forever?

"Why would they have need for violence, especially against each other?" Tio asked as the three trotted along the southern road.

"No living thing is so enlightened," Hali said.

Tio grew quiet.

"Good job killing the conversation," Alim whispered to Hali.

According to Tio it would take at least four days to reach Spirit Arboretum from Wilton. Belsan territory was all new to Alim. People from Grenvel avoided it as if it were an unsafe enemy country, though it was technically part of Grenvel.

Growing up, Alim had wished to visit Spirit Arboretum and try every exotic fruit from the Coveted South. Especially solfruit. It was used in many Solstoran ceremonies and the arboretum was the only place to get it after the Quake created Phantasmal Reef and stranded the north.

"Hey, Tio, ever tried solfruit before?" Alim asked.

"No, don't think so. What's that?"

Didn't you say your mom is a Solstoran priest? "Never mind, was hoping you could help me find some in the arboretum."

Hali said, "It's a fruit from Fion. I'll keep an eye out for an extra juicy one.

"Fion?" Alim asked.

"One of two countries in the Coveted South. The less coveted one."

It hadn't crossed Alim's mind that the south had distinct countries. Why didn't people use their names anymore? "Does Fion not have the fancy technology?"

"Some, but it was more known for nature preservations, like Belsa's Spirit Arboretum. All the technology legends are about Bansil. Both used ether in their day to day lives like Thauma was striving to do. Funny that the Conclave and Gren Consortium both spent an inordinate amount of time failing to cross Phantasmal Reef since nobody cared until the countries were gone. Birds, fish, boats. Doesn't matter, nobody gets through and there's no way around."

"Why don't you talk about all this in your lectures?" Alim asked.

"Because nobody attends them for boring history facts?"

Tio giggled with an abrupt snort. "True! History is at the bottom of my list for sure."

Alim shrugged. "Well, I found it interesting."

Before long, the road veered more west than south and led them to the mage-built mountain, Last Stand. Its grassy peaks were numerous and unnaturally pointed, meant for impaling invaders. Many parts of the mountain were an unfinished painting against the sky, marking where the mages' efforts had halted.

High above the peaks, a jagged green hole marred the sky with a hazy mirage-like appearance. Its edges melded with the surrounding blue into a subtle cyan border. The Lunar Vault. Alim thought it aptly named, since Solstorans believed evil mortals were imprisoned in sky vaults—the three moons.

The green moon had exploded hundreds of years ago, not long before the ethereal plague hit Thauma and the Quake had separated Our Stranded Lands from the mainland by creating Phantasmal Reef. So many catastrophic events back-to-back, it was only natural Solstorans connected the exploded moon back to their legends of monsters escaping sky vaults to end the world. Even if the world was decidedly not ended and no literal monsters had been involved.

Under the shadow of Last Stand, the night sky had a single orange moon visible, giving the sparse grass an orange tint. An anzu flew overhead, the outline of its shaggy white mane and eagle wings barely visible. It roared as it soared towards a dense forest—Spirit Arboretum. Even from this distance, Alim could tell it had more types of trees than they knew existed. It made them want to purchase a botany compendium so they could name everything and impress the others.

"Hey, Hali, can you get some food supplies from my horse?" Alim asked while lighting a campfire with their axe and a flint.

Her disappointment at what she found echoed off the mountains. "Yeast and flour? Were you planning to bake cookies? We need real food."

Alim shrugged. "That wasn't me! As an experienced Refulgent Wastes traveler, I know how to pack appropriate food. Blame Tio."

"Don't call Thauma that..." Annoyance dripped from Hali's words like they'd been soaking in it for centuries.

"Habit." Only scholars still used the name Thauma when referring to Refulgent Wastes.

Tio was off on his own, growing patches of grass for the animals. "Sorry, Hali. I felt bad when Alim mentioned not buying any meat because of me, so I wanted to do something special." He brushed both animals with his hands. "Baking is simple with my flourish."

"How?" Hali asked.

"I'll show you when it's time for dessert. Put simply, yeast is a fungus. I can talk to it like any living thing and convince it to take my ether to help it grow. Speeds along the proofing process."

"Can't wait!" Sweets were Alim's favorite. *Baking by talking to yeast? Sounds more like the books with crazy immortal druids.*

"It created a lot of buzz at school. Medical students thought speaking to simple lifeforms could lead to new ways to heal diseases and wanted to pair up with me. With so few druids to assist, our research didn't get far, so I switched subjects." He pushed several seeds into the soil with a bloody finger.

"Tio, your hand," Alim said.

A bush sprouted and little green dots formed as Tio moved his hands along it. The blood from his finger evaporated, following the exterior-first rule of blood tolls. "It's nothing." Trace amounts of blood lingered on a silver leaf dangling from his bracelet.

"That's not nothing," Hali said.

He filled a bowl with ripened blueberries.

"Tio." Hali had the sternness of a mother.

He walked up and placed a bowl of blueberries into Hali's hands. "Sorry." Tio's jaw moved without his mouth opening, like he was chewing his tongue. "My flourish is weak. All druids, really. Our blood toll only works with open wounds."

Everybody knew druids had dwindled in numbers, but this was the first Alim had heard of weaker magic.

"Aren't runes similar?" Tio sat on the patchy grass near Alim's freshly lit fire.

Alim rustled through Tio's things, looking for a game he'd told them about.

"A common misconception. If you don't paint a rune with blood, it will siphon the toll from you directly. Greedy little things take more than necessary too. I have a potion recipe—"

"Let's play this game, Tio." Alim held out a cardboard box containing *Druid Fake Out*. It had little cartoon druids drawn on it, restoring a forest. One had an obvious wig and over-emphasized evil grin, holding their hands behind their back, an axe in one and fire in the other.

"I don't know… you probably wouldn't like it."

Alim tilted their head. "Of course we will!" They tussled Tio's hair, and he recoiled as if their hand were a spider.

Chapter 6 Alim

With the game unboxed, they scattered wordy cards, colorful dice, little figurines, and a board on a thick feather-patterned blanket. Tio's words all bled together as he explained the rules. It was a miracle they kept up at all. Alim nodded along, while Hali's gaze lingered on her cards as if they were written in a dead language. The three were a team of druids tasked with protecting a forest from a spreading rot. Except one person was secretly on the enemy side, trying to destroy the forest and sabotage the other players. Once the game began, Alim was assigned the glorious role of villain.

"How long have druids needed to bleed themselves to use their spark?" Hali asked.

"Maybe fifty years? We lost other powers over the centuries. Namely healing, long lives, and long-range communication using surges."

Alim played their card with a confident slap. "Wait, druids were really immortal?"

Hali placed a random card as if she couldn't tell what the best play was. "A hundred years is hardly immortal."

"It's not as if long life was ever part of our flourish. Non-druids in Belsa benefited too. Living longer is easy when your neighbor is a mobile hospital," Tio said. "Our archdruid, Bel, is our last remaining healer, and the blood toll is so high she can't make good use of it."

"It's no wonder you're on this mission." Alim grumbled at Tio's card choice. "Come on, really?"

After several rounds of encouragement, Hali still appeared to have no clue. She showed a card to Alim. "Is this one good?"

They grinned. "Oh yeah, the perfect play." *For me!*

Hali set the card on the blanket to end her turn.

Epic music blared in Alim's head like a whole orchestra was inside their helmet as they sifted through their hand and slammed down their card, cinching their victory. "I did it! Sorry, Hali. No hard feelings." They threw a fist in the air and bounced around the campsite.

"I missed something, didn't I?" Hali asked.

Tio gathered the mess of cards into neat stacks. "Alim won."

"Weren't we on the same team?"

"No, one of us was randomly assigned as the secret enemy. Alim in this case."

Alim's shameless hollering was only matched by the distant roars of the half-lion, half-eagle anzus roosting in Last Stand's peaks.

Hali smacked herself on the forehead. "The name *Druid Fake Out* makes more sense now."

Stripes and Alim's horse whined as gray mist flooded the camp. Alim stopped their celebration early, trying to figure out where the mist was coming from. Last Stand? The mountain wasn't known for its fog.

"I'll go see why they're upset," Tio said as he left.

Light dimmed as the campfire dissipated and the glow of the neon orange moon and setting sun were blocked from view. The animals bolted, with Tio chasing after them. At some point Hali must've unsheathed the dagger from her boot because she held it with both hands. The blade had a peculiar rainbow sheen, which the encroaching clouds of gray glided around.

Chills ran up Alim's arms, dotting them with a trail of goosebumps. Flittering like paper caught in a breeze, robe-like tatters floated at Alim and stopped at their face. Puffs of breath crept through the slits in their visor, reeking of rotted wood. Jaw clenched, their hands itched to have an axe in them, even knowing it would be ineffective against an incorporeal phantom.

Rattling their helmet with a disapproving, whispery screech, the phantom swam through the thickening mist towards Hali.

CHAPTER 7

The pungent stench of mold and a low hum marked the phantom's arrival. Gray filled Hali's vision in all directions. Etherite blade holding the mist at bay, her arms tensed as she gripped its hilt tighter.

After all this time, phantoms are still attracted to Kthon.

The phantom's gray tatters circled above, waiting for its time to strike. Hali wished she still had an etherite sword. Or better yet, magic. Anything to keep this unfortunate, discarded human a safe distance from her—and Kthon. The etherite metal in her dagger wouldn't scare it forever.

Heavy footsteps resonated through the mist, startling the phantom. Hali slashed as it dove, only managing to sever a small chunk of gray ether resembling cloth. The phantom's arm twisted around her dagger hand, clenching with damp, freezing wisps.

Alim barged through the mist and tried to tackle the phantom, falling right through it.

Struggling to move against the phantom's hold, Hali made quick, tiny cuts in the dense fog to shape it into a rune. Before the fog reconstituted, she placed her free hand into the symbol to activate it, her veins burning as the magic took its toll and the air roiled. Bursts of wind railed against the phantom, forced it to let go, and created a gap in the fog.

Alim grabbed their now-visible axe and stood side by side with Hali. "Why's a phantom attacking us?"

"Later," Hali said as the fog recollected around them and the phantom disappeared. *Great, it could be anywhere. What I wouldn't give for ethersight right now.*

With silence surrounding them, Alim's heavy breaths became hard to ignore. Hali's eyes darted, looking for where the misty form of the phantom might rematerialize. Alim's helmet turned murky and distorted. Hali kicked the back of Alim's knees, knocking them to the grass as shrieking energy exploded where their head had been. The force of the explosion pushed Hali onto her back and sent her dagger soaring out of reach. Alim's head smashed into the ground. A gnarled visage tore through the rippling air, wailing. With its misty robes unfurled, the phantom's appearance reminded Hali of molding fruit.

Alim groaned as ropes of grass extended and yanked them away from the battle. At the end of the ropes, Tio had both hands against the ground, only letting go when Alim arrived at his feet.

"Hold on, what if you're hurt?" Tio said as he kept Alim from standing and examined them.

Guess I dropped my dagger earlier. Hali detached her book from her belt. *Best to avoid using more blood.* Each rune inside was drawn using ink infused with her own blood, so a portion of the blood toll was prepaid. Hali flipped to a powerful fire rune—flame tooth.

Here's hoping the fire's light gives enough time to let us escape. "Tio, get our companions ready!"

Her blood burned, and heat welled in her throat. Face to face with the phantom, Hali spat a small flame through its head to give it a taste of what was coming—then opened her mouth and unleashed a conflagration that eradicated the phantom's top half and cast a red hue around the area.

Chapter 7 Hali

As Hali took a breath to prepare for her next volley, the phantom's remains wrapped around her throat. Choking, she ripped at it, only for her hands to pass through to her own cowl. Phantasmal fingers latched onto her left arm and pierced her rune. The tattoo burst with black light, and shadows encased the phantom as Hali's veins blackened. The phantom then dispersed along with the fog, leaving behind a searing headache.

As Tio and Alim approached with the okapi and horse, Kthon's shadows morphed into the face of an unknown woman before seeping into Hali's eyes.

Sereia's boots sank into crystalline blue sand. After weeks traversing Clikclik Dunes to find its ether surge, it was a relief to see the massive barrier of color-shifting haze. Awaiting beyond the barrier would be the first eidolon Sereia needed to collect blood from. The runes for Rasal's resurrection didn't activate with her own blood or any amount of ether she poured into them. Malakine hadn't lied—eidolon blood was the only way. As the haze transitioned from purple to pink, Sereia threw her arms apart, splitting the barrier in two and creating a haze-free corridor.

What kind of eidolon will I face here? Will it cooperate?

As if he heard her thoughts and was compelled to respond, Kthon's itchy presence entered her mind. *No cooperate. Kill.* With every word, the scent of freshly squeezed orange juice wafted forth, manifesting from nothing.

I'm not killing an eidolon if I can avoid it.

Rune needs all blood. Kill.

Killing an eidolon? Sereia knew she should consider the ramifications of doing such a thing. What might happen to the spirit linked to the eidolon? To Empyrea? To mortals? Why was Malakine asking her to do this? The answers didn't matter. Not if Sereia could see Rasal. No price was too high, and Sereia would gladly accept responsibility for the fallout when the deed was done.

Once on the other side of the barrier, a small pond surrounded by peach trees awaited. Every surge exhibited etheric imprints in different ways, and Sereia found each more beautiful than the last. This surge's ether manifested as gradients of ethereal pinks, purples, and greens streaked across the blue dunes.

She took a moment to admire the glimmering, color-changing sand, trying her best to delay confronting the eidolon. Of which there was no sign. There was nowhere for it to hide, and even if there were, it shouldn't have sensed Sereia's presence since she wasn't physically touching the haze barrier. With one hand gripping the hilt of her sheathed etherite sword, Sereia approached the oasis pond.

A small bundle of foliage whirled in front of Sereia. Then the mess scattered, revealing a miniature person made of white ash wood, with diamond-shaped ridges. She would be small even for a doll and easily mistaken for one if not for the fact that she flittered about via her own four translucent leafy wings, which resembled a grasshopper's.

The nature spirit—Dryadine—had an echo behind her voice, akin to wind chimes ringing in the distance. "Sereiamina! What brings this flesh to Zergi's domain?"

Sereia let out her relief and frustration with a sigh. Relief because Dryadine hadn't caught on to why she was here and frustration because she couldn't stand her proper name—or being referred to as "this flesh." She had to earn the right for the spirits to even acknowledge she had a name. Each spirit forced Sereia to undergo a trial to better her celestial magic and her connection to Empyrea. Dryadine's was one of two combat trials, so Sereia knew better than to initiate a fight with her.

"My name is Sereia. I told you a hundred times—forget it. I need something from Zergi."

"Oh-oh, it would be an honor to help Empyrea's celestial," Dryadine said, flapping towards the oasis. "I was jealous when I heard Vulkine and Malakine got to help with the plague."

Chapter 7 Hali

Not much to be jealous of. The fire spirit's seed didn't help our research in the slightest, and Malakine failed to protect Rasal.

Trails of etheric haze swirled to Sereia's hand as her blood ignited. The ether vibrated, rippling her skin, until a barrage of pink energy released, contorting into a series of waves and crashing into Dryadine. The spirit's body emanated a matching light and collapsed into shards of bark and leaves. She wasn't dead, but Sereia was hopeful it would keep Dryadine out of the way.

Sereia scratched her right arm, finding a rash forming under her sleeve. The magic use was getting her dangerously close to etheric drought already. *I should be more conservative with celestial magic. My spark will have to suffice.*

After stepping over Dryadine, Sereia caught a glimpse of a wolf before it vanished. *Was that the eidolon?* Scanning the oasis with her ethersight, she found no sign of it.

State your purpose for breaking in and incapacitating my spirit, celestial. Zergi spoke directly into her mind with a calming, charismatic voice matching how Sereia imagined royal speech to sound.

"I need your blood. Enough for one rune." Sereia continued searching for the eidolon, but there was nowhere for it to hide. Except the Path. Sitting between the Corporeal and Ethereal Realms, Zergi would be safe from her until it chose to attack.

You aren't the first to think to use our ethereal blood for magic. More will try after you fail.

"Malakine has asked this of me."

Do you believe Malakine infallible? That they know what's best for all? You don't understand the consequences of celestial magic, even after your last disaster. Look what it cost to cure the ethereal plague. Was it worth it?

As if an air mage had stolen the oxygen from her lungs, Sereia couldn't breathe. Nobody knew about Rasal's death except Rev and Malakine. "I didn't mean for that to happen. Malakine was supposed to—"

Do not put the blame on others. You brought Malakine because you knew the risks.

Tears obscured her vision. "I KNOW!" It wasn't meant to be this way. Sereia hadn't meant to kill her son.

"Good." Zergi's voice projected from behind her in addition to mingling with her thoughts.

Sereia ducked under the leaping wolf and her blood tingled as she intercepted it with a gust. Zergi crashed into the sand, and Sereia winced at the resulting yelp. The wolf was covered in green, orange, and yellow leaves instead of fur. Piercing golden eyes peered out from a crown of roots, which crawled across its spine, peaches dangling from it as decorative orbs.

A tingling sensation crawled up Sereia's spine, and the veins in her face pulsated in sync with her tattoo's writhing ink. Hooked spears of dark mist launched from Sereia's binding rune, homing in on Zergi. Although Zergi bounded between each spear with no effort, each successive dodge left less room for error, and all Sereia needed was one hit. After witnessing how Kthon had bested Malakine, Sereia knew it was her best chance to defeat eidolons, though Kthon's power was something she had yet to become accustomed to.

Wind swirled around Sereia's right hand as she continued guiding the shadowy spears with her left. As her next spell completed, Zergi's fangs bit into her arm and wrenched it aside to redirect the blast of air into a nearby dune. Multicolored sand rained down upon them as Sereia lost focus on her spears, letting them dissipate. She ripped her arm from Zergi's grip and shadows wrapped around her wounds. Without any input from her, the shadow-bandages sewed Sereia up like a twisted version of a druid's healing.

Returning the favor, Sereia slashed into Zergi's shoulder with her sword, crunching into its leafy hide. Vines grew and wrapped around the blade and Zergi vanished again, taking her sword with it.

A familiar eagle screech pulled Sereia out of the fight. Golden-brown feathers, black-tipped beak and talons, and a wingspan so wide it threatened to hide both moons. Orange and yellow light radiated from the moons and illuminated the eagle's rider—Rev.

With pink hair down to her shoulders and vibrant purple and green peacock feathers extending from the bottom strands to her lower back, Rev wore her long blue tunic, dark beige pants, wool-lined boots, and a wool-lined green cloak with a fig leaf emblazoned on it. Her left hand held a twisted quarterstaff of living wood.

You brought your staff? Talking must be out of the question.

Rev dismounted her eagle familiar. "Thanks, Shahbaz." She waved her hand and the gigantic bird soared away.

Zergi appeared, swordless, next to Rev as she spoke. "Sereia, please stop this resurrection nonsense. Come back with me. Let's cleanse Thauma before it becomes a wasteland. I can't restore our home alone."

Nonsense? "I'd rather die than return home without Rasal. Thauma doesn't matter anymore."

Rev leaned on her staff. "You don't mean that. This isn't worth it."

Sereia screamed until her lungs refused to supply air to her tantrum. Catching her breath, she struggled to speak given her sore throat. "Of course it's worth it! I'm bringing our son back—how could you possibly be against that?" She clenched her teeth, biting back the temptation to say more.

The disappointment on Rev's face was clear even before she frowned. That look used to make Sereia feel awful. It always came when Sereia had spent too much time studying or researching, neglecting to spend time with Rev for weeks. But it had no effect on Sereia now. Feeling any lower was impossible.

Within the span of a blink, Rev put her hands against the ground and unleashed whip-like brambles beneath Sereia. They wrapped around her arm and pulled her off her feet. Preparing another spell, the blood toll's tingling crept down her legs. With a twirl of a finger on her free hand, small whirlwinds sliced through the brambles. Sereia tried to move but every part of her body refused her demands.

Arboreal Path

Rev's staff stretched across the oasis and cracked Sereia's jaw. Its length morphed as Rev spun it around, hitting her again on the cheek before contracting to its original shape.

A numbing coursed through Sereia as her mind waned. Blood pooled on the dirt from Sereia's mouth. How long had she been on the ground? She still couldn't move. *Rev must've coated the brambles with paralytic poison.*

Feeling returned one limb at a time, and Sereia reached into a pouch on her belt for an elixir—a blue concoction capable of spurring a human's blood replacement process. It wouldn't bring her back to normal, but it may help eke out a few more spells. If she lasted long enough for the elixir to do its work.

Buzzing. Everywhere. Clouds of shiny dark blue wasps with orange wings surrounded her. Tarantula hawks, if she remembered from Rev's lessons.

Sereia's jaw clicked as she talked. "You care more about eidolons than your own family." Her rune burned against her skin, boiling her blood until the veins swelled and blackened, ready to pop. Her vision blurred and her ears rang. Citrus stung her nostrils. Consciousness became a struggle as Sereia neared the limits of the blood toll she could handle.

Misty tendrils leaked from the binding rune and dashed through the wasps, erasing them from existence. Gathering along the sand, the mist created a painting. A painting of a toddler shrouded in darkness, obscuring all features beyond a silhouette. Dozens of shadowy limbs sprang forth and peeled the painting from the sand and brought it to life.

Kthon, don't involve Rasal in this. Let him go!

Tears ran down Rev's cheeks. "Sereia, what is that? What have you done?"

Attempting to respond caused sharp pain to shoot through Sereia's skull. *I'm not doing this.*

The shadowy child sprinted using the wobbly, inhuman legs sprouted from his back and crashed into Zergi. Bones broke and reshaped within the child. Limbs stretched and bent at impossible angles. His head rotated

Chapter 7 Hali

upside down and spat out an elongated claw. Rev dove between the claw and Zergi, getting snatched in the wolf's place.

Kthon, let Rev go. We're here for the eidolon.

Blood swished within Sereia as the elixir struggled to bring her supply back. Sereia tried to pull Kthon back into his prison, but the rune acted as if she didn't exist. No ether answered her celestial summons, and her air spark did nothing.

Zergi howled, summoning a thick tree root to coil around Kthon. The stretched child phased through the root unharmed and lanced Zergi with a spike-like limb. Leaves vaporized from the wolf one by one as Kthon tossed it into the pond.

Pinned against the blue sand, Rev screamed as shadows poured into her. Ate away her ether.

Stop! A cord of shadow shot from Sereia's rune and attached to Kthon.

Drenched with sweat, Sereia yanked Kthon off Rev. His head sank into his body and came out the other end with a sunken, eyeless face. Was this Kthon's true visage or another borrowed existence?

With renewed strength, Kthon scurried back to Rev as limbs tore from his back and reabsorbed into the binding rune. Kthon exploded open into a maw endless as a star-filled sky and enveloped Rev before succumbing to Sereia's rune. A shadowy replica of Rev's face was the last thing Sereia saw before Kthon faded into the rune.

Sereia limped towards the pond Zergi had been thrown to. *Rev, Rasal, I can fix this. All I need is eidolon blood. Then we'll be a family.*

Sand jostled underneath Sereia as if the desert itself were trying to swallow her. Bright lights flickered around her, and the air tore open a doorway to another realm of existence.

A starportal?

Two shifting tones of hatred intermingled as Malakine floated through the starportal and landed in Sereia's path. "Sereia, my celestial. This should have been easy for you."

Easy or not, I'm almost there. "Move."

"You've done enough. At least with Kthon inside a surge, I can handle it now." Four additional starportals burst open around Malakine. "If I destroy the surges, then their ether will funnel to Kthon through these portals."

Malakine connected all the surges with these portals? Wait... "You can't—that would kill the eidolons and other spirits. I'll have no way to bring Rasal and Rev back to life."

"Spirits gladly die for Empyrea's future. It should be the same for my celestial and your doomed family. You squandered this chance for resurrection and killed your partner too."

A rainbow of ethereal energy gushed from the crags forming in the quaking dunes and from the starportals, bombarding Sereia. As the ether seeped into the binding rune to feed Kthon, Sereia felt power surge within her blood.

"When Empyrea's ether has been returned at last, centuries of turmoil between spirits and mortals will be over. All thanks to your family."

Sereia reached out with both hands and seized the ether within Malakine.

"Cease this, my celest—"

Malakine's two halves unraveled at the seams. Ethereal threads buzzed and ripped. Two of the starportals closed. Sereia's veins threatened to rupture, but she fought through the pain. Using the same technique she'd used to break open the haze barrier, Sereia threw her arms apart. Malakine's lifeless husks splattered the peach trees black and white. Two more starportals closed. Dryadine swooped out from the pond with a half-disintegrated Zergi and soared through the last starportal before it collapsed.

Zergi won't survive. When it dies, Dryadine will die too. Sereia collapsed into the sand. *Resurrection is impossible now.*

Although the starportals were gone and ether was no longer flooding the surge, the earth still quaked from the lingering effects of Malakine's spell. This surge was going to be destroyed. Water from the pond splashed as the land itself cracked and tilted.

The white remains of Malakine sloshed off the trees and clung to Sereia as she slid towards the ocean with the entire oasis. Between the fractures of the world, rampaging roots tore through the earth. Fissures erupted in the wood and leaked gray mist filled with millions of tortured eyes. The phantasmal blood of Empyrea blackened the water as the earthen slide crashed into the ocean, throwing Sereia from it.

Rasal. Rev. I'll be with you soon. Sereia dove into the phantom-infested waters head first, and the last thing she heard was shattering bone.

CHAPTER 8

Tio splashed a pail of cold water onto Hali, hoping his apologetic and worried expression wouldn't be the first thing she saw.

Hali sat upright, staring at Last Stand's grassy peaks as if it might leak more phantoms at any moment. "Are you two okay?"

"Us?" *You're the one who passed out with blackened eyes and veins...* "We thought the phantom got inside you or something."

"Don't be ridiculous," Hali said.

Alim tapped their helmet with a nervous pattern. "How are we supposed to know what's ridiculous or not with phantoms? My old Dreamer camp bordered Phantasmal Reef, and we had phantasmal storms all the time. Not once has a phantom been aggressive."

"What was a phantom doing here to begin with?" Tio asked.

Hali adjusted her cowl, pulling it up until it almost covered her chin. "Phantoms are attracted to areas with an etheric deficit. Last Stand is one such spot."

"Because of how the mountain was made?" Alim offered Hali a hand.

"Exactly." Hali grabbed Alim's hand and pulled herself to her feet. "Using their sparks until their blood ran dry. Etheric death... it makes your phantom unable to find rest. Without any blood, there's nothing to transport phantoms to the spirit tree's roots."

"Druids bury people with a seed to let their body nourish a future tree. We call it 'returning our power to Empyrea.'"

"There you two are with that spirit tree stuff again. Isn't that an old druid religious ritual, like burying soldiers with salt?" Alim asked.

"It's not a religion... it's truth," Tio said. "Some may stretch our old teachings into religious belief, but everything is based on real druid experiences. There's no mystery to it like with Solstora or the Old Faith."

"But you only know it through books and hearsay. What proof is there?" Alim asked like a kid trying to one-up their teacher.

"Our magic is proof. Ether in our blood gives us power. Where do you think it comes from? How do you think the surges form? You're literally trying to get special magic from fruit. Whether it's really a tree or not, all research points towards something from an external realm supplying the world with ether. With or without druid tales as support."

"I see what you mean. Guess it's hard to compare. My family raised me to 'embrace the sun' as it were, but I learned to see religious stories as stories. Otherwise we'd still believe a cosmic frog carries the world."

Hali appeared to be drowning in her thoughts, ignoring the conversation.

"Maybe let's table this." Tio scratched the stubble forming on his chin. "Hali, are we safe here? We can continue to Spirit Arboretum."

"It's my fault my family never rejoined Empyrea." Hali crouched and stabbed at the dirt with a dagger. "My partner never got buried with a tree. She'd hate me. My son would too."

Tio froze. *Does she want me to respond? What am I supposed to say to that?* His breathing became shallow.

Alim kneeled beside her. "Nobody hates you and it's not your fault. We're here to set things right for your family."

Hali nodded. "No more phantoms will come. We're safe to rest under the mountain."

As Hali left to get her sleeping bag, Alim whispered to Tio, "Let me explain her part in all this."

Learning Hali had lost her son and partner was crazy enough on its own, but Tio didn't know how to process the idea that a spirit had killed her family. And Alim was becoming a celestial to help Hali? *To think I almost turned Alim away and only brought them along when they proved helpful. I'm a jerk.*

The discussion shifted back to druids as Tio attempted to explain where to draw the lines of fiction, belief, and fact. It was clear Alim was having a hard time reconciling everything, as they continued to debate until Tio fell asleep midway through.

Spirit Arboretum's signature thousand-flower aroma was never the same. Today it hit Tio with the sweetness of honey, the floral notes of hyacinths, and hints of... *Peanut butter? That's new.*

The dirt path cutting through Spirit Arboretum's abundant foliage went on forever. Days after the phantom incident and Tio was still exhausted. He couldn't imagine how Hali and Alim must feel, considering what they'd experienced.

"We've been at this for half a day and I haven't seen the same tree twice. How can these all grow here?" Alim asked.

Tio could name every tree, but doing so would take longer than it took to walk this far. "Many can't. Without druid caretakers, the foreign trees would wither."

Hali trailed behind them, still as melancholic as she was at Last Stand. "This is Starpath. A healer planted everything here and made sure every tree on the path was unique. Many can't be found anywhere else. Not since the Coveted South got cut off by the Quake."

Beams of sunlight pierced the thick canopy, reflecting off Alim's helmet. "Didn't you say history was boring?"

Chapter 8 Tio

"It's tangentially related to ancient magic, you know," Hali said, shielding her eyes against the helmet's glare.

Although Hali had assured them the surge wouldn't be dangerous, Tio couldn't help but feel unprepared compared to his well-equipped team. Sure, weapons weren't his expertise, but he wanted to find a way to be helpful. As such, he carried a list of plants to keep his eyes open for. Tio spotted several he needed and whispered to the bushes while gathering ingredients.

"What are you doing?" Alim asked Tio.

"Hali gave me a recipe for an elixir. Accelerates blood production."

"No, not that. Why are you whispering to plants? Weird…"

"It'd be stealing to take without asking first. I mean, the words are unnecessary. Magic does all the work, but it makes me feel better."

"You're asking a bush for permission?"

Tio shrugged and moved on to a honey locust tree to pluck its thorns.

Hali kneeled next to Tio and whispered, "See that bright orange fruit? The long, skinny one?"

"With the yellow stem?" Tio asked.

"Solfruit. Use your spark to make it nice and plump for Alim." With a touch of concern, Hali added, "Don't touch your eyes after."

The solfruit filled out as Tio's flourish ripened it, becoming almost as fat as it was long. Seed-filled juice sloshed inside when he plucked it and realization of Hali's scheme hit him.

"Alim, here's that fruit you mentioned the other day." Handing the solfruit over, the tips of Tio's fingers were left tingling.

"Woah, it's bigger than I expected." Alim chomped straight to the stem, splashing a swirly orange and yellow juice on their chin. "Sweet! No, wait—" Hiccup! "Ow, what—" Hiccup! "Water. Water!"

As if prepared, Hali wiped Alim's blemished chin with a wet rag and handed them a full jug of water. Cheeks redder than a cherry and wet with tears, they chugged the water with annoyingly loud gulps, accompanied by exasperated whimpers.

Sitting down and panting like they'd run a marathon, Alim took the wet rag from Hali and raked it against their swollen tongue. "That's no fruit. You're the worst, Hali." They sounded like a bee had stung their tongue. Five times.

"Peppers are technically fruit," she said with the most genuine laugh Tio had heard from her. The way it made her puffy curls bounce would tempt Sir Fluffyboi to swat at them.

"So are tomatoes, and you don't"—Alim inhaled more water—"throw one in a bowl with peaches and strawberries."

"I'm so sorry." Tio had sensed the fruit was spicy when helping it grow but hadn't expect such intensity. Still, he grinned at Alim's exaggerated flailing as he went to get medicine.

Stripes bumped Tio as he dug through his packs. "Can I get one of those fruits? Seems fun!"

"Have at it. They're in those bushes, but don't expect me to ripen any." *I've used my flourish enough as it is.* Finding some medicinal flowers, Tio crushed them into Alim's empty jug. "This will help," he said, transferring water from his own jug.

"Thanks." Alim downed the refilled jug as fast as the first.

Hali poked Alim's helmet between the eye slits. "A new experience to write home about!"

"So thoughtful. My dad will love hearing I'll never taste again because our holy fruit is a hot pepper." The medicine had already improved Alim's pepper-induced lisp.

Resuming their trek down Starpath, Alim kept veering off to punch trees as if spreading their pain soothed the lingering heat.

"Keep that up and the arboretum might hit back," Tio said.

Dropping their hands as if to hide what they were doing, Alim asked, "Am I hurting it?"

"Not like that you aren't." Tio was surprised to hear a question generally paired with sarcasm spoken with genuine inquisitiveness instead.

Chapter 8 Tio

Can somebody without the nature flourish even understand? "Trees can't really feel the way we do."

"Tio!" Belsin—one of the arboretum's mage caretakers—funneled water to a batch of hydrangeas using a nearby stream. "Welcome back. Did you bring friends to study the haze with you?"

Next to him, Zecha used strong, square rotations of her arms to agitate a large patch of empty soil with her flourish. A variety of uprooted flowers waited to be replanted into the tilled land.

"Is Tio back?" Zecha asked. "Oh, look at you in your Conclave cloak. It suits you so well!"

Tio blushed as Alim and Hali nudged each other, neither quite able to hold back their snickering.

Flicking the leaves on his bracelet, Tio said, "Hey, Belsin. Hey, Zecha. We'll just be checking the haze for a bit. Same precautions as usual. Mind evacuating the arboretum for me?" He handed the reins for Stripes and Alim's horse to Belsin. "Make sure they're safe too."

"Anything for the Conclave."

As the two left, Alim let out a belly-propelled guffaw. Their words struggled out through snorts of laughter. "Our little Tio is famous!"

Tio dug his foot into the dirt. "Believe me, I'd rather live invisible. Instead, everybody in Belsa knows who I am just by virtue of my flourish."

Hali patted him on the back, and he twitched away. "That's clearly not true. They recognized you for studying ether and earning the Conclave's trust, not for being a druid. But… Alim is right. You're famous, you know?"

Both erupted in renewed laughter as Tio abandoned them. The trail ended at a fig-tree thicket with a violet haze winding through, forming an impenetrable barrier. He knocked on the dense haze with his knuckles and a twinge hit his blood. A slight pressure, similar to using his flourish. Three knocks, as was his tradition at the start of each research session. Both because the squeezing ether felt nice and the satisfying echo which resembled the high notes hit by a bard singing an energetic song.

Arboreal Path

"It's a big wall of ethereal lights! Beautiful… Are we destroying it?" Alim panted as they caught up.

Hali approached the haze barrier with her book open. "Impossible. The ether will mend itself."

Tio sat on a rough patch of dirt and drew in his notebook, adding extra details to a cat he'd drawn the other day. "How quickly? Will we have time to get through?"

"Safely?" she asked.

Each stroke of his pen made Tio wish his flourish were water so he could erase his abominable creation from the paper. "That's the idea, isn't it?"

"It's not like I've tried this before or anything." Hali flipped pages in her book and ran a hand along the edge of the haze.

As its color faded to green, strands of haze clung to her, yanking Hali against the barrier. She ripped the dagger out from her book and swiped the haze with its smooth rainbow blade. It scattered and returned to the barrier, letting her drop.

Alim ran to Hali with their axe ready. "What happened?"

"Never seen it do anything like that before," Tio said. *It's like the ether was attracted to her. Only seen that with the enchanted artifacts I used to measure the ether.*

"We've been denied entry." Hali sheathed her dagger and wiped off loose grass, dirt, and twigs from her pants.

"Denied by what?" Tio asked.

"The eidolon. It can monitor us through the barrier's ether. Let's see what I can do about that." She propped her rune book against a trunk and put her hand on a wild, jagged symbol on its pages. The haze writhed, twisting in on itself. Small bursts of wind pounded against the barrier and created a small opening.

She's making it look easy.

Alim stepped through.

Chapter 8 Tio

"Don't!" Hali yelled, releasing her hand from the rune.

Tio dragged Alim out of the opened path as the haze snapped shut in their face.

Hali slammed her book. "Don't be in such a rush. That rune was only meant to test it."

"Could've warned me then. Are you going to use a specialty rune this time?" Alim asked. They put a hand on the haze barrier as it shifted to pink.

"You think too highly of me. My plan is to hit it harder."

Hali removed her jacket, revealing the long, sleeveless black tunic she wore underneath. Ocean waves hid in the fabric that could only be seen when the light hit it right. Streaks of white shot across a black tattoo on her left forearm like dozens of wishing stars contained within a circle and an incomplete triangle. Tio fought the urge to take his pen and add a third line to the bottom. *So that's where her family is trapped?*

Drawing in the dirt with her dagger, Hali constructed a large rune. Three wavy lines inside a square. It was big enough that Tio could lie on each of the lines and not cover them completely. Hali dug around in her pack, taking out several candles and vials. She poured the vials' crimson liquid into the carved dirt and placed a candle on each of the corners of the square. Crouched on the middle line, her hands touched the other two.

Are the candles necessary? Don't runes only need blood? For fear of breaking Hali's focus, he kept his questions to himself.

Hali's eyes blackened for a moment. Same as they had when the phantom attacked her.

A new smell hit him. *Orange blossoms?* Was it from the arboretum or Hali's candles?

As Hali threw her arms over the rune, a breeze carried smoke from the candles and whisked past Tio, ruffling his hair. A spicy, earthy scent took over, reminding him of his mom's cooking. Cardamom? The thousand-flower aroma had never shifted so wildly before.

Arboreal Path

A gust of wind smashed past Alim next, nearly ripping their axe away. Trees bent, almost touching grass. Hali's arms shook, and blackened veins bulged across her skin. An eerie whistling rattled Tio's ears as wind circled the thicket. Bark stripped from the trees, and the whistling became a howling crash. The haze tore asunder, creating a clearing to the ether surge. A glimpse of the surge's overgrown bright pink and purple vegetation made everything they were doing real. His palms became slick with sweat. This was happening. Soon, he'd be inside a surge.

"I don't have all day." Hali strained to be heard over the rampaging wind.

Without hesitation, Alim bolted into a full sprint. Tio found himself not far behind, without realizing his feet had started moving. The top of the haze barrier reformed rapidly. Tio didn't want to imagine what would happen if everybody got trapped here. Behind him, the haze barrier had already shut itself, with Hali running ahead of the gushing ether.

Diving through an opening no bigger than a window, Alim crashed into vibrant grass, splashing leaves into the barrier. Tio jumped, grasping for Alim's hand, but the swirling, multicolored haze pushed between them. As if the ground he was running along no longer existed, Tio fell. And fell. And fell. Several leaves the shade of lilac tumbled alongside him. Staring at them distracted from the etheric haze coating him like burning oil, until he stopped, feeling as if his arm might tear off.

When Tio looked up, he saw a black mist rope connecting him to Hali as she dragged him up. *What sort of magic is that?* Every passing moment something drilled into his brain. Was it the shadow or the haze? Both? He clenched his eyes shut in pain.

Hali grabbed Tio by the wrist and hoisted him up with one oversized, boney hand. *Something's not right.*

Gritting his teeth, Tio pried his eyes open as a shimmering white wooden hand set him upon a road of wooden logs. *Where'd Hali go? Who is this?*

The wooden hand snapped back to a distant set of branches, where a glowing person sat with a bored expression. Their body was split in two. One side emitted pitch-black light with feminine features, the other bleached-white and masculine. They looked emaciated, as if they'd been starving for weeks.

Where am I? The road of logs was more like a series of interwoven branches. He was atop a monumental tree the likes of which would have been impossible to miss. Its bark was plain, but the leaves were colorful circles. Most were the ethereal trio of pink, purple, and green. The remaining ones were muted variants of blue, orange, and yellow. Gray mist coiled up the trunk, forming a dense fog crown that blocked the sky. *Nothing like this exists in Grenvel. Is this inside the surge?*

Floating to the branches they'd set Tio on, the glowing person said, "No, you never finished crossing the haze barrier." Their deep, yet soft, voice cracked between words, only the white side showing any signs of life—the other hung loose as if asleep.

Did they read my thoughts? Tio's vision warped and his eyes crossed as he looked down at the distant yellow meadow. He gripped the branch-road tight with sweaty palms and opted to stare at the far-off green sky.

"A power I inherited by sharing a body with Malakine. One I'd much rather be free of."

Malakine... Recognition struck. It was natural to pick up on root words for a couple of dead languages while studying ether. *Malak is book. No, too literal. Maybe mind. Ine is spirit?* Through dimming light, Tio saw bark-like crags running along the white side and star-like speckles throughout the black side. They looked to be composed of ether, though Tio had never seen white or black ether before. "Are you a spirit?"

"When I lived."

"How are you dead if you're speaking?"

"My new existence is an extension of Malakine, as my celestial ether sustains her and ensures she cannot die as I did."

"Who are you then? Originally I mean."

Arboreal Path

"No memory remains of who I once was, save for being killed by mortals and collected by Malakine." Their unanimated side ruined what should have been a wonderful smile as their tone grew energetic and childlike. "Though I do so enjoy the name I've since been given by Sereiamina. Call me Ikazu!"

Mortals can kill spirits? Tio didn't know who Sereiamina was and didn't even want to try pronouncing it. Not a Grenvelian name at all. Another spirit perhaps? "Where are we? Can you help me find my friends? We're trying to find out what's wrong with Empyrea."

"We're nowhere. This is all in your mind," Ikazu said.

Like when I commune with an animal? "How do I return to my body? I need to find an eidolon."

"Oh, you'll find my eidolons don't want to be found. Except by those with matching blood."

"Ethereal blood? Hali mentioned as much but says I can't get it. We're hoping my friend will be able to open the haze barriers when they become a celestial."

"A new celestial?" Ikazu's black edges grew into grasping tendrils as the other half awakened. "Sorry, my waking time is over. You have to leave now."

"Wait, not yet—"

Ikazu poked Tio's forehead with two wooden fingers and shoved him off the branches.

An intense rupture in Tio's skull distracted from the gut-flipping descent into darkness. It burned. Ached. Itched. And a thousand other sensations at once, only dulling when his back touched against something soft as a pillow pile. Sinking through, Tio dropped again until he collided with something far less comfortable.

"Tio, we thought you died!" Alim said, cradling him.

Coughing through his words as if he'd washed up on a beach, Tio said, "Nope, still here. Can you put me down please?" *Was any of that real or are ether-induced hallucinations a thing?*

Hali felt Tio's forehead with the back of her hand. "You're burning up." The veins on Hali's face pulsed as if she were still paying a high blood toll.

Tio swatted Hali's hand away. "You don't have to tell me. Feels like my head is stretching from the inside."

"What's wrong?" Alim asked.

"Don't think he was exposed long enough for ether poisoning. Keep him conscious, Alim." Hali darted through the lavender brush.

Heat radiated through Tio's body. His flourish activated on its own, building pressure in his body and squeezing his organs. Was this etheric death? How long before his body disintegrated? He felt fainter now than after spending a whole day tossing magic left and right.

"Hey, hey. Don't close your eyes." Alim squeezed Tio's cheeks. "You looking forward to any games after this?" They sounded muffled and tinny.

"Games?" Focusing was difficult. He searched through his brain for something related. "*Volatile Lemurs*. Tired of playing games by myself. It'd be fun to play with you two more."

"Sounds strangely violent and I have no clue what a lemur is, but I'll let Hali know." Alim tapped their helmet nonstop. "Are those bumps?" They sifted through Tio's hair, slow and methodical.

Rustling indicated Hali's return. She mashed together several herbs and squeezed solfruit juice into the mixture until it was all an orange paste. Hali smeared the paste onto a leaf and held it under Tio's nose. No smell, but somehow it snapped him to attention, urging him to vomit. He tried to push the gross concoction away, but Alim pinned his arms as Hali dabbed the two swelling spots on his head.

Lulled into a numbed state of half-consciousness, Tio couldn't feel the burning anymore, nor muster the energy to talk.

"What's on his head?" Alim asked, sounding more muffled than before.

"Don't know yet, but this shouldn't be possible. It's as if he's been touched by an eidolon."

"Was an eidolon in the haze? Did you see it while you were in there with Tio?"

"No, haze barriers trap the eidolons inside. Leaving is impossible. Maybe an eidolon contacted him through the ether?" Hali rubbed more paste on the growing protrusions, working it down into his hair. "All we can do is wait until the conversion is complete."

"Conversion of what?"

"His blood. Tio has ethereal blood now."

CHAPTER 9

Pacing between the haze barrier and the nearby grove repeatedly, Alim had already counted every fig tree twice. Seventy-eight. With everything in the surge tinted by ambient ether, a new set of colors graced their eyes every few moments. At first it had been disorienting, but now they barely noticed the ether.

On the other hand, Alim found it impossible to ignore the ceaseless chirping from hidden birds.

Hali determined Tio was growing antlers, saying it was normal for a person with ethereal blood to take on eidolon traits. But the stumps on Tio's head didn't look like antlers to Alim.

Groaning, Tio asked, "What happened?" His hands came away from his hair covered in the orange goop Hali had used to soothe his pain.

"Can you not remember?" Hali asked, handing Tio a damp towel.

Tio wiped his face and hair clean. "No. Everything between you opening the haze and Alim catching me is gone." As he stretched, his bones made a symphony of satisfying-sounding pops.

Alim tried to pop a few knuckles but failed to do anything except get hurt. *Ouch…* "You're going to love your new look," they said. "Antlers are fashionable." *Like a permanent winter solstice costume.* Silly jackalope-themed attire, like antler-headbands, were common in Grenvel this time of year. Alim loved people willing to publicly deck themselves out in solstice attire. "All you need is bunny ears and tiny wings to complete the set."

Tio poked his antlers. "Kind of stubby. You got my hopes up."

At least he's maintained a good mood.

"They're still taking in ether to grow. Give it a few weeks, maybe a month," Hali said.

"Is that how ether works? Share the love. Puberty refused my request for a growth spurt." Alim struggled to reach the top of Tio's head to compare their height.

"Being short is part of your charm," Tio said.

Too good a mood. "I think I preferred you numbed with solfruit paste." Alim retrieved their axe from the tree it was propped against. "Since you're better, what's the plan?"

Tio stroked his chin as if contemplating some genius strategy. "Not a clue." He wiggled a finger, letting wisps of pink ether curl around it. "The ether inside the surge is different from the barrier. It's malleable. I'd love to study it, but I think searching for the eidolon is our more promising venture."

Hali nodded. "Agreed. With your ethereal blood, the eidolon should be less… agitated by our forced entry into its domain. It may even help you learn what's wrong with Empyrea. The fun part will be convincing it Alim is worthy of celestial magic."

"How do I prove that?" The idea of being judged made them itchy like a spreading allergy—it reminded Alim of trying to impress Dreamer leadership.

Hali looked Alim up and down. "Could you try being less Alim-like?"

"Everybody done roasting me? Come on…"

Chapter 9 Alim

"I don't know about Tio, but I have another century's worth of material on you." Hali pummeled Alim's shoulder with tiny punches. "Be ready to answer the eidolon's questions and to do whatever the spirit wants of you."

"Then we'll get a spirit fruit from it and I'll be a celestial?" Alim asked for confirmation.

"You'll be one-fifth of a celestial and start to manifest some power. But for our needs, two or three pieces of fruit is best. That's when you'll really be able to bend ether to your will."

We're so close. "Let's go find us an eidolon!"

The trio trekked deeper into the surge, breaking through tangled bushes to an open glade. Foggy ether coated the trees in a pale, almost white, purple hue. Rushing water signaled an unseen river. Were they near the Trachea?

"Should we follow the river?" Alim pointed towards the sound of trickling water. "It has to drink at some point, right?"

"Can't say I know if eidolons require sustenance," Hali said.

Aren't you the eidolon expert here?

Tio brushed a hand against a tree trunk, nodding periodically as if he was having a silent conversation. "This way." He moved where Alim had pointed to.

"Wait, you can ask trees for directions?" Alim asked.

"Don't be ridiculous. See these fresh scrapes on its bark?" Tio swiped a finger against subtle indents in the wood. "And these shavings? It's clear two different types of trees made this mess. Like a tree rubbed against another tree." He blew a cloud of wooden dust off his finger. "Plus, your water idea makes sense."

"Oh." *I don't understand the rules of his nature gift at all.*

"Don't feel bad, Alim." Hali lingered too long on the word *bad* for Alim's taste. "Took me forever to grasp what talking to plants means. At least animals have human senses and motivations."

"It's not complicated." Tio itched the base of his head-stumps. "Plants are simple. Survive. Grow. Make babies. Repeat."

"Doesn't sound different from people I knew in the Dreamers," Alim said as the search for the Trachea River began.

Tio laughed. "In a way there's much in common. But they can't see or hear or… anything else necessary to think and make decisions. Never had a plant say 'no' to a beneficial trade before. Unlike animals, who are as stubborn as people."

A scream pierced through Alim's response, drowning them out. It sounded human, but were there humans in surges? A small leafy root creature sprouted up from the soil in front of them. Its face was like a white wooden mask with pine needle hair and no eyes or mouth. It had tiny wooden nubs for legs and arms, and leaves wrapped around it, approximating clothes. Its loud wailing continued as it ran away, kicking up a storm of pine needles.

Shielding his eyes from pointy debris, Tio asked, "What was that?"

Hali said, "A mandragora. They don't teach you about those in Belsa?"

"There are hundreds of species—I can't know them all."

Several more screeches rang out. Mandragoras popped out of dozens of little holes and scattered, and puffs of flame burst through the pine-needle clouds as the skinny snouts of pyre dredgers climbed out of the mandragora holes. The fire-breathing moles scurried in the opposite direction of the mandragoras. Something in the air smelled sweet, like cherries. Light blue smoke escaped from the holes. Alim choked as they breathed it in.

"Innoboro poison," Hali said. "This dose is meant for small animals, so we should be fine."

"You'd know, Miss Poison Rune." Alim drew their axe.

The ground rumbled as thick, swampy stalks crept out of each of the holes. One stubby stalk had an eye on the end of it. As it pushed through, the grass and dirt gave way to a living, teeth-filled mess of vines. Cherry-scented blue smoke leaked from its gaping mouth as it wriggled.

Chapter 9 Alim

Tio pushed Alim's axe down. "Let me," he said as he walked to the beast. "Innoboro, please halt. We're simply passing by."

They weren't sure if any of Tio's words got to the creature because a tendril whipped out and latched onto his arm with sticky slime.

Alim sliced through its appendage, grabbed Tio, and pulled him to safety. The ground trembled as the innoboro slammed its tentacles in a tantrum.

Hali's book glowed and the innoboro's oozing smog vanished. *Of course she has a rune to counter innoboro poison.*

"Don't hurt it," Tio said.

"Its limbs will grow back." Hali turned pages in her book and activated another spell. The rampaging tentacles calmed, and the innoboro crumpled over with its eyestalk closed. "That'll keep it sleeping for some time."

"That was a lot. You alright, Tio?" Alim asked.

"Besides being useless, yeah."

"Why didn't your spark work?" Hali hooked her book onto her belt. "Is this because nature magic is weak?"

"If only I had such an excuse. My own weakness is to blame. Animals never respond well to my attempts to talk."

"That innoboro wasn't going to listen to anybody," Alim said. "Other animals like you well enough."

"You only met the weird ones." Tio guided everyone by the sleeping innoboro. "Shouldn't be far now."

A cliff stopped their progress with water finally in sight. Tio pricked a finger against his bracelet and smeared blood on a nearby root. Bursting through the soil, the root curved in and out of the cliffside to form steps to the bottom.

"Good job, Tio." Hali hopped down the roots first.

He blushed, scratching the back of his neck.

Following the river didn't work as well as Alim had hoped. It led to the other side of the haze barrier and Tio didn't discover any new clues.

"Should we turn back?" Tio asked.

Alim tapped their helmet. "What other choice—"

Birds scattered. Trees rattled, swaying as a piece of the canopy moved on its own—towards them.

"Wait, is that tree moving?" Alim asked.

"Eidolons sense everything coming in and out of haze barriers. It must be investigating." Hali's voice quivered as if the eidolon's footsteps were shaking her vocal cords.

"Would've been nice to know that earlier. Is it angry? Can Tio talk to it?"

"Anybody can talk to an eidolon. It's not just an animal—it's part of Empyrea."

"I don't know." Tio jangled the leaves on his bracelet. "I don't know."

"Who are you talking to?" Alim asked.

Tio trembled. "You don't hear that?"

A giant stag stepped through the undergrowth. Branches grew from its skull like antlers, forming a massive tree full of figs. Green leaves floated down as the stag walked, forming a trail behind it. Its brown fur had the same purple tint as everything else in the surge. With each soft, noiseless step, the grass it crushed sprang back taller. The other trees and plants seemed to reach for the stag as if begging for its magic.

All three were still as statues when it neared. An odd tranquility sat in the air as its gaze shifted between Tio and Hali. But never Alim—it ignored them. One of its eyes looked wrong. Instead of a black orb, it was amber with a small black pupil.

The others appeared to be having difficulty in the eidolon's presence. Tio's hands were unsteady, but this was the longest Alim had ever seen him maintain eye contact with anything. He was either dying inside or determined. They hoped it was the latter, because Tio had been through enough today.

With Hali's cold, empty stare, she seemed prepared to justify her existence to a god. The look made the hair on the back of Alim's neck stand on end, and they were glad Hali wasn't directing it at them.

Chapter 9 Alim

Etheric haze rose from the ground, blanketing the group until none were visible.

The eidolon's words mingled with Alim's thoughts and, simultaneously, boomed across the glade and shook a storm of leaves free. "You seek power? To walk the Path?"

As the haze receded, Hali and Tio were gone.

"Not for power's sake. Magic is a tool to protect people. With it I can help my friends."

"Ask Sereiamina how effective celestials are at protecting."

"Who? What did you do with my friends?"

"Same as with you. Once each person's intent is clear, you will be reunited."

The stag stomped the dirt. Rippling water drew Alim's attention behind them to the Trachea as it became frothy with bubbles. *It's gifted with water magic?*

"Will you take on the celestial's burden—to serve Empyrea? Abandon the Corporeal Realm to act as the spirit tree's proxy among mortals?"

"That's a lot of confusing things to commit to on the spot," Alim said.

A cool breeze swooshed through the stag's leaves. "The deed is not done until the Path is completed—a full connection to Empyrea established by the eating of our spirit fruits."

Even if I can back out, this is shady. "If the cost of being a celestial is acting as a servant to you, then count me out."

"The last celestial was of the same mind," the stag said as something damp grabbed Alim's wrist and dragged them splashing through the Trachea's shallows.

Hali didn't mention it might turn aggressive! Alim struggled against the water, but the entire river might as well have been holding them back. Knowing they'd already ruined the chance to obtain magic, Alim unhooked their battle axe and slashed into the stretched watery appendage. Its detached hand remained, squeezing Alim's wrist tighter and freezing.

Arboreal Path

A hand? Did the stag create a water golem? Seems unnecessarily flashy.

Alim smashed the golem's frozen hand against their leg, shattering it. The stag's water golem stood in the deep end of the river with an outstretched and freshly de-handed arm. It had taken the time to mold the golem like a woman with tall tsunami-shaped hair that whipped around, suds gurgling through her with each dramatic, flowy movement.

While the wounded arm retracted and morphed a new hand, the other hurled water missiles in Alim's direction. Without a thought, Alim tracked the golem's stance and arm angles and moved enough for the volley to soar right by their visor, so close it splashed them with droplets. A second assault clipped them on the arm and exploded into icy vapor.

Frost grew on Alim's skin and sent shivers through their body. *Maybe Hali was right. Should've worn sleeves.*

Bubbling underneath Alim, tentacle-like water coiled around them and pulled them face to face with the… golem? Her eyes, one green and one blue, followed Alim's movements. She breathed. *No way is the eidolon showing off this much.* The water-woman wasn't being controlled. She was alive. *Is this the spirit?*

Throwing a left hook at the water spirit, their fist splashed most of her face away. The sight of a nearly headless woman made them hesitate long enough for the spirit to freeze the water around Alim. The ice lifted, with Alim in tow, and launched onto the muddy bank.

Another arm of water gripped Alim by the neck, raising them as the spirit floated over. Ice melted onto the spirit's slowly reforming face below them.

Alim dropped their axe, catching the handle between their legs. With a twist, the blade slashed through the water. Hurtling down, they plopped into a mud-spattering mess.

Smearing mud from their visor, they couldn't see the spirit anywhere. *Where are you hiding now?*

Mucky water rippled underneath them, and they soared out of an Alim-shaped hole in search of their axe. Disgusting, undrinkable water struggled, reaching for the sky from where Alim had landed. Weaponless and unprepared for the next assault, they winced.

Feminine and bubbly, like something was caught in her throat, the water spirit spoke from the puddle. "Vinn, this is our new celestial?"

Alim's helmet clattered as the stag spoke. "Do you not approve, Undine?" The eidolon kneeled to the tiny, rippling puddle as if bowing in respect.

I was right—Undine means lake spirit! Wait... that'd be like me being named axe human. "Hold on, eidolon... stag... Vinn? Vinn, why did you attack me? Sorry I can't be your celestial servant or whatever you said, but I only want to help my friend, Hali."

Vinn stepped over Undine and turned its golden eye towards Alim. "A servant is the exact opposite of what we seek in a celestial. You answered my question correctly, so Undine commenced her trial without hesitation."

A face formed in the puddle, nodding. A tiny hand popped out and pointed at Alim. "This flesh hasn't bested me with magic, so consider the trial failed. Using weapons is cheating."

"My name is Alim, and I don't have magic. I'm pallid."

"Flesh-beings don't get names."

Alim felt grossed out and tried to think of an equivalent term to wield against the water spirit. "This flesh-being defeated a moist-being in battle, so I think I earned a name." Hopefully spirits hated the word moist as much as people did.

"Defeated? This flesh fell on me."

"Doesn't matter, 'this puddle.' I still won," Alim said, kicking mud into Undine. "But..." *Guess Hali never told me the full story.* "What is this celestial burden? Why was that the question you asked me?"

The stag shook its head until a pile of leaves drifted down over Undine. Within moments, she was whole again.

Vinn said, "Because it was the mandate previous celestials followed. To think of the Ethereal Realm before oneself, your loved ones, or the

Corporeal Realm. It turned them into weak-willed tools of the celestial spirit. Only the last thought to defy. After much harm had come to the world. And herself. If the world is to have another celestial, they shall not be weak, and we shall ask nothing of them."

"All flesh is weak," Undine said with a bubbly smirk.

Is Hali the celestial that defied? "Why would you share powerful magic with me for free?" Alim asked.

"Do not mistake Vinn's offer as selfless," Undine said. "A celestial must reopen the Arboreal Path or we remaining spirits and eidolons will die. Otherwise we'd never risk allowing a mortal to take our power again."

"Yet I'm not being asked to do this?"

"Simply visiting the Path yourself should open it for us as well. Enough for spirits at least. Eidolons may need to wait until you eat every fruit."

"I'm still not ready to decide. Not until I see my friends are safe." *Not to mention Hali needs to explain why she left out this celestial burden stuff.*

"Of course." Lowering its head and nearly swiping Alim with the crown of its fig-tree antlers, Vinn said, "Take one. Tread the Path with care."

Alim maneuvered a hand through the maze of five-pronged leaves, seizing one of the figs from its antlers. "How long will the fruit last?"

"Take your time. My fruits do not expire so long as you remain within my surge," Vinn said as its canopy returned upright. "Now for your friends." A multicolored haze rose again, obscuring Vinn, Undine, and everything else.

When the haze receded, Vinn loomed over tall tree roots with a human figure caught within. Tio? *Why isn't he moving? Did Vinn put him in some sort of trance? Why—*

Vinn nudged Tio with its front hoof and green mist wafted out from Tio's mouth.

"Hey, what are you doing?" Alim tried to run, but ice had already encased their feet.

A cold fog reminiscent of Undine whirled around them. "We're protecting Empyrea."

CHAPTER 10

It had been some time since Hali last saw Vinn. Standing in the middle of the purple-stained greenery of the grove, a mere glance brought the taste of sweet figs back to her lips.

Vinn was fourth of the five eidolons she'd visited when she was on the Path. At the time, it was linked with Nomine—the earth spirit—and didn't have the strange golden eye reminiscent of the amber gemstone door leading to Hali's family catacombs.

The stag bowed its head. "Sereiamina, welcome home."

Hali cringed upon hearing her full name for the first time since battling Zergi. Only her father used it, but Rev had introduced her to the eidolons and spirits as such instead of "Sereia." It was the joke that kept on giving.

"Thauma is my home. Besides, I've received warmer welcomes. Your barrier attacked me."

"Did you expect different bringing your artificial spirit here? Dryadine warned us not to let you and Kthon near our surges."

So they know... "I wouldn't have come if I could avoid it. Kthon has shackled Rev and Rasal long enough. Alim must become a celestial and set my family free."

"Then you didn't attack Zergi's surge for Malakine?"

Not for Malakine. "I didn't kill Dryadine and Zergi if that's what you're implying. You can thank me for stopping Malakine from ripping the other four surges apart."

"But you played a part in bringing Kthon to the surge, did you not? You didn't kill anybody, but Kthon killed many that day."

In a hopeless attempt to maintain composure, Hali balled her hands into fists and counted her breaths. *One... two... three...* "Don't expect an apology. Can we move on? I've brought you a new celestial and a druid to guide them. Think of them as recompense for my mistakes."

"You think we'd want to work with another celestial after what you and your predecessors did?" Vinn asked.

"Don't be coy. We know Empyrea is dying. If you could fix it yourselves, you would have by now." Hali relaxed her fingers and exhaled. *Four... five...* "Tio's antlers came from you, exactly as Franz gave Rev her peacock feathers." *Six... seven.* "And you're having Alim undergo a trial with your spirit as we speak, or am I wrong?"

If there was a chance that Tio and Alim could restore Empyrea, there would be no choice for the eidolons but to accept them. To do otherwise would doom their kind.

"It is true Undine is testing Alim. However, Tio's ethereal blood was not my doing," Vinn said.

"Then who?" *There's only one eidolon per surge, so who else could have?*

Water sprayed from Vinn's branches as its canopy rustled. "Besides an eidolon, only a celestial spirit could alter his blood."

Sweat beaded on Hali's brow. "Impossible. I killed Malakine during the Quake. Their ether turned to dust. Wouldn't Empyrea be fine if you replaced them with a new celestial spirit?

Chapter 10 Hali

"There is no new celestial spirit." Grass and flowers sprouted with each step Vinn took away from Hali. "Tio's ethereal blood requires cleansing."

"Cleansed how? Wait, don't hurt Tio. He didn't do anything!" Hali ran after Vinn, getting caught in the dense foliage growing in its hoofprints. *Didn't Vinn say it was linked with Undine? How does it have the nature spark?* Thorns cinched around her neck.

Vinn vanished through a purple haze.

Hali raised her boot high enough to slip its dagger out. Ancient thoughts resurfaced as she cut herself free. *Can two spirits link to one eidolon? Vinn confirmed Dryadine died though.* Was there another way for Vinn to have nature-infused blood? Hali's binding rune vibrated with black energy as if to remind her what Vinn's blood could help her accomplish.

Raspy words punctured her heart, reopening old hopes. Within her, Ikazu's presence became faint, and Kthon filled the gaps in Ikazu, speaking familiar words. *Resurrect. Us.*

Was resurrection still possible? Hali had wasted a lifetime looking for an alternate solution for her family when the original had sat within Vinn all along.

Now's not the time to revisit my plan. I need to find Tio.

CHAPTER 11

Tio never thought he'd see the day being alone was more overwhelming than drowning in swathes of clamoring people. If either Alim or Hali were still here, he'd be hiding behind them from the eidolon's chilling gaze.

Its unsettling eye was bright enough to overpower the etheric fog in the air, with a distinct coloring reminding Tio of the Conclave's yellow warble receptionist. Thinking of the annoying bird only made him fidget more.

"Another lost druid ferrying power-hungry mages into my domain." The trees shook with each word, but it was also as if the stag spoke into his mind. It was nothing like talking to other animals.

Am I being too trusting of Alim and Hali? What if they're just using me?

"Which eidolon gave you ethereal blood?"

Gripping his shaking hands together in an attempt to still them, Tio said, "You're the first I've ever met." *Deep breaths.* He gave his antler-nubs a tap. "These showed up after falling into your haze barrier. We thought you gave them to me."

Chapter 11 Tio

"Antlers they may be but not mine. A side effect of receiving your blood in my surge. Empyrea can ill afford an unvetted druid masquerading with ethereal blood," the stag said as gnarled white roots burst through the grass, twisting amongst themselves and Tio.

Tio expected the roots to squeeze the breath out of him, but they held him with a gentle touch, like his mom had when he was a child. Now eye-level with the stag, Tio flinched as it nudged him with its muzzle. The environment melted away, leaving Tio free to roam in endless white. Thoughts were thrown at him at a startling rate worse than an intense communion with an angry Sir Fluffyboi. A prevailing thought clung to him, containing a name. Vinn.

The void filled in with yellow grass, and an enormous tree scraped the sky. Parts of the tree were muddled and grainy. Others were completely missing, with jagged, shadowy holes in the middle of its trunk, branches, and leaves. Phantoms swirled around the tree along with streams of pink, green, and purple ethereal lights. Etheric haze wafted from the roots into a blue moon in a green sky. Tio reached for a nearby root, but an overwhelming pressure pushed against him like a giant crushing his head.

"Why is this place so familiar?" Had he seen it before?

Trying to remember brought pain worse than whatever prevented Tio from touching the tree.

"It should be. This is where you received ethereal blood," Vinn said.

"How are you showing me this? Are we communing?" If they were, it was far less abstract than he was used to. More recalling a memory than exchanging vague emotions.

"Communions were always this vivid when nature magic wasn't a mockery of its former self."

"Are you saying my flourish is stronger?" Tio asked.

"Nothing your ancestors weren't capable of. Don't concern yourself with power. Once the extraction is complete, you will be pallid."

Extraction?

Pink light extended from Vinn and wrapped around Tio's legs. Though his headache subsided, Tio's blood heated and slopped like thickened oatmeal. Each time his blood smashed against his insides, a freezing color-shifting steam escaped his pores.

"What you're feeling is your ethereal blood returning to Empyrea," Vinn said as its aura crept up Tio's neck. "This memory our communion has recreated is flawed, covered in holes. It's been tampered with. There is no clearer sign your ethereal blood is corrupted."

I can't lose my flourish! A green flicker engulfed Tio's vision. A slithering sensation ran down his body, and when sight returned, Vinn's aura had receded.

Tio's hands—no, his everything was shining green.

Vinn stomped its hoof. "Stopping the extraction will put Empyrea in danger!"

The ethereal steam stopped leaking from Tio and grouped together on its own. It undulated. Hardened. Melted into a shadow. Tio shielded his face as the shadow bowled into him. Instead of feeling its cold grasp, Tio watched as his aura devoured his would-be attacker.

"That was inside me?" Tio asked, patting himself all over as if more things might crawl out from him.

"Impressive. I was mistaken about you. Never would I have expected a mortal capable of quashing corruption on their own."

"What is corruption? Do I have more?"

"Nothing in a communion is real. Think of this as your mind contextualizing what's happening within itself."

So I don't have green light powers. Should've known. "Real enough for you to try stealing my flourish."

Vinn's remaining pink aura disappeared. "Without an intact memory of how you got your blood, I had to assume you'd be a danger to Empyrea. If you're truly here to heal our spirit tree, you'll no doubt have to make similar judgements."

Will I? It's not for me to judge anything.

Chapter 11 Tio

The holes in the all-encompassing tree filled in, and the distortions coating it disappeared. A pink, circular leaf floated into Tio's glowing grasp. Warm ether gushed from one of its roots and nearly knocked Tio over as it shot into the sky and battered into the distant blue moon.

Tio hovered his hand over the wounded root. "Is this Empyrea? Did the Quake injure it?" It couldn't have been a coincidence that the Quake had centered on an ether surge. Tio had always assumed it had played a part, whether it had caused the issues or was a result of the true cause.

"These injuries predate the Quake. Take witness to what started it all—the opening of the Lunar Vault." Vinn stomped one of its hooves and, as if waiting for a signal, an ear-shattering shockwave knocked Tio flat on his butt.

Drizzles of blue debris blocked the sky and tinted it teal. Where the moon once stood, a stretched, distorted scar remained. Empyrea's ether changed colors and rushed past Tio in increased volumes, so much so he thought the Lunar Vault might pull him in too.

The Vault is carrying ether out of the Ethereal Realm?

With a *pop*, everything surrounding Tio faded and left him floating in emptiness.

"What caused this?" Tio asked.

"If I or my linked spirit knew, you would have seen. Memories are the building blocks of communion visions. We only know Empyrea's ether has been stolen and abused since mortals first found it by wielding runes they did not understand."

Who though? Sipherra is capable of harvesting ether, but only recently and the Lunar Vault has been there for hundreds of years. "Are our flourishes stolen then?" Tio hadn't considered whether the ether supplying magic to humans was given willingly.

"No, the very surges you seek to repair are the result of a compromise from the last time spirits and humans clashed. When Empyrea's first celestial spirit died, it was decided to allow ether to drain into the Corporeal Realm to sate mortal desires."

"Mortals killed the celestial spirit?" A flash of a radiant, wooden face appeared in Tio's head. *Why is this face familiar?* "So Empyrea is weakening because the celestial spirit is dead and the Vault is draining it?"

"This is but one such event to siphon significant ether from Empyrea. You weren't wrong with your first assertion. The Quake disrupted Empyrea's flow of ether by destroying a surge. One with the nature spirit and its linked eidolon inside."

"I presume without a nature spirit, there's no way for Empyrea to produce the ether that gives druids our flourish?" *And mages are still impacted because of this… flow disruption.* "Is there any way to reverse this?"

"Spirits are many, but Empyrea is too young to have had other nature spirits to take Dryadine's place and too drained to birth new spirits."

"Birth? Are spirits Empyrea's children?" Tio sputtered over his own words.

Nothing worked how he expected. Every new morsel of information rattled against his existing understanding, eradicating obsolete facts and theories. "Are you implying there are other spirit trees?"

Vinn remained stiller than death.

"Vinn?" Tio waved. *Why're you all frozen?* He poked its leg and the stag cracked as glass would. Pieces of Vinn dropped into the void and shattered. Tio fell as the world shook and distant lights shone inside the fractures. *No! I still have more questions!*

Hopping between collapsing pieces of darkness, Tio tripped and slid into endless nothing as the speckles of light grew and grew. A strange hand grabbed him and dragged him onto wet grass.

Is the communion over? Tio awoke laid out beside the ether-touched plants of the surge with Alim's helmeted face hovering over them. *Is this going to become a thing?* "Where's Vinn?"

Trees crashed next to him as a ring of turbulent water darted after Hali. Vinn followed the madness, and the fallen trees bent upright as the stag passed by.

Chapter 11 Tio

"Hali's taking care of Vinn, so we can escape. She'll catch up."

Tio pushed Alim aside. "What do you mean, 'taking care of?' She can't kill an eidolon!"

"Nobody said kill, but Vinn was taking your gift. We rather prefer you the way you are."

"No, that…" *From the outside world, I may have appeared trapped.* "I handled it. Vinn and I are good." This was as good a time as any for Tio to learn to raise his voice. "Hali, stop!"

Vinn slid against the grove's edge and knocked over another tree. Hali leaped onto the stag and held a dagger against its throat.

"Stop!" Tio shouted.

Hali looked back at Tio without lifting her blade from its deadly position. The ink on her tattoo swirled with rapid fervor as Tio approached.

"Lower your weapon. I'm fine. Vinn is an ally."

The rainbow blade pressed ever deeper into Vinn. Hali's drawn-out breaths stopped. "As long as you're safe." She pulled her dagger away and let it fall into her boot sheathe.

A few drops of blood stained Vinn's neck as it rose. Water drained from its fur and gathered against the wound. In moments the cut was gone, and the healing water morphed into a water-woman.

"Resorting to violence again, Sereiamina? Can't say I didn't expect as much from you."

Who's Sereiamina?

"You're as prone to it as I, Undine," Hali said as she grimaced and held her bleeding shoulder.

Undine must be Vinn's linked spirit. "Let me see your shoulder, Hali." *My flourish is stronger—could I heal this?*

A shock passed through Tio the moment he touched Hali, like she'd been scooting her socks against a rug. As Tio ripped his hand away, a stark but fleeting image shot into his mind. A child with no face, bathed in shadows. Past? Present? Figment of his imagination?

I'm sick of this new magic already.

Hali looked confused. "Don't worry about it. Hardly worthy of first aid."

"I wanted to try—"

Tio covered his ears as Vinn's voice rattled his insides. "Sereiamina, a crippled celestial is of no use to your 'allies.' Allow Alim and Tio to proceed without you slowing them down."

Vinn continued speaking, but this time only in Tio's mind. *Seek out the other eidolons. Our haze barriers will be more cooperative for you.*

When Tio looked for Vinn, the stag was nowhere to be found. "Why would Vinn say that? Of course we need you."

"It's not wrong." Hali held out her runed arm. "Kthon is too big a risk. Every surge I step into puts your mission in danger. The two of you can do this easier without me."

Alim said, "You know more than either of us about ether, celestials, and everything else."

"By now you know enough. Did you eat your first spirit fruit?"

"No," Undine said with a splash at Alim. "That flesh is scared."

"Excuse me for not wanting to become a weapon for spirits. Hali, I need details." Alim led Hali to the other side of the grove.

"A weapon? Why would Alim think that?" Tio asked Undine.

"Celestials were created to serve the celestial spirit."

"The one humans killed?" Tio scratched the base of his antlers where they met his skull, but nothing satisfied the itch. The urge to scrape them against everything he saw rose with each passing moment.

"No, the second—Malakine—became obsessed with returning ether to Empyrea after being forced by the rest of us spirits to create the surges."

The compromise Vinn mentioned. "So, Alim knows this and wants to make sure that won't happen to them?"

"Yes, Vinn's word wasn't enough."

Understandable. "Do you think humans harvesting ether hurts Empyrea?"

"Malakine thought so. Is this flesh ready for the possibility?"

Chapter 11 Tio

"I don't know."

Sipherra is the only group capable of harvesting ether. Too recent to have caused the Vault to open, but could they cause something similar to happen? Grenvel is practically run by Sipherra. I can't waltz into Gren City and demand they cease developing ether tech.

Tio fidgeted with his bracelet and devised a plan while waiting for the others to return.

CHAPTER 12

Celestial burden. Why was the concept so scary? Alim had an instant distaste for it, but now Hali was challenging them on why it mattered. Years of working free as a Dreamer had been quashed and replaced with military servitude when Sipherra bought the mercenary company.

Having control over who to work for made mercenary life tolerable. Alim had never taken unsavory jobs, and the company had never forced them into Grenvel's political squabbles. How would being a celestial be different than life under Sipherra?

Alim scooped some clay from the riverbank and squished it between their fingers. *Vinn wanted me as celestial because I refused to be controlled. But how do I know control isn't an inherent part of the deal?*

"Hali, were you the celestial Vinn said defied the spirits?"

Sat upon a rock with her feet dangling above the river, Hali said, "It's difficult to defy when you agree. Malakine excelled at constructing a narrative to lead me into their plan. I didn't realize how anti-mortal they were." Hali smirked. "Make no mistake though, I did things my way.

Angered Malakine every time. Regardless of trust, spirits have no control over celestials."

"Then what happens if I eat this?" Alim twirled the orangish-purple fig.

"Your blood will get its first dose of celestial energy."

"I'll have ether inside me like Tio?"

"Everybody's blood has ether in it—that's how sparks work. Even pallids have some. Main difference is quantity and how it gets there," Hali said. "The fruit teaches your body to produce higher proportions of ether like spirits do."

"Tio is like a human-eidolon and I'll be a human-spirit?"

"If that's what you got out of this, I need to quit doing lectures. The details don't matter. You'll have your free will. Any other concerns?"

"None."

Hali hopped from the rock onto the damp dirt below. "The conversion process will be painful. Undine has healing powers, so you'll want her nearby when you eat the spirit fruit."

Upon returning to the grove, they found Tio writing in his notebook while Undine prattled.

"Our companions have returned," Undine said with bubbly energy.

"Is it 'our' now?" Alim didn't like her tone shift.

"Vinn asked me to accompany these flesh to ensure a safe journey."

"Have you suffered short-term memory loss? Hali and I made short work of you and your eidolon. We're capable enough without you."

"Neither spirit nor eidolon were ever in danger. Sereiamina's fleshy arrogance has tainted the next celestial."

"I already agreed to link with her," Tio said. "Undine can tag along inside me."

Linking is becoming a host for a spirit? Surprised Tio is okay with that when he dislikes being touched so much.

Hali shook her finger. "Unless you both want to come out of this with ether poisoning, I wouldn't recommend that. Spirits can only link to humans born with a spark matching the spirit's element. Shouldn't you know better, Undine?"

Undine's words fell like angry ice cubes dropping into a glass. "What do I know about linking with mortals? I'm not Malakine."

"Guess you can't come after all." Relieved, Alim clapped their hands.

"Alim was born with the water spark," Tio said. "You could link with them, Undine."

"I'd rather not." *Sharing my body is more than a little disconcerting.* "Can't you follow us without invading my personal space?"

"Death awaits any spirit who leaves their surge without linking. She needs the dense ether to survive," Tio said. "If I'm going to fix Empyrea, it couldn't hurt having one of Empyrea's children with us."

"If spirit plus animal equals eidolon—will linking make me an eidolon?" Alim asked.

"No." The lack of amusement exuding from Undine hit Alim in the heart. *She's going to make this journey feel twice as long.*

"Have you decided if you're going to become a celestial?" Tio asked. "Based on what Vinn showed me and Undine told me, Empyrea's lost a significant portion of its ether. We'll need to find a safe way to repair the flow of ether. Celestial magic may be the key."

First Hali, then Undine and Vinn, now Tio. Everybody needs me to be a celestial. Can't wait to mess up somehow. Maybe if I'm lucky the world will explode, and I won't have to deal with their disappointment.

"Fine, I'll do it." Alim chomped into the fruit, crunching their teeth against an unexpected pit. *Figs don't have pits, do they?*

"Woah, hold on…" Hali said too late.

The inside of the fruit was blood red, filled with little seeds around a large pit. Alim rubbed their jaw, the fruit's sweet juices emitting a slight peachy tang as they chewed. Before they could examine why it tasted so odd, their blood froze. Melted. Froze again. As if their heart were getting dunked in snow and thrown into desert sand repeatedly. Amidst that chaos, a smaller sensation of chattering animals echoed in their head. It was weak, but they could hear chirping birds, croaking frogs, squealing pigs, huffing bears, and more.

Undine placed a hand upon Alim's helmet and disappeared. All the heat drained from Alim as cool water flowed through their veins. Undine floated through their bloodstream and left frosty slush in her wake.

A path of winding tree roots sparkling with ethereal colors formed underneath Alim and cut through a brown sky with constant fast-moving white swirls splashing through it like milk through coffee. Off the road of roots to Alim's left, they saw a faded Hali and Tio unmoving, mid-conversation. To their right, a similarly obscured view of unfamiliar scenery: a tree in a distant golden meadow, the sheer size of which prevented them from seeing its top. A mirror-like sheen reflected Alim's scrawny image back at them, urging them to train harder.

Flesh-beings don't respond well to taking in celestial magic. Rejection could kill this flesh. So this flesh owes me.

I get it, just please stop saying flesh. Where am I?

The Arboreal Path.

Much of the road led to darkened corners, the darkest of which stopped abruptly at a pitch-black abyss. Would walking down the abyssal road result in falling to their death?

Looking down led to instant regret. Nothing but sky lay beneath them. Alim's world spun three times over as they fell on their butt. They straightened their helmet and waited for the churning in their stomach to stop.

Try not to get us killed. Undine splashed around, releasing a soothing warmth in Alim's blood.

I hate being linked already. Arboreal Path doesn't mean anything to me. What is it? How did I get here?

Consuming a spirit fruit brought you here to the in-between—that which connects the Corporeal and Ethereal Realms. Soon, coming here won't require a fruit. Such is a celestial's power.

Blue stars brightened one at a time, hazy trails connecting them. The formation reminded Alim of a whirlpool. Subtle green stars—in no particular shape—gathered next to the whirlpool.

Why would I want to come here? Alim asked.

The stars here align to the elements. Each attunement strengthens this flesh's connection to the Path and to the Ethereal Realm. Once complete, a celestial's potential is unlocked. But returning to the Path regularly is necessary to recharge. Otherwise, celestial blood will boil itself away and lead to etheric death.

Okay, so if I don't return, I die. If I do return, I might fall to my death. Love it. What a magnificent place. Alim looked to the darkened roads. *Where do these go?*

Each represents a connection to the Corporeal Realm and provides entry into the surges. One exists for every spirit, and the Path grows in strength as new spirits are born. Though dim now, each fruit this flesh eats appears to re-energize the Path similar to the formation of new spirits.

On the opposite side of the Path, the abyssal road's shroud throbbed, threatening to encroach on its neighboring roads.

Does that one lead to the Ethereal Realm then? Why is it so dark?

Yes. That darkness filled the Path and blocked it from us. Though the surges are now unblocked and partially lit, the Ethereal Realm appears to still be barred from us. Perhaps completing the Path will open the way to the Ethereal Realm.

So I need to get to every surge and attune to every element, then spirits can return to Empyrea and restore it?

I hope so. Let us return to this flesh's physical form. I will need to rest a few days.

Physical form—am I not really here? A few days?

No response. The cooling sensation in their blood breathed in and out as if Undine was snoring. As the Arboreal Path vanished around them, Alim found themself back among their friends.

Chapter 12 Alim

"Must've been an intense flavor," Tio said in a way that convinced Alim the reason he was such a loner was because of all the punchable things he spewed.

"Ready for my training, Hali?" Alim asked.

"You only just ate the fruit. No ether is going to respond until your blood finishes attuning to water. We've spent long enough in a surge though—it'd be best if we left."

Swatting at clingy fog, Alim said, "This place sucks anyway." They headed towards the cliff with Tio's conjured root-steps, but Hali stopped them.

"No need to backtrack. Nothing is linear in an ether surge, so if we leave through here"—Hali pointed at the green and pink swirling wall in the distance—"we could end up anywhere along the barrier's other side."

Tio put his notebook down with a ridiculous smile. "The surge is rotating independently of the outside world?"

Alim peeked at Tio's notes to find that there weren't any notes at all. Only random triangles, cubes, bubble words, and a drawing of a cute cat. *This is what he does while he's talking? Here I thought he was writing for the book he promised Barbaroli.*

Hali stepped over a pile of fig leaves left behind by Vinn. "You can think of it that way, but not in a literal sense. Whatever causes it also messes with time. The effect varies. When I last measured it, seven days had passed for the outside world after one day in a surge."

"No, no… crap." Tio's dejected eyes poked little holes in Alim's heart.

The sincere use of 'crap' reminded Alim of their childhood. Alim put on their best mom impression. "Such language! How could you say that under the sun's embrace?"

Tio broke out of his shock with a giggle. "Did your mom say that too?" He scratched his antlers with nervous urgency. "I already sent my letter of introduction to Gren City before we left Wilton. If we've been in here almost a week—Gren City is five days away. Great first impression…"

"Let's worry about that when we get there, okay? How do we open the haze barrier? Do we have to use brute force again?" Alim asked.

As if disappointed, Hali said, "No brutalizing this time unfortunately. Tio, touch the barrier."

"Like this?" Tio poked it like it would bite him if it noticed his presence and the haze parted around his finger. "Oh, it tickles!" he said, fighting back a smile.

Alim and Hali walked behind Tio as he diverted the haze. This was how Alim imagined the ethereal lights would look if they could sit on the Lunar Vault and enjoy the show. Pink swirling inside of green, purple splitting the other colors, merging, splitting apart again. Shy pink trying to be alone, swirling inside an overly affectionate green sharing its love. The homewrecking purple cutting through both, splitting them all apart then merging them together into a single entity, before tangled webs of all three shot out as wispy tendrils. And—

Frustrated thumping bounced from their helmet. "Tio, could you not? You're ruining the ambiance."

Continuing his incessant giggling, Tio said, "Want to borrow my blood and do this yourself? I can't help being ticklish."

Once through to the other side, Team Ether Cleavers arrived in an unfamiliar section of Spirit Arboretum. Both moons rained their light down, mixing into a mellow, cool orange. Unlike Starpath, this road only had one type of tree. But it wasn't one they had seen before. Droopy tufts of teal begged to touch the dusty moonlight-tinted dirt from easily snappable branches.

"This is the outer edge of New Fion." Tio scanned the area with his map out, getting his bearings. "If we pass through Pasture Downs, Gren City should only be a couple days away."

"See, it all worked out in the end," Alim said. *I can't wait to get to Tovaloreande Sanctuary and see where magic gifts began.*

Tio let out a loud whistle and a fierce screech echoed his tune in

Chapter 12 Alim

response. Two more sets of whistles and screeches and a large bird with a hooked beak and angry eyebrows landed at Tio's feet. It looked like a cross between an eagle and an owl.

"Can you find our friends? A horse and an okapi. Have them meet us—"

The owl-eagle-thing squawked and bounced.

"No, no that's not what I meant. Don't eat them. Tell them to find us in the valley with lots of sheep." He pointed north. "That way. I'm sure you know the one." Tio tied a paper around its leg. "And deliver this to the big human city. Follow the pigeons. And no, you can't eat those either."

The force of beating wings reached all the way to Alim as it took off.

"Wait, that's how you do it? You just talk to them like people?" *Don't know what I was expecting. Animal noises? Thought he was playing a trick on me when he walked up to the innoboro with casual conversation.*

"Sort of? I consciously use my flourish to translate, otherwise animals won't understand. Takes a few attempts before I get it right, as you saw. Much easier to translate what they say. Almost happens without me thinking."

"You did fine. Nobody uses every aspect of their spark perfectly," Hali said.

It didn't take long to leave Spirit Arboretum behind. For the remainder of the night, they journeyed through fields of verdant hills covered in vegetables and flowers. These hills held numerous farms, collectively called… Hillfarm. Sometimes Alim felt the people responsible for naming things hadn't put much effort in. They were always mashing two words together or, worse, using their own name. *Maybe there'll be an Alimton one day.*

Baaing let them know they'd arrived in the desired meeting place the next morning. Going through a whole night without sleeping was weird, but it hadn't been a day for them yet. Alim worried their sleep schedule might get confused. Noisy white and black puffballs roamed between the hills. Tio ran down and started talking to and hugging sheep like they were long-lost family. Alim went to join him, but Hali stopped them.

"Stay. We've got training to do before you get too tired."

"But—sheep!" As much as Alim wanted to learn magic, fluffiness was calling to them.

"They'll be here when we're done," Hali said as she flicked their visor.

Hali held one hand in front and one behind, legs ready to lunge like she had a rapier in hand. "Stand like this."

"Really? I'm more the smash-with-big-weapons type. Is there a different stance?"

"Not one you're ready for. This is better for the basics. You would have had to use similar flowy posture for your water spark, if you weren't pallid."

True. Alim had spent too much time as a kid practicing the stances for water magic, hoping one day their gift would arrive. This wouldn't be too different.

Every time Alim held the pose, they wobbled worse than gelatin in a windstorm, and Hali directed them to change something. But improvement never came.

"Put those abs to use for onces—I know you have them," Hali said, prodding their arms and legs into uncomfortable angles. "There—better."

"Don't think my body was meant for this." Alim thought their legs might snap off.

"Stop blubbering—you'll get used to it." She thumped their cuirass. "There's a reason mages opt for a leaner build and lighter clothes. Might be easier if you didn't insist on wearing armor."

"Hey, I'm lean." Alim flexed their arm.

"Then I'm a walking skeleton. Put that away and get back in the pose."

Trying again, it felt a little more natural.

"Do you feel anything?" Hali asked.

"My insides are trickling. Like my blood is getting hit with a drizzle. Is that the blood toll?"

Chapter 12 Alim

"The beginnings of one at least. That's how you know the stance is right. It feels different for everybody and gets more intense as you use more complex magic. Mine ranges from a warm tingle to boiling."

"For me it's a pressure," Tio said, squatting behind them.

How long has he been watching? Alim felt their cheeks redden.

"Sorry, didn't want to interrupt. Stripes and Majesty are here with our things when you're ready for a break."

"Majesty?"

"Your horse. Stripes says she's a princess and deserves nicer things. You should get on that."

The animals are plotting against us—I can feel it. "Why can't animals pick normal names?"

"Some do, but names aren't something they use in their own lives so it's not important to them. They think of it as a codename for speaking to druids. Besides, human names are dumb too when you realize the meaning and origins."

"Tio, do you mind setting up camp for us? We'll be down soon," Hali said.

He nodded and returned to the sheep valley.

Hali returned to the lesson by entering the rapier-like stance. "Make sure to pay attention to the blood toll taken by each technique you learn. Count how many uses it takes before you're unable to continue. This isn't something you want to misjudge in the middle of combat."

"Okay, what next?" Alim asked as they mirrored Hali.

"There's ether everywhere. Sense it. Firmly grasp it. Bend it into whatever you want. Celestial magic is flexible compared to other sparks but costly."

As Alim's limbs ached, a pink sheen floated through the sky. So small they would have thought it a figment of their imagination. The trickle in Alim's blood turned to a gush as they grabbed onto the etheric speck. Tugged on it with smooth arm movements. But what were they

Arboreal Path

supposed to do with it? Were there limits? They trembled as the ether fought against their influence. It split into three, each a different ethereal color, and burst. A vivid shockwave knocked Alim back, rolling them down the hill. Counting each full revolution, it seemed as if they might set a world record until they finally bowled into something cushiony that brought them to a halt.

Upside down with the world doing flips, the urge to hurl was imminent. A pained baa came from the sheep that had apparently broken their fall. Underneath its white fluff, one of its legs was bent at a frightening angle.

Oh no, what should I do? Alim's head pounded. *Tio should be able to get some wood to make a splint. There's got to be bandages in our supplies, or I can use my cloth straps.*

Nothing worked when Alim tried to stand. *Where's Hali? Did she get caught in the blast too?*

"You okay?" Tio shouted. Crouching between Alim and the sheep, he examined the damage. Panting like he'd run the whole way here, he grabbed at his bracelet. "I can fix this—I can fix this." His breathing grew erratic and he started whispering "deep breaths" like a motivational chant.

As Tio touched Alim's arm, a warmth ran through their bloodstream. All their cuts fizzled with green light as they sewed shut. Every bruise faded. Their headache disappeared.

"Healing?" *I thought Tio said that power was gone.*

"Seems so. Okay, keep the sheep from squirming," Tio said without giving Alim time to realize their limbs were responding again.

"Of course." Alim sat behind the sheep and held through its wool as if giving it a hug.

It struggled against them, trying to kick Tio in the process.

"Hold still. We're helping you."

The sheep responded with a weak baa and stopped wriggling. Until the wince-inducing tug Tio gave its leg to straighten it. With a swift kick to Tio's face using one of its uninjured hooves, the sheep pushed until Alim's

Chapter 12 Alim

helmet was filled with wool. They regained control and Tio pressed his hands against the realigned leg, releasing the same shiny glow.

"You can let it go now." Tio wiped blood off his cheek and applied pressure to the already-swelling injury.

With one last elongated baa, the sheep hopped away.

"Wow, that's a rude thing to say," Tio remarked.

Alim pulled on Tio's arm. "Hali might be injured too—come on."

"No need—your etheric blast didn't have much power behind it." Hali clapped. "Healing though? Did the ethereal blood restore your spark?"

"Partially." Tio shrugged as if it didn't matter. "I got camp set up. You two hungry? Pie should be ready soon."

Was Tio really going to gloss over his new ability? Alim decided not to pry, but Tio's lax attitude never grew any less jarring. "Oh, what kind?" Dessert sounded amazing after training.

"Solfruit."

Alim's lips swelled at the mere mention.

"Kidding. It's fig. Of the regular, non-spirit variety."

Tio dragged the others towards his campfire, where Stripes and Alim's horse were waiting.

The horse trotted over with an excited whinny, nudging at Alim. "So, Majesty huh? We're not supposed to name our steeds, but I guess I'm not a Dreamer anymore. And you're more than a steed." Alim patted Majesty's neck.

With a thick mitt on his hand, Tio grabbed an iron skillet off the fire. "Pie's done!"

Hali cooled it off with a weak air rune and sliced it with her dagger while Tio went to grow fruit for the animals.

"Sorry about earlier," Alim said as Hali handed over a plate of pie.

"It's part of learning." Hali sounded melancholic as she sat down next to them on the feather blanket and dug pie filling out with her fork, swirling it around her plate.

"You feeling okay? Is this about what Vinn said?"

Hali wrapped her cowl tighter around her neck, like a purple and green constricting snake. "Have you ever wondered about fate?"

"In what way? Preordained destiny style fate or coincidence fate?" Alim asked.

"Both. My father used to talk about it all the time. He—" She paused as if she couldn't remember a specific word. "He knew a lot about the Old Faith. The religion was all about fate and unavoidable misfortune."

Sounds depressing compared to Solstoran beliefs.

Hali continued, "When an opportunity you thought lost appears again, you take it. That's the attitude he always touted because misfortune comes regardless. In my father's eyes, it was worse to wonder 'what if' than to make the wrong choice."

"That's what we're doing. Only a couple more pieces of fruit then I can help free your family, right?"

"What if there was a way to get my family back without you? I've already learned more than I thought I would in that surge, and Tio needs you more than I do."

"I'm not sure I follow. Wouldn't you have done so already then?"

"Never mind, I'm pretty tired, you know?" Hali scraped her slice of pie onto Alim's plate. "You can have mine. I'm going to sleep…"

"Rest well." The words came out in an unintentional whisper.

Hali left to retrieve her sleeping bag from Majesty in silence. Tio glanced at her, and then at Alim before returning to feeding Majesty grapes and brushing her hair. Alim set their untouched plate of pie aside and lay on the blanket, observing as the twin moons and sun dwindled in the darkening sky.

CHAPTER 13

The towering, spiky glass churches of Gren City were ahead of the group, peaking over the city's large walls. It didn't take Barbaroli's map to know Tovaloreande Sanctuary was the next ether surge. This surge was common knowledge due to its permanent haze barrier, even if most didn't know what it was. Tio was adamant they get permission to enter the sanctuary, which had been locked down by Gren Consortium for two years now. But what would the cranky old Consortium be able to do about it if they waltzed in?

Despite the ethereal plague being cured, many still believed it lingered. A theory about pallids spreading a weaker plague, causing babies to be born without sparks, had recently gained significant popularity. This theory was exactly why there was a line to get into Gren City. One they had been stuck in for far too long. It seemed paranoid guards were scanning people's blood to find pallids. Nobody else worried about it, but Hali knew better. If Hali or Alim showed up pallid on the machine, it could take weeks before their entry into the city was approved.

Oh joy, we're next.

Hali hoped it was warmer beyond the city walls. It had grown chilly in Pasture Downs and the constant wind hadn't helped. She regretted leaving behind her jacket before entering Spirit Arboretum's surge. It hadn't crossed her mind that they wouldn't exit in the same spot. *Should've known better given how much time I've spent in surges.*

As they entered through a smaller door on the gate, a man in a long red coat came in from the next room with a steel crate. The sleeves of his coat read Sipherra under the company's mountain logo.

"Here's another batch of ethometers. Try not to break them this time," the scientist said to the guard, dropping the crate. He left as quickly as he'd come, taking ridiculous strides the whole way back through the cramped room.

The guard plucked a scary handheld rectangular device with claws on one end from the crate.

That's how they're scanning people? Hali had never seen anything less elegant. Machines from Diya had begun to grow in popularity in Grenvel but were expensive. The least the knock-offs could do was make it less obvious the process was going to hurt.

"Nice jackalope costume. Way to be in the solstice mood," the guard said as he latched the device onto Tio's trembling arm. Tio yelped while the guard read off the device's screen. "Nature. Next!"

Machines ran on the same principles as sparks. Pay the blood toll, get a result. Most were simple compared to spells but analyzed data well enough. *Perfect for mundane gate duty.*

Alim stepped forward and had their blood checked. "Water. Next!"

What a relief. The device must've detected Undine as a spark.

"Hurry along." The guard pushed Tio after noticing he was waiting for everybody to get through.

Alim grabbed Tio, and the two headed to the bag-inspection checkpoint with the animals.

Chapter 13 Hali

"Oh, we got a beauty here." The guard whistled while preparing his ethometer.

A beauty? Whether a harmless compliment or a ploy to get a date, it was annoying all the same. Hali was sick of people commenting on her appearance as if it were the only thing worth mentioning. At least partially because she saw it as a nicety people said without meaning, no better than asking a stranger how they were.

The machine stabbed into her arm, siphoning blood in tiny gulps. A jingle of beeps and boops indicated it had met its quota and examination was beginning.

"My shift ends after eighth bell. How about dinner?"

And there's the proposition. I'd rather headbutt your face into mush.

Before Hali could give him the rejection of a lifetime, his eyes bulged out of his head while reading the ethometer's screen. Blocky green text wrote out "Plague."

They can detect the ethereal plague?

"Sipherra tech is so unreliable these days." The guard reached over to replace the ethometer. "Hold on, let me try again."

I'll never be allowed to leave Gren City. Sipherra will swarm me if I get the same result.

Hali snatched the guard's wrist and twisted until the device fell from his grip and shattered. He struck her across the face, escaping as she let go of him.

The binding rune on her forearm activated, leaking out dark mist. Shadows snaked across the stone floor, formed into a claw, and yanked the guard by the ankle, smashing his nose against the ground and dragging him. His mouth opened to scream. No sound came. Instead, darkness seeped from his mouth, eyes, and nose. The shadows fused and shaped itself into a human man.

I let things get out of hand again... "Ikazu. Make him forget." *You're always forced to clean up my messes.*

The shadow's head unfolded into wing-like hands, wrapping around the guard's face and burying in his skin. Pained expressions faded from his face as Ikazu's fingers wriggled through his head, searching through memories like one might flip through folders in a desk. Each one flashed in Hali's mind for brief moments. Pressure for grandchildren. A series of bad first dates. Until Ikazu found his most recent set of recollections. As precise as Ikazu had become with Kthon's shadow magic, collateral damage was still likely.

Ikazu dropped the guard and returned to Hali, wrapping around her until he was face to face. *That smile again…* She reabsorbed the shadow spirit into her rune and shuddered. *I knew entering Gren City was a bad idea. This guard may not remember, but his dreams will never be the same.*

Hurrying through the gate's little door and a winding hall, Hali made it to the next checkpoint. Tio was already through and guards were examining Alim's belongings.

Alim glanced back when Hali slammed the door behind her. "Took you long enough," they said.

"Pallids take longer to get processed, you know that. We're lucky I got through without weeks of bureaucracy." Hali shook her head while getting her things ready for inspection. "I think you have the right idea. With the helmet."

Alim looked surprised, at least from what she could see of their face. "I'd love to agree, but what does that have to do with anything?"

"People don't make assumptions about you. Under your helmet and armor, you could be anybody, you know?"

"Not true. Assumptions are made about me every day." They put on a screechy, mocking voice. "Like, 'Must be one ugly mug under that bucket.' Or my favorite, 'Dreamers send children into the Wastes now?'"

Guess people find a way to judge everybody's appearance. She rubbed her cheek. A new bruise for a new day.

"You've been acting weird since Spirit Arboretum—want to talk?"

"Don't worry your pretty little helm about it. Been a long trek."

"The offer to talk still stands." Alim left with their things as the guard finished poking around for contraband.

Hali had spent the whole journey from Spirit Arboretum to Gren City conflicted, contemplating what Vinn had told her. More than that, what it hadn't told her. If the nature spark lived on in Vinn, then resurrection was still possible. But would Tio and Alim approve of getting eidolon blood? Of bringing the dead back to life?

Kthon's murmurs brought aches and itchy blood. *Resurrect. Us.*

"Hey, Hali, hurry up!" Alim yelled.

Grabbing her things from the guard, she caught up with them through the last checkpoint door. The stench of horse blasted her nostrils the moment she stepped onto Gren City's paved main road. Worse than that was the fruit vendor she swore should be renamed citrus vendor.

Tio whispered to the animals before saying, "I'll make sure they get a nice stable."

The okapi rammed into Tio's back.

"Correction. Luxurious stable. Only the best for Stripes and Majesty."

Hali chuckled as she remembered Rev's eagle familiar. Its constant dour mood was a fun counter to Rev, and it had an appetite to rival Alim's. Tio was better with animals than he thought he was.

"Never had reason to come to the capital before." Alim ran ahead and examined every nook and cranny. "I love it here already!"

"Everything in Gren City clashes—what's there to love?"

"Look at all the people! And their sense of style—so much variety! Maybe I should get new clothes here."

Hali scoffed. "Alim, seriously?"

The older residents wore burlap tunics and dresses, so there was no way Alim meant them. Better were the younger crowd with their beat-up duster jackets, fur caps, knit shawls, and patchwork dresses, but still everything about the outfits screamed "found this in a trash heap" not "wearing this for the aesthetic."

"Sure, why not? A little character never hurt anybody."

"Remind me to take you to Diya sometime and show you real fashion."

Other cities had a gradual change in design, or one or two newer districts, but Gren City was a mishmash, as if somebody had avoided any semblance of a city development plan. On each street, rotted-through wooden homes stood next to cramped steel hovels and giant stone churches with spiky glass ceilings.

Repurposed Old Faith churches occupied every corner of Gren City. The tallest buildings by far rivaled Belsa's trees, and each had a bell to help citizens tell time. Fancier churches had a giant clock built into them too.

Alim sat on a stoop in front of the glass church, overtaken by vines and pink geraniums. "Look, grumpy, let's have that talk."

Not taking no for an answer, are you? Rubbing the front of her neck, Hali asked, "How far would you go to undo a mistake?"

"Doesn't the answer depend on the mistake?"

"What if you'd harm somebody by fixing it." She pinched her tattoo, wishing for sleeves to cover it with. It was a surprise she'd got this far with nobody noticing its animated ink.

"Solstorans have a prayer. 'Cooperate with your neighbor and the jolly sun forgives the mistakes and sins of the faithful faith… people?'"

"Did you have a stroke or just give up halfway through?" If Alim meant to amuse her, their plan had worked. Though she'd prefer getting her friend's opinion, not jokes.

"Yeah, I choked. Solstora doesn't even have the concept of sins. I'm jealous of people that get to give motivational religious speeches."

"Works better if you use a real prayer or proverb and actually believe it."

Alim traced one of the crescent moons on their helmet with a finger. "Mistakes are the worst. Whatever is haunting you, I understand. To answer your question, I regret several choices from my days as a Dreamer. Not enough to try and 'undo' them, especially not if there's a chance to make things worse for others."

Chapter 13 Hali

"What's your worst regret?" Hali asked.

"Not going back to see my family in the Mudplains. They'd think I'm dead if not for the money I send them."

"Alim, we weren't far from there. We could have taken a couple days from our journey for that."

"Last time I spoke to my dad, I told him I wasn't coming home until I had gifted blood. Obviously didn't think I'd actually succeed."

Tio strode by in a blur, faster than Alim attacking a cupcake, and pressed his face against the glass window of the church. He wiped dew off to see inside. "Wow! Is this a greenchurch? Never thought to see so many plants in Gren City."

"Food produced by greenchurches is free," Hali said. "Take some if you're hungry."

"Other people need it more than me." Tio grazed the vines with his hand, sprouting raspberries along its length. "Must be hard to maintain these without druids."

The fruit reminded Hali that she had to finish carving a statue for Rasal.

A bell rang out four times to indicate afternoon. In her head, it resonated with Kthon's relentless demand. *Resurrect. Us.* Kthon was getting louder than shout-whispering scum in a library.

Hali scrunched her face, trying to ignore the internal racket, until Alim brought her back into their mundane conversation.

"Did you hear Gren Consortium rejected an attempt to shut down greenchurches?" Alim's excitement didn't match the topic in the slightest. "Wouldn't think a group with Sipherra as one of its heads would reject a money-making scheme, but they told the complaining merchants to offer a better product! At least that's one good thing Sipherra has been involved in."

"Not that surprising. Greenchurches are a drop in the bucket compared to what Hillfarm produces. Wouldn't be worth upsetting people depending on the free food to survive." Hali peeled Tio off the glass like a stubborn sticker. "Can we go now?"

A maze of claustrophobic buildings led them to the Consortium Promenade's courtyard. Extravagant houses designed with structurally unnecessary pillars flew large gaudy flags representing their spark. Flags with mixed colors and symbols represented married couples of differing sparks. The pride in one's spark and flagrant lavishness was not unlike Hali's upbringing.

Her family's manor contained the biggest library in Thauma. Up-and-coming mages came there as part of the "elemental tour," in which they visited major cities to learn about each spark. Thauma believed there was something to be learned from every spark, even if a person didn't have it. Hali had loved the glamour and prestige back then, but now it irked her.

Tio pointed at an old person with a tall hat and vest. "Alim, you should replace your helmet with one of those!"

"Black is more Hali's color. I need a splash of vibrancy!"

"Like them?"

An approaching mob was full of young people who had that never-worked-a-day-in-their-lives air about them. Each wore gaudy, puffy silk shirts and lace dresses lined with exotic furs.

It only took a glance for Hali to feel her age creeping along her bones. *I love a nice dress, but modern fashion is ridiculous.*

Fussy clamoring picked up as more joined and formed a circle around them. Gawking onlookers pointed and heckled Tio about his antlers. Hali gripped the hilt of her book's dagger and stepped in front of Tio. Shouts of "witch" joined the druid-themed jests as the crowd noticed the writhing ink of her rune.

Alim raised their yellow-strap-wrapped arm to signal they were a Dreamer. "Out of our way. Stop acting like you've never seen people dressed for winter solstice before."

Chapter 13 Hali

The crowd groaned and went back to whatever it was idle nobles did as Alim shoved through the remaining loiterers with Tio in tow.

"Sorry, Tio," Alim said. "You'll blend in better once festivities start. Bet you're wishing Vinn gave you a less obvious feature."

Alim's Dreamer trick works here too?

Tio wiped the sweat building on his forehead. "Thanks. Both of you."

Past the library bookchurches, they arrived at Consortium House, where Gren Consortium met. It was surprisingly quaint compared to its surroundings. Small and unnoteworthy. Inside, it was pristine. Long halls in every direction marked the deceptively large size of the building. If somebody had told her they'd invented a spell to make the building bigger on the inside, Hali would have believed it. Red carpet acted as a road through laminated wooden floors, leading them to a receptionist desk covered in knick-knacks and framed children's art. A little serpent-shaped fountain of Gren City's mascot—the leviathan—spurted water on a soothing loop.

Tio took the lead. "The Conclave sent me. I'm Tio."

"Yes, we got your letter of introduction and the rescheduling request. We weren't expecting three."

He stumbled over his words, losing all sense of credibility. "These are my… research assistants."

"Of course, very good." The receptionist looked over a binder, swishing back and forth between its pages. "I'm sorry, your audience appears to have been downscaled to a meeting with one representative. One moment please." The receptionist tipped his tall hat and bowed his head before leaving to another room.

"Assistants?" Alim glanced at Hali.

Tio stuttered and stared at the ceiling. "H-How else was I supposed to explain it?" He winced and pushed against the swollen cut where the sheep had kicked him.

"Why didn't you heal your busted lip?" Alim asked.

Arboreal Path

"Tried. It didn't work on me. Must be a limitation."

Druids know so little of their spark these days. How was all that knowledge lost?

A mural of the Old Faith's betrayal caught Hali's eye among the myriad portraits of previous Gren Consortium members and other historical events. It depicted a young woman bleeding five elements surrounded by cherry blossom trees. Torrents of beautiful pink flowers caught in the wind. Whoever painted it must've spent months getting every detail right. The title at the bottom listed it as *Tovaloreande*.

At the end of the mural, the receptionist opened a door and peered through, calling them over. It hurt Hali's brain trying to piece together how the building's floor plan connected those rooms and how he'd got there so quickly.

Tio smacked his antlers against the top of the door frame, grimacing and rubbing them. Hali shot a glare to stifle Alim's laughter.

"Still not used to these things," Tio said with pep as he sidled into the room. "Felt kind of good though? Maybe I should take up headbutting as a hobby."

Ignoring Tio's embarrassing doorway encounter, the receptionist said, "Help yourself to the coffee bar. A representative of Gren Consortium will be right with you."

No sooner than the receptionist left did Tio bolt to the coffee. "Want any?" he asked while rubbing the base of his antlers.

"No thanks," Hali and Alim said in unison as they sat at the table.

"You're allowed to laugh. I appreciate you two looking after me out there but relax a little. Can you believe I still forget I have these things? I'm going to have to remodel my home."

He can brush off so much pressure and responsibility yet crumples in social situations where nobody has any expectations of him. Do the opinions of strangers matter so much?

"I have no problem laughing at your expense, believe me," Alim said. "How are you not nervous about this meeting? They downsized you and you don't even know who we're going to meet with."

Chapter 13 Hali

On cue, the receptionist peaked round the door. "Geno Sipherra. Head of the merchant ring and president of Sipherra."

A woman with glued-down brown hair entered, seated in a floating three-quarters orb lined with red cushions. Her buttoned-up white jacket was a more elaborate version of the red lab coat the gate scientist had worn. Gold accents and fancy red embroidery led to Sipherra's spiky mountains logo on the shoulders. She tapped against the orb's side using a matching golden cane with a mountain-shaped ruby.

This is the leader of Sipherra? Hali looked over at her teammates. Alim gently tapped their helmet while Tio spun his bracelet around his wrist, staring with such intensity she thought he was witnessing the meaning of life.

"Thank you for adjusting your schedule to see us, Geno," Tio said.

"How could I not? Your research papers are popular amongst my company's scientists. I believe many recent innovations at Sipherra have you to thank." Geno adjusted the monocle on her left eye, switching to one of its other lenses. "Is your deformity common among druids? Perhaps Sipherra could treat you."

Great, I hate her.

"That won't be necessary." Tio gulped his coffee as he took a seat between Alim and Hali. "I like my antlers. Can we discuss business?"

"Are you here to accept my job offer?" Geno asked.

Tio was offered a job at Sipherra? Maybe he really is famous.

"If you'd read my letter, you'd know I'm not. Same as when I originally declined, I'm working with the Conclave to solve an important matter for all Our Stranded Lands. Magic is dwindling, and if we don't do something, mages and druids will both become extinct."

"As much as I respect your opinion on ether, what you say can't be true. My scientists assess Sanctuary's surge monthly. No such signs exist."

Tio set a scuffed teapot with a screen bolted onto it on the table. "This is an enchanted artifact. It absorbs ether, measures it, and releases it safely."

"We've tried such artifacts. None work," Geno said as her orb stopped at the head of the table. "You expect me to believe this teapot isn't inert?"

Tio shrugged. "Belief doesn't factor in here." He whispered to Alim, "Think you can push a little ether into the spout?"

"I don't know if I have the necessary level of finesse yet…" Alim whispered back.

"Just get it close then." Tio lifted the teapot.

Alim waggled a finger, clearly struggling to get any ether to respond to subtle movements. With only a few days of practice, it was no wonder—Hali had entered the full stance for months before learning.

Despite the difficulty, enough must've gathered because the artifact whistled as its display rotated through characters and numbers. The screen landed on "133eb A23 W26 E19 F31 N1."

"Is that readout supposed to mean anything?" Geno rested her head against her hand as if she were bored already.

A slightly pink steam jetted from the teapot.

"It's a measurement. The listed 133 ether blocks is significantly less dense than last year's average of 300–400. Interesting that nature showed in the elemental split. Recalibrating the device for decimals is normally necessary before my element is listed." Tio returned the teapot to his bag. "My instruments are more sophisticated."

Geno grabbed her cane and leaned on it for support, arms shaking as she stood upright. Golden braces clamped down on her creased red trousers. "I didn't take you for a braggart, druid. State your purpose or leave."

"I want permission to enter Tovaloreande Sanctuary and Refulgent Wastes to continue my research."

"No. Only Sipherra employees are granted access to either location. However"—Geno rapped her fingers against the top of her cane—"I'll reconsider if you give us your artifact and you explain the wonderful design of your friend's tattoo."

Chapter 13 Hali

"This artifact isn't mine to give," Tio said, confidence melting with each word.

"And there's nothing special about my tattoo except enchanted ink from Diya." *My usual excuse works well enough on the ignorant masses, but the head of Sipherra? Does she recognize it?*

Alim showed off their Dreamer-wrapped arm again. "Surely you can make an exception for a Dreamer."

A gruff cough pulled their attention to a lone man in the doorway. Gray speckled his blonde hair and light, barely visible stubble dotted his cheeks. "Yellow napkins won't convince us."

Knew that wouldn't work forever.

"Allister?" Alim banged their head against the table and spoke under their breath. "Great. The two worst possible people."

Ever the dramatic one. Not sure we'd be any better off with Gren Consortium's librarians or mage academy headmasters. At least with the leaders of Sipherra and the Dreamers we have a connection.

"Ex-Dreamer or not, you're not getting into our restricted areas for free."

Alim pounded the table, knocking over Tio's empty coffee mug. "Sipherra and Dreamers, both as unreasonable as ever. Surely some artifacts will turn up while we're in Refulgent Wastes. Let those be payment."

Excuse me? How did this turn into an offer to plunder Thauma?

Allister adjusted the collar of his cloud-patterned tunic. "Alim, your discovery was the first of any significance in decades. Do you expect me to believe you'll find more?"

"The insides of haze barriers are untouched, and we can get inside." Alim was irritating Hali more with each word.

You're telling them too much.

"Thaumic artifacts are no longer of interest to Sipherra. Give us the teapot or tell us how to enter the surges, or your request is denied. Final offer."

"No."

Geno sat back in her orb with impeccable posture. "An unwillingness to cooperate is surprising in an emissary for Belsa's Druid Conclave and our leading ether expert. You're dismissed."

Allister shook Tio's limp hand. "I'm sorry, kid. Would've been a joy working with you." He flicked his wrist and the receptionist funneled the three of them out of the room.

As soon as the receptionist slammed the door shut on them, Hali shoved Alim into the wall, tilting a row of portraits. "What the hell, Alim? Want to ask the rest of us before you offer graverobbing services?"

"It's not graverobbing to preserve Thauma's culture in Grenvel's libraries."

"My culture is not to be a museum piece for Grenvel's entertainment."

"It educates people. Reminds everybody Thauma existed. What good is that knowledge to the dirt?"

"I thought you were done being a Dreamer."

"Sorry," Alim said. "It was the only thing I thought might sway Allister and Geno. The cache I found before I left the company settled Grenvel's feud with Diya, so if we found something even more rare and pristine in the surges… Never mind. Doesn't matter anymore."

"Did I miss something?" Tio asked.

"Forget it." Hali wiped the frustration off her face.

On a long, silent walk of defeat, they arrived at an inn on the south side of Gren City. The building was so ancient that a stiff wind might knock it over.

Hali sat on the front step. "Why didn't you take the job, Tio? Or hand over the artifact. Not like you need it anymore."

"Vinn made me suspicious of ether tech. This meeting only made me more worried about what Geno is doing in Tovaloreande Sanctuary and Refulgent Wastes. Stopping their development of ether tech may be as important as healing Empyrea."

Chapter 13 Hali

Alim laughed. "Tio the lawbreaker. Has a ring to it. If Sanctuary always has a surge and Refulgent Wastes contains most of the marked potential surges, they're hardly optional destinations."

"If my suspicions are right and Sipherra causes another ether catastrophe on the scale of the Lunar Vault or the Quake, I don't think Empyrea will survive it. We'll lose magic on the spot. If Our Stranded Lands doesn't sink into the ocean this time."

"Well, with Hali we may stand a chance against a Dreamer patrol or two." Alim clapped Hali on her back.

"I'm not going." Hali looked at her binding rune. The weight of it could tear her arm off.

Alim frowned. "Is this about the artifacts? I'm sorry—we aren't going to take any."

Hali laughed, shedding a tear. "That was a jerk move, Alim, but that's not it."

"You're serious though? Then why?"

Tio's eyes glistened as he avoided looking directly at Hali.

"I decided before we got to Gren City." *You'd both blow up on me like Rev if I explained.* "Look, Vinn was right. Going with you all is a disaster waiting to happen. Undine would agree if she were awake."

"What are you going to do then?" Tio asked.

Bring my family back. "Vinn showed me there's another method to defeat Kthon and free my family by myself." *With eidolon blood.* "Vinn left before I got what I needed." *The nature-infused eidolon blood I had thought lost all these years.*

The two looked at each other, and then at Hali with renewed confusion.

Alim sat on the stoop next to Hali. "I wouldn't even be completing the Path without you. How am I supposed to figure out this celestial stuff without you?"

"Undine can teach you in my place. She knows enough." Hali thumped Alim's visor. "It's better to keep you away from Kthon. If something went wrong, he could latch on to you as he did to me." *Or we could unleash the plague upon Our Stranded Lands.*

Alim grumbled. "Don't make decisions for me. Your safety matters as much as mine."

No, it doesn't. "Regardless of safety, Tio's need of you is greater than mine. Rest assured, I won't die, so if I fail, you can help me afterwards." *If I don't fail… there may be no eidolons left for you.*

"When my celestial powers are complete, I'm finding you. Your family comes first."

My family does come first. "Something to look forward to then." Hali hugged Alim tight until their breastplate was crushing her ribs. "Take care. Armor is still a bad idea, by the way."

Digging through her things, Hali handed a novel to Tio. "This is *Ferocious*. Give it a read for me, okay? You'll love it, even if it doesn't have romance."

Tio nodded, his loss for words clear on his face.

"Goodbye, Team Ether Cleavers," Hali said as her rune burned.

Kthon crawled into her thoughts and croaked his familiar words. *Resurrect. Us.*

CHAPTER 14

On the outskirts of Tovaloreande Sanctuary's cherry-blossom-filled landscape, Tio squeaked as Alim yanked him below a pink petal pile. Alim signaled for quiet with a finger against their lips as a pair of Gren City guards wandered by.

How did I let Alim convince me to do this? Tio's heart rampaged as he controlled his temptation to touch his bracelet. *I'm home. Playing games with a cake in the oven. Deep breaths.* The pleasant smell of fresh marble cake was almost real.

Flinging their brunette locks with all the sass of Sir Fluffyboi, the first guard said, "Hey, you think Geno will leave Sanctuary soon? Things get tense when she's around. All the Dreamers especially get serious. Are they scared of her or something?"

The second guard whacked on their skullcap with a mace like a less intelligent knock-off Alim. "Can't blame them—she's practically their boss nowadays." A bright rectangle danced on their cheek.

"Hold up. There's something on your face."

Maybe this explains why stealth scenes in books always take place at night. Tio blocked the light bouncing off Alim's helmet with his hand.

Sassy Brunette said, "Never mind, it's nothing. Light's always bouncing off these stupid blossoms."

Skullcap whined and smacked their friend. "Hey, what did the flowers do, kill you in a past life? They're pretty."

"Less pretty when you find them in every crevice for days. You'll see."

With Skullcap and Sassy Brunette a ways down the grassy trail, Tio followed Alim into the pinkness that was Sanctuary.

Alim let out a quiet victory whoop. "If those had been Dreamers, we'd be in chains right now. Or dead. Probably dead."

"Lucky us. There's bound to be more, right?"

"City guards? No. A place like this, with sensitive information, is going to be exclusive to special Sipherra-branded Dreamers. The whole mercenary company might as well be Sipherra at this point though." They sighed. "Enough of that. We finally made it!"

"Please don't act excited to be in the middle of enemy territory."

"No, no, it's not about that. Aren't you the least bit eager to be in a place with 733 years of history? The birthplace of modern magic! Where's your enthusiasm?" Alim did their helmet drum routine.

Tio gave the weakest "woohoo" he could muster to make it extra salty and patronizing.

"Seven hundred and thirty-three years, Tio!"

"Figure that out all on your own, did you?" Considering the event marked the start of a new calendar system, there wasn't even math involved. "Save the history ogling for when we're safe."

With all the facts Alim had spewed about Pasture Downs and Gren City over the past few days, Tio could fill two concussion-grade books. Somehow, Alim had managed to stay quiet during last night's monthly moon eclipse at least. The overlapping yellow and orange moons had bathed the inn with beautiful green light. Eclipses were more difficult to

Chapter 14 Tio

appreciate in Belsa's thick forest. *Too bad Hali wasn't there to enjoy it with us. I hope she's doing okay.*

Alim scoffed. "Fine, be like that, but when you get murdered and spill out new magic for the world, I'm not starting a revolution for you."

Tio laughed. It wasn't that he didn't care, but it was hard to be invested in something from so long ago. Tovaloreande established the first nature-centric culture in Grenvel, and her death was thought to have been what gave people flourishes, sparks, or gifts—whatever people wanted to call it. The first druid—Drassil Ren—had been part of the revolution against the Old Faith after their betrayal. Standard learning in Belsa, but not something Tio yearned to know every detail of.

A shockwave blasted etheric haze into their direction with spinning pink dust devils as birds dotted the sky and numerous critters darted from the bushes.

"Wait, is Hali here?" *But why? If Sanctuary were her destination, she'd have joined with us.*

"Do you know anyone else capable of that?" Alim ran off the trail, through the brush.

"Could you not?" Tio bounded after them, praying to the sun—his mom would be proud—that they wouldn't run into any more guards.

Branches slapped him in the face as the forest grew denser and forced him to move with careful steps to avoid making too much noise. The deeper they got, the more petals and flowers covered the grassy floor, until it was as if they were stepping through more blossoms than grass. Tio crouched behind a tree across from Alim and peered into an extensive Sipherra alchemy outpost.

The perimeter was guarded by Dreamers with yellow straps the same as Alim wore—except for an added red Sipherra mountains design—wrapped around arms, legs, waists, and even necks.

A large stone battering ram with tiny rainbow spikes was set up against the green haze barrier. A team of earth-gifted mages filled cracks along the ram while red-coated scientists examined beakers with etheric mist floating within.

It wasn't Hali after all. All that noise and it doesn't look like their battering ram made a dent.

"Would you care to repeat that, Osanshia? Remember, your place on Gren Consortium is on the line," a familiar-sounding voice said to one of the earth mages.

Another angle confirmed Tio's intuition. *Geno Sipherra is here. Did we fluster her into checking or is this operation important enough for her to be here in person?*

"Breaking the barrier is impossible. How do you know that ex-Dreamer told the truth?" Osanshia asked.

Osanshia looked to be the lead mage. Tall, with orange hair braided like erratic tree branches held together with strings of amethysts, her violet-lined lavender robes were light with a thick leather Dreamer strap keeping them from flowing. Exactly the type of mage-appropriate clothes Hali hounded Alim to get.

Geno propped her head against her hand with a bored stare. "With but an inkling of comprehension you'd know not to doubt one of Allister's precious Collectors. If Alim says they got inside a haze barrier, then they did. Whether it was Alim or the druid or the witch."

How does Geno's orb float anyway? Her flourish maybe? Isn't she a bit young to need a cane?

Geno continued, "Are you telling me I've wasted millions manufacturing etherite for this ram?"

Millions? Did money even go that high? Maybe if somebody were trying to buy a whole country. And what's etherite?

"Of course not. We made progress. The last impact deformed the barrier for the first time. But we—"

Dragged by his feet, Tio crashed into something before finding himself upside down with a face full of his own cloak. There was nothing but

Chapter 14 Tio

an invisible swirling pressure holding him. A Dreamer weaved his hands through the air, matching the rotations of the magic holding Tio in place. The strap of his grass-woven satchel snapped, and his belongings scattered.

Alim was gone from their hiding spot. *Please tell me you escaped, Alim.*

"An intruder?" Osanshia said, flipping Tio's cloak out of the way and tugging hard on his hair. "And a druid too. Hey, Geno. This your guy?"

"How many druids do you think skulk about haze barriers wearing the Conclave's fig leaf?" Geno pushed her cane into her orb and floated to Tio. "Druid, you chose to trespass. Disappointing, but maybe seeing my company's hard work first-hand will change your mind. Let's be cordial."

"Hard to be cordial upside down." *Also, I have a name. You obviously know it since you read my research.*

With a snap from Geno, the air locking Tio in place released, and he fell antler-first onto the blossomy ground. Blood dripped into his hair from where the grayish-brown velvet had torn on his left antler. *Headbutting hobby looking mighty enticing right now.*

Geno reseated herself, back so straight Tio became all too conscious of how much he slouched. "Imagine a world in which ether pumped through cities into every home. Powering machines without a need for gifted blood. The rate at which we could innovate would be unmatched by any previous civilization."

"You want Grenvel to become like the Coveted South?"

"Sipherra will make the South quaint by comparison, and I'll prove it by conquering Phantasmal Reef where our ancestors failed. The first step in our technological journey is the leap from blood-based ether to surge-based."

If I worked for Sipherra, I could ensure the ether is extracted safely and prevent dangerous tech from developing. It would be an amazing opportunity… but I can't trust you, Geno. "How do you expect me to help?"

Geno stroked her chin. "Show us how to get through the barrier."

"You've got the wrong person. Another was responsible." Tio wiped the blood off his antler.

"Those are real?" Osanshia asked.

"Haven't you read the stories? I'm so druid, I'm half-animal." Authors sensationalized nature magic like it was otherworldly compared to "normal" flourishes. Shapeshifting was one such ridiculous power.

"Druid, quit the games. It couldn't have been Alim. Was it the witch? How did she do it?"

"It wasn't complicated. She hit the barrier like… really hard." Tio walked closer to the haze.

An amethyst from Osanshia's braids floated down, revolving around her palm. "No amount of magic would have broken the barrier without killing the mage."

True. Hali never mentioned why her rune worked. "Come on, uhh Tree Braid? You seem capable. If my friend could do it, so can you." Tio retrieved a blue bottle from the grass and shook it about. "Old Thaumic recipe. Restores blood and keeps the magic flowing."

Irritation soaked Geno's words. "We're well aware of elixirs and how rare their ingredients are."

Right. The mages that died building Last Stand used elixirs to extend their lives so they could keep working. Tio gave a sassy shrug. "No ingredients are rare for druids. Let me go back to Spirit Arboretum and collect some for you."

"Elixirs don't make magic stronger, no matter how many you chug." Osanshia's amethyst vaulted between her hands. "Don't lie to us."

Tio backed into the etherite battering ram. *A little further…*

Osanshia's arm shot forward, rocketing her amethyst at Tio, and he flinched hard enough to feel every crease he'd have in old age.

The gemstone clanged against metal. When Tio opened his eyes, Alim was there with the amethyst lodged in the side of their helmet.

"Osanshia, what were you thinking?" Geno said as Alim's throwing axe blurred by her and clipped through one of Osanshia's branching braids.

Chapter 14 Tio

Tio smacked the ground with his bloodied hand. Faint pressure built as the blood toll connected him with an underground network of tree roots. With an intense squeeze taking hold in his veins, tangled roots burst through the soil and tossed clouds of pink into the air. His thoughts focused on defense—the trees did as he suggested and molded into two towering walls, forming a lane through the Sipherra outpost.

"Alim, this way." Tio grabbed them by the hand and sprinted to the twisting purple barrier. Same as when exiting, the haze parted to let them through and closed rapidly behind them.

This time it didn't tickle. Instead, it felt like he was trudging in circles through heavy snow with wind blaring like distant cries for help. As if the ether were resisting him, he began to feel as if he were being forced through a tiny tube until he crashed to the other side into a heap of singed blossoms.

"Great job back there." Alim clapped Tio on the back and returned his grass satchel.

"Thanks for getting my bag," Tio said, unable to hide the strain in his voice.

"Are you injured? Undine's still asleep, but she'll take care of you soon."

"My skull feels like a hardboiled egg, and it's not just because of my antler." Nausea built in Tio's stomach.

"Get some rest. We're safe now."

Constant wailing crept into Tio's skin, prickling him everywhere. "I won't be able to sleep with this noise."

"All I hear is how out of breath you are. Come on, sit."

This pain... it isn't mine. It was as if Tio were connected to the entire forest. Feeling what it felt. "Something's wrong."

Barren trees in every direction. That shouldn't be possible. Unlike in Diya, cherry blossom trees never stopped flowering here. Even without druids. Tio dashed through dim piles of ethereal-colored blossoms. He heard Alim's heavy steps trail after him, but he didn't wait.

Arboreal Path

The deeper he got, the worse his headache became. Fewer and fewer blossoms littered the grass, and those that did had taken on a gray tinge. Trees went from flowerless to wilting to rotted. Arriving at a blackened grove, broken glass crunched under Alim's boot as they caught up. Tio followed the agonizing screeches to the rapidly decomposing corpse of a colossal lynx.

CHAPTER 15

Flipping through her rune book, Hali reviewed her available spells. *Two poison. Two nightmare.* She flicked the falling cherry blossoms off the pages. *Two force. Two wraithstep. One invisibility.*

An even spread, except for the invisibility rune she'd used to bypass patrolling Dreamers. She didn't know what magic would work best, and time was limited. Making more might have put her at risk of fainting from blood loss since she'd used most of her stored blood vials at Spirit Arboretum.

Nearly overlapping yellow and orange moons peaked through the pink canopy. *The monthly eclipse will happen tonight. I'm sure Alim is forcing Tio to stay awake to see it.*

Hali stepped through green-tinted haze-touched flowers and brushed her hand against the barrier, letting its maw chomp her. Casually walking through would alert the eidolon to her presence, but she wasn't a celestial anymore. Forging a path through the ether like she had when breaching Wolloisha's southern surge wasn't possible. Not that it had helped much then. Zergi had been able to smell her coming from the beginning.

Coating her arm in Ikazu's wispy shadows, she pushed against the biting haze. Every step was met with a sting worse than being injected by a doctor. Over. And over. And over.

Just as she thought the haze's assault might make her regret ditching Tio and Alim, Hali was out. Instant relief—all the pins and needles prodding her departed.

Hali scanned the dim forest. Ahead, she spotted a disturbed pile of blossoms. No doubt the eidolon had been sleeping here and awoke as she passed through the barrier.

This would be simpler if I could still sense its ether. The last thing she'd expected was to be longing for her celestial magic back.

Everything took on a dark emerald hue between the color-shifting ethereal cherry blossoms and the now-eclipsing light of a singular green moon—the spitting image of the Lunar Vault pre-destruction and the reason it was called a twin eclipse.

Rustling. Hali opened her rune book to a nightmare rune. Inspired by the sweet-smelling smog of Fion's sludgy plant beasts—innoboro—this rune was the sleep-inducing cousin of the poison rune. Its jagged, circular shapes shone on the page.

The trees wobbled as a giant lynx leaped from branch to branch. A cloud enveloped it. Descending from the tree unaffected, the lynx circled to Hali and swiped with claws coated in the same etherite rainbow metal as her dagger. She jumped backward, escaping disembowelment with narrow margins.

If nightmare did nothing, poison won't work either. I wanted to get its blood without a fight, but that plan is ruined. This is why I don't plan things. Hali found the page with a force rune.

As the force rune's square and triple waves lit up, a whistling gale battered against the lynx and deflected its second strike. Not the devastating impact she was hoping for—the rune hadn't done much more than inconvenience it.

Chapter 15 Hali

It let out a low growl and invaded her mind and ears with its voice. "Sereia. First you break into my surge, then you cast spells on me," Sulin said. "Explain your purpose, celestial."

Sulin was small by eidolon standards but still stood as tall as Hali—far larger than the wild cats she'd seen while journeying with Rev. Weathered roots ran from its front paws, up its legs, neck, and ears, and the tips of its furry ears had cherries swaying from the lingering blow of her magic. Gray spots covered its white fur from head to stubby tail.

Kill. Eidolon.

Stop talking or I'll cut your rune in half.

An idle threat. Hali had already tried ruining the binding rune. The shadow always crept out and protected itself. No amount of strength let her touch it.

"Give me your blood. Please."

"For what, feeding your artificial spirit?" Sulin doubled in size as its fur stood on end. "I haven't forgotten how Malakine nearly destroyed my surge to do the same."

"I didn't ask for Kthon, nor am I doing anything for his gain. This is for Rev and Rasal." *I don't want to hurt you.*

"Does it matter? A spell developed by Malakine, using Kthon as a conduit for eidolon blood... do you expect to control the resulting magic?"

"I didn't blindly trust Malakine. It took me years to ensure the runes had a chance to work."

Sulin backed away. "You cannot have my blood. Not for a chance."

Hali flipped to a rune of pointy spirals, activating it with a touch."

Multicolored blossoms kicked into the air and Sulin appeared behind Hali as if teleporting. Its attack hit her shoulder and sent her tumbling, cracking her cheek against a trunk. Blood gushed from her shoulder and her ears rang. With no time to breathe, Sulin was already upon her, tossing more flowers in its wake. Claws raked down Hali's face and she recoiled, only to find herself unharmed.

About time, wraithstep. The delayed intangibility of the phantom-based wraithstep rune was always difficult to time. *Not many offensive options left in my arsenal. How can I make good use of my temporary invulnerability?*

Hali's blood boiled. As its intensity increased, the bubbling became loud enough to hear. Shadows leaked from Hali's tattoo into a dark puddle, expanding and raising off the flowery ground until Ikazu took on Rasal's masculine figure.

This is the hard part, Ikazu. Don't kill Sulin. Besides the potential environmental destruction, killing Sulin would render her friends' goals unattainable. Alim wouldn't be able to become a celestial without attuning to every element. Tio wouldn't be able to restore magic without a celestial. Hali had made things hard enough by abandoning them in Gren City, but the possibility of resurrection wasn't something to pass up.

Ikazu lunged at Sulin, erasing any part of his body its claws tried to eviscerate. The black mist radiating from him formed thick tendrils and latched onto Sulin's legs. She tried to suppress the joy she felt from using magic in combat again. The adrenaline rush. The buzzing in her veins. Fighting with runes paled in comparison to the personal sensation of utilizing her air spark or bending ether. This was a distant third. But this wasn't a sparring session with Rev or an academy student. It wasn't a battle against nameless, faceless enemy soldiers where she could numb herself. Sulin was a friend. An important part of the world. There could be no joy if this ended as it had with Zergi.

Sulin fought to break free, but Ikazu wrestled the lynx to the ground.

Unsheathing her dagger from her book, Hali approached the trapped lynx and placed the rainbow blade at its shoulder. "I'll be gone soon enough, Sulin."

A shallow cut and the deed was done. Hali collected the ethereal, multicolored blood in a glass vial. But flames erupted from the blood, shattered the vial, and combusted Ikazu, releasing his hold on Sulin. Hali's blood seethed as Sulin bit down on her leg. The cord linking her to Ikazu

Chapter 15 Hali

undulated rhythmically, pouring her power into the shadow. Sulin threw Hali into a tree and its branches buried her with uncountable blossoms.

A rash streaked Hali's right side, snaking up her neck as Ikazu trembled. The fire dispersed as an arm sprouted from Ikazu's side. Pulling on its own body, the upper torso of a shadowy woman hung from Ikazu's left side. Ikazu tackled Sulin, grabbing hold of it and pinning it with four hands, while the Rev-like woman hanging from Ikazu reached through the lynx's body and pulled out wisps of etheric light.

The way Sulin convulsed, it reminded Hali of plague victims nearing the end of their lives, blood turning to dust. Kthon's shadow magic was much the same. Repulsive. And yet, these same shadows preserved Hali's loved ones and would be the key to resurrecting them. *I can't back out now.*

Ikazu sank into themself as the lynx overpowered them. With a sharp roar, a conflagration whirled from Sulin's mouth and melted Ikazu, forcing them to retract into Hali's rune.

I can't stay conscious through summoning Ikazu again. No useful runes left. Sulin's too fast to engage with weapons. Hali's blood burned, though it was a relief compared to her last two boiling-level blood tolls. *If I don't do this right, Kthon will be unleashed and consume Sulin.*

Hali's rune ejected shadowy tendrils flailing into the air. Each exploded into smaller spikes. Waves of fire deflected most, but Sulin's defense failed. Four spikes got through and lanced Sulin's heart. The eidolon collapsed, and a light-headed Hali with it.

Tears rolled down her face as she retrieved her dagger and a second vial. *Sulin, it didn't have to go this way.* Was her family more important than the eidolons—than magic itself? Hali's clenched her jaw, remembering the impact of Rev's staff. *Rev will hate me when she's back, but I'll never forgive myself if Rasal isn't given a chance at life.*

Nearly falling over twice, Hali finished filling several vials with Sulin's rainbow blood. Her vision blurred. The only eidolon rune she thought might help was Egress. Short-range teleportation. With it, Hali could return to Gren City and rest. Vial in one hand and paintbrush in the other, Hali drew a rune on an empty page of her book. Once finished, it resembled leafy vines with unblinking eyes watching from each leaf. In the language of spirits, it translated to "travel where the mind gazes."

Activating the Egress rune had no result. *Suspected as much. Sulin's blood isn't compatible with this eidolon rune.*

In this condition, Hali would never reach Gren City. Resting close by would have to suffice. *I can't leave Sulin like this. Maybe a druid-style burial would be appropriate?*

But right as Hali stood, her vision went dark.

The crackling of a campfire soothed her ears as she regained consciousness. When the world came back into focus, her hands, shoulders, and head had been bandaged. Her frayed auburn hair was still matted with petals, but her surroundings were nothing but the sparse red and brown of Grenvel's trade plains. Hali saw Tovaloreande Sanctuary's pink canopy to the north.

A tall, gray-skinned old man wearing a wide-brimmed hat grimaced as he tasted soup from a ladle. Water trickled down his rain-catching hat, funneling through a tube into a large jar on his back.

Did it rain? How long have I been out?

"You're awake!" the logu said with glee that contrasted his sharp orange eyes.

Her mind was still fuzzy, but something about the logu agitated her. *Did this guy get into the surge somehow and pull me out here?*

"Found you crawling through the forest, out of your wits." The logu paused at Hali's reaction. "Don't look so confused. Your injured ether drew me to you."

Logu ethersight differed from a celestial's. It could see finer details. Like injury, apparently. Logu always made Hali feel like they were seeing her soul, judging her.

Chapter 15 Hali

"I was making my rounds through the Sanctuary. Paid an arm and a leg to get in there, mind you. Ridiculous. Anyhow, I noticed the barrier had some weak spots—no, sorry, more like spots with no barrier at all. Seemed like those spots were growing rapidly, too You were on the other side."

"And the lynx?"

"You weren't near any lynx if there was one. Like I said, you crawled. I didn't bother going any further in after I saw you needed help." He gave an inappropriately timed bellowing chuckle.

Hali picked a petal from her hair, finding it absent of ether and colorless. "Thanks, but I must be going." Hali commanded her body to move, but it didn't budge.

A second booming laugh escaped the logu. "It wasn't a problem. Name's Barbaroli Pensa, and a Pensa always helps those in need."

Why is that name familiar?

Barbaroli handed Hali a bowl of soup. "Those wounds aren't going anywhere. Eat."

Nothing could be less appetizing. The soup was about as pungent as feet on a sunny day. Alim's specifically. The helmet never came off, but Alim's boots came off too much. Famished as she was, Hali sipped a spoonful and hoped for the best. Although eating caused aches, the taste wasn't abhorrent enough to stop Hali's spoon from hitting an empty bowl before she knew it.

"Fifty-seven…" Barbaroli took inventory of his fruit as he packed them into a steel crate. "Eighty." Crate sealed and ready to go, Barbaroli heaved it into his wagon with ease.

Watching him made Hali eager to have the same energy levels, so she could get back to Gren City and plan for the next surge. *Wait, one of my eidolon runes can help.*

Hali opened her pack and retrieved her painting supplies. It took all of Hali's concentration to keep her arm from shaking as she kept it raised

Arboreal Path

for painting. Stroke after stroke, the image of a misshapen claw holding an orb materialized on the page. With a claw representing stealing and an orb representing the sun, it roughly translated to "steal energy," but Malakine had called it Sapper. The rune glowed even without activation. Hummed. The Sapper rune had responded to Sulin's blood.

Hali turned one page back to a nightmare rune and activated it. It may not have been effective on Sulin, but Barbaroli wouldn't be as lucky.

"Do you have family near? If you—" Barbaroli collapsed against his crates of merchandise.

Now for Sapper. The page lit on fire for a few seconds before fading and leaving the paper blank. Hali slammed the book shut and her pain drained away.

Standing gave Hali no resistance, and her pack swung over her shoulder as if it weighed nothing. Not only had the rune been successful in stealing Barbaroli's strength, Hali felt stronger than ever.

She set a small pouch stuffed with colorful money into Barbaroli's hand. *Payment as thanks.* Not exactly the nicest reward for the kindness he'd shown Hali, but at least this one would live with intact memory and nightmareless sleep. That was more than others could say after meeting her.

The trek back to Gren City took the rest of the day and consumed most of her borrowed vitality. At the gate, a lone guard was letting in a family. Hali opened her book to her last invisibility rune. Her body shimmered before disappearing, allowing her to follow the family through the checkpoints, careful to maintain enough distance to not be smelled or heard.

Luckily, there was an inn next to Gren City's entrance. She hobbled past the stables and an abandoned greenchurch before arriving at the inn. Her invisibility wore off right as the door shut.

She tossed a bag of coins on the counter. "Give me your best room."

"You don't have paper money?" The innkeeper's agitation was clear on their face.

Chapter 15 Hali

I gave all my Grenvelian money away to that merchant. "This is all I have right now. It should net you plenty at an exchange."

The innkeeper opened the bag and couldn't hide their ridiculous crooked smile, handing over a room key without a second complaint.

Limping through dingy green halls and entering her room, Hali prepared for her first new eidolon rune since binding Kthon. A series of candles spread cardamom-scented smoke as Hali lit them with a weak fire rune. The pleasant fragrance would block the horrid citric tang of Kthon's magic.

What little shadow came out traced along the edges of Hali's arm before returning. Hali's thoughts drifted to Rasal as she examined and cleaned her rune-carving needle. When this was all over, everything would be worth it. Hali would finally meet Rasal. The real Rasal. Her little raspberry lion.

She poured vials of rainbow blood into the needle—then, jaw clenched, Hali pierced her right arm. Each light jab replaced brown skin with rainbow ink. No spot shared the same colors or patterns. Flesh burned. Vibrant hues parted. Shadows filled the gaps and spread throughout the incomplete rune.

Unlike past experiments, the candles did nothing to stop the whole room from reeking of oranges. Hali covered her nose with her cowl and wiped the welling blood from her throbbing arm. Now black with splotches of vibrating color, the Sapper was almost a recognizable shape.

You'll be with me soon, Rasal.

CHAPTER 16

Under an immense bonfire of dead trees awaited the eidolon's last charred bone fragment. Alim had to crawl among the smoldering wood and hope embers didn't fall on their bare skin. Stretching their axe as far as they could, Alim raked the crumbling bone out from the bonfire and tossed it into Tio's mortar, holding their blistering fingers to their lips to cool them off.

The sounds of Tio's pestle grinding the fragment along with the others was enough to make Alim beg for Undine to drown it out. But she was still asleep, churning within Alim's veins as if she'd been stuck in a nightmare since entering Sanctuary's surge.

Tio added soil in with the fine gray powder until the two were indistinguishable and dumped the mixture into the burial mound.

Burning fur and flesh still clawed at Alim's throat and eyes as they sat on wilting grass. As if the etheric fog itself had died, the grove was coated in various shades of blandness. Gray dirt and grass, a black puddle as dark as Phantasmal Reef, and even Tio's hair had lost its leafy luster, appearing muddy.

Tio opened a jewelry box, and the blinding light within pierced the fog and returned vibrancy to the sanctuary. At least, next to Tio. He grabbed a glowing seed and inserted it into the mound of ashen soil.

"Should you be using Empyrea's seed for this?" Alim asked.

"It's an eidolon. What other seed is worthy?"

Logical, but he'd said past attempts to plant these seeds hadn't done anything. "How do you know it'll grow?"

"Doesn't matter. Being buried with the seed is enough. There's no shame in a burial tree that doesn't grow." Kneeling at the mound's base, Tio recited, "Death brings life. Return to Empyrea and be reborn in the joining."

Alim reached under their visor to rub their eyes. The words reminded them of Solstoran eulogies they'd heard at their mom's funeral as a kid. The exact phrasing escaped them, but rebirth had been mentioned for sure.

Instead of grief when remembering that day, Alim thought of the music, dancing, and great food. Not to mention the pleasant things everybody had shared, whether fond memories or their mother's achievements. The beautiful, resonant hymns stuck in their mind as vivid as the day they'd heard them—a synchronous hum of thousands of Wolloishans as the priests lit the pyre at the peak of a blue dune to signal the sun to ferry her to a new life.

Finger pierced by his bracelet, Tio smeared blood across his palms and placed each on the burial mound. The soil shifted. Pulsated. Parted, making way for a twig. He wiped his brow with his forearm and sighed, sounding as tired as he looked.

Alim grasped Tio's shoulder. "Definitely eidolon worthy." They started dismantling the cooled bonfire so it could be used as compost for Tio's restoration efforts.

"Let—Let me handle that," Tio said, tripping on his words. "You did enough building it and keeping it lit."

"Got it. I'll see if there's any signs of what happened." *Though I don't know what I'm looking for... Hali would know what to do. I'm not much of a celestial without her.*

As Alim explored the darkened woods, they found other dead animals, flowers, and trees rotting as if days of decay were happening in minutes. A chill stirred within Alim like jingling ice cubes.

You okay in there, Undine?

No, Undine said.

Any idea what happened here?

No.

Alim banged their helmet right on its amethyst-embedded dent, hoping Undine would feel it like an earthquake. *Come on. I need your help finding clues.*

This flesh is close to the forge. Take me there please.

Oh, a "please" for the flesh bag? Lucky me, I'm honored. No counter jab? *Sorry, show me where to go.*

Undine directed them through the decrepit forest. Was the whole sanctuary dying? The death of an eidolon—what effect did that have?

A web of interlaced trees lay ahead in the gray and black clearing. The thick center where the trees combined had a door, a window, and a chimney.

This it? Alim waited for a response, but the water spirit had fallen quiet again.

Pushing the door open, its creak grated at their senses. A single large room made up the interior, with an anvil and forge taking most of the space. Alim ran their hand along the bottoms of the hammers, tongs, chisels, and other tools hanging from the wall. Slamming their foot into something heavy, they tripped, and the floor's rotted bark cracked under their weight.

What is that? Alim lifted the bulky dark orb that had taken them down. *Obsidian?*

Holding it in both hands, their helmet warped like their brain had grown five sizes in the black glass's reflection. Their twig of a neck looked as if they hadn't lifted a day in their life. Distorted or not, they hated looking at it, so they held it out of sight under their arm.

Chapter 16 Alim

The only other things in the room were dark gray ingots piled in the corner. Everything in the forge was immaculate, like Hali had overseen it. This orb was the only item out of place. With nothing else to see, Alim left the forge, hoping Tio might have some insight.

Partway through the clearing, the orb ignited and became so unbearably hot they let it drop. Orange energy swirled within, coalesced into a fireball, and launched into Alim. With a crash, Alim found themself back in the forge, having been thrown through its wall.

Lingering embers danced off their cuirass like the sun engraved on it were alive. Head turned away and blood swirling, they held out both hands. The spinning, blazing sphere stopped in mid-air, caught in a vortex of pink and green ether between their hands. Color returned, if only in Alim's vicinity.

Just as Alim tossed the fireball aside and stomped out the flames, another hurtled in their direction. A chill left their body, and water splashed, engulfing the latest attack. The droplets in the air merged until Undine sprayed into existence.

"That flesh does not wish you harm, Vulkine," Undine said, motioning towards Alim.

The burning orb expanded in a fiery vortex, forming legs. Arms. A head. They looked like a child. "Undine? How are you here?"

"I am bound to that flesh. It is through their blood I exist in your surge."

Infernal hair flickered in rhythm with Vulkine's speech. "I can't remember anything. Except, I think I died." The fire spirit poked a strange gap in their shoulder and whimpered. Alim could see right through it.

"You're safe." Undine held Vulkine's hand and steam billowed as the two elements collided. "What's the last thing you remember?"

"A nice lady. The one bound to Empyrea. She grew these pretty trees for me."

Undine's voice entered Alim's mind. *That was long ago. Vulkine has lost everything.*

Sanctuary's namesake—Tovaloreande—had started this forest to protest the Old Faith. If Empyrea and spirits had been involved with her, then maybe it was true her death had brought the gift of magic.

Is the memory loss related to Vulkine being a child? Alim asked, unsure if Vulkine had always been like this or if spirits even aged as people did.

Their body reverted due to low ether. The memory loss is not normal.

"Does this flesh walk the Path?" Vulkine asked. "Sulin's fruit will attune this flesh to fire."

"The lynx? Sulin is—" Alim's blood chilled and teeth chattered as if ice was building on the inside of their helmet.

"The trial comes first, right?" Undine's frozen fingertips steamed as they returned to liquid.

"Trials! My trial is fun, and nobody can walk the Path without creating etherite! Plus, it's educational. Nothing teaches how ether works better." A thin line of fire followed Vulkine as they skipped into the forge.

Undine?

Spirit and eidolon are intertwined. When one dies, so does the other. If Vulkine can hold out a little longer, I think they would enjoy one more trial. Do that for us, please?

Even if attuning to fire was impossible now, Alim knew the trial was the right thing to do for Vulkine and Undine both. *Of course.*

They followed Vulkine through the Alim-shaped hole in the fused trees. Vulkine crawled up the forge and stuck their face in to ignite it, giggling.

The room filled with warm light as Vulkine ran through, breaking the gray fog. The fire spirit then climbed to the top of the pile of glimmering rainbow ingots.

"Vulkine, is that etherite?" Alim asked. *I've seen that metal before. Hali's daggers and Sipherra's battering ram. Even the festival golem back at Wilton. How is Sipherra making etherite if they don't have celestials?*

"Yes, yes! Isn't it pretty? But what will this flesh craft? A sword?"

Chapter 16 Alim

No weapon was as ineffective in Alim's hands as a sword. "A spear—wait, I thought I was going to create my own etherite."

Vulkine hurled an ingot at Alim.

Catching it nearly pulled their arms out of their sockets. *How does haze turn into something so heavy?*

"Smelting this is the first step. Then create your own to finish the weapon."

Using tongs, they placed the ingot into the blazing furnace. Alim waited. And waited. It didn't soften. "Am I missing something?"

"Silly, etherite is too strong for fire without weakening first."

"Weakening how?"

The fog twisted into tiny Alims, marching through the air. Vulkine was wiggling their fingers in step with the army. "Celestial magic."

"Use your magic to 'see' ether. Truly see it," Undine said.

Seeing with magic?

"That's cheating. You revealed the trick, Undine," Vulkine said, their hands on their hips.

Undine blew little bubbles at Vulkine, each bursting into steam puffs on their cheeks. "You're only the second trial for Alim, so they didn't know about ethersight yet."

"Oh! Sylphine would have helped with that. She should have been first."

There's an order? Hali could've told us that before we chose a surge.

Closing their eyes, Alim's blood surged as they reached out to the surrounding ether like Hali had taught them. "I don't see anything."

A cool, damp hand touched Alim's cheek. "Use the inner eye. Look at me."

What's an inner—

Circular splotches of color burst in front of them like a vivid version of the lights one sees with shut eyes, flamboyant dust lingering before clinging together and vibrating. A second explosion sent Alim reeling, but they got no further away from the light show until they stumbled into a crate.

Myriad old tools and blocks of gray wood clanged off their armor. "Whatever you did, I think it worked?"

Undine generated frothy bubbles where her heart should be with her chuckles. "Now try the druid. Ignore distance. It is irrelevant for ether."

"I can see Tio from here? Will I be able to tell where he is?"

"Once mastery is attained, but for now interpreting location is beyond this flesh's skill."

Could've dumbed it down a bit by saying "not until you get good."

Alim returned to darkness. The tingling of their blood toll lit small puffs of indistinct ether, and a chaotic presence stole their attention. Like splattered paint smelling of flowers thrown against a canvas with no care or precision. Each new splatter was different in size and texture. No rhyme or reason. No color scheme. Attempts to peel their gaze away were thwarted by an intense desire to witness each new flawed addition like Alim examining their unsatisfactory physique in a mirror.

A less distracting stem of light with a little flame at its base sat in their periphery under a rogue splatter. Its comforting warmth invited them away from the chaos, allowing its mess to fade. Alim's veins stretched against their skin like a god were remolding their physical form. It felt as if they were in multiple places at once.

Tunneling through thick, muddy ether, Alim found a new display of light. Like puzzle pieces laid out awaiting a solution. With a poke they connected perfectly with colors fading into each other. But a central piece was missing. When Alim lingered on the emptiness, an overwhelming energy scraped their insides. Was somebody humming? Or crying?

Quiet, garbled words projected in Alim's mind. *Resurrect. Us.*

A moistness smacked them across the face. "What did this flesh see?" Undine asked.

"I saw three things, but I don't know what to make of any of it."

Chapter 16 Alim

Vulkine's flames had become as small as a fading torch. "Those are etheric signatures. All things have a unique pattern."

Like a mental fingerprint.

Focusing on the forge, Alim found the ingot was like a thousand small etheric signatures cobbled together. Within their mind, they reached into the little pieces of ether and unraveled them like gooey cinnamon rolls. Returning to reality, they found the ingot emitting a ring of purple light with white at its center. Its integrity compromised, the metal bar drooped.

Vulkine watched, seeming more a proud parent than entertained child.

Alim grabbed the sagging ingot with the tongs and set it on the anvil. Holding it in place, they hammered.

No effect.

Alim reinforced each swing by swirling ether around the hammer's head, and dents formed as the metal mashed. Strike after strike until it shaped into a diamond-shaped spear head.

Vulkine examined the metal. "Amateur work, but it passes," they said. The tone reminded Alim of their dad—always unwilling to give genuine praise.

The blade wasn't smooth, with obvious dips and angles where the hammer had struck. "I'm no blacksmith, but it works for me. Is it time for phase two?" Alim hooked the spar onto the hip strap their dearly departed throwing axe had rested in.

"Yes, yes! Let's make etherite!" Vulkine pranced to the knocked-over crate of tools and discarded junk, tossing things left and right. "Perfect for the spear shaft."

Alim's muscles twinged at the thought of maneuvering with an etherite spear. "I could barely lift the ingot."

Shrill cracking echoed, and Alim shielded their face as pulses of heat barraged them. What little of Vulkine was left sucked into itself, returning to their previous black orb form, thick smoke crowding the forge as a deepening fissure snaked across the orb.

CHAPTER 17

What was once a twig had grown into a sapling. *So much progress. This normally takes days. Weeks. Empyrea's seed works fast.*

Grayed ether whirred past Tio and absorbed into the sapling. Pinching one of its miniature leaves, he tuned out the forest's cries and connected his mind to transfer more of his ether into the tree. This would be the last he could afford for the day without experiencing etheric drought. Nothing was worse than breaking out in a rash for days because of one too many spells or, worse, not being able to use his flourish at all.

Tio owed it to the eidolons to make sure this tree matured, but he couldn't allow himself to overdo it or the whole process would be delayed. With luck, this would be enough to let the tree grow on its own, so Tio could leave with Alim to find the next surge. Once the journey was over—whether Empyrea was mended or not—he would return to add a memorial.

Last drop of blood taken by the toll, a burst of color blinded Tio, and when his vision returned, the tree had sprouted a lynx kitten like a fruit. The branches snaked up its ears with tiny dangling cherries. Roots wrapped around its neck and front legs, and dark gray spots dotted white fur. Its claws were ordinary, not the rainbow metal present when Tio had found the adult body. The kitten plucked itself from its stem and fell to ashen soil, stretching and yawning as if it had woken from a deep sleep.

Drab gray was eradicated by bright pink and green as the fog's color restored and the flora revitalized. The agony of the trees faded, replaced by a low hum.

Unable to resist, Tio scratched the kitten on the head. *Do eidolons like being petted?*

The kitten rubbed along his arm before jumping into his lap. Its head rammed into Tio's chin and the world melted into a black void. *Another communion.*

Emotions flooded in. Gratefulness most of all. As Tio floated, the lynx flew into view. Its name flashed. Sulin.

"Can you show me what happened to you?" Tio asked.

"No. I remember dying, but nothing before." Given what had happened, Sulin's collected demeanor surprised Tio. Or maybe the surprise came from how misaligned the kitten's resounding, gruff voice was with its appearance.

Maybe I can delve into our communion and stimulate Sulin's memory?

A green aura flickered from Tio's hand. Setting it upon Sulin's head, the void filled with ether-coated cherry blossoms. However, substantial sections of the landscape were missing—gaping holes leading back to the communion's void. What parts did show were fuzzy, as if Tio needed thick glasses. *Sulin didn't forget. The memory's been corrupted worse than mine was. What could do such a thing?*

Black mist stuck to Tio's hand as he lifted it from Sulin. He bathed it in his green aura as he'd done to the corruption in his own mind. "We may need to repeat this process again later. I can't promise you'll remember when we're done, but you'll sleep easier." He'd repeated the process for himself nightly since he'd met Vinn, but he still couldn't remember who'd given him ethereal blood.

Arboreal Path

Tio sat next to Sulin on a blurry pile of colors. "For now, let's figure out what you *can* remember. What about the people harvesting ether from your surge? Did you know that was happening?"

"Perhaps. Perhaps not. I only remember Empyrea pushing me into the Corporeal Realm to defend its celestial spirit from mortals." Sulin let out a high-pitched kitten growl. "Mortals love stealing ether. Even after we compromised and gave them magic with our surges. Let them have it. We'll make more and laugh as they destroy themselves with their prize."

Sulin's cute whiskers bounced with a bellowing laugh Tio would have found intimidating coming from anything other than a kitten. "The day they can alter the flow of ether is the day I'll be scared."

"Like a celestial?" Tio asked.

"I don't know what a celestial is. But if it can reroute ether, then it could destroy or create on a whim. Even Empyrea would require aid if ether's flow was disrupted."

"That's why I'm here. The flow did get disrupted, and my friend is becoming a celestial to return Empyrea's ether."

"If you are sure, then you must find what is obstructing the flow. It should be clear in the Arboreal Path," Sulin said as its fuzzy image rippled out of existence.

Tio returned to his real body, and Sulin looked ready to pounce on him. *Even eidolons can be cute!* Tio dragged a stick along the freshly rejuvenated ground, and Sulin gave chase with the tiniest of hops.

"I'm back!" Alim shouted, carrying a black orb with Undine trailing alongside them.

"What did you find?"

Alim set the orb down. "This is Vulkine, the fire spirit. But… how is Sulin alive?" They tapped on their helmet.

"Empyrea's seed must have done it. It was absorbing the faded ether and growing faster than any tree I've ever seen."

Chapter 17 Tio

Sulin put its front paws on the orb, rolling it around like a toy. Orange light coated it as the crack closed, then flames engulfed orb and lynx both until a fiery kid carried the kitten out of the dissipating inferno.

"Thank you," Vulkine said, clinging to Tio with a warm hug as Sulin climbed to the druid's shoulders.

"That flesh is a Keeper," Undine said to Alim as if in awe.

Alim said, "I mean, yeah. I'd keep him around. Tio's nice."

That's sweet. Hope they know I can hear.

Undine said, "No, not like that. A Keeper. As in, Keeper of Empyrea."

Tio peeled Vulkine off his leg and placed Sulin on their head. "Is that special? Did Empyrea choose me or something?"

"No flesh is more special than another. All are equally inadequate. Keepers just have Empyrea's seeds in their pockets."

How disappointing. Pai would've loved hearing I was Empyrea's chosen. "Did you know the seeds would do this?"

"No, but now I see why it was important for us to track Keepers. More so now that no new seeds are made."

"Well, I have five left."

"So few?" Undine's insides swirled around.

"I'll take good care of them." Tio hoped he could keep that promise. The seeds already emitted less light than they had when he'd left Belsa.

Day turned to night. Vulkine, Undine, and Sulin played around the forest with pink petals swishing by them, while Alim sat upon a rock, drawing in a thick book near their campfire between spoonfuls of steaming stew. After spending most of the evening checking on Sulin's health, Tio sat next to Alim assured the eidolon would be fine.

"Hey, do you know anything that can erase memory?" Tio asked. "Sulin is in great condition, but its memory is in tatters. Most are gone."

"Vulkine was the same. And you had that lapse in memory from the arboretum's barrier. Before you got your antlers." Alim flicked their pen against their helmet. "The ethereal plague comes to mind. I learned the symptoms while in training. In the last day or two before death, most were said to forget their loved ones. Paranoid people may think the plague lingers in Refulgent Wastes, but it's long gone."

"Those same paranoid people blame druids for not curing the plague. One of many reasons we're hated…" Tio scratched his stubbly chin. "Not sure if the plague is the right line of thought here, but I'll study up on it."

"Couldn't possibly be as interesting as what I studied today!" Alim presented a sharp rainbow metal. "Check it out! Made from etherite."

"What is that supposed to be?"

It twirled around and pointed at Tio's face. "It's my new weapon!" Alim announced with too much pride.

"Is dramatic flair part of your fighting style?"

The chunk of metal morphed into the shape of a throwing axe and Alim hurled it. It soared overhead, spinning the whole time as Alim flicked their hand, beckoning for their weapon. Answering the call, the axe arced around and continued its death spin in Alim's direction. They dove under the whirling weapon and it scraped their helmet before sinking halfway through the rock Alim had been sitting on.

Tio burst out with laughter. "Maybe you need more practice."

"Lessons were learned. Etherite is sharp—" Alim tilted their head in the usual investigative manner, getting uncomfortably close to Tio's face. "When's the last time you washed your face?" They spat on one of their yellow cloths and rubbed it on his cheeks.

Tio flailed about, kicking Alim off. "One, don't touch me. Two, did you really just wipe your spit on me?"

"Sorry! But—" This close, Alim's gentle eyes were clear as day behind their visor. "It's like you have freckles now. Gray ones, like Sulin's spots."

"Huh. More eidolon traits? Neat, I guess."

"You're way too casual about this. Again! Where's your excitement?" Alim struggled and pulled up the axe so they could sit again. "Did you learn anything new about Empyrea at least?"

Chapter 17 Tio

Tio thought the moons were growing larger, as if they were falling and would crush him at any moment. "Precious little. Sulin said the flow of ether should be visible to a celestial in the Arboreal Path. Not sure what or where that is."

Alim revolved their etherite, shaping it into a spearhead. "Oh, good. More responsibility for me… that's not the least bit nerve-wracking." They snatched it out of the air. "Vulkine and Undine taught me to see ether, so Sulin wasn't wrong. If ether flows to Empyrea through the Arboreal Path, there was a big ol' abyss blocking the Ethereal Realm. Maybe it's because not enough ether is getting to it? Next time I go, I'll check it out with my ethersight."

"I hope so." Tio poured himself a bowl of stew. "Can I see what you drew earlier?"

"Don't spill on it or you'll regret it." Alim handed over the thick book.

A bestiary. When Tio opened it, he found a series of animal sketches, including several he had never seen. The back had empty pages, as if meant for adding new entries. The last two pages with entries had the eidolons and spirits. One with Vinn, accompanied by Undine; the other, Sulin, with Vulkine.

"Where did you learn to draw?" Tio was a tad jealous. The best images he could conjure were little more than wobbly lined cats a child could outdo.

"Sometimes it got boring on expeditions. Good way to pass time."

"Speaking of expeditions—what's the best way to enter Refulgent Wastes?" Tio wasn't looking forward to traversing the wasteland. How would it feel to be so far from plant life? Thinking about it was enough to make him lonely.

"The Dreamers' normal route around Runegate would get us caught. Cutting across North Lung by boat might be risky."

"That's too bad. I would've liked to see Runegate." Tio realized the impossibility of his statement. "Visit. Visiting Runegate… would've been…

neat." Tio coughed to cover his awkwardness. *You can't see Runegate, Tio! It's invisible.*

"Next time." Alim tossed one of the dead branches into the flames. "Refulgent Wastes is smaller than Grenvel, but we can't afford detours. We'll be there for two or three weeks as it is."

"Go under the lake," Undine said as her tall wave-like hair rippled.

Alim jumped up. "Of course! The water gift helped Grenvel forces infiltrate Oressa. By creating a giant air bubble and moving soldiers through it, they got into the city unseen and liberated it from Diya."

"We don't have an army of water mages. Is 'giant air bubble' feasible for one spirit?" Tio nervously traced his antler with a finger.

"For Alim, I will try my best. As thanks for helping Vulkine."

"I have a name now!" Alim cheered, spilling their stew on the grass.

"Don't celebrate too hard. Even with you as an anchor, sustaining myself outside surges only lasts a short while. But by transferring ether between our link, you can borrow my power."

"I'll get to use my water gift after all." Alim finished whatever little was left in their bowl. "Borrowed or not, that's always been my dream. I'll practice my stances every day."

Tio pointed to Refulgent Wastes on the surge map. "There are three surges here. At least one has a confirmed barrier between the Lungs. The other two are north of Sky Tower, and somewhere east of Stoneport. Should we head back to Wilton first?"

"No, we should go straight to Oressa. Crossing North Lung near Runegate should be safest. Plus, Oressa's library may have some books to help me hone my technique."

Sulin wandered into camp and stared at Alim with cherries dangling from its ears. "Eat," it said with an eerie calmness as its voice dug into head and ears simultaneously.

Alim plucked a couple of cherries. Tio imagined they were looking at the fruit like a lost lover under their helmet.

Chapter 17 Tio

Realizing how inedible the fruit was, Tio slapped them from Alim's hand.

"What's wrong with you, Tio?" Probably the only way Alim would sound more upset would be if he had spat on their pancakes. Maybe he'd try it sometime just to see.

"Sorry, let me examine them first." Tio held the cherries, connecting to them with his flourish. "These are poisonous." Most cherry blossoms didn't produce fruit people would want to eat, but this was worse.

Vulkine laughed. "No fun at all. It wouldn't kill!"

Tio removed the poison with his flourish. "We don't have time for Alim to be stuck on a toilet." He tossed the cherries over.

"Thanks, Tio!" As unceremoniously as one treats popcorn, Alim plopped the fruits into their mouth. Right away, they fell backward. Warmth radiating off Alim blasted Tio like a scorching summer day from across the campsite. It quickly became tolerable, and Alim wiped sweat off their cheeks. "Intense. You want a turn?"

"Absolutely not. This celestial business is all you. I take it you're okay?"

Alim nodded with a slight grimace. "No Arboreal Path this time though."

"It won't be automatic anymore. We'll go when you need to recharge," Undine said.

A distant, foreign pain took hold of Tio and drowned out whatever Alim was saying. Heat exuded from antlers to chest, worse than during Alim's attunement.

Alim stopped mid-sentence. "You feeling alright, Tio?"

The burning was directional somehow, pulling him east to where Vulkine and Sulin were playing. "Maybe I caught a cold?" Tio sniffled and rubbed his itchy eyes. "Or I'm allergic to Sulin."

Undine splashed a wet hand against Tio's forehead. "This is your ethereal blood warning you an eidolon is in danger."

"Is whatever killed Sulin still here?" *Could the haze barrier be weakened since its eidolon died? I should measure it.* Tio searched his grass satchel for his teapot artifact, but it was nowhere to be found.

"Sulin's haze barrier is restored—it would know if another was inside with us. You may be suffering from lingering effects."

"Well, how long will that safety remain? How do we know Sipherra's battering ram wasn't what killed Sulin to begin with? And now they have the means to advance their technology."

"Did something change?" Alim asked.

"I dropped my artifact back at Sipherra's camp. Sipherra got what they wanted. It's only a matter of time before they accelerate their ether harvesting and make things worse for Empyrea."

CHAPTER 18

The ethereal-colored, claw-shaped rune on Hali's right arm threatened to leap off her skin with its constant pounding. Wavering back and forth in a tidal rhythm, the three ethereal colors splashed against black ink.

It had only been two days, so a swollen and tender arm was to be expected, but each clash resulted in bouts of pain—worse, more ever-present than Kthon's binding rune had caused. The new tattoo may as well be tearing itself from her skin.

How am I supposed to write? Can't focus like this... A twinge propelled up Hali's arm and clamped her hand shut over her pen, scraping it across the page. Mangled and useless, the pen joined its fallen brethren on the desk's pen graveyard. Rune-induced spasms hounded Hali as a constant distraction from the poem she was composing in memory of Sulin.

Nothing like this happened with my first rune. Am I crazy to think the eidolon blood is summoning me somewhere? It's too precise to be incidental.

Unlike the binding rune, the Sapper's ink always shifted in the same direction. Green ink swam to Hali's right, wiggling through pink, swirling with purple, then bursting back to pink. Raising her arm only made the ink slosh to the left.

Fresh pen in hand, Hali completed the last line of her poem and shut her book with satisfaction. *The story of Empyrea and its children will live on through this book. Should my efforts result in Empyrea's fall, know my lineage will always be indebted and honor the role the spirit tree played in our renewed existence.*

Hali cleaned her new tattoo again in the washroom sink. Thanks to Ikazu's protective shadows, it hadn't scabbed and was practically healed. Still, it was best to cover it for another couple of days. As Hali wrapped it in gauze bandages, the pulsing ink quickened, matching her heartbeat.

What might the eidolon blood be showing me? The angle the tattoo pulled changed as Hali moved, consistently pointing east. *Could this be leading me to the other eidolons? Tovaloreande Sanctuary's surge is eidolonless... where else? Tio's map had East Peaks and northern Thauma marked. Must be one of those spots.*

Two potential locations. This was perfect. If the direction changed as Hali traveled, then her crazy thoughts would win. *Either spot would only take a week or two to reach. Can I really fight another eidolon so soon, even with Kthon's healing?* Fighting Sulin had taken more effort than Hali had planned for. Not only would travel slow her healing, but restocking her book's runes required her to draw a substantial amount of blood.

There's only two months to find four more eidolons. There may not be another opportunity if Tio is right about nature magic only lasting one more solstice.

Hali left the inn for the market to prepare. This early, the streets were devoid of people, with only merchants configuring their stands. Browsing and chatting with said merchants, Hali bought everything she could carry. First a grappling hook and torch. East Peaks hadn't had a barrier when Hali had walked the Path, so she didn't know whether its surge required climbing, spelunking, or both.

Chapter 18 Hali

Dried fruit and jerky were next, since what Hali had brought with her from Wilton was depleted. *Alim had a veritable mountain of food. Should've borrowed from them when I had the chance.*

Last on the preparation checklist was the stables, where Hali had put in an order for a swift travel horse yesterday. One requiring less rest and capable of being left at Oressa before heading into Thauma. Taking an animal to Thauma wasn't wise, considering how limited resources were there. These specialized horses also knew their way home and were trained to abandon their renter after waiting alone too long. *If I die, a horse isn't going to die with me.*

Upon arriving, the familiar reek of oranges and manure hit her like a dictionary to the face as horses nibbled on discarded orange peels. The stablemaster gave her the reins, and she was off on a sleek chocolate horse before the smell gave her a migraine.

Every night, Hali painted a new rune in her book using blood-infused ink. The pulsing changed directions in gradual increments until, about halfway through the journey, it was pointing northeast across a stream—the old border between Grenvel and Thauma—towards snow-covered mountains.

It might've been prudent to take a southern detour, following the trees floating down the stream to Oressa's lumbermill. Resting there would calm her nerves. Watching the water mages retrieve the trees and funnel them to the earth mage to chop with sharp stone saws... Hali could do that all day. Compelled by impatience, she waded through the shallow water instead.

On her seventh day of travel, Hali arrived at an expansive hole leading into the mountain. One of many such entrances making up Yinsen Caverns throughout southern East Peaks. The pulse, now so strong Hali was numb to anything else, didn't lead to the obvious entrance, but north of it. Hali gave her horse some feed and hugged its neck. *Roam free, friend. If I take more than a day, you know what to do.*

No ground-level entrance showed itself as Hali searched the northern face of the peak. Only a small crack no bigger than a person and too high up to reach. Slinging her grappling hook into it, Hali climbed and slid through. Upon landing inside, she discovered the corridors were cramped and wet—enough room to raise a torch, but not much else. *My longsword would have been useless here. For once, Kthon breaking it will be a benefit.* Hali had long since grown used to wielding daggers, but the longsword would forever be her weapon of choice. While recovering the etherite to make daggers at all had been a blessing with her dwindling celestial magic, Hali still regretted not restoring the weapon to its original form.

Screeching bats panicked and scattered as Hali lit her torch and sidled through the corridor until the cavern opened into a more comfortable size. Bright green luminous moss and pink flowers coated the walls. As she progressed, Hali couldn't help thinking of Alim and Tio.

I've really screwed things up for them. Alim will never be able to attune to every element with Sulin dead. Will all magic disappear if Empyrea dies? All in exchange for two lives… Am I making the right choice?

Right. Choice. Kthon itched within the binding rune.

Hali resisted the urge to scratch. *Don't speak to me.*

Resurrect. Us. Kthon flashed the image of a rune. The outlines of leaves hooked together in a helix with snakes piercing where the leaves meet. *This next.*

Help me if it pleases you, but you're a tool, Kthon. Nothing more. I've redesigned the eidolon runes to consume your ether as fuel.

After studying Malakine's eidolon runes for years, Hali had determined the purpose of each and how they linked together for the resurrection spell. Originally, activating all six runes required drawing upon Empyrea's ether within the Ethereal Realm, as if Malakine had never intended Hali to successfully use it without some alternate power source. But Hali's adjustments would allow the spell to work anywhere, with less eidolon blood required, and…

Chapter 18 Hali

In the end, the resurrection you so eagerly goad me about will kill you.

Deeper and deeper through the cave's corridors, moss grew thicker and blossomed with more flowers. When Hali arrived at the haze barrier at the passageway's end, its fog transitioned from purple to green. Once more, it was time to face an eidolon and do what must be done. Hali steeled her resolve. *My family is worth any cost.*

This haze clung to her skin worse than Tovaloreande Sanctuary's, as if walking too fast would flay her in an instant. *Ikazu, I need help getting through the barrier.*

Ikazu sleep. I help. Kthon's garbled words bounced in her head as shadows exploded from her binding rune and eradicated the barrier.

Fog destroyed, a vast chamber opened to Hali, dotted with stalagmites glittering with ethereal sparkles. Color-changing moss coated the walls, and sunlight peeked through large gaps in the stalactite-covered ceiling to illuminate the pit Hali found herself in. Tree roots invaded through the same gaps, like they were stretching the ceiling open.

Atop a dangling root, a barely lit silhouette with bright eyes observed Hali. It looked to be a barn owl with its head on backward. *Judging by the size, the fact that it's looking right at me, and my rune's nonstop thumping... that's the eidolon.*

The owl's head spun around as it dove off its perch and circled around to her, talons extended and persimmons hanging from its tail feathers.

No hope for peace? Hali's blood seethed as she activated the Sapper rune for the first time. Strands of ether poured from the owl's wings until it stopped midair, flapping erratically as it crashed.

With the sapped ether seeping into her skin, Hali felt like she could lift a hundred boxes of books. Far more effective than borrowing from the merchant had been. As the spell finished, Hali's binding rune roiled. *It worked—the rune took half its blood toll from Kthon.*

An eruption of air knocked Hali airborne as the owl beat its wings and gave chase. Before she was skewered, Hali flipped her rune book to

Arboreal Path

the flame-tooth rune. The intricate rune evaporated off the page while a burning sensation rose in Hali's throat.

An inferno spewed forth from Hali at the flying eidolon as it spun out of the way, flames licking its wings. Although Hali adjusted her aim, she couldn't keep up and blasted everything unfortunate enough to be in her line of sight.

Scorched and melted rocks. Mossy walls ablaze. But no damage to her intended target. Flame tooth required a lot of blood to paint, so she only had one more prepared. A direct hit would have resulted in an early victory, if only Hali could immobilize her foe.

A talon scraped across Hali's cheek as the owl soared over her head, circling around, poised for another strike. As Hali turned to a page in her book with pointy spirals, the owl's talons dug into her shoulder as it screeched in her ears, wind raging with its wings. Hali bit back her excruciating scream while slapping her hand against the wraithstep rune. The rune disintegrated from the page, and the owl fell through Hali.

One wraithstep down. Only two left. What else would pair well here? *Invisibility.* Hali turned several more pages, activated another rune, and vanished as she ran to a nearby stalagmite.

Taking the dagger from her book, Hali carved into the rock. With a hand on the symbol, blood surged, siphoned by the greedy magic. A bright yellow hue ignited under the rune, and burning tensed Hali's fingers. The owl flew, skirting below the gathering smoke clouds, in search of her.

Chunks of the stalagmite broke, collected bit by bit, and soared at the eidolon like bomb shrapnel. Gusts of wind diverted hundreds of shards and embedded them in the walls, with only a few getting through and pelting the owl's wings. Plummeting, the eidolon crashed near Hali.

"I'd rather not kill you," Hali said as she became visible again. "Can I at least know your name?"

"Anemo," it said, returning upright. "Whether you kill me or take a paltry blood sample, I'm effectively dead regardless, celestial."

Chapter 18 Hali

A couple vials of blood wouldn't kill an eidolon, unless I'm missing something? "Explain."

"No!" Anemo's voice shook the cave and rattled Hali's brain as a tunnel of air cut through the smokey cave and carried her into the ceiling, impaling her through the lower abdomen.

Vision blurred and Hali tried again to call upon Ikazu. No response. The rune refused to activate. Not even Kthon answered. *I've used too much magic already?*

When an ordinary spell was cast, it took as much of the blood toll as it could, even if the result severely injured or killed the caster. Hali didn't have that luxury, as the shadows prevented her from using any spell that might kill her. Who the protection came from was difficult to say. Rasal and Rev through Ikazu out of love… or spite for locking them up with Kthon. Or Kthon himself, keeping her alive as a vessel. No matter what Hali did, dying was impossible.

As much as she wanted to test if Anemo could thwart Kthon's protective shadows and kill her, she activated another book rune before impacting the stone floor. Thick shards of bark chipped off her skin as she lay within a small crater. Barkskin. A rune inspired by Rev's eidolon-given ability to turn her skin to impenetrable bark. Tio had inspired her to draw it again and now she wished she'd painted more than one.

Shadowy energy emanated around Hali's wound, wrapping it and sealing it shut, pressure pounding in her head. As exhilarating as battling was, Hali wanted to run away. To read books, curled up in the safety of a library.

Anemo's wind gathered around Hali and spun her, churning her stomach. She activating another wraithstep rune, and the magic passed right through her, eroding the ceiling with a ferocious typhoon.

Hali struggled to her knees, carving another shrapnel rune into the cave floor. With the flip of a couple of pages, the last flame-tooth rune appeared. Combining the two, Hali breathed flame into the launching rocks. Molten stone pelted the owl and its surroundings. More moss combusted, and thick smoke stung Hali's eyes and forced a hoarse cough from her.

Anemo leaped onto Hali and clawed furiously at her chest and shoulders, leaving deep scratches in her clothes and wooden body.

As if there were a god monitoring the battle for well-timed humor, her barkskin receded moments after the strike. Anemo then drilled into Hali's shoulder in the same spot and forced her to drop her book and dagger.

Eidolons are a vindictive bunch... If Anemo wanted to go for a killing blow, it'd had ample opportunity.

Right arm unusable, Hali reached to her boot with her left, flipped the dagger upright, and swung wildly. Forgetting her borrowed eidolon strength, the dagger sliced deep into its sinewy talon. Anemo stumbled backward and flapped furiously. Unable to lift off, it didn't get far before tumbling. Hali forced herself up, ignoring every pang of remorse. The only solace lay in the hope that the air spirit would restore Anemo the way Kthon restored Hali.

Anemo looked at her, judging her as all eidolons did, before going still. Was it accepting death or surrendering to live another day?

Hali gathered enough vials of blood to practice drawing the rune before the tattoo process. "You won't die. It's like I said, I'm here for the blood. Not cooperating was your choice. Sylphine will find you and heal you."

"Not if Malakine finds me first…"

Malakine's dead. "Why…" Hali struggled to speak. The shadows clinging to Hali's wounds weren't working fast enough, and her borrowed strength was dwindling.

Hali blinked and found herself surrounded by shadowy tendrils. Another blink and she was outside the cavern with her rented horse nudging her. Without any semblance of thought, Hali climbed into the saddle with pained breaths. Blood seeped through her shadowy bandages. This was bad, but Hali had recovered from worse. Kthon or Ikazu or whichever

Chapter 18 Hali

wouldn't let her die, but she needed to recover faster to get to the next eidolons before solstice.

Night fell and consciousness became a challenge. Hali nearly fell off the horse as the shadows abandoned her, having used up the last of her ether reserves. *I could really use Tio's healing right now...* No way he'd help now. If abandoning him wasn't enough, there was no question Tio would hate Hali for what she was doing.

"Are you okay?" A woman with a long red coat held out a flame with one hand and grabbed the reins of Hali's horse with the other. "You're wounded! We have doctors at the Sipherra Mining Outpost. It's nearby, come with me."

Try as she might, Hali couldn't respond, and consciousness trickled from her grasp as the scientist led her further east.

CHAPTER 19

Crouched against Stripes's legs in the middle of a pumpkin patch, Tio applied pressure to his burning gut, pretending it helped in the slightest. It had been three days since Sanctuary, and the "eidolon-danger" sickness still lingered the whole trip through the Trade Plains' sparse autumnal grasslands, ever-pointing east. To think Tio had been worried about the cherry poisoning Alim.

Alim held a rainbow-swirled bucket under Tio's face. "I got you, buddy."

Tio pushed it away. "Get that out of my face. I'm not puking into your weapon-turned-bucket."

"Better than on the pumpkins. No worries, it'll clean right out." Alim banged on the bucket as if to say, *Come on, you know you want to.*

"Today is better. I don't need it." Tio's cheeks inflated as he prevented himself from permanently hating the taste of pumpkin pie. *Shouldn't have eaten an entire pie… Alim is a horrible influence.*

"Is that why you're curled up in your 'I hate people' ball?" Alim nudged the bucket closer. "I'll hold back your hair."

Chapter 19 Tio

A good giggling session was the cure he needed. Tio's pain subsided, and he felt renewed. "No more stops, I promise. Let's go to Oressa." Tio wobbled his way onto Stripes.

Alim morphed the bucket back into a throwing axe and sheathed it onto their hip. "Will do, boss."

"Back to riding already?" Stripes asked. "More rest would be better, Tio. I can hear your stomach yelling."

Tio patted Stripes on the neck. "I appreciate the concern—"

Alim clapped as Majesty and Stripes crossed out of the green vines and orange grass onto a patch of pure white dirt. "Welcome to Refulgent Wastes," Alim said, as if they'd been waiting to do so all day.

"This is the Wastes?"

"The outskirts. You can tell from the splotchy bleached spots. Though don't call it that to anybody in Oressa. They consider themselves part of Grenvel's trade plains, even if cartographers took a few centuries to agree. Just look at your map."

Huh, it does label this area as the Wastes. Guess I assumed it was East Grenvel like our modern maps. "Isn't it odd to imply a place people live is a wasteland?"

The random pearlescent areas could have been mistaken for snow from a distance, but up close their cracked, craggy appearance gave them away as something far less fluffy and fun. Beautiful in their own way but jarring next to the surrounding ordinary grass and dirt.

"Yeah, but all this land was a former part of Thauma, which became Refulgent Wastes. Sort of anyway. Northern Thauma—where we are now—was always an outlier away from Thaumic mage culture."

Majesty bumped into Stripes, nearly throwing Alim into Tio.

Alim pulled on their reins. "Woah, come on, Majesty. Walk straight."

"Black and white suits you, Stripes," Majesty said. "Looking as shapely as ever."

Alim tousled Majesty's mane. "Don't argue with me."

Do I tell Alim their horse is flirting with Stripes... for the fourth time?

Stripes said, "Thanks for noticing, princess. I worked really hard on it for you."

"Could you not do this in front of me?" Tio whispered, once again wanting to die. *I wish I could turn my flourish off.*

It took two more days to arrive at the town's gates. If the ethereal-colored lights plastered on Oressa's outer walls and buildings weren't enough to make the town seem alive in the dead of night, the crowds were. He thought it might be quiet enough when he stabled Stripes and Majesty, but the streets only grew more congested the further into town they traveled.

"You going to be alright alone, Tio?" Alim asked. "I need to brush up on my water stances at Oressa's library."

"O-Of course. I'll get us an inn room." Tio flicked his bracelet charms.

"Hang in there. If you need me, use your flourish. I'll see it with my ethersight and come find you." Alim tapped their helmet.

Onto the search Tio went. It should have been a simple enough task, but Tio immediately allowed himself to get caught in a sea of people. The waves carried him through the town's main road to a residential area filled with brick homes.

Deep breaths.

Visible puffs of breath escaped his lips as he followed his mantra and poked his fingers into the dull sides of his leaf bracelet. Oressans were notorious for being harsh to outsiders. What if somebody noticed he was a druid? Would he cause a scene like in Gren City? Would they kill him?

Deep breaths.

Plenty of others were dressed in bright colors and hats. Some had dyed their hair ethereal pink, purple, or green. There were even a few with jackalope antler headdresses. His own antlers had grown considerably since leaving Spirit Arboretum. The tines hadn't all grown in, but doors

Chapter 19 Tio

were going to be even more of a problem for him than ever. What if people noticed his weren't part of a costume? What if they saw his strange gray freckles?

Something Alim had said yesterday came to mind. "Nobody's going to take a second glance at you. You'll blend right in with the festivities. And if not, let me be your bulwark again."

Though Alim's words made sense, Tio's brain wouldn't let him accept it as truth as if twisting the wisdom to further his anxiety-driven mania.

All the light-entangled homes blinded Tio, their ethereal lanterns reflecting off the snowdrifts hugging the glittery, gemstone-infused brick walls. The biting cold made him wish his cloak were three times thicker. *If we had more time, I'd wait for summer.*

Large people with armor, stamped with the cloud and moons of the Dreamers, patrolled the streets. Even unarmored soldiers with yellow cloth tied around their heads, legs, or arms mingled with each other on each street corner. Half touted Sipherra's mountains like the Dreamers at Sanctuary. Alim had warned Tio this was the Dreamer's home base, but he hadn't expected so many to be on duty. Not even outside the city was safe as past the south wall lay yellow, orange, and red mercenary tents engulfing the space between Oressa and North Lung.

Every Dreamer Tio passed made him more uneasy. Surely Geno put Sipherra and the Dreamers on high alert. Was there a bounty on his head? *Stop thinking about this, Tio. Ask for directions and move on.*

Shutting down as soon as he tried speaking to somebody, Tio succumbed to his inclination to escape the crowds. Trying his best not to bump into anybody while refusing to ask people to move, Tio finally found a path to break from the pack into a circular plaza of aging stone-built shops. None were an inn, but there should be one close. Hopefully.

Deep breaths. Unable to take it anymore, he sat on a bench and counted pebbles in the dirt road. Approaching the hundreds, Tio lost count as high-pitched singing broke through the numbers in his head.

Arboreal Path

> *Deer boy all sulky and sad*
> *Find cheer from fresh solstice fad*
> *Hair like grass and antlers tall.*
> *Uplift his spirits, snowball!*

Chilling cold broke through Tio's anxiety and crunched against his cheek. As he scraped snow off his face, the goofy lyrics, broken rhythm, and snowball battled in his head for credit in breaking his stupor.

"How can you be so grumpy dressed for the festival?" a child with long blonde hair asked while taking the seat next to him on the bench. Soot covered her face and blue dress, like she'd been standing too close to fireworks all night. A golden cloud-shaped locket hung from her neck.

"Consider the grumpiness gone, little bard."

"Those look neat!" The child pointed at his antlers and invaded his personal space to examine his face. "Where'd you get them? And this gray face paint?"

I knew somebody would notice. "Uh—a friend. I had to get ready for Oressa's festival after all."

"You're not from around here, are you?"

"Am I that obvious?"

"Nobody says 'OH-REH-SAH.' You gotta say it cool. Like 'Or-suh.'"

"There's no way I'm cool enough to skip syllables."

"Try it!"

"Did anything else give away that I'm not from Oress—Or-suh?" What an unnatural way to pronounce something. Why not alter the spelling at that point? Even if his stay in Oressa would be short, Tio didn't want to call attention to himself. Maybe Alim could help him practice.

"Yeah! Your hair doesn't look dyed. Does that mean you're a druid?"

Attentive kid.

The child continued before Tio could respond. "My pops tells me outsiders are bad luck. Didn't want me around the other outsider I met—a patient at Doctor Shell's office! She's real pretty, with reddy-

Chapter 19 Tio

brownish hair and neat glowy tattoos! We can't get her to wake up, but we're trying really hard!"

Hali is here? Did she get hurt?

"Pops didn't like her tattoos. Said they made her ugly and called her a witch. But I talked to her while she slept, and I haven't had any bad luck at all!"

Alim had mentioned that Oressa, as a former Thaumic city, had stricter policies against Old Faith practices, including runes. Since runes weren't used anymore, this generally meant Solstoran symbols, whether used for casting magic or not. Anyone caught with something reminiscent of runes or religious iconography was labeled a witch.

"Not all outsiders are dangerous, but your father is trying to keep you safe. Don't trust everybody you meet, Oressan or otherwise."

"I'm not afraid of strangers." The locket around the child's neck burst open and four gems twirled between her wiggling fingers. Blue and green gems cut like jagged blades. Yellow and orange gems cut into sharp crescents.

"Noted." If the dent in Alim's helmet was any indication, it was best not to get hit by an earth mage's gem. "So, you're not just a bard… what's your name? I'm Tio." *Almost forgot introductions again!*

"I'm Charlie." Charlie grabbed Tio's hand with both of hers and shook violently, like they had finalized an important business deal. "Being a bard would be a dream come true! But Pops says my gift is meant for building golems."

Tio's mind went back to Hali. "Where is Doctor Shell? I'd like to visit your new friend."

"You like witches too?" Charlie laughed, not understanding how derogatory the term was. "Follow me!"

Charlie ran full tilt down an empty alleyway to a dead end. Lagging behind, Tio did his best to keep up without running. The building at the end had a small sign outside to indicate it was a doctor's office. Charlie pounded on the door until somebody opened.

"What's the ruckus? It's way too late—Oh it's you, Charlie. Can I help you?" An old man peaked through the cracked door with not a hair to be found on his head or wrinkled face.

The doctor's red-brimmed glasses and matching long coat made Tio's heart drop until he realized there wasn't a mountain symbol to be found. Not Sipherra at all, this was just stereotypical Grenvelian doctor attire.

"We want to see the new lady!"

Shell looked at Tio. "At this hour?"

"Your patient is a friend of mine," Tio responded.

"Well, I'm afraid your friend isn't doing well." Shell adjusted his glasses. "She was found unconscious near Sipherra Mining Outpost and hasn't been awake since. There are signs of magic-induced internal bleeding and several external injuries. I've done all I can, but this isn't something mages normally recover from."

"Maybe I can help. I'm a healer."

"A healer… I apologize, your manner of dress threw me off."

"Druids like festivals too." *Can't I enjoy my antlers without everybody assuming I'm some sort of clown?*

Shell guided Tio through the entranceway, past a desk with little carved figurines of cute animals. Mostly puppies and fuzzballs meant to represent pyre dredgers. Quite the collection. Besides that, the rest of the room was plain, with light brown plank floors and walls. A skinny man was splayed out in one of the waiting-room chairs.

"Some people don't know how to celebrate in moderation." Shell thumped the man on the head. "My son among them."

Shell's son groaned and tucked his legs into the fetal position.

In the next room, a woman with Hali's unmistakable auburn curls and rune tattoo slept on a white bed, hooked up to a murmuring machine.

"I have to warn you," Shell said, "this patient's blood tests came back pallid."

Chapter 19 Tio

"What, do you believe pallids are contagious, that we might become pallid by being near her?" Tio's eyes rolled so far back into his head he could see his insides.

"That garbage?" Shell chuckled. "No. But many people do, especially since Gren City locked down. Oressan law forces me to reveal pallids for the 'safety of the public.' Of course, with so many signs of magic use in her condition, this was an unexpected blood test to be sure. I half wonder if my old machine is finally broken."

"It's almost as old as you, Mr. Shell," Charlie said.

"Doctor." Shell sounded as if he'd corrected Charlie hundreds of times today alone.

As Tio sat in a stool next to the bed, the deep, pale scar on Hali's neck drew his attention. Like something had nearly decapitated her many years ago. *Could anybody survive something so severe?*

Hali's chest, shoulder, and abdomen were wrapped in thick bandages, and she had a new tattoo on her right arm—a claw. Rather than the black-and-white ink of her original, this one had the three ethereal colors swimming amongst each other against a black background. *A new rune tattoo... is this part of her plan to free her son and partner?*

Tio pricked his finger and examined Hali with his magic. *She should be dead. What happened?*

Peeling back each of the bandages showed the wounds had scabbed over already. Something was accelerating her recovery. Under any other circumstance, Tio would assume Hali had been recuperating for months. Despite being half mended, Hali's condition was worse than anything Tio had seen. The only injury of the same severity he'd seen had occurred when one of Belsa's druids had made a bad deal with a wolf and had their hand bitten off. Tio and the medical students had got the hand reattached with a mix of stitching and several flourishes. If healing powers had been an option at the time, the process would've been far less messy.

"How long has she been here?" Tio asked Shell.

"A day. She spent two at the mining outpost, and two more traveling here. We see patients in this condition once or twice a year. Classic signs of an anzu attack. Beasts'll venture out pretty far when food is scarce."

The injuries do line up with an anzu. A lion head for the bite marks on her leg and talons for causing these shoulder lacerations. Still, something's off here.

An invisible force repelled Tio's hand from Hali's abdomen wound, preventing him from getting close. *This feels similar to a haze barrier.* Tio tried again, struggling through the strange permeating aura. Shadows danced in his periphery. Something gripped Tio, like thousands of beetles burrowing into his arm. *This blood toll is intense… and odd.*

Tio's veins tightened and twisted as he concentrated on Hali's external wounds, healing them completely. The last drop of blood from Tio's finger evaporated as it dripped from his shallow cut. *Hali's still bleeding and overheating internally. It's as if she's continuing to use magic in her sleep.* Tio tried to do one last examination to find the source of Hali's magic use, but his flourish froze.

Did I use too much ether? He hadn't had his flourish stop responding before, but the healing he'd done should at least slow whatever was draining her. Tio retrieved a blue potion from his bag and handed it to Shell. "When she returns to consciousness, make sure she drinks this. As much as she can keep down. It will stimulate blood production."

Shell placed a finger into a Diyan machine, wincing as it drew his blood with a hidden needle. A sheet of paper with numbers printed on it ejected with nothing to catch it. Without looking, Shell snatched the paper. "Already much improved! With any luck, she'll recover soon."

Charlie cheered. "Thanks, Mr. Tio! I should get Pops, so he can meet you!"

"I don't think that'd be a good idea, Charlie," Shell said as he placed the printed results into a red folder. "Your father is much too busy preparing for another expedition. Another time, I'm sure."

Chapter 19 Tio

What a relief. No more new people for today please.

"Will you be staying in town a while?" Shell asked Tio. "We could use your help."

He wanted to make sure Hali was okay and offer help, but if her recovery took too long, they could run out of time. "No, my other friend and I leave Oressa tomorrow."

A musical knock came from the main door. "Another visitor? Does nobody read the hours on my sign?" Shell grumbled to himself as he headed through to the other room.

"You're welcome to come back tomorrow at our slated meeting time, Dreamer," Shell shouted through the closed door.

A Dreamer? Glad it sounds like he doesn't want to open the door. What if they recognize me?

Charlie asked, "Do you have to leave, Tio?"

"Yes, I'm doing important work for the Conclave, and it has to be finished before the solstice."

"Isn't she your friend?"

"Of course, and Hali's recovery is important too. But I trust you and Shell to take care of her," Tio said as two sets of footsteps approached.

Shell walked in the room with Alim in tow.

"Don't look so surprised, Tio. I said I'd come find you if you used your gift." Alim's tone changed when they saw Hali. "Hali's here? What happened?"

Tio said, "All signs point to excessive magic use."

"Did she…" Alim assessed Hali while tapping their helmet.

"We can discuss theories when we're alone."

Alim noticed Charlie at the foot of Hali's bed. "Wait, is that you, Charlie? You've grown!"

Charlie looked baffled, tilting her head as if a different angle might solve the puzzle.

"What, don't recognize the helmet?"

Arboreal Path

Charlie gasped and hugged Alim. "You've been gone so long! Look, I'm Shell's assistant! I get to work on his machines. And my earth gift has gotten strong—Let me show you later!"

Tio dug into his grass satchel while Alim and Charlie caught up and handed Shell a pile of ingredients. Copying from Hali's recipe, Tio scribbled instructions onto his notepad as legibly as he could manage before ripping the page out and handing it to Shell. "Mix these according to this recipe, and you should be able to make two more elixirs. One per day, half in the morning and the rest in the evening."

Shell bowed. "Grenvel could use more wandering healers. I may not have your gift, but druids inspired me to become a doctor after seeing the good they did for villages in need. Those days are sorely missed."

How old was Shell if he remembered when the Conclave still sent out healers? Eighty? Who had he met? Had to be Bel. Few other healers had traveled Our Stranded Lands in the last century.

Tio and Alim said their goodbyes to Hali, Charlie, and Shell before heading to the nearby inn. The streets had calmed down, and a single yellow moon shone down on them.

On the way, Tio asked, "How do you know Charlie?"

"She's Allister's daughter."

Tio was extra relieved he didn't have to meet him again. Not after trespassing in Tovaloreande Sanctuary and having that run-in with Geno and Osanshia. Allister would hand Tio over to Sipherra in a heartbeat. Then they'd have both the artifact and one of the people who'd made it.

"I don't think that doctor likes Dreamers very much," Alim said as they removed the yellow strap from their arm.

"What makes you think that?"

"He wouldn't even open the door until I mentioned yours and Hali's names, and still bombarded me with questions before letting me inside."

"Right..." Tio's mind trailed off as the duo made it to the empty plaza.

"You thinking about Hali still? Can't believe she turned up here."

"Is it wrong to leave her?"

"You said she was fine. Besides, Hali made it clear she has her own goals."

"Dangerous goals, clearly. She needs us. What if she dies next time?"

Alim sat on a bench, patting the space next to them. "Do you think Hali used her tattoo?"

Tio took the invitation to sit. "I don't know. She's pallid, so it's that or runes. There wasn't much left to heal by the time I got there, and she was covered in a layer of invisible protective ether. Maybe the spirit in her rune?"

"Undine, could a spirit do those things?" Alim nodded along as if somebody were speaking to them. "You're on the right track, Tio. Must be Kthon."

"Then Kthon makes sure she lives? I suppose it makes sense. A spirit dies when its linked host dies."

"Between you and Kthon, Hali is safe. But her new rune…" Alim shrugged. "The library closed before I could find all the books I wanted, so I need to take another trip tomorrow. We can look up Hali's claw tattoo while we're there."

Tio locked his gaze on the yellow moon. Alim was right. Hali could be out of commission for a week or more and they only had a month at best. *Sorry. Time's not on our side, Hali.* Tio pulled out his box of seeds and opened it. Inside, one of the five seeds crumbled to dust. *Did… I cause this? Bel said they rotted slowly over years. What if I'm making things worse? Do we have even less time than I thought?*

"What's wrong?" Alim asked.

Tio slammed the box shut and stammered without a single coherent word escaping his lips. *I can't burden Alim with this. They're having a hard enough time grappling with celestial magic.*

"You realize I can see through the box, right? There's one less seed in there."

Right. Ethersight. "Sorry, Alim. I can't do this. I've only made things worse. Sipherra has my artifact and is reverse engineering it as we speak,

Grenvel itself has become our enemy, eidolons and spirits are dying, Empyrea's seeds are rotting faster than ever—if more eidolons need our help or these seeds become key to restoring Empyrea or we're too late… or—"

Alim rose from the bench.

Are you leaving? You should. My mission is doomed.

"You just saved a life, Tio. A friend's life."

An itch skittered across Tio's arms. *Did I?* The feeling of burrowing beetles returned. *Today? I can't remember what I did today… Is my anxiety that bad?*

"Don't look so confused. Hali's ether was so low I couldn't detect her, and you changed that."

Hali? Tio scratched his arm until the incessant prickling stopped. *That's right. She was wounded.* "I did what anybody would."

Alim extended their hand to Tio. "But that's just it."

Tio grabbed Alim's hand and let them pull him up from the bench.

"Nobody *could* do what you did—both today and back at Sanctuary—and many wouldn't regardless if they could. Empyrea is in good hands."

Does Alim never feel doubt? Maybe it's wrong for me to feel this way. "If you say so." Staring at the moon again, he saw a subtle, black ring wavering around its amber rim. "Do you see that?"

"It's beautiful as usual. Always love a good moongazing, though it's a shame there's only one tonight."

The black mist dissolved, caught in the wind. *I guess it was nothing.*

CHAPTER 20

Alim shielded themself from the accursed morning sunlight glaring from the glass ceiling of Oressa's ancient magics library. When Hali had described the library, she'd neglected to mention it was more of a campus. Four buildings with different topics of focus. Ancient magic, gift magic, literature, and history. The ancient-magic wing was the smallest by far. With only a single story, it was smaller than Wilton's library, but the shelves were densely packed. Alim presumed this was where most ancient texts discovered in Refulgent Wastes ended up.

Despite being a Dreamer for years, Alim had always been based in other locations, so they'd never had a chance to see Oressa's library in person. They studied using whatever books people brought into the mobile camps on the border between Wolloisha and Refulgent Wastes.

The corridors were narrow enough that Alim thought they might become the meat in a bookshelf sandwich if anybody so much as bumped one. Despite being the most prolific type of magic before Tovaloreande's death, there was precious little information here on runes due to their association with the Old Faith. Alim picked out a book with an obvious, but promising, title—*Complete Runic Compendium*. The back stated it had been updated with each new finding, with the last update being… Alim hated having to convert calendars. Modern books at least had the courtesy to list both formats.

"Tio! What's 'Year 10 under Rasalas's Shadow, 37th Cycle' in AB calendar?" Alim yelled. An echo repeated what they asked three times over. *Good thing this place is as crowded as the line for mayonnaise banana smoothies.*

"AB 698. You'd think the history buff would be able to convert OF to AB," Tio said, roaming by with a stack of books cradled against his chest.

Then the last update was over thirty years ago. A cursory glance through the pages revealed a paltry eighty-seven runes.

Several aisles over, Alim found the ether section. Each book was dustier than the last, with pathetic, thin bindings more appropriate for children's picture books than comprehensive collections of a subject. What little was there referred more to the mystery of ether than any substantive knowledge.

How did Tio study this? There's nothing valuable. Alim was sure Tio must've already read everything here, but they tucked one under their arm.

Sitting at a granite table, Alim set down their findings and slipped the ether book to Tio.

Tio spun the book so he could read the title. "I've read this before."

And confirmed!

"Don't frown—it might have its share of clues. There's an entire section on surges. Maybe it'll jog my memory or spur inspiration."

Alim flipped through the compendium of runes. None of the symbols looked like anything they had seen Hali use, but reading the effect of one reminded Alim of when Hali trounced the guard hounding Tio at Wilton.

Poison rune. Nature aspected.
Found in classroom texts, it was used to teach
children how to draw runes. The effect is little

more than indigestion.
Like all runes, scholars believe it is based on a gifted creature, though it is not known what creature has such magic.

Finally, a familiar-looking rune. A square with three wavy lines inside.

Force rune. Air aspected.
Based on the devastating anzu of Last Stand and East Peaks, it is believed this rune's wind blasts were used by ancient Thaumic peoples to clear dangerous fumes from mines.

Hali had used the force rune at Wilton and again to break into Vinn's surge. Such vast levels of power for a single rune. That was the last page with anything written. Every other page was blank, waiting for reports of a new rune.

"Not a single match. Hali's tattoos aren't in here." Alim slammed the compendium shut. "Hali told me creating new runes is why she came to Grenvel. In lectures, she said runes were crafted using bits and pieces of other symbols, like building a phrase, so I assumed by 'create' she meant using pieces of other runes."

Peeking over his book, Tio said, "Ancient magic was her expertise, and she was a former celestial. Not to mention her Thaumic heritage. Given all that, Hali must have other resources."

"Then why come to Grenvel? Most of this 'complete compendium' is sourced from Thaumic descendants. Only a scant few were discovered in Thaumic ruins. Surely we have no more to offer her here than… wherever she's from." *Why was Hali so secretive about where her family had lived?*

"Maybe spirits have special runes?" Tio suggested with about as much confidence as Alim ever heard from him. Little to none.

"Undine, thoughts?"

Runes are our language, and mortals have but a fraction of our words, but I didn't recognize the symbols either, Undine said. *Random words, as if*

Sereiamina thought they were pretty without knowing the meaning. It'd be like saying "fire flower" and expecting it to be a spell.

We both know she's not tattooing runes because they're pretty. Could Kthon show her new words?

I hadn't considered Kthon. Possibly. He's not a spirit born of Empyrea, so I don't know what his knowledge of our language is.

Where did he come from then?

Your guess is as good as mine. We didn't know Kthon existed until he killed Dryadine. It was assumed Sereiamina created him, but now I'm unsure.

"Hey, Alim? Find anything out?"

"Sorry, Undine loves to chit-chat."

Undine froze the veins under Alim's wrist. *Define "love."*

Stop that—it was a joke. "Wouldn't rule out the possibility. Apparently humans haven't come close to discovering every word used to construct runes, but Hali's tattoos were unfamiliar to Undine as well."

"Doctor…" Blood dripped from Tio's nose as he stumbled for a name or word. "Who… who was it?"

"Shell? From last night? Did you have a rough sleep or something?" Alim tossed one of their yellow straps to Tio. "Clean yourself up."

Tio fiddled with the cloth like he didn't know what to do with it before wiping his face. Slapping his cheeks, Tio whispered to himself, "Deep breaths."

Rough week for you to be sure. Nothing's gone your way since Sanctuary. Alim poked the amethyst freeloader lodged in their helmet.

Tio did as he instructed himself before continuing. "Just some weird nightmares kept me up is all. Shell mentioned Hali had a run-in with an anzu. Her wounds were caused by talons and big fangs, and she was at Sipherra Mining Outpost, coming from East Peaks."

The half-lion, half-eagle creatures were formidable opponents. The bestiary's gifted animals section recommended a party of five if confronting an anzu became necessary. But something about the situation didn't line up.

Chapter 20 Alim

"What could Hali need in East Peaks?" *And how does it relate to her new tattoo?*

"One of the map's unidentified surges is supposed to be there." Tio placed his book on the table as gently as one would treat a tall, extravagant cake.

True. Why did she need to go alone if her destination was so close to a surge? Maybe she didn't remember, but she could have asked. "Learn anything from the book?"

"Kind of? It reminded me that while ether has notes of one of the elemental flourishes, it's ultimately its own element. It's both a source of our magic and a type of magic itself."

"Meaning?"

"Remember how you exploded some ether back at Pasture Downs?"

"I'd rather not." *Poor sheep. Good thing Tio was there.*

"Maybe you were skipping ahead in your celestial training. Other flourishes have recommended orders to learn techniques. Steps on a ladder if you will."

Hali wouldn't rush my lessons though. Unless she'd already decided to leave us?

"Have you tried again since attuning to fire?" Tio asked.

"No…" Alim didn't want to hurt anybody again. Learning celestial magic without Hali was worse than walking in the dark. Rushed or not, Hali knew celestials from a human perspective. Undine's teaching didn't always translate well for Alim. "But I've been studying water-gift stuff every day." Alim slapped the elemental gift technique books in their pack.

"Ready to take us under North Lung then?"

I believe in us, Alim.

Thanks for the vote of confidence, Undine. "Of course. Let's get going."

Based on the maps Alim had studied, a bubble of air would need to be maintained for only a short distance if they approached from the eastern side of North Lung. Luckily, that was also sufficiently far from Dreamer camps.

Arboreal Path

Alim sat outside the stables and waited for Tio to retrieve their animal companions. Bringing Stripes and Majesty to Refulgent Wastes wasn't an option. Once outside Oressa's walls, Alim hugged Majesty.

"Goodbye! Be safe," Alim said to Majesty.

"Stick to the trade plains for a week or so. If there's no sign of us then meet us in Belsa," Tio said to Stripes.

The okapi and horse galloped west, while Tio and Alim made their way south, to North Lung.

Black clouds obscured the sun and moons, dumping an endless torrent of rain. Distant bolts of lightning joined the Lunar Vault in cracking the sky, illuminating the mangled emerald scar with a thundering crash. Abysmal weather, but Tio had an extra bop in his step—a complete turnaround from his dour mood the previous night.

Let's link, Undine. I need practice.

Alim felt as one with the water spirit as their blood turned to flowing chunky ice. Lifting a hand up above their head, rain droplets deflected away from Alim and Tio as Alim created an invisible umbrella. Same concept as walking under the lake, but nowhere near the same scale. Baby steps.

Arriving at the lake a few days later, grasslands transitioned to mud at North Lung's shore. The stretch of pristine water reminded Alim how unprepared they were for the task.

You should recharge in the Arboreal Path before you go, Undine said.

Forgot that was a thing. Am I low on juice or something?

This will put an immense strain on you. Let's at least give you a fighting chance.

"Tio, can you watch over me for a bit? I need to meditate for uh… celestial reasons."

"Going to the Path? Look out for ether flows while you're there. And don't take too long. As much as I enjoyed the rain, if it starts up again, I'm leaving you here."

Chapter 20 Alim

"Your antlers are plenty umbrella enough." Alim sat on wet, sandy mud and concentrated.

What am I doing exactly? This would be the first time Alim had entered the Arboreal Path on their own. The spirit fruit had done the work at the arboretum.

Cool pressure built in Alim's forehead as Undine said, *To visit the in-between in your mind, we must leave your body behind.*

How?

Remember the inner eye you use for ethersight. Open it. Gaze into it until it opens into a starportal for your consciousness.

Eyes closed, Alim sat in darkness and stared into wandering rings of color. Thoughts meandered, bouncing between subjects faster than Alim could identify them. Blue dots formed a lotus flower. Looking upon it dulled Alim's senses.

Thoughts faded. A slight tingle replaced the gentle wind and sticky mud. A string swung underneath the lotus and drew Alim closer each time it changed directions. Alim pulled on it, unraveling the world around them and revealing the brown sky underneath.

Alim crashed onto the Path's interwoven roots. *Not as smooth of a landing as when the fruit does it.*

Shy, milky tornados stretched downward from the sky, not quite willing to leave and wreak havoc upon the glowing road. The whirlpool constellation's stars had grown brighter and shifted to a cyan hue, and the road almost reached far enough to stand under it. The Path forked in the center, leading to a blinding orange constellation set in a spiraling inferno formation. Eating the overly bitter and sour cherry must've added that one. Elsewhere, faint green stars still drifted on their own, unchanged from Alim's last visit. The remainder of the Path was still dim, with the Ethereal Realm cut off abruptly by the abyss.

Scouting around, whatever small puffs of ether Alim saw stood still as statues. *I don't see any "flow" here. Any clues, Undine?*

Arboreal Path

The Path is a two-way channel. Ether comes in to Empyrea from the Corporeal Realm and then sends it back. Maybe the abyss is blocking ether as well as us.

Wouldn't ether from the Corporeal Realm be flooding the Path then? Ether is blocked from that end too, even though we can come in. How does ether get here?

Only the celestial spirit knows. Ferrying ether to Empyrea is their duty, Undine said.

And the flow stopped when the celestial spirit died, right? Maybe it's dependent on one existing. Is there nothing we can do?

Another spirit could take on the mantle of celestial spirit, as was done by Malakine when mortals killed the first, but nobody can link to Empyrea without entering the Ethereal Realm.

Alim tapped their helmet. *Sounds like unblocking the Path and letting all you spirits through is our first step then.*

No, our first step is for you to recharge.

Standing around isn't enough?

Unless you want to be here for months, you'll need to draw ether out from the constellations yourself.

Alim hated the pose for pulling ether in. They stretched their arms out wide in the air and stared straight into the burning stars. Ether hurtled from the stars as gassy meteors, crashing into Alim's helmet and bursting into ribbons of ethereal colors. The ribbons absorbed into Alim, and they felt more rejuvenated than after a full night of sleep.

Ready? Undine asked.

Absolutely not.

The Arboreal Path disappeared, and Alim returned to the lakeside where their vision was filled by a wide grin and gray freckles on golden-brown skin.

Alim jolted backward and hit their head against sand and mud.

"That's what you get for always invading my personal space." Tio's piercing giggle bounced around in Alim's helmet.

Chapter 20 Alim

"Fair enough, I won't make a habit of it if you don't." Alim wiped sand off their… everything and linked with Undine.

"Did you see anything in the Path?" Tio asked.

"It was more about what I didn't see. We need a new celestial spirit to re-establish the flow."

Lavender water hyacinths skimmed across the lake's surface. A gentle stirring flowed within, and Alim threw their arms apart. The stirring turned to raging rapids as the water parted. The two stepped through the mud left. Tio lagged, helping fish back into the water.

"Tio, leave them be," Alim said with struggle already clear in their words. "The water will return to the fish as we move."

"Sorry, sorry."

As they trudged forward, the lake formed around them, pushing against Alim's gift. Heart pounding, blood gushed through Alim like an internal tidal wave crashing against a coastal village. Before the wave hit, an opposing chilling wind repelled it. The internal rapids churned, calmer and colder than before.

Careful, you almost dropped the lake on us, Undine said.

I'm starting to think this was a bad plan. Thanks for helping.

Outside the dome of air, brownish red and green curly weeds wavered as hundreds of minnows swam by. Among them, rainbow-scaled fish jetted by at ridiculous speed. Alim recognized them from their bestiary—ikatere. Ikatere fish used the air gift to propel themselves but weren't as dangerous as other gifted animals. One leaped into their safe zone and slapped Alim's face like a stray splatter of bacon grease.

Water closed in as the dome shrank from lost focus. Tio caught the wriggling jerk and whispered while getting it to safety, leaving Alim to repair the air bubble with rotational, flowing arm movements.

Ikatere continued alongside, and Alim swore they heard an irritating shrill voice begging for food over and over. Everything was testing their patience. *Not a fan of animals right now.*

With each sloshy stride, the sticky ground threatened to steal Alim's boots. Undine's frozen dam cracked and veins bulged in Alim's arms. Not much further—

Tio slammed into nothing and fell backward.

"Runegate." Alim hadn't known the invisible wall extended into the lake.

"Should we turn back?" Tio asked.

"No. We go around." As stupid as it sounded coming out of their mouth, it seemed like a good idea in Alim's head. Maybe it was the blood loss?

Following Tio as he grazed his left hand along the invisible wall, water trickled from the dome's ceiling, pitter-pattering on Alim's helmet. *How much longer is Runegate? This is ridiculous.*

Ahead, the annoying school of ikatere swam through the barrier. "There!" Tio shouted.

Tio should have saved one of those elixirs for me. "I don't know if I can make it."

"Not long now—hold on."

The eastern shore was close. Alim's arms seized up, and Undine's assistance faltered, unleashing a storm into their veins. Bright, cracked rashes broke out on Alim's hands and they fell to one knee. Water gushed into the dome as it collapsed.

Alim snapped a finger, evaporating away more blood and freezing the surrounding water. Despite the cold weather, the ice already dripped. Exhaustion took hold and Alim found themself face-first in the mud. Soothing warmth embraced their hands and arms—Tio's healing touch.

Ice shattered and an instant flood overtook both Tio and Alim. Water choked Alim before they realized holding their breath was necessary. Crunchy and wet noodle-like appendages grabbed onto Alim's arm. Too weak to pry themself free or lift their axe from its hook, Alim was helpless as the noodles dragged them through the lake. Rushing water eradicated

Chapter 20 Alim

the mud clinging to Alim right as the noodles tossed Alim onto shore and renewed their muddy coat.

Alim wiped their helmet clean and spat until the chunky grime filling their teeth was gone. If there was one advantage to being immobilized by the pain of their blood toll, it was how it distracted Alim from tasting anything. Through fuzzy vision, Alim watched curly green plants recede into the lake.

A pink bottlenose dolphin pushed Tio ashore, squeaking and doing a backflip into the lake. Water ejected from Tio's mouth and nose with a cough. A blue glass bottle made its way from Tio's pack to his hands. *He had one more after all.*

Tio rushed to Alim and poured the drink into their mouth. The reaction was instant and reminded Alim of biting into a bursting juice-filled candy—except their heart did the bursting. Alim jerked upright and began spitting again as taste returned. *As if mud wasn't bad enough. That potion tasted like fish oil and grapes.*

"Couldn't you have given me this drink earlier?" Alim asked.

"It wouldn't have kept up with your blood toll and may have hampered your focus." Tio helped Alim walk further inland to dry sand. "At best you'd have lasted a dozen more steps."

"Not a pleasant experience, for sure. And I didn't even get to the 'disintegrate yourself' etheric death part." *More credit needs to be given to the mages that built Last Stand. Chugging elixirs and withstanding their gift's blood toll until it killed them? I can't imagine.*

"I'll see if I can find kindling for a fire. We need to get dry."

No need, Undine said, reaching a hand from under Alim's helmet.

Hundreds of droplets seeped from clothes, bags, and everything else and drained into Undine's hand until it was like nobody had taken an unfortunate dip into North Lung. It was too bad Undine couldn't operate freely outside ether surges without Alim holding her back.

Let me sleep. That was a tough day. Undine's link faded, and the icy feeling in Alim's veins turned to a numbing trickle.

After a few hours, the elixir's residual effects completed and Alim felt good as new. Mostly.

"What now?" Tio asked.

Alim pointed at the map. "Stick to the plan. We head to the permanent haze barrier between the lakes before trying the others. It should have the next eidolon for the Path."

Tio tightened his grass satchel's strap. "This isn't so different from Grenvel so far."

"Refulgent Wastes proper is still a day away. You'll know it when we get there."

As they walked, brown grass gave way to arid, white wastelands. Uneven ground shifted up with enormous cracks in rigid dirt. Every step crunched like dried leaves.

Night didn't provide much shade or protection from the blaring heat thanks to a permanent second sun in the center of the Wastes. The closer to the center, the longer the days and brighter the nights. At the ruins of Hearth, no night existed—but nobody went to Hearth unless they had a death wish. It was at the core of Bleached Brambles, where the Wastes were more bramble than land. If a Dreamer got lost there, they were assumed to be rotting in the suns.

Every breath was like inhaling barbs from the pale thorn bushes. Alim hadn't missed this place at all. Lifting a thick, spiky vine for Tio to pass under, they found a hidden road through Bleached Brambles.

"This is Plague Tollway. Should take us right to the surge."

"Alright, nerd, give me the background. I know you want to."

"Nerd? You're one to talk, ether-boy," Alim said, laughing as they clapped Tio on the back. "If you insist. At the peak of the ethereal plague, this road took people to Thauma's last safe quarantine zone. Which I would guess is behind the haze barrier. Und dal Sylph Manor I believe. Most taking the road got infected, like their lives were the cost for using it. Hence the name."

Chapter 20 Alim

"Riveting," Tio said with a fake fancy accent.

Alim scoffed. "Remind me why we're friends?"

After a couple of days on Plague Tollway, they found a forest of rotted stumps and logs. Huge, colorful mushrooms contrasted the bleak ground and dead trees they grew over. Some were larger than Tio's head, longer-than-ever antlers included. *Are his antlers ever going to stop growing?*

Small patches of grass grew and wilted as a rabbit-like critter hopped by. Tio's giddiness radiated through his smile. "What's that?" He looked like he wanted to pet it three times to Malakday.

"That's a jackalope. I thought they were extinct." As the mascot of winter solstice, how could Alim not love the miniature antlered rabbits. Even their tiny vestigial white wings were cute.

"If they were extinct, winter would never end," Tio said with words that had soaked in sarcasm for a few decades too long—obviously playing off the myths of how winter was only over once a jackalope had left its burrow.

"Original. Have I mentioned I preferred quiet Tio?"

"Why can't the grass it grows stay alive?" Tio picked at the crumbling blades.

"Same reason druid attempts to restore Thauma failed. The Wastes doesn't support life."

The jackalope hopped into a grassy burrow nestled under half-white, half-brown thornbushes, with a gradient of flowers sprouting from inside.

Tio pointed to the burrow. "Their flourish overpowers the rot if they stay put. No need to forage for food, only water."

"Guess it's easy to survive when your gift provides food." Alim pointed up the steady climb. "The surge is close."

Outside the haze barrier, they discovered a strange machine near a long-extinguished campfire. Chunks were missing and wires hung loose, but Alim recognized the oblong cube shape and metallic blue sheen. It had Sipherra's mountain logo etched onto the bottom half.

"Another Sipherra experiment," Tio said as he brushed a hand past the red mountain logo etched on the bottom half and unlatched a hidden compartment.

"Yeah, I've seen this before. Though it wasn't a machine at the time. It was one of the artifacts I found before I quit the Dreamers." In fact, it was part of the haul that had earned Alim their helmet and the title of "Collector." Gren Consortium must not have given all the artifacts to Diya when brokering their trade agreement.

"Seems your artifact was turned into a shell for a complex piece of technology. They bolted a series of smaller machines onto it, not unlike what I did to my teapot artifact. Sipherra learns quick if they've pushed my tech this far already."

"But the artifact I handed over was inert, same as any other."

"Yes, but Sipherra has a live one in their possession thanks to me. Doesn't seem this experiment worked, but no doubt they're close to reproducing Barbaroli's enchanting process. The next surge Sipherra tries may not be so lucky."

"Creating a machine to mimic a logu's enchantment? Isn't that a bit farfetched?"

"For one getting a direct supply of ether from a surge? I'd be more surprised if Sipherra ran into any limitations at this point. It's more a matter of time. Think about it—once you can manipulate ether, you can do anything magic can do."

"Hali said the same about celestials. Given enough training, a celestial could utilize every form of magic known to humans."

"Right, so why wouldn't that include logu magic? The ability to enchant magical properties into objects is no different than our flourishes. Both essentially consume ether to produce or control something."

"Sipherra stripped it for parts," Alim said as they circled the machine. "Their crew must've been in a hurry or maybe the experiment ruined whatever's left here."

Chapter 20 Alim

Tio yanked a piece of faded rainbow cube from behind scorched wires. "Never seen this component before."

"It's etherite, like my throwing axe." Alim whirled the rainbow chunk of metal from its holster and reshaped it into an axe.

"Not nearly as vibrant. It's lost all its luster."

Looking at the cube with ethersight showed the metal had no ether left inside. "Sipherra may have been trying to use etherite as a power source." *Then they're not trying to emulate my teapot to analyze ether. The machine is meant to make the ether easier to transport.*

"Right, but it seems the haze barrier absorbed the etherite instead of the intended reverse. Though I can't figure out why." Tio tossed the cube aside and approached the haze barrier's wispy edge. "I've seen enough. Ready to go?"

Stepping through was as easy as it had been in Tovaloreande Sanctuary. Maybe easier. Rather than resisting, the haze almost aided them with the way it opened at Tio's touch. And Alim never heard a peep due to Tio's ticklishness, so they were able to watch the ethereal majesty in peace.

A lush meadow greeted them on the other side with thin purple fog tinting the green grass and colorful wildflowers. If not for the haze barrier, Alim would swear this wasn't a surge at all. The colors never changed, and the density of ether was no greater than it had been outside. In the distance, a run-down mansion and several smaller homes perched at the edge of a cliff. Better condition than anything else in Refulgent Wastes by far, but not a prime living arrangement either.

Tio was already rolling around the flowers, distracted by jackalopes bouncing around him and blue jays fluttering about, chirping cheerful melodies.

Have fun with that. I'll get to looking for the eidolon or spirit.

The manor's splintered door swung open with a slight touch. Faded and chipped red-painted walls were like a firestorm against the disheveled bookshelves. The haze barrier here was permanent, yet the house seemed to have been ransacked. Not everything had been taken, but somebody had searched the place, looting whatever they thought might be valuable.

Every book Alim checked was written in an unfamiliar Thaumic dialect. What little they understood pointed to the books being fiction. If it didn't seem to have to do with magic, most looters weren't going to bother. What use were make-believe stories in a language few could translate?

The next room over was even larger than the main hall. Endless bookshelves lined the walls from floor to ceiling, which let in sunlight through a sizable breach. Same as before, everything here was unreadable fiction or incoherent scribbles.

Downstairs, the library turned to a basement of blue sapphire bricks. It looked out of place, perhaps added to the manor after the fact as part of a renovation. Everything within was immaculate, like somebody had cleaned it in preparation for Alim's arrival. Three sarcophagi carved from gemstones lined the rune-smeared far wall with ethereal-colored lanterns between each. Clear quartz on the left, blue aquamarine in the middle, and yellow tourmaline on the right. Behind them, deep scrapes and scuffmarks led to a door of pure amber—a known marker for Thaumic crypts.

Must be important people to have gemstone coffins. If that door leads to a Thaumic crypt, why are the coffins under the library?

Alim borrowed a lantern. *How is this still lit?* They could sense it was ether inside rather than a flame, but what method of celestial magic let one create light? Every step of the way, Alim felt less and less suited to being a celestial.

Hali could've explained the trick behind this. Her insight on this room would've been invaluable as well.

Starting their investigation from the left, Alim placed the lantern near the quartz coffin's plaque.

Chapter 20 Alim

> *Here within is the Thaumic druid*
> *You kept Thauma safe*
> *Rev Und dal Sylph*
> *191–226 AB*

A druid from Thauma? Nobody there had ever been born with the nature gift. At least, not according to history books. The name Rev reminded Alim of the orange moon, Revati.

Next, Alim went to the aquamarine coffin. A deep crack snaked across its lid. *Did somebody try to get inside?* The text on the plaque had a clean slice in it with a slight reflective, colorful sheen, but Alim could still read it.

> *Here within is Thauma's second celestial hero*
> *Savior of Nihali, cleanser of ethereal plagues*
> *Sereiamina Und dal Sylph*
> *193–226 AB*

Sereiamina—that was the name Undine used for Hali, and this person was a celestial too. *Two celestials with the same name, five hundred years apart. I wonder if Sereiamina is a common Thaumic name, or if Hali was named after her?*

The title and achievement engraved on the tomb were equally perplexing. Nihali was the green moon's name, before its destruction created the Lunar Vault.

If this celestial was responsible for closing the Vault and curing the plague, how are they not famous across Our Stranded Lands?

The smaller tourmaline coffin had numerous statuettes surrounding it. Green lions holding raspberries by the stem. Each looked so close to the last, it was easy to mistake the statuettes as identical. But the shade of green was different by the time counting hit fifty, and brown could be seen underneath. The fifty-first and last lion was reddish brown with only minor flecks of green and sat upon a sheet of paper.

Alim had seen similar patterns before on copper pots. Dreamers used copper for all their cookware. Something about the taste of metal building character. Nobody did anything to stop the green tarnish from taking over the cookware either.

The last plaque's text illuminated as Alim's light approached.

> *In your naming is existence acknowledged,*
> *importance confirmed, and impact actualized.*
> *In your naming you are not forgotten.*
> *You are Rasal Und dal Sylph, and your mark*
> *on the world lives on through all who know*
> *your name.*
> *224 AB*

Rasal. Derived from Rasalas, the yellow moon. The tribute on the plaque matched almost word for word with a Solstoran naming rite used for unborn children.

These three were buried together as a family. The parents died only two years after the child. Feeling a pit growing in their stomach, Alim grabbed the note from under the newest lion statuette and read it.

> *Rasal & Rev*
> *Today will be my last day at Und dal Sylph Manor. I'm sorry I've failed to release you from Kthon. With my celestial blood drained, I am no longer tethered to this surge. Please wait for me while I look for a way to give your phantoms peace without hunting eidolons. Don't worry, I'll take breaks to check on you both every year. Until the end of time.*
> *Sereia*

This sounds exactly like Hali's story, except… hunt eidolons? This can't be about Hali. Did I mess up the translation? I should read it again.

An explosion of water soaked the note as Undine poured from Alim's helmet. Ink spread into unreadable blobs and parchment broke apart in their hands.

Chapter 20 Alim

"I was reading that! Four days of sleep and this is what you do first?"

"Sorry! The strange ether here interfered with my reconstitution."

"What do you want, puddle?"

"This flesh wounds me with words." Undine's puddle-face rippled into a grimace as she took her humanoid form. "I was coming to inform you this surge has no eidolon or spirits tied to it. Something else created it."

"Is that important?" Alim asked.

"Find anything useful?" Tio yelled from the library.

Alim motioned for Tio to come down. "Yes, but you have to see for yourself, and Undine destroyed a vital piece."

Undine gurgled and patted the paper, absorbing the water but making it no more legible. "Not like I meant to. What were you reading?"

"Was kinda hoping to reread it until you ruined my plans. It was difficult for me to translate. The handwriting was horrible and my Thaumic isn't great."

Tio approached with slow, uneasy steps. "Uh, coffins? Who would be buried in a surge?"

Alim tapped their helmet. "'Who' depends on how Undine answers my next question. How many years ago did you meet Hali?"

"Spirits don't measure years."

"How many times have you linked to different eidolons since?" Tio asked.

"Twelve," Undine said without delay. "I was linked to Franz. Haven't been linked to the peacock since, but I'm hoping for next cycle."

Tio wore confusion as a mask. "Between 479 and 520 years ago? That can't be right."

Lifting a small scrap of dried paper, Alim said, "This note was written by a celestial named Sereia, who was leaving this surge to free her family from Kthon." Alim put a hand on Hali's sarcophagus. "This coffin marks the supposed grave of said celestial, dead at the age Hali claims to be, in the date range Undine said she met Hali. Few too many coincidences, don't you think?"

"Then the other coffins…"

"Are for Hali's family. The very same people trapped by Kthon."

Tio didn't look convinced. "Okay, so let's say Hali happens to be this celestial. Why does it matter?"

"Thing is, Hali's not just 'some celestial.' She closed the Lunar Vault and cured the ethereal plague. Tio, Our Stranded Lands is beyond indebted to her. You and I wouldn't exist. If people knew what Hali did, she'd be treated as a legend."

Though... what did she mean by hunting eidolons? Did she mean the Path, or was she killing them? Is Hali doing it again... the way she fought Vinn, she easily could've killed Sulin. I can't tell Tio that.

"Am I supposed to be angry Hali hid all this or sad about history forgetting her?" Tio shrugged. "Hali is still Hali. I'm not treating her any differently because of her past accomplishments."

When you put it like that... "I guess not. Can you imagine being stuck in this surge for however many countless years though? Unable to defeat Kthon. Unable to free her son or her partner. I'd have given up."

"I'm with you so far, but there's something missing still. Yes, time is wonky and slow in surges, but if the difference was so stark, we'd have left Vinn's surge to find several years had passed." Tio played with his bracelet as he read the plaque on Hali's coffin. "A lifetime in a surge is still a lifetime. When druids had powerful healing, the long-lived among them were described as any other elderly human. So how has Hali not aged?"

Undine's single word splattered and roared like a waterfall. "Kthon."

CHAPTER 21

Sereia hadn't been known for good choices. Her body broken, she'd had abundant time to think on every inadvisable decision she'd ever made. The latest of which being summoning Kthon inside a surge.

It's my fault Kthon absorbed Rev. My fault the eidolon blood I needed for Rasal's resurrection is gone. Why did I think Malakine was helping me? Spirits only care for themselves.

The elemental-themed constellations in the Arboreal Path's brown sky dimmed with each passing day—if Sereia even knew what a day was here—as Kthon's shadows mended her obliterated bones and failing vital organs using the Path's abundant ether. Sereia had hoped falling into the ocean would kill her, but it seemed the plague-puppeted spirit had no intentions of letting his host die.

As soon as she was able, Sereia crawled along the glittering road of woven wood towards the growing darkness shrouding the Path.

Kthon, you can't keep me alive forever. Sereia rolled off the Path. Etheric clouds rushed by in smeared blurs with no bottom to the world in sight.

Each dense packet of ether Sereia touched only quickened Kthon's healing efforts until she crashed and landed on something hard as rock.

Groaning and aching, Sereia looked up at the hole she'd left inside a familiar roof. *Kthon opened another starportal? I'm home.*

Sliding off the blue crystalline platform, Sereia realized what she'd fallen on. A lone aquamarine sarcophagus with her name on it, waiting its turn to be taken through the amber door to the Und dal Sylph catacombs. *How long have I been gone for people to think I'm dead, and who built this?* The description on the plaque said it all. Sereia's father was the only Magister she'd told about the cure. *Father, I thought you evacuated. Did you leave the coffin outside the family catacombs in hopes I'd return?*

Sereia slashed the plaque with her sword, leaving a rainbow gash down its center. *Savior of Nihali? Cleanser of the ethereal plague? Don't laud me as a hero. Not when I wrought far worse than anything I prevented.*

Spinning the blade around, Sereia thrust it towards her gut. Etherite split into two and one of the shards flew into the bookshelves upstairs as Kthon's shadows shielded Sereia from herself.

Gripping the hilt of the fractured sword, Sereia pressed it against her throat. A shadowy claw held the weapon back, and Sereia's arms rattled as she exerted all her strength. *You don't get to choose if I live. This is my body. My life.* Sereia removed one hand from her sword and used it to collect the surrounding ether. Embedding it onto the edge, Sereia went for another swing. Shadows cleaved and diffused, and Sereia slumped onto her coffin, gurgling as her blood spilled over the light-blue gemstone.

<hr />

Hali's eyes creaked open as the nightmare-fueled memory ended, feeling as if she still needed another twelve hours' sleep. An immense pressure kept Hali from moving. Skin tingled. Hoarse, crackly breathing. Not her own but nearby. Pitch-blackness slowly gave way to vague shapes as Hali's eyes adjusted to the dark. Cold, orange-scented gasps grazed her cheeks as an

Chapter 21 Hali

empty, smooth face stared from the dark. A thin layer of purple fruit-like skin stretched over its hollow sockets and ever-open mouth.

Gangly limbs with knobby, long fingers pinned her by the head and chest. Crouched over the bed, he was squatting on her legs with feet planted on the floor. Hali wanted to scream. To look away. To do anything. But paralysis forbade it. Forced her to return Kthon's gaze. The plagued spirit had its body back. All Hali's work to keep him bound, all Rasal and Rev's efforts to hide him beneath the façade of Ikazu—everything was unraveling.

Sharp fingers brushed across her scarred neck, and fear tingled along her spine. The urge to vomit rose, if only to feel a sense of relief from the roiling in her stomach. Kthon's face fizzed and contorted, sunken features filling in and rounding out until Kthon appeared as a malformed woman.

A new face? When…

Kthon pinched into Hali's head with wriggling fingers. Having her skull split open would have been more bearable. Memories peeled back within Hali's mind like skin flayed from bone, and flashes of each moment the shadow touched appeared. When Kthon took Rasal. When he absorbed Rev's phantom. When Hali took her own life, hoping to allow her family to rest in peace. It bent the memories, mashed them together. Linking them with a thread of shadow and pulling.

Let them go. Life unburdened from the past is a happy life.

"NO!" Hali struggled against the gnarled limbs holding her then grabbed the first thing her hand found in the darkness and smashed it into Kthon's head.

Orange pulp spattered against her cheeks and her improvised weapon shattered, cutting up her palm and scattering against the floor. Lights blinded Hali as she sat up, screaming into her bleeding hands. Kthon was gone, and an old man with a red doctor's coat stood in a glaring doorway. Whatever the doctor was saying was dominated by incessant beeping.

Where am I? Am I hooked up to a machine? A hospital bed?

The doctor leaned Hali back and poured a foul drink into her mouth. *Elixir? How did he get the ingredients for it?*

"Where am I?" Hali asked with such low volume she wondered if she'd only thought it.

"You're in Oressa and I'm Doctor Shell. Looks like you did a number on my blood analysis machine…" He wiped Hali's face with a towel. "What is this? Oranges? Must be pyre dredgers again. Dratted moles get in the vents and leave their fruit about. I'm so sorry about this."

Broken glass and machine parts littered the room. *Was I hallucinating? No, Kthon was too real. Hold on a little longer, Ikazu. I only need two more eidolons.*

"Charlie!" Shell shouted.

"Yes, Mr. Shell?" a little girl asked as she skidded through the door. "Oh, what a mess!"

"Can you fix this? It'll take months to get a replacement."

This girl is an engineer? At her age? She didn't look a day older than eight.

Charlie's front tooth waggled as she spoke. "In my sleep, Mr. Shell."

"Stop calling me 'mister.' I know your dad hates titles, but I'm a doctor."

Jabbing her loose tooth with her tongue, Charlie looked at Hali. "You're awake, miss! It's too bad your friends had to leave Oressa." She pointed at Hali's binding-rune tattoo. "What is that? It's pretty!"

Shell bonked Charlie with a foam piece of wrecked machinery. "Stop befriending patients, girl. She needs rest and you have work to do."

Charlie sighed and rolled her eyes, opening her locket and levitating a sapphire to her hand. Grabbing it, she reshaped it into a wrench, then the three other gemstones became a variety of other tools Hali couldn't recognize.

An engineer and an earth mage strong enough to control gems?

Metal and gemstone pounded as Charlie cobbled together the pieces into a spiky patchwork mess. She pressed a button on its side and its beeps and boops joined those of the other machines in the room. "This'll work

Chapter 21 Hali

for now, but it'll need new ether conductors soon. Pops will order some for cheap."

What a tone shift. She almost sounds like an adult. Hali tried to speak, but her throat stung from Kthon's lingering grasp.

Shell took the repaired device and placed one of Hali's fingers into it. "Your name was Hali, right? Maybe you've done me a favor here. After twenty years, it's time I get a new blood analysis machine."

"Mr. Shell, we call them ethometers these days."

"And we called doctors Doctor in my day."

Charlie shrugged and took the device from him, plugging it into a bigger humming cabinet-shaped machine. She poked at her tooth while waiting for the noisy printing process to make its slow progress.

"I'm going to pull that tooth out for you if you keep that up," Shell said.

"What? This?" Charlie hit the tooth with her wrench and knocked it out with a squeak.

Hali laughed, coughing specks of blood into her hands.

Running up with her tooth in one hand like some sort of trophy and her other cupped under her mouth to catch the blood, Charlie said, "My work's done. Tell me about your art! Are you a witch?"

Shell held linen against Charlie's mouth and began to speak up as Hali finally found her voice.

"The proper term is runekeeper." Hali was almost transported back to her lecture room in Wilton, where she'd given this talk near daily. *And this isn't art. It's the embodiment of my failures.*

"Woah, your accent is neat. Say more things!"

In a sudden bout of weakness, Hali slipped backward into her pillow with heavy eyelids.

Charlie squeaked and tugged on Shell's coat. "Is she okay?"

"Yes, but the mixture of elixir and muscle relaxant is making her drowsy. Let's—" Shell's words warbled out of existence.

No, I can't sleep. Not now.

Passing blades of grass tickled Sereia's nose, fluttering in and out of reality. She mumbled and turned herself over only for dozens of flowers to take the grass's place. A cord of shadow emerging from her wrist rune hauled her through a thorny rosebush as she found herself smacking into the side of her family manor and scraping up its walls.

Again, death was taken from me. Sereia traced a line of rough dried blood coating her neck with her free hand. *Have I given Kthon free reign by weakening myself?*

On the roof, the cord ended attached to a trembling shadow, its shape fluctuating violently between a deformed corpse, a toddler, a woman, or an amalgamation of the three. Deflated arms ejected from Kthon and clutched the shingles in vain, unable to drag his unstable form. Lanky and stubby legs alike pushed Kthon along an aimless route.

Planting her boots into the uneven roof tiles, Sereia fought against the cord, yanking hard enough to topple Kthon. Shadowy body melting onto the roof, Kthon's head oozed from his neck to his back to see Sereia. Three faces rotated around the head's surface, grinding like teeth and puffing citric vapors in every direction. Absorbing the vapors, one of the flattened arms filled out into a gnarled claw and snatched Sereia, pulling her close. The faces halted, and pulsating, hollow sockets stared through her.

Struggling did nothing. Screaming did nothing. A thin, translucent shadow wrapped from her rune up her arm. Soft and fleshy, the shadow-skin pulsed in time with Sereia's quickening heart as it wound her body into a tight cocoon. Stinging citrus juice dribbled from the dimly lit orange interior. Her breathing slowed, and soothing thumps echoed within as Sereia's blood pumped to her tattoo and through Kthon's cord. Rising, warm liquid clogged nose and mouth without obstructing her breaths.

Chapter 21 Hali

A comfort not unlike what Sereia would expect from death swaddled her. *This is what I deserve. Will I become a part of Kthon? A perfect punishment. Rasal, Rev, I'll share in the prison I made for you.*

Cradled and suspended, consciousness slipped.

The cocoon jostled. Blinding white light emanated from the binding rune and traveled up the cord, spreading through the cocoon's branching veins. Shadow-skin tore and Sereia sloshed out the shredded flaps, coated in viscous, orange fluid. Vomit and violent shivers followed.

Wailing pierced through Sereia's sickness, and a small white blotch in Kthon's abdomen split as serrated luminescent fingers of wood squeezed out. Two hands propelled upward and dug into hollow eyes, peeling the shadow-skin from the sockets. Kthon's impossible howling stopped only when the wooden light had turned the shadow spirit inside out, reverting him to a faceless silhouette smashed against the roof.

From behind, the unknown entity appeared as little more than the suggestion of a woman. *Is this the spirit I created Kthon from?*

Kneeling to Kthon, the wooden light-woman liquefied as she stepped into Kthon's skin. Black and white painted the roof with each clash of the two molten spirits, until white speckled the black as stars. The nightesque inky mass rose in two blobs. One taking the form of a toddler, and the other the exact outline of Rev. The two held hands before combining into a single entity and vanishing into Sereia's binding rune.

CHAPTER 22

Cracked white cliffs peered down to Stoneport's gray stone quarry and idyllic beach. The three couldn't have been a more mismatched sight.

For the last hour, Alim hadn't stopped talking about how the town was both an excavation pit for precious gemstones and one of the cornerstones of Ether Bazaar's trade ring. Something about how Iogu enchanted anything people brought from around the world. Alim spoke so fast it was difficult to keep up. Tio didn't care in the slightest about an ancient culture's top ten exports but enjoyed Alim's passionate lectures all the same. It was a good distraction from thinking about how many surges were left to check with only two months left.

As he had done every day since leaving Oressa, Tio peaked into his jewelry box. *One. Two. Three. Four.* Just to be safe, Tio counted three times.

"Tio, watching your seeds isn't going to make them last longer."

"I know… I can't help it. What if next time I find we have no seeds left?"

"Then Undine will stop calling you Keeper. There's no use fretting over it. The course we plotted is the most efficient we could think of."

Chapter 22 Tio

"We assumed the last surge would have an eidolon because of its barrier, and all we found was Hali's pile of secrets. I didn't plan for having to find two more at this point."

"All I heard you say was 'only two more left.' Stay positive."

"Positive? What if Barbaroli's marks are wrong? We could search every spot in Refulgent Wastes and find nothing, then the only remaining locations are on opposite sides of Grenvel. There's no time to visit every surge, and you can't be in two spots at once, Alim."

"Don't worry about worst-case scenarios. Trust the map. We'll figure out what to do when the time comes. Stay focused on the now." Alim looked out to the beaches. "Get through Stoneport. Search the mangroves for the next surge. Simple."

Tio sighed and crouched at the cliff's edge. "How do we get down?"

"The normal way is using an earth gift to create an elevator."

"And for us?"

A coil of rope snaked out from Alim's pack. They secured it to a rock and dangled it over the cliff edge. "This is the shortest cliff. A fall from this height would only break a few bones."

"Reassuring." Tio had flashbacks to the physical fitness test he'd had to pass to work for the Conclave. On a scale of one to ten, that memory scored a solid negative-seven. And in this unyielding sun? Tio was looking at a negative-eight experience for sure.

"Don't worry, I'll catch you if you fall." Alim rappelled down without a care.

Tio clung to the rope with both hands and feet, shuffling down like a caterpillar. *Deep breaths.* On his tenth breath, the safety of solid ground embraced him.

Alim clapped Tio on the back so hard he nearly rammed the cliff with his antlers. "Didn't think you had it in you."

Tio let out a nervous chuckle. "My life is in danger so long as you're around."

"And don't you forget it!"

Alim recovered the rope and led the way to Stoneport. Its buildings were remarkably well preserved, with rounded curves instead of sharp corners, and many pillars and arches that seemed to serve no function beyond looking pretty. They were crafted from a mix of marble, granite, and some from gemstones. Tio couldn't name them, but every color of gem was represented.

One building must be worth more than Gren City's entire Consortium Promenade. "Why doesn't anybody loot these gemstones?" Tio asked.

"Between Thaumic earth gifts and logu enchantments, simple mining tools aren't effective on these buildings. Nobody wants to invest what it'd take to set up a proper mining operation in Refulgent Wastes."

Tio stared into the quarry's depths. Each tiered descent was twice as far as the cliffside they had climbed. Thauma must have based everything around their flourishes because nothing was safe here, with not a single guardrail or warning sign. Only steep drop after steep drop.

Clucking cockatrices battled each other at the bottom of the quarry, pecking scaly rocks from each other's wings. A smaller group of the rock-encrusted chickens, crowned with sandstone combs and dangling wattles, loitered ahead on a diamond bridge leading to Stoneport's golden beaches. Every step away from the quarry onto the diamond bridge reduced Tio's irrational fear of falling into the pit and being pecked to death.

He pointed at the lighthouse on the beach, feeling childish for asking so many questions. "What's that for?"

Less extravagant lighthouses sat in the cliffs Tio had explored as a child between Meisha and Ahsiem. Each lighthouse marked a side of the Mudplains cliffs, and sailors navigated between them to sail safely from The Sigh into Trachea River. This one didn't seem to serve such an obvious purpose.

"Texts describe it automatically alerting Stoneport of incoming ships. Trade, invasions, whatever."

Chapter 22 Tio

It must be a machine then. Did Coveted South engineers design it or Diyans? Tio understood the appeal of history better now. So much of the forgotten past would improve lives.

Rough, uneven steel barricaded the bridge with a small brick building connected to its edge.

"We have to go through the checkpoint," Alim said as they stepped inside. "This was their way of trying to keep infected people from escaping quarantine by boat."

"Is this going to be on the test?"

Rattling. The whole building trembled, and a green gemstone cabinet fell and blocked Alim.

A red-coated scientist peeked over the cabinet and let out a thick, phlegmy cough. "Dreamers?" He sounded ragged, like he'd spent a lifetime swallowing sharp rocks.

The etherite throwing axe at Alim's waist twisted horizontal on its own, extending into a spear as Alim grabbed it. They poked its tip into the mountain logo on Phlegmy's coat. "Not anymore. Where's your escort?"

"Dead…"

"What do you know about an artifact at the western haze barrier between the lakes?" Alim asked.

"The failure project? Nothing—"

Alim prodded Phlegmy with their spear.

"It was supposed to tear down those weird barriers for good. Don't ask me how. Ether and machines aren't my field—I source materials." Stone flaked off as Phlegmy scratched the craggy, gray patches on his arm.

Busting a hole in a haze barrier would be an ambitious first step for Sipherra. Destroying them is on another level. "Isn't Sipherra trying to build ether cities? Why would you destroy surges if they're a self-sustaining source of ether?"

"I told you, not my—" Phlegmy cringed as Alim scraped along the edge of his petrified arm with their spear. "Phase two is Phantasmal

Reef. Geno hyped up the next ether reactor design's ability to run from Phantasmal Reef's energy instead of ether. It could cut a path through the Reef. Maybe drain the whole thing dry if we're lucky."

Is there ether in the Reef, or has Sipherra discovered a way to use phantoms as a power source? If that's really possible… that's why Sipherra deemed it acceptable to destroy surges. Build a city on the Reef and any person that dies will be sucked into their reactor. Forever. No need to worry about how surges move every cycle or how to transport ether between locations.

"What happened to your arm?" Tio asked.

"Pissed off a catoblepas while hunting for basilisk eggs to build a casing for the next ether reactor. I'm as good as dead." A chunky coughing fit cut into Phlegmy's last couple of words.

Alim shrunk their spear and hung it from their hip. "When? Here?" They paced, tapping on their helmet as if trying to keep up with an energetic song.

"Maybe an hour ago? I only escaped when cockatrices attacked it. You'd think creatures with the same gift would like each other more."

"Doesn't make people any friendlier." Tio tried to examine Phlegmy's petrification with his flourish. "I'm a healer."

Phlegmy pushed Tio. "Don't bother. Who knows how many pebbles are lodged in me and my earth gift couldn't get any out. What are you going to do? Heal them away?"

Before Tio could even try to help, unbearable alarms squawked from outside alongside furious clucking. *What's going on?* Tio rushed to the window.

Dust clouds spread across the beach while cockatrices scattered up the cliffs. The largest bird continuously screeched until the flock had all escaped the dust, which was fast approaching the checkpoint.

Alim turned Tio around and wrapped his face tightly with their yellow cloth. "Hold your breath if that stuff gets in here. Unless you want to be like our Sipherra friend here."

Chapter 22 Tio

"Don't you need one too?" Tio froze as the scientist shrieked in torment.

Alim hefted Tio over their shoulder and leaped over the cabinet-barricade. A small *pop*, and little drums sounded off as thousands of objects pelted the cabinet. When the vibrations against his back stopped, Tio peeked to see the scientist's chest had erupted in a bloody mess with insignificant pebbles spilling from dozens of holes. Dents, punctures, and scrapes riddled the cabinet.

"That's why you don't breathe in catoblepas dust. Earth gift plus tiny rocks equals mess."

Alim towed Tio back out of the checkpoint and set him against the diamond bridge.

As if the deafening cockatrices weren't enough, Stoneport's lighthouse blared musical horns and illuminated the approaching creature climbing out of the ocean with ethereal spotlights.

The catoblepas's sunken, bearded face scraped along the beach, secreting dusty fumes from its stone-tusked, pig-like snout. A long neck with scraggly strands of hair collided with the checkpoint, while rock-coated legs shook the world. A wispy tail ending with a spiky growth like a morning star trailed behind it, flicking at the water.

Dust cascaded over the roof, pouring in their direction. Tusks scraped along the bridge as the catoblepas's head peered over the checkpoint. Tio skipped the exhalation step of his usual "deep breaths" mantra, and Alim stood unflinching with axe in hand.

The catoblepas stepped onto the bridge with its front legs, snapping it near the checkpoint. The section below them collapsed, kicking Tio and Alim into the beach below. Collecting his wits and wishing he had landed on the loose mounds of kelp leading into the ocean, Tio retightened the cloth on his face. Above, the catoblepas searched over the remains of the bridge. Being underneath made it clear how large it really was. Easily as tall as ten buildings.

Squealing and snorting accompanied the blasts of killer dust shooting from its nostrils as it searched.

Alim groaned and straightened their helmet. "Make a run for it. I'll immobilize the catoblepas for you."

"I'm not leaving."

Veins bulged in Alim's arms as freezing water climbed up the catoblepas. Ice shattered at the smallest shift in the creature's weight. Its spiky tail crashed into Alim's chest, slamming them into a diamond pillar.

Tio moved without thinking, his bracelet gouging a deep wound in his hand. Grabbing kelp by the frond, he sensed it was alive. Using this connection, he called to the undersea forest. With a splash, hundreds of pieces of giant kelp darted out and wrapped around the catoblepas's neck and legs. It squealed as the kelp tightened and wrenched it onto its side.

Salty water sprayed Tio as his felled opponent crashed into the beach. It snorted out a barrage of dusty air at him. Almost tumbling backward, Tio dug his feet into the sand. The fumes dissipated, and Tio approached the catoblepas's giant head with stinging, squinted eyes.

Tio placed a hand on its dry snout. "What ails you? I—"

It responded by spewing, and the cloud bypassed his mask with no problem at this distance. Tio wheezed uncontrollably as sharp pain trailed into his lungs. While his body tried in vain to expel everything he'd inhaled, Tio jabbed his hand with his bracelet again and smeared his blood onto the catoblepas's face, forcing a communion.

Anger. All Tio saw was an endless red light surrounding the creature. A calming green aura emanated from Tio but did not budge the red when they collided.

"Let me help you," Tio said.

"Humans do not help." The catoblepas's red aura pushed against Tio's, gaining steady ground.

"My friend and I aren't here to hurt anything. Why are you angry?"

Chapter 22 Tio

"Humans stole basilisk eggs. Basilisks are friends. Dying friends. Blinding light pushed them from homes. Now humans finish them off.

Legs crossed, Tio meditated and concentrated on projecting pleasant thoughts. He remembered home. Sir Fluffyboi. Bel. Stripes. Alim. Hali. With a burst of renewed energy, his green aura clashed with the red, forming yellow blazes at their edges. Green enveloped the catoblepas, erasing the red and its anger with it.

Tio broke the communion and the kelp unraveled to release the catoblepas. Pain rose in his chest, forcing him to hack pebble-filled mucus into his hands.

"I'm sorry, druid. Forgive me."

Pebbles vibrated inside Tio. With one final cough, a beige cloud escaped and followed the catoblepas as it wandered into the sea. Each breath felt like swallowing glass, even without the rocks in his lungs.

Alim limped over. "Have you been holding out on me? How did you do that?"

Tio shrugged. "I stayed positive."

"Real funny, throwing my own words at me." Alim let their big and little axes drop and sat between them.

"It wasn't a joke. My flourish lets me share feelings with animals and plants. Though it's usually less effective."

"You forced the catoblepas to be happy?"

"No, we came to an understanding through emotions. I only made it easier for the catoblepas to think clearly."

"Can you do that to me?" Alim asked.

"Communions don't work on people. Besides, your mind is probably a scary place." Tio sat next to Alim and grabbed a handful of sand to play with. "Let's take a break for now. The next surge can wait."

CHAPTER 23

Three swigs of cranberry juice later and the taste of muddy grapes, fish oil, and vinegar yet remained on Hali's tongue. The horrid combination had awaited Hali every morning since she'd woken three days ago and reminded her how indebted she was to Tio.

Without the healing and elixir, this endless process of medicines and examinations would last another month and the nature-aspected eidolon blood would disappear before Hali was strong enough to retrieve any. Returning the favor for Tio didn't seem possible. Not when Hali may yet have to kill another eidolon. *Anemo's survival was a fluke. My next encounter may not go my way. Not with Kthon beginning to overpower Ikazu.*

Hali looked through a window of an overgrown greenchurch. Nobody inside—perfect. Rickety doors creaked open and Hali sat on a rusty metal bench inside. *This must be the last greenchurch in Oressa.* Old Faith churches outside Gren City had been mostly demolished as atheism took hold, especially in Thauma. But Oressa had always been more Grenvelian than Thaumic, even when it had been part of Thauma.

Chapter 23 Hali

I volunteered to upkeep this greenchurch so many times in my teens. No doubt this bench is the same as back then. Hali set a fresh novel on the seat next to her. *It was always an excuse to do more reading than actual work. Some things don't change.*

Charlie tumbled through the greenchurch doors and face-planted into the wooden floor. If her front tooth hadn't already fallen out, it'd certainly be gone after a fall like that.

"Be careful—you might bring the whole greenchurch down." Hali's arms burned and her back cracked as she picked Charlie up and dusted off the kid's blue dress.

"Sorry, Hali!" Hearing Charlie's endearing, self-inflicted lisp had been the highlight of Hali's days in Oressa.

"Don't apologize for that. You okay?"

"Do I look okay?" Charlie asked with a frustrated whine.

Hali looked her up and down. Skinned knees aside, no damage done. "You'll live."

Charlie giggled. "I have something for you." She reached into her patch-covered satchel—Hali recognized none of the patches except for the wrench indicating engineering apprenticeship—and handed over a small orange box.

Hali tugged on the lid—

Little hands forced the box closed. "Not in front of me! It's a goodbye present." Embarrassment flushed Charlie's cheeks.

"Worried I won't like it?"

Hali flinched when a loud bell clanged from above. "Isn't it almost time for school?"

Charlie closed her little satchel and squeezed her cheeks in dramatic shock. "You're right! Pops might not take me to Wilton's solstice festival if I'm late again. See you after school!"

Hali waved goodbye as Charlie scrambled out the doors with the same voracious energy she'd used to enter.

Arboreal Path

Cracking open her novel, Hali's pain subsided. There was no such thing as a bad book. Each was unique and had something to teach. Reading every last one had been a goal since Hali was young, to the point where knowing there wasn't enough time to do so had depressed her. Now? Every book in the family library had been read thrice over in the seventy-odd years she'd been holed up in her artificial surge.

Has it truly been more than seventy years since Ikazu suppressed Kthon?

She'd never expected Ikazu to hold him at bay this long. Though meant to keep Kthon from the outside world, the ether surge Hali had manifested with her celestial magic had also prevented her from leaving—same as the barriers did to eidolons. Due to being created through her celestial magic, the barrier came with the additional benefit of immunity to being controlled by anybody other than Hali. Once ether has been manipulated by a celestial, another couldn't repeat the process on the same ether.

With her lack of ability to breach the haze and the surge having no connection to Empyrea, Kthon would've been trapped forever. Or at least as long as Hali needed to find a way to free her family. When Kthon had begun draining Hali's magic, she was forced to leave the safety of her surge.

The book in her hands trembled. Too unsteady to read. *I was an idiot then and I'm an idiot now. What do I expect to do against Kthon?* A small breeze was all it would take to make Hali fall apart. *I need to think about something else. Anything else.*

Hali put away her book and retrieved Charlie's gift. Unimpeded, she removed the lid and found a note and a ring inside.

The front of the note said, "I know it's not good, but I wrote a song to go with the ring." The kid had all the confidence of a miniature Tio. Hali flipped to the back.

From upon their vault celestial,
The gods gave a quake most bestial.
Dark reef stranding us with decay,

Chapter 23 Hali

Hero Hali frees phantoms gray.
North and South cleansed, our savior wins!
Together a new age begins.

Eyes watering and throat constricting, Hali tucked the note into her pocket. Not exactly the distraction she'd been looking for. It was her fault for telling Charlie about her binding rune's power over phantoms. What harm was there in retelling old children's stories about phantoms and runes though? A heroic rune, capturing phantoms to save the day. Is that what Hali had thought would happen? Slap a rune on her arm and Rasal would live? Rev would forgive? Maybe not expectations so extreme, but reality had been far worse than her gravest fears.

Examining the handmade ring, she found it was a perfect replica of the binding rune. Bent titanium formed the band, and the rune was yellow tourmaline for the twin lines and aquamarine for the circle. Charlie obsessed over Hali's tattoos, but Hali didn't want to be emulated. *I'm no role model.* Still, knowing Charlie viewed her in a positive light warmed Hali's thrice-dead heart.

She put the ring on and let the emotions and craftsmanship marinate in her mind. It reminded Hali of her own crafts, so she searched her pack for her last project and placed a brown copper lion in her lap, only to realize she needed a dagger. Doctor Shell had hidden Hali's weapons from her as if she were a danger to herself. The statuette's mane and tail needed finishing touches, and the raspberry still needed to be carved.

I can afford to take a detour to give this to Rasal. One last time.

Orange skies and purple clouds glided over the glass ceiling and reminded Hali of the time. *I've been out longer than I thought.*

Taking as brisk of a pace as her lingering injuries allowed, she made it back through the slums to the plaza right as the sky turned dark with not a star or moon to be seen. Solstice lights sputtered on and off in the alley leading to Shell's office. As gaudy as they were lit, the flickering was more annoying.

A crash came from inside the office. Hali peered through a window, seeing a woman with plate armor, a sword stashed on her hip, and a red bandana tied in her hair. The bandana had mountains drawn all over it.

Is she Sipherra or Dreamer? Both? That's right, Alim did mention Sipherra had bought the mercenaries.

Shell backed against the wall as the mercenary flipped his reception desk.

"Where is the witch? Today was the agreed-upon transfer date. We've waited long enough for you to patch her up," the mercenary said.

"Maybe if Sipherra kept my equipment up to date at the mining outpost, we wouldn't have had to bring her here to begin with." Shell pushed up his glasses. "I never agreed to hand her over. Runes or not, I'm not holding anybody hostage for Sipherra."

"This isn't some petty rune-vandalism case. Geno Sipherra herself is looking for this witch in connection with a group of trespassers who ransacked Tovaloreande Sanctuary and assaulted two members of Gren Consortium. Geno believes the witch's runes are responsible for their escape."

"Well, as I said from the start, my patient is gone. Geno should look herself if it's so important." Shell puffed out his chest and got in the mercenary's face. "And if Sipherra ever pulls a stunt like this again, Allister will hear about it."

The mercenary punched Shell in the gut and he crumpled into a ball. "Allister is but an extension of Sipherra now."

Enough of this… At least Shell didn't confiscate my "art supplies."

Using what remained of Sulin's ethereal blood, Hali painted a gnarled claw on the wall and a square with three wavy lines onto her hand. Shell's door slammed shut, and the mercenary stepped into Hali's line of sight. The Sapper rune illuminated the alleyway and filled Hali with the mercenary's stolen vitality.

"Who's there?" the mercenary shouted, clutching her head as glaring light faded to a blanket of darkness.

Chapter 23 Hali

Obscured by night, Hali approached with quiet, slow steps. A flicker of purple light exposed her.

"Hello?" More flickering, and the mercenary panicked. "Stop!"

A gloomy abyss took the alley as the annoying decorations died for good. Sprinting, Hali was upon her opponent in an instant and crunched the mercenary's plated gauntlet at the wrist. Hali smeared her painted hand onto the cuirass as she tossed the mercenary into the alley's wall, cracking it and scattering chunks of brick.

Sword drawn, the mercenary got to her feet and dashed at Hali. Clenching a fist, Hali activated the rune she'd wiped on the mercenary's breastplate. It shone, and the metal armor collapsed in on itself, crushing the mercenary's chest. The mercenary fell against the damaged wall, blood leaking from her mouth. Hali wiped the remaining eidolon ink onto the mercenary's bandana.

The trespassers she mentioned must be Tio and Alim. Are they being hunted too? My rune was mentioned too, but I doubt the "escape" theory was the full story.

As much as Hali wanted to replace her ragged, patchwork clothes and visit the library, staying in Oressa longer was too big a risk.

Tendrils of shadow snaked across Hali's eyes until her vision was eclipsed. She gripped the mercenary's limp head and her fingers stiffened as Ikazu's magic poured through her. Hundreds of trivial scenes played out in her mind.

Memories lasted mere moments after death. *Come on, Ikazu. Find something.*

Not able to afford the blood toll to summon Ikazu, Hali had to channel the memory-stealing power through herself. Doing so was a severe bottleneck for Ikazu, leaving Hali with minimal clarity and precision. Every memory blurred together. Tio's name appeared alongside the insulting alias for her homeland, Refulgent Wastes. Hali's hand snapped back with sharp pain as the connection severed early.

Sipherra has tracked Tio and Alim to Thauma? It's good they haven't been caught yet. Which way would they have taken to get around Runegate? Maybe I can follow their trail and make sure they're okay.

With the last of her borrowed strength, Hali lifted the corpse with one arm and tossed it over the wall, then hobbled into Shell's office.

"Hali?" Shell rushed her into the back, where Charlie poked her head out from inside a storage bin of red coats.

"It's late, Charlie. You should be home." Hali sat on the hospital bed and took the last elixir from Shell.

"I promised to see you after school!" Charlie said as she climbed out.

"From inside that pile of clothes? What happened?"

Shell rubbed a soaked cotton swab on Hali's arm. "Sipherra is looking for you."

"Does that matter?"

"Yes! Sipherra's intentions for you were dubious from day one—every hour they tried to collect you back at the mining outpost." Shell squeezed Hali's arm and poked a needle in, drawing blood. "While it was true we needed my equipment to monitor your health, you were clearly recovering without our help. My counterpart transferred you here as a cover."

"Don't you have a contract with Sipherra? Why are you helping me?" Hali asked.

"Patients come first for us, same as it was for traveling healers. Your runes, whatever they do, are none of my business. What's the point of upholding a deal made with revolting people?"

Rev had said the same when dealing with the ethereal plague. "I'm all too familiar with the patient-first mentality, though revolting sounds harsh for a tech company."

"With what they had planned? Sipherra is tightlipped around contracted medical personnel, but rumors at the mining outpost after the transfer alleged Geno has been experimenting with runes. That Sanctuary nonsense was only an excuse to get their hands on you. You would've been

Chapter 23 Hali

a test subject. Every Dreamer and wannabe Dreamer in this city will be after you. Cover your tattoos. Dye your hair. We can hide you."

"Hide? Sipherra is no threat to me, and I've done enough of that." Hali's tattoos throbbed, ink and pain both pointing south to Thauma. "My friends are the ones in danger. I have to go after them."

After chugging the disgusting grape concoction, Hali gathered her things and held out her hand to Shell. "Daggers please."

"Be careful." Shell relinquished her blades at last.

Charlie clasped her arms around Hali's legs.

Crouching down to Charlie's eye level, Hali said, "Thanks for the ring, Charlie. I couldn't have asked for a better gift."

"There's more where that came from!"

"Focus on your studies. Become Oressa's top engineering bard!"

Goodbyes done, Hali left Oressa behind.

By the time she arrived at Runegate, the aches had dulled. Columns of transparent white runes pulsed from ground to sky, marking the invisible wall. The pulses repeated several times per day, but blink and it was over. Beyond Runegate, the land was bleached white by centuries of ethereal lights bombarding it.

Once a year for the past four years, Hali had made a pilgrimage into Thauma, but somehow, she'd forgotten the rune for opening the gate every time. The only memorable part had been drawing lines to indicate how much of the gate to bring down. Forgetting that was impossible after having brought the entire gate down by accident during the ethereal plague quarantine.

After a brief review of the rune book's reference sheet to refresh her memory, Hali got to work drawing in the dirt with a dagger. Curved squares linked by curly lines. Each square contained odd shapes that reminded Hali of trees or fruit.

After marking the rune off with vertical lines about as wide as two people, she poured Anemo's blood in the tiny trenches, and a rectangular section of earth under Runegate rose. No need to use her own blood after having just recovered. Pieces crumbled until a doorway took shape. Hali kicked dirt over the rune and smooshed it, leaving no sign remaining.

Sweat beaded on her forehead the moment she stepped through the doorway to the land of two suns. Daylight never left Thauma now. The earth behind her submerged with a low rumble.

Hali recalled Tio's surge map. Without knowing which path into Thauma they'd taken, which direction to go from here wasn't clear. Not too far east there should be a surge, though it wasn't one her tattoo was guiding her to.

No eidolon there, but they wouldn't know that. The back entrance into Overlook Plateau is near there, and my pulsing is leading me to Overlook's surge. Two in one, so east is the clear choice.

On the way, she saw no trace of people. No Sipherra. No Dreamers. No Alim or Tio. Only periodic basilisk tracks, and that was the last thing Hali wanted to encounter. Not a problem under normal circumstances, but if she found her way into a nest by accident, those reptiles would tear her to pieces.

After a day with no sighting of anybody or anything, Hali knew her friends hadn't come this way.

Hali set up a small fire and lit her cardamom candles. *Let's go with the left calf for the Control rune.* Etching the helix leaves one jab at a time, Hali retreated into her thoughts, drawn back to Charlie's note.

Hero Hali. Thauma once believed in me like that. My own grave regards me as a hero. Tio and Alim were relying on me, and I turned on them. Now they're being hunted while I'm off killing and wounding eidolons. Would Hali be able to face her family—or Tio, Alim, and Charlie for that matter—after this? What if Tio and Alim caught her mid-battle with an eidolon? Tio's reaction alone would break Hali's heart. *My methods are unacceptable. I can't kill anymore eidolons. No, I can't even fight them. No more violence. This time, the eidolon blood will be given willingly. There must be a way.*

CHAPTER 24

Alim swatted at a cloud of buzzing mosquitos and trudged through bicep-deep brown water. "Can you blame me? These things are awful." Being bombarded with the odor of rotten egg didn't help either.

"They're living things too," Tio repeated with a raspy voice. At least he wasn't ranting like he had been when they first reached the mangroves. Since Tio's height meant the water was only waist-deep for him, he was carrying both packs to keep everything dry. He hadn't let Alim forget that either.

"So, you like mosquitos?"

"What? No, they're the worst. Everybody hates them." Tio hiked the two bags up on his back as the water rose above his waist.

Alim smacked their helmet. Druids were confusing. It must be difficult treating life as such a precious thing. "I give up—can you ask them to go away?"

With a few whispers, the cloud scattered. Not a mosquito in sight.

"Tio. We need to have a talk later. If it was that easy, why'd you wait half a day?"

"Their conversations were more interesting than yours." Eidolon-gifted freckles jiggled with Tio's cheeks as he laughed.

You're getting too comfortable pushing people's buttons.

If they were still at the beach, it might have been bearable. But as soon as it had transitioned into this horrible rainforest-swamp hybrid abomination, Alim's patience had shrunk to the size of a corn kernel. Creepy reptiles and insects at every turn. Even the mangrove trees gave them the jeebies the way roots splayed out of the water like thick spider legs. Picturing them as noodles didn't help either. That just made Alim think of haunted food coming alive to strangle them.

Alim punched Tio in the shoulder, a bit too hard to be considered a playful jest. Tio yelped and caught himself just before face-planting into the gross water.

He rubbed his shoulder. "That's the thanks I get? I heal you—you break me?" Tio let out a soggy cough.

"Sorry! I'm an idiot!"

This flesh really is dumb, Undine said.

Every time Tio wheezed, it reminded Alim that he'd stood against a catoblepas. And won! Not in a million years would they have guessed Tio would be good in a fight. He didn't need a bulwark after all. Beast tamer had been added to the list of Tio traits alongside good, if occasionally annoying, company and healing. *It's too bad his gift can't heal himself.*

"Not at all—it's my fault." Tio pointed to the amethyst lodged in Alim's helmet. "Clearly I didn't learn my lesson."

"I should have—"

"Done what, recklessly attack a camp of mercenaries? You got us away at the first opportunity. Don't beat yourself up over it."

Maybe, but Alim still felt pathetic. They hadn't done enough. Even if Alim had protected Tio in that moment, he was the one who'd got them safely to and through the haze barrier. Alim's only contribution had been getting struck in the head by a gem.

Chapter 24 Alim

"I have to beat myself up about it. Hali's out saving her family." *Though she might be killing eidolons to do it.* "You're protecting magic itself! Both of you had such honorable goals. And here's me. Like a kid throwing a tantrum because they were born without magic, I'm here because I was jealous of power I didn't have."

Tio stopped dead in his tracks and cleared his throat. "No. Without you, I'd likely be stuck crying in a corner in Wilton. Or dead in an alley after upsetting the wrong guard. Alim, your first response to my mission wasn't about yourself, but others. Pallids. Hali's family. You may want magic, but you've hardly been selfish. Protecting magic can only be done by a celestial. At best I'm your eidolon-sanctioned travel guide."

He bowed, grazing the water with his long, pointy antlers and almost swiping Alim with them. It was good those things had stopped growing, considering he still hadn't gotten the hang of having antlers.

Alim squinted and wiped tears out from under their visor, hugging Tio tight right as he came up from the bow. Tio gave them an awkward pat and wriggled his way out of their grip.

"Thanks, Tio." *Seems he doesn't hate people after all.*

"That's your one hug. Don't come at me again or you're getting headbutted."

"Noted." Alim resumed the awful slog through the mucky water, losing count of how many times the mud tried to steal their boots.

After being soaked through for almost a full day, Alim wanted to give up. At this point they were a walking prune soldier. Probably tasted as awful too. What if they'd passed the surge already? It felt as if going any further north would lead back to Oressa.

Tio whistled a birdcall, waving to Alim from behind a mass of tangled roots. He was only knee-deep in water now and pointed to an outcropping of dry rocks. Finally! Rushing through cloudy water, Alim soared onto the rocks like they were soft, bouncy pancakes.

The low roaring of water crashing against water came from the north, and a light pink mist drifted across their face as they drank from their water jug. With every sip, Alim had to pinch their nose under their helmet, so the taste wasn't tainted by the foul air. They rolled out sleeping bags and started to set up a campfire.

"We made it," Tio said.

"Huh?"

"Don't you see the haze in the air? It's coming from Overlook Falls."

Alim had been too tired to put two and two together. "But we're not even dry yet."

"Get over it, you armored baby. Undine will dry us later. The sooner we check it out, the sooner we can leave."

Tio made his way to the waterfall, and Alim sighed.

Not going to follow the Keeper? Undine asked.

Have you ever walked through a mangrove swamp in heavy plate?

I've seen heavier.

What do you know? You don't even wear clothes.

Taking careful steps back into the water, Alim left behind the cozy camp without having enjoyed the chance to use it. A real break would've been nice. They hadn't had one since Oressa and needed at least five naps. Yesterday, preferably.

The thunderous rumble of the waterfall spritzed Tio with pink and purple mist. The wall of water climbed to Overlook Plateau's lake, far beyond where Alim could see. They had no idea how to get to the top, but Alim had always wanted to go there to climb Sky Tower. It was supposed to have a telescope that saw across most of Our Stranded Lands. They'd heard at least one claim it could see as far as the Coveted South on a clear day.

"Any ideas?" Tio asked.

"It's a dead end."

"No, I can feel flora behind the waterfall. Can you freeze it?"

Chapter 24 Alim

Freezing rushing water wouldn't work. Undine hadn't even been able to freeze a calm lake for long. "Maybe rerouting the water will work?"

Linked with Undine, the water banged against an invisible force as Alim blocked it, pushing enough aside to see behind the falls. A haze barrier waited for them.

After both had made it through, Alim's borrowed gift released, and the waterfall became complete again. The haze felt nice and cool compared to the muggy, damp air of the mangrove swamp. Tio struggled against the barrier as if it did not wish to open.

Each movement felt like Alim had hefty weights holding them down. Being elbow-deep in water wasn't doing them any favors either.

Something slithered past their legs, and Alim nearly jumped out of their armor, tumbling through to the other side and landing on damp grass beside Tio. Ahead, a winding trail of pink water coursed beside walls of thorny orange brambles before turning a sharp corner. An alternate route to their left was filled to the brim with the same brambles. Clanging metal echoed in the distance, past the thorny jungle.

"That sound must be another spirit forge," Alim said.

"It is," Undine said as she squeezed the slimy liquid off Alim like they were a human snot rag.

"Does every surge have a forge?"

"Yeah, in case Nomine or Vulkine get assigned there. You'll really like Nomine!"

I wonder where the forge was in Spirit Arboretum?

Tio had a worried look as he strode to the pink water. "The eidolon is upset. You go on ahead to your trial—I'll find it."

"Wait." Alim sloshed the water off Tio with Undine's power.

"Remind me to get better shoes for this. Some big boots maybe? Like, boots up to my eyeballs."

"Sure, next time we're in town we'll have a grand shopping adventure. Stay dry, Tio. If you run into any trouble, please call for me with your

Arboreal Path

flourish. There's a lot of ethereal noise here, so make it big if you want my ethersight to see anything."

Squeezing between prickly vines and brush, getting scratched everywhere, Alim cursed traveling with Tio once again for instilling guilt in Alim about hacking and slashing a bush. *Not everybody can beg thorns to play nice.*

As if they had willed it themself, the thorns receded into the vines and a path formed through a winding grassy grove. *Did I do that?*

They felt Undine clinking against their veins like swirling ice in a glass. She splashed out from under their helmet. "All me, sorry."

"You have a nature gift?"

"Not with full effectiveness." One of Undine's eyes flashed green. "With what little of Dryadine's ether remains within me, my control is weak. No better than Tio's magic."

Like healing. "How did you take in the nature spirit's ether?"

"Dryadine spoke to me through the Path before she died. I retrieved her core and fused it with my own before her ether faded." Undine seeped back into Alim.

Will we bring Dryadine back, like we did with Vulkine?

I miss Dryadine dearly, but such an opportunity has long since passed. When Empyrea is restored, we will one day have a new spirit with dominion over nature magic. Until then, I must hold onto this power.

Two more spirit fruit, and then Empyrea is as good as restored!

Undine bubbled around inside Alim. *These linking sessions have tired me. Let me sleep.*

All you do is sleep. It's not fair, one day, we're going to swap places.

As the trail ended and the raucous hammering grew louder, Alim arrived at a massive tree billowing black smoke into the bramble canopy. Fiery light fluctuated, breathing, from inside. The noise stopped, and a lanky vine-covered man constructed from mashed together gravel stood in the tree's large opening.

Chapter 24 Alim

Waving about a smithing hammer, Nomine motioned as if to say "come in." Inside, tools hung along bark walls. Etherite ingots were stacked high near sizable shards of thick golden bark. A pleasant warmth radiated from the active furnace. Nomine dragged out a stone chair near a circular bark table growing from the trunk floor and slapped the seat with a gentle smack.

"Don't talk much, do you?"

Nomine slapped the seat again.

Alim took the hint, and the earth spirit slid over a granite mug of steaming tea. Taking a sip, they found it plain for their taste—it needed honey and milk. Nomine sat across from them with his own tea, never losing eye contact. Did spirits need to eat and drink?

"What are we crafting?" Alim asked.

His gaunt face was unmoving. It reminded Alim of a radical sect of Dreamers that took a vow of silence until their dream was achieved. Which seemed as pointless as dipping sweet fruit into sugar.

Nomine sipped his tea and it flowed down the cracks in his gravelly body like a gentle stream. He directed their attention to the pile of wood with ether pulsing off it and a workbench.

Try as they might, Alim couldn't budge the wood. *This is worse than the etherite ingots!*

Acquainting themself with under-utilized muscles, Alim skidded a chunk of the golden wood along the floor until it pressed against the workbench.

Nomine clinched the wood with two fingers, lifting it to the workbench with an I-need-a-vacation look in his eyes.

"Thanks, buddy." *Celestial magic is the trick again, right? Easy.*

Closing their eyes and visualizing a round shield, Alim picked at the ethereal threads holding the wood together. Unable to get a solid grip, the threads slipped from their fingers at each attempt. *Something's off. But if I mix the ether with something easier to control, maybe...*

Arboreal Path

Alim reached for the shifting green and purple fog in the air, folding it into the wood. As the two merged, the wood became malleable. When Alim opened their eyes, the wood had been molded into an imperfect targe. Uneven and wobbly, but what wasn't in Alim's life? They added one of their yellow straps, and the shield was complete. Heaving it up with their off hand, it was almost weightless. Alim had picked up heavier things with a fork. It was as if Alim had combined the wood and ether to create something entirely new.

I don't want to carry another unwieldy thing. My axe is bad enough. Their throwing axe came to mind. Alim was able to shape it into almost anything. Could the shield be condensed in the same way?

First, I'll need somewhere to store it. They whirled a ball of ether into their hands, shaping it into a dome as they modified it. Forced it into a hardened metal. Etherite. Alim affixed the etherite dome onto the shield's center.

Alim dug deep into the ether's internal structure and tweaked it. The wood wrapped in on itself, shuttering into the etherite center. Strapping the dome to their left forearm, Alim pushed on the ether inside the shield—bark shot out and quickly filled a circle around the dome, reforming the shield. *Convenient!*

Nomine grunted and nodded, startling Alim. *Forgot he was here.* Stone hands invited them to sit again.

Where was Tio? His etheric signature didn't seem any closer or further away. Had he run into trouble? "I'm done, right? My friend needs me."

The earth spirit shook his head and motioned at the seat again. A fresh mug sat on the table. Was the trial not over yet? Maybe he wanted to examine their work.

Something about the tea smelled different. Taking a sip, an overwhelming sweetness hit with a slight bite, similar to a plum or green apple. Alim downed the entire glass, feeling refreshed.

Undine shouted, *No, no, no! Alim, that was part of the trial.*

Chapter 24 Alim

The water spirit's essence spread through Alim's veins, feeling as if she were trying on Alim's skin as a coat. They were going to burst at the seams. Gut-wrenching pain overrode every other sense as blood formed into rounded chunks, rolling and sloshing around as a landslide. Undine ejected from Alim, knocking over the table, and bumping Nomine into the forge. Both spirits faded from sight.

Alim fell onto sparkling roots, bouncing off the side of the Path. Reaching for the first thing they saw, Alim grabbed hold of a dangling thread of ether and plummeted as the milky sky unraveled before their eyes.

CHAPTER 25

Anxiety sprouted little stems of doubt, coiling around his mind, strangling every thought with uncertainties. *Splitting up was a bad idea. Books prove that every time.*

Tio walked along his flourish-influenced road of elevated neon-colored mangrove tree roots. Given the sheer size of previous eidolons, Tio assumed he would have seen it by now. The pink water was shallow enough that any sizable animal would have nowhere to hide.

Globules of pink dripped onto his antlers. Was it raining? The sky was dark but without a single cloud. Distorted and wavy. Hundreds of shadows ran by as if cast by a school of fish. A lake? *Am I under Overlook Plateau's lake? The surge's haze barrier must hold it up there.*

Something spiny grazed his legs, jerking him forward. But nothing was there when he looked. Tio scanned the water, but cloudy ripples of bright green and purple mud obscured the shallows. Little bubbly swells popped and released an intoxicating, sweet scent. It would've made for a wonderful perfume if Tio had something to bottle it up with.

The roots creaked and fluctuated as something pushed on the road from underneath. If he were still carrying those heavy bags, he'd have gone for an unwanted swim by now.

Fear flooded him with a gnawing, prickling jitter in his bones. Death. Tio was going to die here. He had seen it and, somehow, knew it was around the corner. Would Alim be the one to kill him? Hali?

Tio poked his fingers into his bracelet. *No, stop. These aren't my feelings.* Tio shook off the imported emotions, realizing something had coiled around his legs.

Another rush of foreign anxiety flooded his mind as Tio was yanked from his road and splashed underwater. As he was dragged through the shallows, Tio's antlers snagged on a stray mangrove tree, plucking him from whatever had him in its grasp. He climbed out of the water using the cluster of spindly roots.

A spiky, triangular snake head surfaced and clumsily swam at Tio. Rough, pointy neon-yellow scales glimmered purple as it slithered onto the branches, baring fangs dripping with venom.

Seems the eidolon found me first. But bush vipers are tree-dwellers... what compelled it to be in water?

While clambering upwards, blood trickled from Tio's snagged antler. Wiping the blood onto his palm, Tio concentrated on the tree. In a shiny purple and yellow blur, the snake zoomed across the trees to strike.

Branches expanded into a dual pronged pole and constricted the snake's neck against another tree's trunk. The size of the snake's maw reminded Tio it would have no problem swallowing him whole and dooming him to live digestion.

Wriggling as it dangled from the tree, the snake splashed the water with its manchineel-covered tail. The apple-like green manchineel fruit was toxic, so Belsa was the only place in Our Stranded Lands where a person could eat one, since druids removed their poisonous properties. Would Alim have to eat this? *If the cherry would have given Alim a bad* time, this manchineel might kill them outright. Maybe it's part of the trial to remove the poison?

Tio hopped across the tangled trees to the snake, climbing to its pinned head. Placing a hand upon it, fear crept in once more. The snake's fear. "Can I help? What are you afraid of?"

"Saw—I saw it. You're going to kill me. Like Zergi, Sulin, and Anemo. My time is short. This ethereal prison will be my grave."

Did it go into the water hoping to kill me or to get away from me? Tio let his own emotions mingle with the snake and its squirming body calmed.

"Slay—you aren't here to slay?" The spines on its head shuddered. "You are the other. Tio."

"You know my name?" *Can eidolons talk to each other? Or spirits? Maybe Vinn gave the other eidolons notice?*

The eidolon's tail whipped up and spiraled around Tio's wrist.

Once again in emptiness, a coiled snake materialized in front of him. Its name was Orbi. Fear subsided. The darkness writhed with the dead, churning whirlpools of gray phantoms. *Am I above Phantasmal Reef?* Tio didn't think phantoms made noises, but the agitated waters sounded too close to weeping for his comfort.

Orbi's tongue flicked out. "Terrain bereft of ether. Severed from Empyrea."

Tio catapulted northward across the sky, to the snow-kissed mountains of East Peaks. An invisible hand plopped him into a cave, covered in incandescent green moss blooming with pink nettle flowers. Thick, pungent smoke overwhelmed him as the flowers caught fire.

Brought back to reality, Tio almost fell into the water, but the snake's tail caught him and lowered him to safety.

"Is Phantasmal Reef what's weakening Empyrea?" Tio asked.

"The reef is a symptom. Find what stops spirits from entering the Ethereal Realm, and you find what leads phantoms astray."

"You mentioned Sulin… the lynx isn't dead. We revived Sulin."

Chapter 25 Tio

Orbi's relief coursed through its every word. "Nomine hasn't heard from Vulkine in the Path. They must be weak still. Perhaps when I die, you'll bring me back too."

"Why are you so sure you're going to die?"

"Many cycles ago, our fallen celestial spirit needed me. The other eidolons may have forsaken Malakine for the Quake, but I forgave. I linked with Malakine to save them, but our connection failed to hold." Orbi lowered its head. "I dream of my death every night. Each a different method, delivered by a different hand. My punishment for dooming Empyrea."

Malakine again? The celestial spirit caused the Quake? "Malakine is dead."

"And I will be too. Malakine's curse will take all eidolons soon enough."

"It won't come to that," Tio said. "My friend and I will protect you."

"The new celestial?" Orbi's tone shifted and its speech relaxed. "Yes, Undine told Nomine about Alim. I want to help. My fruit will attune Alim to earth."

"No offense, but your fruit might kill them and there's no telling if I'm capable of removing such a strong poison either."

"Such is known. Nomine distills it into a tea. If the celestial drinks it first, they will become partially attuned and protected. Enough to make the poison not deadly."

"And if I remove the rest, it should have no effect at all." Tio snagged one of the manchineels from Orbi's tail. It shriveled as he removed the poison until it looked less like an apple and more a green prune.

"I will take you to Nomine's forge."

Tio grabbed hold of the spines near Orbi's head as it slithered along the mangroves. "The cave you showed me. Was it a surge? Why was it on fire? Who were the other two eidolons you named? Where—"

"One question at a time, or you're going for a dip," Orbi said with the same level of affectionate irritation Tio's mom had often used. "Yes, the cave was Anemo's surge. Trapped as we are, it took our spirits much time in the Arboreal Path to map out Empyrea's roots to get our locations for you."

So the Path connects all the surges together. I never thought about how eidolons wouldn't know where they are. "This… I appreciate it! Knowing where to go for Alim's final attunement will let us finish with more than enough time to unblock the Path." *Pink nettles are the key. Only one cave in the entire Yinsen cavern system has those flowers.*

"Hold on. What do you mean by 'was' a surge? Anemo… that's one of the eidolons you mentioned." Tio's mood darkened.

"When Sylphine returned to her surge, it was ablaze. She extinguished the inferno, but Anemo was gone. No body, no feathers, no bones, no etheric dust. Gone."

If Empyrea's seed had revived Sulin by taking in the surge's lingering ether and mixing it with the lynx's ashes, was Anemo a lost cause at this point? "Is Sylphine okay?"

"No sign from her since she relayed that message. Nomine has always been mute, but he's been silent even in our mental link since."

"Is that how you knew my name? Spirits can speak to each other across surges?" *Sounds similar to what druids could do.*

"Precisely. When Alim ate their first fruit, the Arboreal Path opened enough for Undine to relay a message to the other spirits about the two of you working to restore Empyrea." Orbi stretched onto the elevated road Tio created and continued towards the crossroads where Alim had left for the trial. "You see, we would very much like to live, so all the spirits and eidolons agreed to help. Eidolons cannot move about freely in the Arboreal Path and can't enter the Ethereal Realm at all, so if our surges cease to exist, we die and our linked spirits with us."

"Undine linked to Alim, so couldn't the other spirits all link to humans to survive?" Tio asked.

"No, mortals do not have sufficient ether to sustain a spirit alone. Without Vinn, Alim would be unable to host Undine. Although a spirit could sever the link and live in the Arboreal Path until the next cycle, eventually every eidolon's fate will be the same. With the Ethereal Realm blocked to the spirits, there will be nothing supplying them with the ether they need to live."

"We'll investigate the final surge. And I promise to do what we can for Sylphine and Anemo." Tio itched his shoulder, pricking a finger on a thorn. Pink flowering brambles wrapped around his upper arm. He gave them a weak tug, only to find they were a part of him. *That's mildly inconvenient.* Much of his sleeve had been ripped by it, so he tore it off. *Pretty as they are...* The thorns receded. *There.* It seemed he could control them with his flourish.

As Orbi and Tio passed through divided brambles, they found an empty spirit forge. No Alim, Nomine, or Undine to be found inside the hollowed-out tree. A jumbled mess of tools and knocked-over furniture and tables were all Tio saw.

Orbi hissed at sparkles drifting in the air. "A starportal. The spirits retreated to the Path. Strange… I will call for Nomine through our link."

Tio set one of the tables upright and placed the dried manchineel on it. *Retreated from what? Is Alim in the Path too? Their meditation doesn't physically take them there, but Orbi said the tea would partially attune them. Maybe their celestial power is strong enough to enter the Path now?*

Scouting the tree's perimeter alone, Tio followed a set of small tracks to a red bush. A fuzzy beige mouse poked its head out.

"Excuse me, have you seen a person wearing armor around here?" Tio asked.

"I can't understand your accent, mate. Bit like a pinkie if I'm honest. You a druid or somethin'? Thought you was legends." The mouse's words were almost drowned out by a droning buzz in the distance. Like countless mosquitos hovering near Tio's ear.

Great. Foreign animals with no concept of talking to druids still thought he sounded like a child. "My friend. Metal hat. Giant muscles.

Did you see them?" Tio gestured to outline big biceps and a bucket head as wisps of etheric fog trailed past his head.

"Hanging with the nice rock-guy that feeds us? Course I seen 'em."

"Where are they now?"

"Sorry, mate. No help there. Up and disappeared. Didn't even leave nothin' for us either."

Guess they really are in the Path. "Thanks for confirming."

"Can't wait to tell the kids their pa met a real live druid!" The mouse scurried away.

Orange light whizzed by Tio's head, and he dove, grabbing the mouse. An instant inferno engulfed the bushes and trailed up the forge's trunk. The mouse climbed Tio and hid in his vines.

"Is your family in there?" Tio asked while assessing where the fireball had come from.

"No, we live in the tunnels."

"Those?" Tio pointed at a tiny hole in a dirt wall far from the blaze.

"Course those. You daft?" the mouse squeaked with agitation in Tio's ear.

Come on, can't I get some respect after saving your life? Scrambling towards the mouse's tunnel entrance, an arrow sank into the ground in Tio's way.

Molded bumps in the wall led up to a perch with a crouched archer nocking another arrow. *Sipherra? How did they get into a surge?*

A hiss echoed through the underground grove and the lake above rippled as the earth shifted. Rectangular columns of stone shot from the wall and smashed into the ground against a group of three armored mercenaries Tio hadn't realized were behind him. The archer lost their footing and Tio ran to the hole, dropping the mouse off.

"Thanks, pinkie," it said as it vanished into the tunnels.

A steel boot kicked Tio's side.

Cornered. Two more mercenaries emerged. One had fire frolicking between their hands. The other brandished a sword and looked like they

Chapter 25 Tio

were wearing a golem suit given how much armor they had. They made Alim seem underdressed.

Run. Run where? "Let's talk this—"

The fire mage seized Tio by the shoulder, snatching their hand back when it grazed Tio's new thorns. They convulsed on the spot, collapsing onto the rocks with fiery foam leaking from their mouth. Golem Suit backed away. Tio advanced, stretching the thorny vines along the whole length of his arm. He imagined the priceless look on Alim's face underneath their helmet when he told them the story of his victory against Sipherra.

"Leave this surge. Sipherra doesn't belong here," Tio said with rising confidence.

Golem Suit slashed Tio's vines and tackled him, grabbing his antlers, and crunching his face against the ground. "We're here for you."

Tio's newfound confidence melted as his antlers threatened to snap. *Should've known Sipherra would be looking for us. This is it. I'm dead. At least Alim isn't here. They can finish the journey and heal Empyrea without me.*

Relief. Golem Suit wasn't on top of Tio anymore. Tio rolled onto his back in time to witness Golem Suit sink upside down into a spinning pile of sand.

Orbi slithered to Tio. "Nomine and Undine are safe, but they don't know where Alim is. I couldn't feel anybody entering the surge and the ether grows thin. My barrier must be destroyed."

The scientist we met at Stoneport was right, but how did their tech advance so quickly?

"We should withdraw to my forest. It's safer—"

Hauled off by an invisible force, Orbi slammed through the burning tree forge, knocking it over and scattering chunks of flaming bark across the grove. As the brambles leading back to the crossroads became a hellish blockade of fire and thorns, Tio connected to any flora he could and asked for aid. But what little remained refused his flourish's call.

As Orbi floated helplessly over the wreckage, purple and yellow flakes snowed down like its scales were being ground up. With another hiss, the flakes surrounded Tio and formed into a protective bunker. Nausea bubbled in Tio's gut as he heard a horrible ripping sound. Explosive booms from large, unseen things impacting each other.

Deep breaths.

Something smacked against Tio's barrier. Repeatedly. "It's no good, Osanshia. My gift can't dent this stuff. Don't think it's made of stone."

Deep breaths.

"Do the Dreamers accept academy dropouts? Step aside," a familiar voice said.

No sooner than she had finished speaking, Tio's protection crumbled and left him face to face with Gren Consortium's Osanshia, with her recognizable tall, orange hair in its usual tree braids. Sans one branch thanks to Alim's haphazard axe throw.

Tio rammed his antlers at Osanshia, but she grabbed onto them and flipped Tio onto his back. With a flick of her wrist, one of Osanshia's amethysts flew at Tio and shattered part of an antler.

CHAPTER 26

Vaguely pink water trickled onto Hali's hair as she ducked underneath large, dew-laden blue leaves. Between the impenetrable canopy and the magically uplifted lake overhead, the neon green bioluminescent fungi and vivid yellow fireflies were the only source of light.

Brushing abrasive, puffy curls out of her eyes, Hali cursed the hidden rainforest's humidity. *I should've designed a water rune to sap air moisture and throw it in the garbage. Or had the foresight to bring hairbands.*

Part of her would rather have taken the long way round, through Thauma's blighted crags. At least she would have been able to see Stoneport's beach first… though the mangroves made for unpleasant travel in their own way and would be terrible news for her new tattoo since it was still healing underneath the linen bandages.

Descending through the rainforest, Hali made it to the water-filled mangrove. The water had a hint of faded ethereal color to it, like the rainbow reflections of oil. She cracked open her rune book to a page with a tangled mess of lines and a triangle in the center. Activating it, a tiny, turquoise orb hovered over her fingers. Cool mist poured off it and swirled into a vortex as it collected ice. Once the frozen orb was the size of Hali's head, she tossed it at the water. It exploded off the surface when it hit, freezing patches as it bounced. Hali vaulted between chunks of ice all the way to a conspicuous trail of elevated roots.

This wasn't here last time. Only a druid could make such an unnatural growth pattern. Hali wasn't ready to face Tio yet—she simply wanted to make sure he and Alim were safe. Her only hope was that they had already met the eidolon and moved on.

Following Tio's root-road reminded Hali of the Arboreal Path. The last time Hali had been here, there was no barrier and Rev had been collecting seeds to create Spirit Arboretum. It was here Rev came up with the idea for Starpath—Rev wanted it to represent Hali's "hard work" by emulating the Arboreal Path. As if Hali could've done it without Rev. Hali had been lost when Thauma's Magisters—her father included—planned for her to become a celestial, and it had been Rev who'd made the connection between the original celestial and the ether surges. Rev opening the haze barriers had allowed Hali to accomplish something.

Though, at the time, Hali had hated making such frequent stops for Rev's seed collection. Walking the Path was supposed to take precedence, but the journey had taken three times as long with the number of deviations they'd made.

Hali recalled Rev's sour, yet playful, tone right away, always saying something along the lines of, "Sereia, relax. There's time for celestial burden nonsense later. Druids need hourly flower-smelling breaks. You mages wouldn't understand."

Of course, Hali knowing Rev didn't believe in any celestial burden infuriated her more than the comments themselves. "I'll relax when the Conclave sends me a more competent druid," Hali had said numerous different ways. But there had been no other druids capable of such feats. The eidolons only spoke to Rev.

Chapter 26 Hali

It wasn't until Hali and Rev made it to the southern countries, in Bansil's blood forests, that Hali had started to appreciate Rev's Spirit Arboretum aspirations. And enjoy the resulting extra moments with Rev.

A simpler time—huh? Hali's tattoos pulsed wildly, jolting in every direction. With a dagger in each hand, Hali spun around to meet the eidolon.

Nothing in sight. Not even a slight rustling or rippling to hint anything was near—only dripping water from the elevated lake. The pulsing stopped entirely, a calm Hali hadn't experienced since tattooing the Sapper rune in Gren City. Had something happened to the eidolon? No, the surge's ambient ether was gone. The previously colorful water was now plain and muddy.

My tattoos must need ether to track the eidolons. Should be plenty of ether in the air, even if I can't see any. Unless… Was it even possible for all ether in an area to be gone? *The eidolon won't last long in these conditions.*

At the end of the root-road, Hali smelled smoke. Burned brambles crumbled on ashy soil. Small clouds of smoke piled against the ceiling, funneling out to a deafening waterfall. The air glittered.

She jumped out of the way as a jagged rectangle ripped into existence, folded open, and spat a person out. They groaned and rubbed their signature crescent helmet before collapsing. Alim's lips and chin looked burned, as if they'd botched a fire-swallowing street performance.

Alim shifted towards Hali, their teeth chomping between words. "I couldn't possibly eat another bite."

Why did it not surprise her that Alim's hallucinations involved food? Did their nightmares involve evil pasta?

Something similar had happened to Hali when she'd eaten Franz's kiwi. Rev had put together a remedy for Hali and forced her to memorize it in case of future allergies. Except the peacock eidolon's fruit had caused ether poisoning, not an allergy, but the remedy had worked all the same.

Reducing the amount of ether to avoid poisoning is necessary for some spirit fruits. It's part of the celestial trials. If I'd been here, I could've warned you… I'll fix you up, Alim.

Back to the rainforest. Hali ventured through the mangrove, thankful the ice hadn't melted yet, gathered several glowing mushrooms, a blue leaf large enough to be worn as a dress, and black-green gradient petals, then returned to the squirming Alim.

She chopped all the ingredients and tossed everything in a small iron pot filled with water. A weak flame-tooth rune from her book let her breathe hot air onto the concoction until it boiled, the heat triggering acidic oil to leak from the chopped mushrooms and dissolve the ingredients into a turquoise soup. Hali poured it into her three remaining vials, corking two and holding the last one over Alim.

Hali propped Alim's head up and they said, "Don't put swamp water in my mouth."

"Says the one that eats things they find on the floor." Hali poked their helmet's visor between the clouds.

"You're not my mom—"

Hali dumped the turquoise liquid down Alim's throat, making sure to hold their mouth open. Alim jerked back, knocking their head against the ground and coughing.

"Hold still." Hali lifted their head again and emptied the vial. *That helmet needs to come off.*

A lightning-quick Alim gripped Hali's wrist as she touched the metal. Their grasp loosened and fell to the side as the concoction induced sleep.

"Fine, keep it on," Hali said as she lowered Alim's head down.

Where's Tio? Surely, he would have detected and cleansed this poison with nary a thought. *Did the two have a fight or get separated?*

Venturing through burned brambles, Hali found where the fires had started. Flat purple and yellow gemstones had been flung about in craters; rotted wood torn in half with the dismantled remnants of a spirit forge

Chapter 26 Hali

within. The forge's special flames didn't spread, so it couldn't have caused this. Taking a closer look at the gemstones, Hali realized they were more like scales.

Eidolon blood, Kthon whispered while flashing a peculiar shape in Hali's head. If she looked at it with the right angle, it resembled a farmer's scythe piercing the sun.

As much as she wanted to stop hearing Kthon creep into her thoughts, it was almost a relief to find she'd be able to get eidolon blood from these scales. But what had happened? It was as if a powerful earth mage had ripped the gemstone scales off the eidolon's skin. *Cruel. Somebody capable of this—I wouldn't think twice about letting Kthon have them.*

Spicy smoke wafted from lopsided melty cardamom candles as Hali prepared for the next rune. She filled her needle with the ethereal blood she collected from the scales and poked it into her left arm. This would be her third eidolon rune, Lux. She added it as Kthon—and Malakine before him—had shown her, with the scythe's handle running from her left shoulder to elbow and its blade wrapped around her forearm. The blazing sun sat just above her binding rune.

Lux was the most dangerous of the eidolon runes, and Hali had spent years altering it to make the results more palatable. The original design emulated etheric death, burning ether. Generally, the sun symbol in runes represented ether. While the scythe-ish shape was more unusual, Hali had discovered it to mean inevitable. Or delayed result in this case. Put together, with the sun being pierced, it became "volatile inevitability." Minor alterations to the proportions tamed the impact. While death was still the end result, at least the affected people wouldn't be stuck in the Corporeal Realm as phantoms due to etheric death.

Hali wrapped the tattoo in fresh bandages as her binding rune excreted black-and-white tangled shadows. *I haven't seen white shadows since Ikazu first fought Kthon.* Since winning the last bout, Ikazu had been in full control over Kthon's body, so there hadn't been a need to operate separately.

Thoughts of the mucus-covered membrane Hali had been trapped in last time Kthon had battled Ikazu sent a pervading stickiness crawling down her arms. Grasping the hilt of the dagger in her boot, Hali only got it past her knee before Kthon's shadows wrenched Hali's fingers back until she dropped the blade. Wood-textured light overtook Hali and Kthon, and she sank. The world melted, and Hali watched as Ikazu's white shadows drank Kthon, becoming a Rev-shaped star-filled night sky.

Rev-Ikazu signed with her hands, "You're making Kthon stronger."

Ikazu's never been so coherent before. It's more like Rev lecturing me... "Kthon may feed on the eidolon blood, but I can control it. I can bring you back."

"Every new phantom Kthon obtains. Every new eidolon rune on your body. Every time Kthon heals you. It all adds to Kthon's power. Ikazu, as you call us… we will not succeed next time. We will be so buried as to no longer exist."

"Rasal deserves a chance to experience life, and you the chance to take back the life I stole."

A masculine silhouette tore out from Rev-Ikazu's shoulder and signed with his own set of hands. "Forget us. New family."

"No, how can you ask me to forget?" Hali clenched her fists. "I'm getting the last eidolon rune and you're both coming back to me."

Rasal-Ikazu signed again. "New memory please. With new family."

"I want new memories with you, not anybody else."

Rev and Rasal reached out with Ikazu's four arms and hugged Hali. "Let us go," Rev said aloud, speaking for the first time since their battle at Zergi's surge.

"Memory please," Rasal-Ikazu signed as he pressed his forehead against Hali's. "Last time."

Chapter 26 Hali

Rev poked Sereia in the forehead. "The Arboreal Path sounds so… beautiful! Though the name could use some work. You're literally lighting up constellations! What does that have to do with trees?"

Sereia grumbled in protest. Taking time away from the Path to collect seeds was a waste of time when the Lunar Vault could dump devastating amounts of ether onto Grenvel and Thauma within the year.

"Ignore your celestial-burden nonsense for two seconds. Have some fun." Rev's pink hair had become grimy with bloodsap from Gorweald's ashen-barked trees. Even the purple and green peacock feathers dangling from the back of her hair were stained with dark red globs.

"Easy to say when the Magisters aren't expecting you to solve all their problems." Thauma's leaders didn't approve of Rev's idea to try asking the spirits, but the hate letters had stopped when it had been proved to work. Sereia had already attuned to two elements. Now the Magisters sent letters with all their plans for making more celestials and what they could do for Thauma.

"Does knowing the seeds are for you help? I'm going to recreate the Path as part of Belsa's forests in your honor. Though I'm giving it the proper name—Starpath!"

Sereia laughed. "Pretty sure the spirits named it after the road, you know? The one made from Empyrea's roots?"

Rev held a goop-covered black acorn in Sereia's face. "Laugh all you want. Soon, everybody west of the Great Haze will want to see the amazing Starpath and its infinite variety of trees!"

"Infinite? Somebody's got high hopes."

Rev shoved Sereia into a pile of sticky red leaves, where she fell through a deep unending hole.

"Are you sure you want a child?" Rev asked Sereia. The two were seated on a bench at the top of Sky Tower, waiting to use the telescope.

Sereia put on a thoughtful façade, acting as if she weren't sure. "If it is with you, of course I do."

Rev frowned. "You know what I meant. Ever since you completed the Path, you haven't had time for anything. Magisters control your entire schedule…"

Sereia got up from the bench and stared down at Overlook Plateau's lake. She could barely make out the shimmering cyan scales of a leviathan as it skimmed the water's surface with its winding serpentine body. If the fall wouldn't break every bone in her body, Sereia would jump off the tower to play with the leviathans. Anything would be better than meeting with the Magisters again. They were worse than Belsa's Conclave and Gren Consortium combined.

"You alive over there?" Rev squished Sereia's cheeks together and forced her to pay attention. "Don't make me throw you into the lake. Sit down."

"Oh, have you been working out? Last I checked, lifting rice was a challenge for you."

Rev flexed the unimpressive stick she called an arm and wove it with Sereia's, leading her back to the bench.

Sereia chuckled into a snort. "I'm shaking in my boots." The two locked hands, and she twirled the peacock feathers in Rev's pink hair.

"I have a name picked out," Rev said. "Rasal."

"Sticking with the moon theme? You'll even share the same first letter. I'm feeling a little left out."

"Well, we wouldn't want that…" Rev twiddled her fingers together in her usual deep-thought pose. "We could call you Hali."

"Excuse me? I'd prefer not to be named after a destroyed moon. Are you calling me a mess?"

"Well, I'm not *not* calling you a mess." Splaying out on the bench, Rev kicked against Sereia as if trying to make sure she didn't have to share.

"We can call him Razz for short." Much better. "Rasal is so formal sounding." Sereia imagined a lion munching on raspberries and giggled.

Rev asked, "Nicknaming him already? What are you going to do if combining celestial and nature magic together doesn't work?"

"It'll work. Think of it like insemination."

"Never. Ever. Say that word again." Rev gagged and kicked Sereia off the bench.

Dazzling pinks, greens, and purples reflected off the sparkling waters of the twin Lungs as ethereal lights danced overhead. A stream of ether flowed from the distant scattered emerald remains of Nihali—Hali's new namesake moon.

"Like this," Hali said as she made rune-like symbols with her hands. "It means 'good morning.'"

The shadowy child stared at her, wearing what looked like a young Rev's face. Her little legs dangled off the edge of Und dal Sylph Manor's roof, hands phasing through each other as she failed to mimic Hali. Not a single successful word in the bunch, but Hali smirked all the same.

"You'll get it next time," Hali said as she tried to hold the shadow's hand, passing through it like she'd tried to grab thick smoke. Wisps of black ether smeared from the child's body, drifting towards the endlessly tall dome of ethereal haze. Hali's jaw popped as she clenched it to control her quivering lower lip.

The child's features shifted from girl to boy. Face changes had become less frequent since Kthon had stopped showing up. Hali traced the deep scar on her neck. *If things stay like this, maybe it won't be so bad. Will Kthon ever come back?* It didn't matter right now—spending a calm moment with her family was enough.

Hali channeled Rev's obscene level of pep and clapped her hands. "I gave your name some thought." In the Old Faith, Rev and Rasal's namesake moons were represented by the rainbow-scaled fish—ikatere—and the lion-headed eagles—anzu. "What do you think about Ikazu?"

Clumsy fingers signed the word "Good."

17

Alim's weak voice came from behind her. "Hali? Are you crying?"

"It's nothing." Hali wiped her tears onto her binding rune.

Rasal and Rev both want me to stop, but… I can't. Their resurrection must continue or what's the point of everything I've done?

"Already moving on your own, that's great. How're you feeling?" Hali asked.

"Like I spent last night drinking lava."

"An ordinary day in the life of Alim."

"Where's Tio?" Alim asked.

"I don't know yet. I was hoping you would know if he was safe. This place is a disaster—there's a lot to sort through." *And my greedy self prioritized this tattoo instead of looking for signs of Tio…*

"Why are you here?" Alim asked, swaying with exaggerated clumsiness as they walked. "You really are hunting eidolons. Did you kill this one too?"

How… Und dal Sylph Manor was marked as a surge on Tio's map. They must have gone there first, and Alim can read basic Thaumic—they know everything. "I didn't intend to kill any eidolons." *Though I expected I might.*

"Eidolon blood is the 'blood rich with ether' you mentioned back in Wilton. That I get. If the world is down one eidolon, I presume that's why you stopped hunting them, but what did you learn from Vinn that made you start again?"

"Nature magic was thought gone, but we discovered Vinn has both nature- and water-aspected blood. How could I not resume my hunt?" Hali tugged on her cowl. "My son and partner are my number-one priority, you know?"

"Which is why I agreed to help to begin with!"

"I know, and now I've messed things up for you two." Hali's binding rune burned. "Sulin died because of me, but I promise this surge was in shambles when I arrived."

Chapter 26 Hali

Alim crouched at a pile of brown and white shards. "Hold that thought." They examined one shard up close. "This is from Tio's antler! Was this... you?"

"Me? I'll accept I'm a monster, but Tio is the last person I'd hurt. Whatever happened to this surge and its eidolon, Tio was caught in the fray." Hali picked up scraps of red cloth with half a mountain peak squashing it. "Sipherra."

Fumes practically jettisoned from Alim's crescents as they stomped into the fallen spirit-forge tree. "Sipherra must've followed us from Sanctuary. We had a run-in with two Gren Consortium members, Geno and Osanshia. Either would have the clout to send Dreamers after us. They invented a machine to absorb ether." Alim sifted through the forge and punted a little ball backward into Hali's foot. "We need Undine."

"What's this?" Hali brought the ball close, discovering it to be some sort of dried fruit. "I believe this is yours, floor-eater." Hali tossed the spirit fruit to Alim. "There's no time to wait on Undine. Sipherra captured Tio and may well have killed this eidolon."

"Why would Sipherra kill an eidolon?"

"To defend themselves... or for a new experiment." Hali's tattoos began to pulse again with new ferocity. If the eidolon were dead, it would point west—to Spirit Arboretum and the last remaining eidolon, Vinn. But instead, it pointed south. Sipherra had Tio and the eidolon, and they were on the move.

CHAPTER 27

Following South Lung's shore for a day, the mixture of bleached and unbleached soil transitioned to ghostly blue fields. Each blade of blue grass was thin enough to see right through. Patches of orange flowers swayed in the breeze across gentle hills. Weeping Pass. It got its name long before Phantasmal Reef or Refulgent Wastes existed, but the name had taken on more meaning afterwards. Between the eerie whistling breeze, the dark reef, Refulgent Wastes, and Iron Swamp, everybody avoided Weeping Pass. Everybody except Dreamers.

"When are you going to eat that fruit? From the looks of it, Tio prepared it for you." Hali had brought it up every day after leaving Overlook Falls, as if she'd forgotten the response.

Tio's chaotic ether shone like a green beacon to the southwest.

"After we find Tio." Maybe extra explanation would deter her. "We don't have time for me to mess around with the Arboreal Path or some sort of poison." *Even if Tio dulled the poison, it's got to be worse than the tea I drank.*

Chapter 27 Alim

"When's the last time you recharged? Running out of ether right as we run into an army of mercenaries would be bad timing, you know?"

"It's fine. I was in the Path after drinking the poison tea."

Hali sighed in the way only a teacher could. "For all of a second before accidentally opening a starportal and falling on top of me. Do you realize how high the blood toll is for a starportal? And you want to waltz into Strago and say 'hello.'"

Now that she mentioned it, Alim did feel oddly warm and light-headed. They had assumed it was because Undine was gone. And Strago was the main camp for Dreamers to train at, so it was guaranteed to be packed. Alim sat among orange flowers and said, "Use a rune or something to snap me out of it if I'm gone too long."

"How about I smack your helmet with a rock?" Hali crouched and hefted one bigger than her head.

"I miss Undine. She's less violent."

Odd green plum-thing held between two fingers, Alim opened their food prison and threw it in. Chewy. Sourness scrunched Alim's face and a familiar landslide sensation rushed through their blood as meditation brought them into the Arboreal Path.

The new constellation danced in the sky already. A subdued, amber mountain had joined the whirlpool and flame, growing brighter by the second. *The tea must've started the process already.*

There's more green stars now, and brighter too. Could those be forming another constellation? Maybe from the nature gift inside Undine? The fig I ate back then did taste like two different fruits.

There was a simple cloud or ball floating over a part of the Path with no road leading under it. Even the abyss had a road. Was the road missing because there was no nature spirit?

Okay, recharge and get out of here. Tio needs us.

Alim raised both arms wide, soaking in ether from each of the star formations. The energy swished in their veins as if Alim could feel their heart pumping. As soon as the swishing calmed, Alim twisted their hands to bring themself back to the Corporeal Realm.

"Welcome back," Hali said, bouncing a smaller rock between her hands.

Alim tapped the etherite dome on their arm and their wooden shield shuttered out. "Try me." The tap was unnecessary, but establishing a physical connection seemed to lower the blood toll for celestial magic.

"Neat trick. You've advanced pretty far without my help. I doubt there's much left I can teach you."

"Or maybe I'd be calling down meteor showers and hurling entire star systems at people if you hadn't left us, you know?" Alim made sure to hit the "you know" with the same emphasis and accent Hali used.

"Celestials can't do either of those things," Hali said as she tapped against her curls.

Alim pretended to be taking notes like Tio. "Oh, sorry, was I supposed to be paying attention? I was adding whiskers to this cat."

Both laughed as they had in their after-lecture discussions about utter nonsense back in Wilton.

Walking and talking, Alim asked, "What really happened after you left us? You were laid out with grievous, fatal wounds in a hospital like two weeks ago. Maybe three? Yet you're good as new. And you said Sulin died because of you."

Tio-level insecurity washed over Alim as they nervously manipulated the ether in their etherite throwing axe, stretching it into crazy shapes. "I wasn't ready to hear it before. But now I need to. If you're going to rejoin Team Ether Cl—"

"Cleavers, yes that glorious name again. I don't think the name applies anymore. When's the last time you cleaved a barrier with Tio's new powers?" Hali poked Alim's helmet and frowned. "Kthon killed Sulin. Or maybe I did with Kthon's shadows. Regardless, Sulin wasn't supposed to die. You weren't wrong, I'm hunting eidolons. Same as I did five hundred years ago, but I modified my runes so the eidolons wouldn't need to die."

Chapter 27 Alim

"Did you ever intend for me to help, or was this your plan the whole time?"

"Forcing you to become a celestial to solve my problems was always 'Plan B' for me."

"You weren't forcing me," Alim said. "I volunteered."

"Only because I dangled the temptation of magic and tacked on a sob story for good measure."

"Hali, stop. Tio and I want to help you. Neither of us care what risks are involved with facing Kthon. You don't have to do this alone, especially not if doing so requires you to endanger yourself and eidolons."

"It's not only that." Hali massaged her jaw. "I—I need eidolon blood. To bring my family back to life."

"That's really possible?" Alim asked.

"Honestly, I don't know if it's possible. In theory the combination of runes would allow it, so it's something I have to try. I owe it to Rasal. And Rev too."

"Five hundred years though? That's a long time, Hali. You sure they want that?"

"You think I haven't thought about it a thousand times? What I'm doing is selfish. I know, and I'd appreciate it if you didn't lecture or try to convince me to stop." Hali rubbed her eyes like she was holding back the tide. "And for the record, I'm closer to 108 because I spent most of the last 507 years in a surge. I left my family's manor four years ago."

"Did you create that surge? Everything about it was weird and there was no eidolon."

"Yes, so Kthon wouldn't be able to escape if he ever took over. Kthon won in the end though when he stole my celestial magic as punishment, leaving me without any way to save my family on my own."

"So, your 'anzu' injuries back at Oressa. Were those an eidolon's doing?"

"Some were Sulin. Most were from an owl eidolon, Anemo." Hali spun a ring around her finger; it had a striking resemblance to her original tattoo. A circle with two joined lines. "At least Anemo got to live. I don't want eidolons to die. That's why I changed the designs of the five eidolon runes to need less of their blood."

An owl and a lynx. I see how they got confused for a half-eagle, half-lion. "That ring's new right? Looks like your first tattoo."

"A girl gave it to me back at Oressa. She thought the rune's design was beautiful. Never left me alone until I told her what it did. I left out the gruesome details… all I told her came from old children's stories about binding runes. She wrote a song about it too."

"Charlie?" Alim asked. Allister's daughter had been working at Doctor Shell's office as an engineering assistant, and it didn't surprise Alim in the least that she would pry information from Hali. Nobody could deny her puppy pout.

"The one and only, the engineering bard. When this mess is over, I'd like to see her again." Hali tugged on a curl and let it pop back into her face.

"For sure. Charlie would get a kick out of seeing the three of us together." Alim nearly lost their footing as the blue hills changed to sharp drops. "We're close to Strago."

"Ideas for getting inside?" Hali asked as she slid herself down the less vertical but still steep side of the hill.

"You have invisibility runes, right?"

"Can't get you in that way—those runes only work on the caster."

Alim hopped down, and clouds of ether puffed below to slow their descent. "What we need is a solid distraction. When I was in training here, the whole camp was in disarray one morning with basilisks everywhere. Heard a fresh recruit stole a basilisk egg on a dare." Based on what had happened at Stoneport, the recruit was lucky catoblepones only roamed between the Wastes and Diya.

"Basilisks? You could learn a thing or two from the way a basilisk uses its spark, but I don't think it's a good idea to agitate one on purpose. Much

Chapter 27 Alim

less a whole nest of them. Even if we had Tio to talk to and guide them… we'd be as likely as the Dreamers to get holes punched through us."

"What if I go in and negotiate with Allister? He's usually in Strago this time of year." Alim may not be on the greatest terms with Allister anymore, but they didn't believe Allister was unreasonable. *Unless Sipherra has changed him.* "We trespassed, but Allister knows we had good reason to."

"Allister didn't exactly vouch for us at Gren City, and you said Geno Sipherra holds all the power over the Dreamers now. With the number of mercenaries I saw wearing Sipherra's logo and colors in Oressa, I can't disagree. Unless you think you can negotiate with Geno in the same way, I think your distraction idea is better."

"Fair enough. Geno would sooner run me over with her floating orb," Alim said. *Not sure how often Geno or her loyal employees check in on Dreamer camps.* "What's your suggestion then?"

"Phantoms. Remember Last Stand? Kthon attracts them. Strago is close enough to Phantasmal Reef that we could rile up a whole storm of them."

"How is that not riskier than my basilisk plan?"

"Because the phantoms will only be after me, and I can't die." Hali pulled down her cowl and showed her scarred neck. "Kthon doesn't allow it."

CHAPTER 28

A grimy boot kicked Tio into a cherry-wood cage. They had arrived at the mercenary camp mere moments ago, but the cage was waiting like he'd been expected. *That must be what Osanshia was doing when she rode ahead.*

Sitting in it made Tio uncomfortable. Regular furniture and homes were one thing but using wood for a cage twisted his insides. What if a tree had been killed just to make this? Lived its life, only for its corpse to be fashioned for trapping other living things. *There's plenty of nonliving materials to use. I'm convinced Osanshia killed a tree herself to build this as an insult.* Even if the cage was hundreds of years old and its original tree had died of natural causes, Tio could still be its thousandth prisoner, and that thought made him tremble.

Picking at the cracks in his broken antler, Tio peeled off loose slivers and flicked one between the cage's bars onto the blue grass, a little way short of the snake eidolon. Orbi's pink, scabby skin only had half its scales left, and none had any shimmer. Its face spines and fangs had been broken

Chapter 28 Tio

when it had tried to flee yesterday during a venom extraction. Now dozens of tubes hooked Orbi into a noisy, rotating machine-artifact hybrid.

Whatever the machine was, it had drained Orbi's surge of all its ether and now seemed to be pumping said ether back into Orbi, but Tio didn't know if it was preserving or subduing the snake. Perhaps both, considering eidolons couldn't survive outside surges.

Sorry, Orbi. Yesterday I was useless. If we'd been somewhere my flourish worked, maybe we could have escaped. Tio reached through his cage and connected to an orange marigold. It grew slightly, without needing him to draw blood.

Discovering his flourish worked without injury a couple of days ago would have been celebration worthy if he hadn't been a prisoner. In addition to his enhanced flourish, being outside of Refulgent Wastes had reinvigorated Tio. He felt like he could outlift Alim. But what good would grass, flowers, and vines be against an army?

Tio flicked another antler sliver, this time hitting Orbi's tail. The world became dark and glossy, as if Tio were looking through black glass. *You hanging in over there?* Tio asked Orbi as a weak connection established between the two.

Mortal. Am I alive? Orbi's thoughts had a squirmy, wormish quality as they wriggled into Tio's mind like it were soil.

So long as I breathe, I'll ensure you survive until I can get you back to your surge. Alim can track us. I've been using my flourish every day to make sure my ether stands out for them.

The celestial? Against so many? I accept this. Let me die.

No, that—

Their connection halted early, as if the eidolon had closed itself off from Tio. If Sipherra meant to kill either of them, they would have already.

The caravan of mercenaries expanded tenfold as a team of earth mages lifted Tio's cage towards the hands of a less hefty but still squish-all-humans-sized golem. Bulky steel fingers clasped the cage, carrying him deeper into the ruined city, away from Orbi.

Where there weren't yellow and red tents, golden brick walls were conquered by zigzagging orange marigolds on green vines. Blue overgrowth peeked through cracks. Based on what Alim had told Tio, this was the Dreamers' main camp for expeditions into Refulgent Wastes. In the ruins of Thauma's old capital, Strago.

Being outside Refulgent Wastes proper, this city would have been the least risky for looting and it showed. Only the carcass of a forgotten era remained.

Alim would be providing me all sorts of cultural insight into Strago right now. Tio wanted to be able to stroke his newfound beard and nod along to Alim's ramblings.

Rows of steel golems sat propped against each other like their puppeteers had been too lazy to make them stand on their own. With a camp this huge, the golems must be used for construction, demolition, and hauling their supplies around. There were better, less clunky designs when it came to combat.

I guess I count as supplies right now.

Tio lost his footing and bumped into the wooden bars of his cage as the golem tossed him aside like a boring toy. It fell limp as the puppeteering mages released control.

A wide golden structure stretched as far as he could see to his left and right. It looked like the surrounding ruins, except somebody was taking care of it. Either a perfect replication or refurbishment by an appreciator of Thaumic architecture, with the same pillars, arches, and rounded corners of Stoneport's gemstone buildings. The doors swung open, revealing Osanshia with her looming orange braids and lavender robes.

A guard opened Tio's cage and dragged him out. Not one step had he taken outside before a rock pelted him in the forehead, adding another welt to his collection. Osanshia had been using him as target practice the whole trek.

Chapter 28 Tio

Luckily avoiding his antlers. After the bloody mess Osanshia had made the first time, she probably didn't want Tio to bleed out. It seemed they wanted him alive, but wasn't death the punishment for trespassing in Refulgent Wastes? Tio rubbed his head, wincing with each impact site he grazed.

Geno may want me alive to work on her ether city. But I'm not interested if she's going to destroy surges to make it happen.

Osanshia prodded him into the building with her mace. Dark red carpet led the way through three long halls until Tio arrived in a grand room of shiny obsidian mirrors. At the center of the chamber, Allister leaned forward on an obsidian throne as a bald man with a bushy black mustache whispered in his ear.

Osanshia struck the back of Tio's legs, forcing him to kneel.

The bald man said, "In the Hall of Dreamers, anything is possible. If Allister dreams it, it shall be. Our collective dream shall unite Our Stranded Lands as one Grenvel—"

Allister's gray-streaked blonde hair soared as he pounded a fist into the claw-shaped arm of his throne. "Enough! Tio knows who I am, and as you can see, Dolio, there's nobody here. A formal introduction is unnecessary." He rested his chin against an upraised fist. "Welcome. Did I not warn you against trespassing?"

Tio said, "I—"

"Don't need to speak," Allister finished for him. He brushed the shoulders of his brown trench coat and dusted off his yellow and red tabard as if wiping away Tio's attempt to talk. "You're lucky I got you in here before Geno arrives this afternoon."

"Why, do you plan to set me free?" Tio hacked up a speck of rock no bigger than a grain of sand. *Can't wait to be done with catoblepas dust clogging my lungs.*

"I could be convinced if you worked for me. We have our first schematics for an ether reactor." Allister sifted through documents handed to him by Dolio. "Here's the one."

Dolio delivered a red-tinted paper with white outlines shaped almost exactly like the machine hooked to Orbi.

"How many of these have you built?" Tio asked.

"Address Sir Allister properly." Osanshia smacked Tio upside his head.

"Osanshia, please." Allister's icy blue eyes glowered at her. "Titles have no merit in real conversation."

"Sorry, sir!"

Allister crossed his legs and leaned forward. "The reactor you saw is only a small prototype. A proof of concept if you will. Not to the proper scale we need for a city."

They'll get bigger? This one drank the surge dry. Tio ripped the schematic into shreds.

Amethysts expanded, forming a gauntlet around Osanshia's hand as she backhanded Tio across the jaw. A coppery taste coated his mouth, and his brain rattled.

Allister's gaze shot to Osanshia again. "If you're going to keep interrupting with trivial quibbles, you can leave. You're lucky to be part of Grenvel's leadership. Are you going to let your attitude ruin that?"

Osanshia's face flushed as she stomped out of the room.

Tio rubbed his cheek. "I don't understand… shouldn't you be upset?"

"If you think that was the only copy, you must think us idiots. Second." Allister stepped down from the throne. "Dolio, please make sure our privacy is assured. Lock the palace down."

"Of course, sir." Dolio trotted away like a half-person, half-horse.

If I ever feel weird, I'm going to think about that guy. "So, this is a palace? Fancy throne? Do you think you're some Coveted South king?" Tio's throat tingled, drawing out another ragged cough. His naked wrist called to him as he desperately searched for something to fidget with.

Allister sat at the bottom step. "Princes, not kings. But there is no royalty in the Coveted South. You should read fewer novels and brush up on history."

Chapter 28 Tio

"Same thing, right? Extravagance for the sake of extravagance from the land of infinite technology. Is that not your goal? You've stolen a precious eidolon from its home and then made sure it had no home to return to by destroying it with that reactor. Your technology is an abomination—"

"Tio, sit with me," Allister said with unchanged calm.

"Okay…" *Deep breaths.* Tio settled for pinching the skin of his wrist.

"My goals are not Geno's. I wanted a city, but not if I don't understand the cost. I have no idea what an eidolon is, so you're going to have to explain. Do try to keep your voice down. Dolio can only do so much on his own."

"Why are we being secretive?" Tio asked.

"Few in my company remain loyal to me, I'm afraid. Now, please, catch me up."

After explaining what had happened at Sanctuary, Oressa, and Overlook Falls, Tio was no closer to understanding what was going on in Allister's head. He had as many emotions as a golem. The complete opposite of the melodical Charlie. But he did seem receptive as Tio explained how the eidolons had confirmed the surges were necessary for people to have magic. Without them, everybody would be pallid.

"I've let Sipherra do as they please in my camps for too long. Geno's reactor is not what we planned for. It sounds more like a weapon than an energy reserve." Allister picked up one of the red schematic scraps. "See this part? Our reactors are two-way. Filters the ether and pumps the unusable aftermath back to the surge. This was our original plan."

Ether without its power? What form would that take? "How is that safe?" *And is that what they're doing to Orbi?*

"No tests have been done at scale, but surges reconstitute the ether in a matter of days. We tested this at Sanctuary by restoring its haze barrier."

"You put the ether back in Sanctuary?" *It did seem to recover quickly once Sulin was revived. Recycling ether… could we do something similar with Empyrea?*

"Sustainability is important for my ether city to stand the test of time. Geno was more concerned with transporting ether."

This is not the direction I was expecting this conversation to go. Is Allister really opposing Sipherra? Having Dreamer support would go a long way in ensuring Empyrea's ether isn't stolen by humans anymore. But he hasn't done anything to stop Sipherra.

"As glad as I am to hear you considered the long-term health of what you were doing, how could you let this happen?" Tio took another scrap. "This is clearly meant to store far more ether than is necessary."

And another. "This part ejects consumed ether like you said, but at a rate that would be closer to firing haze barriers out a cannon, endangering everyone and everything around it."

And another. "Don't forget this, which allows ether to be extracted from and injected into living things. Exactly what your 'prototype' is doing to Orbi. How is any of this necessary for your city?"

"I'm not an engineer, Tio. By the time I knew these aspects had been integrated into the reactor's design, Geno Sipherra had already taken my company out from under me." Allister sighed, drooping in his uncomfortable-looking throne. "My city was supposed to tempt Wolloisha and Diya into joining Grenvel. By offering technology the other countries could never dream of achieving on their own, their people would clamor for it. Instead of being stranded neighbors, we would truly be united and live up to the name Our Stranded Lands."

"Noble of you to assume we're not better off separate countries." Tio turned and hacked up gravel. "Do you think Geno would use this reactor as a weapon?"

"Perhaps, but I believe its purpose is for crossing Phantasmal Reef to the Coveted South, though how is unknown to me."

The cannonesque portion of the reactor was large enough for a person or a small golem to walk through. *Fire it to create a long haze-barrier tunnel and have a person walk along it from the inside, protected from the phantasmal*

Chapter 28 Tio

storms. A sufficient enough plan until Sipherra drained enough phantoms from the Reef for it to return to simple water.

"The weaponized aspect is plenty effective as a threat alone. Geno has a meeting in Belsa in less than a week to discuss building our ether city at Spirit Arboretum's western edge. I expect such threats will be made if the Conclave denies her."

Tio stroked his beard. "Geno has no intention of building a city at any surge. Phantasmal Reef is her real target. I haven't pieced together how she's doing it, but the ether reactor will be powered by phantoms." *Nothing in the schematics referenced anything besides ether.* "Belsa has no army or defense—I need to warn them."

Would it even matter? This reactor could level a city Belsa's size and turn it into another Refulgent Wastes.

Allister held painful levels of eye contact. "If you leave tomorrow, you can get there first."

"Wait, are you saying"—Tio turned away to loose another hoarse cough—"you're actually helping me?"

"All I ask is you work with me on my ether city when the time comes—the right way. Let me worry about releasing the eidolon. I can ferry you across the Trachea to Spirit Arboretum, but let's get your cough checked out first. Sounds awful."

"Catoblepas dust."

"Nasty stuff. We have earth mages that specialize in extracting it. Dolio will escort you to our medical building while I make preparations."

"What about Alim?" Tio asked. "They were with me back at Overlook Falls."

Allister locked his hands together. "No word of Alim yet. Without a doubt they're safe. If Alim turns up, I will offer the same refuge." Allister stood and flicked his wrist in a circle. "Dolio?"

Dolio's bald head appeared from behind the throne. "Follow me."

Was he there this whole time?

Arboreal Path

Tio was known for long strides and a fast walking pace, but he had trouble keeping up with Dolio. Was he some sort of champion speed walker? Navigating past the obsidian mirrors, Tio couldn't help but notice how the light of the room bounced between each mirror and Dolio's head in an intense reflection contest.

Back outside the so-called palace, South Lung's crystal-blue water distorted the image of the Lunar Vault. Based on the positioning of the green tear meandering through the sky, winter solstice was less than a month away. Getting to East Peaks alone would eat up most of that time. Much less investigating what happened to Anemo and Sylphine. Was it even possible for Alim to attune to air at this point? And what about Belsa? *Do I really have to choose between Empyrea and my people? Belsa has no chance. We'd have to evacuate, but to where?*

Gray clouds gathered east of Strago as Tio arrived at the southern end with Dolio. *Is a storm coming?* "Dolio, do you think I can get my stuff back?" If it rained, Tio wanted to use the opportunity to finish the book Hali had lent him.

"That can be arranged. Nobody will suspect anything if your pack is delivered here for 'examination.'" Dolio opened the door to a long red gem building. "Right this way."

Most of the medical building's rooms were packed with sick and wounded people. Mercenaries and civilians alike. *This is busier than I expected. Should I help while I'm here?*

At the end of the hall, Dolio led Tio into a room filled with beeping, boxy machines with blinking ethereal lights. A woman wearing an unmarked red coat spun around in her chair. Her face was emaciated, with deep bags under her eyes. A blue ribbon tied her hair into a puffy ponytail.

"Our druid friend here is a friend of Allister. Has an issue with lung dust, and Allister would be most appreciative of your discreet cooperation." Dolio bowed and left the room with a trot.

Chapter 28 Tio

"Oh, druid friends now? Times have changed." Blue scooted towards Tio and placed three fingers against his chest. She raised them slowly, a discomforting burn rising in tandem within Tio's throat, then clenched her hand into a fist, heaving a small cloud through Tio's nostrils.

Tio let out what he hoped was his final cough for the year. "Thanks."

Blue pulled out one of those bitey, scary ethometers from Gren City's checkpoint. "Hold out your arm."

I hate these things. The device bit down, tooting out a musical jingle to make the experience more pleasant as if Tio was a child. And it worked—Tio hummed along.

"Hold on," Blue said as she slotted the device into her big beeping cabinet. "Sorry, Allister hasn't upgraded to the new models with screen readouts." A symphony of whirring, hacking, and pecking made him think the paper was being demolished rather than printed.

Tio stared out the window and watched as the gray clouds whipped into a frenzy. A silver bolt of lightning struck the distant earth. He counted to five before everything in the room quivered with a reverberating grumble. Even his antlers trembled. "What was that?"

"Phantasmal storm. Happens all the time this close to the Reef. Nothing to worry about," Blue said as she ripped a piece of paper from the machine's ejection slot.

Those are phantoms? I assumed "phantasmal storm" was less literal. Tio couldn't tear his eyes away from the clouds as they whirled towards the blue hills with a constant, building roar. Orange dots ripped up from the ground as a tornado touched down, adding colorful flair.

Blue gasped. "How is this possible? You have the ethereal plague?"

The door swung open. "Fascinating news." Geno Sipherra floated into the room on her cushioned orb. "We'll do everything we can for you."

CHAPTER 29

Climbing to the top of an orange crested hill, Alim spotted Strago ruins down in a deep valley. It brought back memories of getting ready for expeditions. Running around camp, collecting food, gear, people, and more food. Yellow and red tents dotted across decrepit buildings and arches overgrown with grass and flowers. Mercenaries and civilians wandered, going about Alim's old daily routines.

Over the past day, Tio's chaotic etheric signature had faded. Now Alim had no idea where he was within the camp, and Hali was off rounding up phantoms at the Reef's edge. Based on the howling tornado forming behind Alim and the gales whipping their helmet with orange petals, they assumed progress was well underway. The plan was to split up since Hali could track the eidolon with her tattoos and Alim could find Tio with ethersight. If their ethersight stopped working, everything would fall apart.

Come on, Tio, give me something to work with. Alim reached into their pack and held on to Tio's antler shard. *Searching the whole camp will take forever, but we'll get you out of here, even if we have to tear Strago to the ground.*

Alim focused their ethersight. There had to be some hint of Tio's whereabouts. A trail of sparkling ether leaked from the antler as it crumbled to dust. The sparkle skimmed down the steep hills, shifting left. Alim rushed after it and hid behind a broken column of gold as Dreamers walked by, chatting about Wilton's solstice festival. As much as they wanted to listen in, Alim kept after the sparkles until they halted at a set of wagon tracks heading further west.

The sparkles lingered on the tracks, where something was lodged in the dirt. Alim dug it out, finding a sliver of bone. The same familiar chaotic ether radiated from it. *Another antler shard.*

Alim repeated their accidental ethersight trick, and the sliver evaporated into a new etheric trail as a thunderous boom rattled Alim's helmet and gray light bathed the camp. *That was closer than the last bolt. Hali's phantoms are getting closer.*

After waiting for a passing golem and its mage puppeteers, Alim crossed the road to the southern district. Peeking from behind a crumbled wall, Alim watched as the trail seeped into the camp's ruby-encrusted medical building. Five Dreamers guarded the inside, based on what Alim could see through the windows.

A gust of gray ether knocked Alim on their back and phantoms soared over them, circling each other in a whirlwind of blue and orange debris. The wails became distant not a moment later as somebody pulled Alim up.

"Dolio?" *What's Allister's assistant doing at the medical building? Wait, I recognize that grass satchel.* Alim grabbed Dolio by the collar. "What've you done with Tio?"

"Nothing." Dolio gently removed Alim's hands and placed Tio's bag into them. "Apologies, Collector Alim."

"Don't call me that. How long have you worked for Allister? No titles." If there was one thing Alim agreed with Allister on, it was how ridiculous titles were. Sir, Dame, Chaser, Collector, whatever. It didn't matter. Besides, Alim had abandoned the artifact-collection life in protest of the exact people who held Tio captive.

"Geno arrived earlier than Allister expected and has taken custody of your friend. Allister is working to extract him. You can meet them at the Trachea tomorrow."

"Tell Allister now's too late to have grown a heart and spine. I'm getting Tio now, or have you not noticed the phantasmal storm?" Alim gestured at what was now three tornados tearing apart Weeping Pass on their way to Strago.

"The disturbance is hard to ignore, Collector, but phantoms cannot enter these Thaumic buildings. They're warded—"

On cue, a new outpouring of gray wind ripped the ruby building's roof off and disintegrated it. People dove out the windows and doors, scattering and shrieking. Dolio wasn't wrong—phantasmal storms had never posed a threat to Strago before. Spooky, sure, but nothing like this. *Hali did say the phantoms would be aggressive, but why are they leaving the people alone?*

Alim unhooked their axe and pushed through the fleeing mob. With careful steps, they broke through the raging gray mist. There were twisted faces in every direction. Breathing felt as if tiny, humid hands were brushing against Alim's innards. Moans of the sick joined the wailing phantoms shredding the building apart. A doctor with gaunt features and a white ponytail funneled the sick into a basement. Alim recognized her from all the training injuries they'd suffered.

"Doctor Hentola? Do you have a druid patient here? Grassy hair, antlers?"

The doctor grabbed Alim and walked them down the basement steps. "So, you're a 'friend' of Allister's as well?"

"They are," Dolio said from behind.

Alim jerked back, gripping their etherite chunk. *He is far too good at sneaking about.*

Chapter 29 Alim

"Your druid friend is in quarantine," Hentola said.

Quarantine? Seems overkill to lock Tio up so securely—the quarantine room's meant for treating the ethereal plague hundreds of years ago. "Is that really necessary? He's not a killer."

Hentola got close and whispered, "His blood tested positive for ethereal plague."

What? How? Could the plague have been hiding in the surges this whole time? Hali cured it though, right? Maybe she could do it again? Or show me how?

"He's under guard, but I can get you through. Follow."

Hentola led Alim and Dolio through corridors packed with red-coated doctors, patients, and murmuring machines. Not a phantom in sight. Not even lingering gray ether. If it weren't for the disturbing clamor upstairs, Alim would think it a normal day. Hali was right—she was the only one the phantoms were after. Two guards with Sipherra-branded red cloths stood at the thick steel quarantine door.

"Doctor Hentola, what's going on up there?" one the guards asked.

"Phantasmal storms. Little more severe than we're used to, so our staff is bringing all the patients down here for safety. Can you let us in to see Patient Zero?"

So diligent. Won't leave even when the world is ending above their heads.

"Protocol says not to let anybody in except you."

Hentola banged on Alim's helmet. "Surely a Collector is worthy of exception."

What? Why would... With an epiphany, Alim grabbed their etherite throwing axe and molded it into a vase. "I discovered this artifact on an expedition into an old Thaumic quarantine zone. We think it can extract and contain the plague. Dolio and Hentola will be assisting me."

Hentola and Dolio nodded along with Alim's thinly veiled fabrication.

"Oh, that helmet! You must be Collector Alim! Heard about you. Your last haul brought peace with Diya. If you think it'll work..." The guard unlatched a series of locks and the door hissed as it cracked open with a blast of citrus.

Alim entered first, finding Tio strapped to a bed, a tube draining small flecks of black-and-white ether from his arm into a strange rotating egg-shaped machine. *Strange color for ether.* Bruises covered his gray freckles and one of his antlers was broken at the tip. *What happened? Who hurt you?*

"This wasn't here when I left," Hentola said, examining the tube. "Doesn't seem to be doing anything."

She can't see the ether? Must be too trivial to show up without ethersight. Alim smacked the machine, hoping it'd crack open like its eggy design implied. "It's siphoning ether from him. How do we turn this thing off?"

"This is one of our prototype reactors." Dolio opened a hidden panel, flipped several switches, and yanked out a cyan wire, discarding it on the steel-paneled floor. The whirring petered out as the reactor stilled and its beeping, flickering lights dimmed. "Collector Alim, did you not retain your basic engineering training?"

"Excuse me, what's basic about this contraption?" *If Dolio's this good with machines, that explains why Allister keeps him around.*

Hentola removed the tube and wrapped Tio's arm with a clean bandage as he groaned, then mumbled and rubbed his eyes.

"Is this what animals hear when you talk? Explains why they can't understand you." Alim lifted Tio off the bed.

Pushing Alim away weakly, Tio said, "No, get away. I have the plague, Alim. Your celestial powers should be strong enough to breach barriers on your own now—fix Empyrea without me."

"Don't be ridiculous. Hali and I aren't leaving without you. She'll teach me to cure you."

"Hali's here?" Tio asked.

"With an army of phantoms, yes."

"You brought this storm?" Hentola asked.

Chapter 29 Alim

"Don't ask how—it's complicated," Alim said. "It was the only way to get Tio out of here. Judge me later."

Dolio pocketed gears and wires from the reactor. "Allister was to extract the druid tomorrow. He's still deliberating with Geno Sipherra, so preparations have yet to be completed."

Alim motioned to the etherite vase with their head. "Hentola, take that. We can convince the guards it worked—"

Metal screeched from above, and steel panels rained with columns of dirt. A flash of orange braids, and Alim's shield unfolded in time to block a flanged mace from hitting Tio. Osanshia kicked the air, and one of the fallen steel panels spun at Alim. They pulled Tio close with one arm and outstretched the other. Ether blended in the air at Alim's command as their veins sloshed and tightened. With a squeeze of their fist, the ether stiffened into a miniature haze barrier with the panel stuck inside it.

Is Osanshia's gift bending metal? Wasn't gemstone control impressive enough? This explains how she became headmaster of an academy and a Gren Consortium member at her age.

Alim set Tio down and unhooked their axe, tapping the amethyst lodged in their helmet. *She's not going to hurt you again, Tio.*

Shield raised, Alim proceeded against a torrent of dirt and metal shards when steel wrapped around their boot. Recalling the etherite vase, Alim caught it and reshaped it into a blade, sawing at the steel. Osanshia stomped, uplifting a panel, and wrapping her weaponless arm with it. Alim dropped the blade and blocked a punch with their shield, but Osanshia's mace struck Alim across the helmet. Loud ringing accompanied the coppery taste of blood in their mouth. Ether burst in Osanshia's face, tossing her into a stripped-clean dirt wall.

Alim finished cutting themself free, sheathed the blade and ran at Osanshia with their battle axe ready. Osanshia slammed a fist into the dirt behind her, crumbled it into a tunnel, and retreated into it. With another haze barrier, Alim stopped her at the tunnel's edge, where it led outdoors to a blue cliff overlooking Phantasmal Reef's blackened waters. Silver bolts of lightning crackled in the sky, and streams of phantoms swirled through the cliffside.

Shoulder-tackling Osanshia against the barrier, the ether shattered, and she tumbled into the flower-covered grass. Alim swung their axe overhead, but it halted as a string of amethysts screamed like a cracking whip and wrenched the weapon from Alim. The earth itself shifted under Alim's feet and flipped them onto their back. Metal crunched. Sharp pain, then nothing but numbness. Blood filled their visor and blocked their blurred vision. The ringing was now earsplitting, overtaking the phantasmal wails.

Struggling to remain conscious, the blood pooling in Alim's helmet boiled, and they grabbed at any ether they could sense. Assembling a cloud of it, they compressed the ether until it exploded. Churning blood evaporated as sparkling pink, green, and purple lights outlined the environment for Alim's ethersight. Alim rolled as Osanshia's revealed outline swung her mace again. They bashed her with their shield, pushing her towards the cliff's edge.

Silver light overwhelmed Alim's ethersight with a loud boom, and Osanshia spun Alim aside. A chaotic green beacon stood behind her as she propelled a pillar of earth underneath Alim and knocked them over the edge and into the Phantasmal Reef.

CHAPTER 30

Invisibility rune fading, Hali bolted across a stone-paved road, stopping behind the rubble of what used to be a Thaumic academy. Her rune book had far more blank pages by this point than she'd planned for, even for Hali's loose definition of plan—which constituted of hurling runic magic at phantoms and running.

It had taken ten different runes to make it this far, and that was only to deal with one phantom at a time. One more barkskin, gaze, wraithstep and invisibility remained.

What happens when the storm catches up to me? Hali found herself wishing a phantasmal storm could outpace Kthon's healing despite knowing full well that wasn't the case. Kthon had kept her alive through drowning in Phantasmal Reef, so a storm would be child's play.

At this proximity, all three of Hali's eidolon-blood tattoos pulsed with blinding colors and crippling intensity.

"What do you mean the druid is quarantined?" somebody asked from within the ruined academy.

"We're following your protocol, Allister, lest the ethereal plague spread," another said.

The plague? Impossible when it's all in me. Unless… did I spread it to Tio somehow? No, Kthon's trapped. Is this some sort of trick to keep Tio captive?

"There is no plague, Geno," Allister said. "Even the most paranoid person in Grenvel knows that. Not a single recorded case after thousands of expeditions into Refulgent Wastes."

"Except we did have one case before today." Thumps from Geno's cane smacking something echoed. "An ethometer detected the plague in Gren City. The day the druid visited. If you wish to dispute the results, feel free to bring it up with Doctor Hentola."

Destroying the ethometer wasn't enough? Does Geno know it was me? Is that why she's been studying runes? Or has she been doing that all along?

Hali peeked over the rubble into the academy's lunch hall. Yellow banners with crescent moons and clouds on one side, red banners with mountainous lines on the other. Workbenches covered in tools and scrap metal replaced the long dining tables, and inactive golems lined the far wall where Hali had once trounced a bully during her elemental tour. Strago was the last stop on the tour, where fledgling mages dueled using everything they'd learned at the other Thaumic cities.

Having assessed where she was, Hali followed the academy's perimeter until her tattoos began to pulse downward. *The labs?*

Suddenly it made sense how Sipherra had made so many advances in technology after becoming involved with the Dreamers. This was where Thauma's Magisters had experimented with creating celestials with ether injections. On student volunteers, of course. Rev had saved Hali from that fate.

"Your request is denied. Neither the druid nor the spirit beast are yours, Allister. I'm much too busy to hear more of your prattling. My guards will escort you to your palace."

Spirit beast… Geno must mean the eidolon.

Chapter 30 Hali

"Get your hands off me," Allister shouted. "This is my camp, Geno. My company."

Yelling came from inside. Clanging weaponry. Windows burst and glass flew over Hali's head. Allister flopped onto the ground, a spear jutting from his leg.

I don't have time to get involved in a company squabble... Hali felt the wind picking up from the incoming tornados, glad phantoms were slow when congealed into a gigantic mass.

"You—" Allister tossed his sword aside and fashioned a flame in his hand. "Here for your friend?"

"You're casual for somebody who just lost his company to a coup and got skewered in the process."

Allister ripped the spear out from his leg and scorched the wound. "Tio's in quarantine on the south side."

Holding her breath from the wretched smell, Hali said, "Alim is handling Tio. I'm here for the eidolon."

"Afraid I'm no help there—Geno wouldn't tell me where it is." Allister grunted as he stood.

"Didn't ask for any. Leave if you don't want to get disemboweled by phantoms." Hali moved away from the building and carved a rune of interconnected swirls, squares, and circles.

Allister limped after her. "Tio told me everything. Allow me to—"

Blood burning, the dirt sank into the depths of the academy as a set of spiraling stairs.

"Witches are good for something after all," Allister whispered in awe.

"Wish I could say the same," Hali said as she descended with Allister trailing behind. "Heard you think my tattoos are... what was the word Charlie used? Ugly."

"And you've only added more it seems."

At the bottom, Hali's makeshift earthen staircase had squashed an alchemy station. She stepped over the broken glass and spilled colorful liquids strewn about the diamond-tile floor. Loose papers on the ground had random shapes scrawled on them—obvious failed attempts at runes. As Hali sifted through, the shapes progressed closer and closer to the binding rune before taking a turn to integrating the binding rune with three other symbols Hali didn't recognize.

Geno tried to recreate my rune? Doesn't look like it worked, but these latest drafts indicate successful trials. Successful at what? Nothing says what it does. Hali stashed the rune documents for further study and left the room.

"How do you know where you're going?" Allister asked while Hali led him through a series of increasingly advanced laboratories.

Hali sighed. "The fewer questions you ask, the happier I'll be, Captain Graverobber." Allister helping Tio hadn't done anything but add perfume to a wet skunk. As far as she was concerned, the Dreamers were still an awful organization for looting Thauma for profit.

In addition to the pounding eidolon-blood tattoos, Hali's binding rune scraped at her insides. *Calm down, Ikazu. Nothing's wrong.*

The next room opened into a vast chamber, where the eidolon was coiled around an etherite rod behind thick glass. Two spinning machines pumped gray ether into its scaleless skin. Hali shed tears at the sight, gripping her dagger. *The disrespect for life. Geno, I hope you're ready. I'm going to repay you in kind.*

Sipherra scientists studied their screens and printed reports without giving Hali a glance.

Allister hobbled ahead of her, loosening a jug from his belt. "Stand back." He tossed the jug into the air, lit both hands ablaze, and concentrated a stream of fire into it.

Combusting, fiery black liquid rained onto the scientists as they finally realized they weren't alone. Their screaming only intensified as phantoms poured in from above, seeping through the vents. Hali opened her rune book to the gaze rune, putting all her hope in the water-sparked basilisk-inspired rune. Feeling as if the blood toll were stabbing her, the air crackled

Chapter 30 Hali

in front of Hali. Sounding off like dozens of popping balloons, an invisible stream of superheated steam pierced the phantasmal clouds and fractured the glass encasing the eidolon.

Hali had hoped it would do more to the glass but was equally relieved it hadn't cut the eidolon in half. A basilisk's spark was one of the most dangerous, being called a death gaze, since people assumed whatever a basilisk looked at would die on the spot. She ran over to the enclosure, jumped, stabbed one dagger into the cracks and twisted. The crack stretched to the floor, where Hali slashed furiously with both blades. But even etherite only scratched it.

A sparkle of ethereal colors within the cracks caught Hali's eye. *Is this... crystallized ether?*

Air shoved Hali against the crystal cage face-first. Her jaw popped as she reached for her rune book again and spun around. There was Geno, sitting in her posh, ridiculous orb, protected by two Dreamers. Hali flipped a dagger, caught it by the blade and flung it at Geno's head.

The dagger stopped short, floating harmlessly as Geno struggled to her feet with her ruby cane. Grabbing the blade, Geno nodded as if approving. "The craftsmanship is top notch. Etherite, is it? Not the strongest material one can create with ether, as you see." Geno tossed the dagger aside as her guards cornered Allister and Hali.

"You are part of the druid's crew, yes? The witch. I must thank you all. Between Tio's thoughtful artifact donation and the weakening haze barrier from whatever you all did in Sanctuary, your group was key to Sipherra's monumental progress this last month. We'll have cities greater than the wildest novelizations of the Coveted South."

Weakening haze barrier—it's my fault? I gave Sipherra what they needed to capture this eidolon?

Geno continued, "Crystallizing ether went from theory to reality. Our reactors are twice as strong as we predicted. Truly a breakthrough. No more thoughts of complicated methods for traversing Phantasmal Reef. Why do

Arboreal Path

that when we can drain the Reef dry and store it in this… eidolon was it? The Coveted South will be rediscovered. No longer will we be stranded."

The clawed Sapper rune glowed as Hali's blood burned, and tendrils of ether funneled into her from Geno's Dreamer guards until they passed out. Thrusting her dagger into the cracked prison again with borrowed might, Hali yanked on the handle as a lever.

Geno threw torrents of air, slamming Hali into the eidolon's prison and whirling her to Geno's orb. "Are you done? You can't break—"

Allister thrust his borrowed spear into Geno's shoulder and lit its wooden shaft aflame. Geno screamed, repelling Allister and his spear with blustery waves.

Hali spat blood in Geno's face and gripped her neck with a shadowy claw from her rune. Then, without a care, Hali eradicated every memory in Geno's mind in order to keep her stunned while Hali guided another shadow to the crystallized ether. Once attached to her dagger, she bent its hilt until it shattered along with the prison wall. Dropping Geno and grabbing her remaining dagger, Hali ran in and sliced each of the tubes attached to the eidolon. Each severed tube flailed and spewed gray-faced mist.

The eidolon squirmed. Struggled. Thrashed! The etherite spines holding the snake to the rod exploded out, destroying what remained of its crystallized prison. Its cat-like eyes shone silver, and puffs of gray ether escaped its nostrils with every breath. A dissonant mix of hissing and wailing escaped its cavernous maw as it slithered forth, battering Hali and Allister aside. Flurries of wind rippled its skin and dangling half-attached fangs and scales until Geno tucked herself in her orb and it closed itself into a protective ball. The eidolon smashed it into the air and swallowed it whole.

Metal grates popped from the vents, and thousands of phantoms whirled in at once, silver lightning dashing between them. Squeezing by the eidolon and Allister, the raging hurricane formed an eye around Hali. One brave phantom among the storm trickled forth and grabbed Hali by the wrist with shriveled, mold-coated fingers; Hali jabbed her blade into its arm, spilling silver juice and spreading the pungent odor of spoiled fruit. Crying and recoiling back into its collective, the phantom's grip left behind burning divots in the same pattern as a peach pit.

The binding rune unleashed black ether and repelled the gray mass. Shadows rose into a writhing humanoid shape with a cycling face. Wooden. Rasal. Rev. Phantom. Owl. Kthon.

Kthon took Anemo? Hali's skin prickled. What did it mean for Kthon to have stolen an eidolon's face?

Phantoms grew closer. Rev-Ikazu darted through the clouds, leaving obliterated silver dust in her wake. The air crackled as a growing silver light filled the room. Ikazu's tether of ether zapped Hali and snapped as the two collided. Memories blasted through Hali's mind faster than she could process as Ikazu dragged Hali by the rune and leaned her against the broken crystalline prison. His face was Rasal's now with a glint of silver where his eyes should be.

Did Ikazu absorb those phantoms? "Ikazu, you have to stop. Kthon already gets stronger with the eidolon blood. Don't give him phantoms to protect me."

Shadowy hands morphed between numerous symbols. "New family. Forget us."

"I'm not forgetting." Hali snatched her peacock-feather cowl and tossed it away. "I won't go through with the resurrection… I'll get Alim to return you to Empyrea…"

Ikazu ripped his head open into a gateway of stars. A flood of silver poured into him, dragging Hali's cowl along with them and disintegrating it.

"Rasal! Rev! Stop!" *If Kthon gets that many phantoms, how am I supposed to stop him without you?* Hali stabbed into her wrist only for white, wood-textured shadows to block every would-be puncture.

Streams of phantoms fought against Ikazu's pull, but none were able to break free of the shadowy vortex. Inundated with silver faces, the shadow warbled as it struggled to match the pace at which the phantoms altered its shape. All the wailing winds ceased, and the unstable shadow dribbled into the binding rune. Hali no longer felt Ikazu's presence within, as if Rev, Rasal, and their spirit ally were in a deep sleep.

Coiled in the corner, the eidolon emitted an aura of gray ether as it approached Hali and filled her view with its silver eyes.

"Celestial, kill me," the eidolon said in her head and ears alike.

Hali wiped her eyes and tear-stained cheeks. "Wh-Why?" *I won't make that mistake a third time.* "My friend can heal you. We can take you back to a surge to recover."

"Eidolons are only eidolons when linked to a spirit, and these mortals severed my link. Forced me to link to phantoms. As I am, I can never link to a spirit again. Even a surge will not give me sufficient ether if I'm not linked."

Linked with phantoms? Hali noticed something carved under the eidolon's chin. The rune Sipherra had designed. *That rune… it stores phantoms? No. It converts the phantoms into ether. There's nothing left of the people afterwards. They're just a power source.*

The eidolon hissed. "Kill me and set me free. Me and all the phantoms infused within."

Set free… such should be the fate of all phantoms. It's what my family wants me to do. Set them free and move on.

Resurrect! Us! Kthon shrieked, louder and clearer than ever.

Tio's gentle face frowned in her mind. *Would he want me to kill this eidolon?* Hali dropped her dagger.

Allister shuffled in front of Hali. "Allow me to do my part." He held up a sword one of the Dreamers had dropped. "Go get Tio. He should still be in the southern end of camp."

"No, I'll do it." Hali stood and the Lux rune's scythe glowed on her left arm. "What's your name, eidolon?"

"Orbi," it whispered in pain.

Chapter 30 Hali

"You will be returned to Empyrea in death, Orbi." Hali gripped the ether within Orbi with her Lux rune, igniting it as if forcing a blood toll. She kneeled, waiting for the delayed combustion. Orbi twitched for mere moments until the spell ran its course and its body calmed.

"Allister, are you familiar with druid burials?"

"Cremation?"

"Prepare the body. Tio will want to give Orbi a ceremony."

Collecting her shattered dagger on the way, Hali climbed out the academy lab in a daze and traversed south to find Alim and Tio. *Is the earth spark gone now, or can Tio bring Orbi back? This was my fault. Sipherra tortured and killed an eidolon because of me. Can Empyrea recover from another devastating ether deficit—*

Far ahead, Tio slammed Alim's axe into a woman with orange braids and knocked her into the azure grass. Sparkling amethysts spilled over the precipice into darkened waters.

Hali ran. *Why does Tio have Alim's axe?* Her chest and legs burned. *Is Alim dead? Is that woman the one who's been tracking them?*

Vines crept up the woman, restraining her, as Tio approached with his cloak billowing in the wind.

Dagger ready, Hali took aim. *I can hit her from here.*

Tio strained to keep the axe aloft as he sank it into the woman's side with a clumsy chop.

Vines ripped. A scream echoed, and the woman tumbled over the edge, dragging the axe with her over the cliff into Phantasmal Reef as Tio crumpled to his knees.

CHAPTER 31

Today was the day Alim would die as Tio's useless bulwark and Hali's feeble student. They might as well have been a paper shield for how well they'd protected Tio and their celestial magic had stood no chance against Osanshia.

With a splash, Alim crashed into the Reef, unable to see anything except distant, flickering silver lights in an empty void. Immobile as they drifted to the bottom of the sea, Alim struggled to get a response from any part of their body.

I can't let this be the end. Tio and Hali still need me. I'm their celestial.

Fingers and toes twitched first, then feeling returned to their limbs. Flailing as they figured out which direction was which, Alim swam upwards.

Ethersight picked up gray ether all around them. Alim burned the blood dripping from their face. But nothing. No ether reacted to their magic.

Am I too weak or is this ether different?

Cuirass and bracers unstrapped, Alim let each piece of armor sink.

Chapter 31 Alim

Shocking pain jolted through their face with every attempt to lift their smashed helmet.

Blood sloshed from under their visor.

The silver lights closed in. Alim inhaled and coughed as they saw upside-down bloated corpse-like phantoms floating around them. Each dangled like fish bait, tied by their feet with ropes of ether to empty depths.

Flailing about as they propelled themself upward, Alim didn't get any further from the drifting moldy faces. Ghastly, agape mouths shone silver spotlights from a mass of intertangled heads soaring between the corpses, nearing Alim with outstretched arms.

Maybe I should have embraced the sun more after all. Will the sun still ferry me to my new life if I die down here?

Lungs clogged. An icy hand grabbed them. Dragged them. Threw them onto warm, dry, and bumpy ground. Cold, moist fingers pried Alim's mouth open and shoved in. Alim coughed uncontrollably, ejecting glowing black water.

Sparkly blue light gathered in a puddle next to Alim instead of soaking into the dirt, forming a familiar face.

Alim wiped their mouth with the back of their hand. "Did you have to stick your dank fingers into my mouth?"

Undine's constellation-like face rippled. "I've been unlinked too long. Direct contact was necessary to remove the water!"

Alim tried to lift their helmet visor again, but each attempt had the same blood-curdling effect as last time. It was jammed in good. "Thanks, puddle." Blood trickled down their face from reagitated wounds.

"I'm only a puddle because I helped this flesh. Give me a hand or I'll die."

How was Undine able to travel this far? *You risked your life for me?* Undine would claim it was in Empyrea's best interest, but it warmed Alim's heart all the same.

Alim dipped a finger into the puddle and Undine wrapped around their arm, absorbing into their skin.

I missed that feeling.

Me too, Undine said.

Splaying out on the cliffside, Alim took sharp breaths until sleep took over.

"This is bad," a chaotic green light said, sounding a day away. "I can't heal this."

"Just be ready on three," an orderly purple light with a black hole in it said. "One... two... three!"

Agony. All encompassing, torturous agony. Overwhelming and inescapable. Alim screamed for longer than they thought possible. Through blurred dots, a blob of purple light appeared holding their demolished helmet.

A soothing, green glow held Alim down. The warmth almost lulled them back to sleep.

The green light shrank and then exploded with fury. "Hali, what were you two thinking?"

Is that Tio?

"That saving you was the right choice?" Hali said with dancing lights.

The warmth of Tio's healing moved along Alim's eyes. "I'm not worth this. You two could have finished without me. And phantoms? Seriously?"

Alim wanted to respond. To tell Tio he was worth everything, but speaking was impossible.

Hali dropped the helmet and helped Tio hold Alim down. "Don't underestimate your importance to others."

"You both could've died." Flesh weaved itself back together on Alim's face as Tio pressed against it. Cheek bones crunched together, reformed. "And for nothing. The plague will finish me regardless."

"Tio, you don't have the plague. Your spark is fully functional, you recognize us, and you're still alive."

"Why would the ethometer detect the plague then?" Tio asked.

Chapter 31 Alim

"I don't know—machines aren't perfect. It was an excuse to experiment on you!"

"At least Sipherra left me intact. Look at this mess, Hali. I can mend Alim's bones and bruises, but this eye is beyond repair. The other?" Tio wiped his brow and choked up. "Alim may never see again."

"Look, you're healing without your bracelet. Your spark is stronger than ever. Alim can be healed…" Hali sounded like she was trying to convince herself more than Tio.

Tio's healing light faded, looking as if he was clasping his wrist. "I don't know how much longer I can go today. I'm already woozy."

Alim's voice returned. "Empyrea needs us."

Tio poked and prodded at Alim's remaining wounds as if adding finishing touches to a disappointing painting. "Our mission is over, Alim. Orbi showed me the East Peaks surge was destroyed. There's no eidolon. No fruit. No spirit."

Destroyed? But didn't Hali mention she didn't kill that eidolon? What happened to it? "We brought back Sulin, Tio. Don't give up."

"Even if the surge is somehow recoverable after this long, we can't get to East Peaks before winter solstice."

"Alim can," Hali said.

"How?" Alim pushed Tio's green light away to see Hali.

"Starportals." Hali wrapped Alim's head with rough, scratchy cloth. "With three attunements you should be able to make one, but you'll need more ambient ether."

Alim heard Tio rustling in his bag. "Iron Swamp has a surge with no barrier. Will that be sufficient?"

"Perfect," Hali said.

Alim sat up, taking in the blurry darkness around them. The only things of substance were still Hali and Tio, except for the mangled gray and black energy pulsing from Phantasmal Reef behind them.

"What happened to Osanshia?" Alim asked.

Arboreal Path

Tio stammered and his light dimmed.

"Swimming with phantoms," Hali said.

Did Tio…?

"I'm sorry," Tio said.

"Never apologize." Hali's light clashed with Tio's. "She got what she deserved."

"Nobody deserves anything." Tio intensified, almost reblinding Alim. "Good, bad, whatever. Things happen to people regardless of deservedness. I'm not sorry for killing her. I'm sorry for everything. This whole mission is a disaster, and I convinced you two to join me."

"Pretty sure you needed convincing first." Alim crawled towards Tio and latched on to him. His light burned Alim as it flared. "We needed you as much as you needed us. Like it or not, we're a family now!"

"A family…" Hali said under her breath with a puff of purple.

"Stop, you're squeezing the life out of me." Tio gently peeled Alim off. "And you're way above the allocated hugs we agreed on. Don't touch me again. For at least a decade."

Alim laughed through piercing pain. "We can still make this happen. Hali's back on the team and we only need one more attunement before I can remove the blockage in the Arboreal Path and take us to the Ethereal Realm."

Cheerfulness entered Tio's speech at last. "I get it—all this positivity is going to kill me worse than your hugs. How's your eye? Can you see?"

Alim waved a hand in front of their face, seeing only a vague distortion with their good eye. "Nope. Not unless you sprinkle a little ether first."

Undine yawned, *Could I help, Alim?*

You tell me.

How much ether does it take for you to see?

If I don't need to see detail, less than my ethersight requires, but more than the air and people have normally. Just enough to make something sparkle.

Use my ether. While we're linked, you can draw upon it as you need. Such trivial amounts won't hurt me, and I'll recharge alongside you in the Path.

Chapter 31 Alim

Alim exhaled, breath as visible as on a freezing winter day. Star-like sparkles clung to the ground and everything in-between like a glitter bomb had exploded. "Never mind—Undine solved it. Can we go now? I'm kind of sick of Strago and don't want to be here when Sipherra does clean-up."

"You're alive!" a shiny Allister-shaped constellation shouted as he limped through a cloud of Alim-breath. "Sipherra won't bother you. They'll be too busy picking a successor. One I can deal with easier, if I can help it."

Geno is dead too? "Won't Sipherra question why their president died in a Dreamer camp?"

"Ether experiments are dangerous," Allister said. "As far as the public is concerned, Geno brought the phantasmal storm upon herself and destroyed our labs."

"Won't Sipherra pick Geno's son?" Alim asked.

"Geno was a visionary prodigy. Her son, not so much. The vote will be contentious."

"Why not take the Dreamers back and disband Sipherra?" Alim asked.

"For what it's worth—and I know you don't trust me—Sipherra learned more from Thauma's ruins than we Dreamers ever did. Together the companies can do more good."

Of course I don't trust you. How many times did I warn you not to work with Sipherra?

"Ether technology can't continue," Tio said. "Not without significant guidance and restrictions. Current designs need to be abandoned. Start from scratch with Empyrea in mind. I know ether experts are rare, especially in Grenvel, but this is an opportunity to work together with the other countries of Our Stranded Lands."

"A unified effort to construct an ether city with safe technology? I'll take your suggestion to heart. This whole ordeal has been more than enough to convince me there's more to druids' Empyrea." Allister held a hand against his heart. "When Gren Consortium next meets, we'll be filling three seats. A replacement for the merchants, a reinstated seat for druids, and the last"—he bowed to Tio—"if you would be a part of our journey to better Our Stranded Lands, I would have you take a seat as our advisor on Empyrea and ether."

"There won't be an Empyrea if we don't succeed," Hali said.

Yes! Hali's on board!

Tio's light fluctuated in intensity with erratic patterns. "When this is over, I'll suggest somebody better suited than me for the seat."

"I hope you'll reconsider." Allister crouched and lifted something. "Your helmet… Alim, I'll have it repaired for you."

"No need." Alim took the crumpled chunk of metal. "It's fine as it is."

Hali thumped the ground with her boot. "Time's short, remember?"

Allister snapped his fingers. "Dolio will escort you through Strago."

"Yes, of course," somebody said loudly as if they were right next to Alim's ear.

Alim instinctively grabbed for an axe that wasn't there before realizing it was just Dolio. *Did he somehow get by all my ether clouds untouched? Too sneaky…*

"These belong to you." Dolio had two glowing silver urns tucked under his arms.

Eidolon ashes. Sanctuary all over again. Tio and Hali grabbed one urn each, and their burning auras became waning candles. How quickly would Empyrea fall with two more eidolons dead? The nature gift had only lasted this long because its spirit lived on in Undine. *Maybe Tio was right. This was a disaster. Some celestial I turned out to be.*

CHAPTER 32

Hidden frogs serenaded each other as the sweet smell of mangos wafted by a yawning Tio. With no trees in sight, it was like the ether itself were scented.

Gray iron ore deposits jutted from the morass, looming over Tio and reminding him of his destined profession sans flourish. The sides had been mined out, like a giant, starving Alim had walked up and taken a bite. From the hunger-rumbles coming from Alim's direction, Tio presumed that may become reality soon.

"Do you need a break, Alim?" Tio asked as he scooped a frog from the muck.

"Shouldn't I be asking you that?" Alim tapped their short hair, bouncing a finger between silky black braids. The lack of fancy helmet and the sleeveless, loose yellow shirt might have made Alim seem meek if it weren't for their ridiculous physique.

Hali meddled with Alim's hair. "You sure you don't want me to braid the other side of your head too?"

"I like it better this way," Alim said, tugging shaggy strands of hair on the unbraided side down to their lips as if to gauge its length.

"Tio, what's that pink glob you have?" Alim asked.

The frog hopped onto Tio's head and climbed his antlers like a tree.

"This little pal?" Tio plucked the decidedly-not-pink frog from his broken antler and set it in Alim's hand.

Alim recoiled, dropping the frog into muddy blue grass. "Sorry… wasn't expecting something alive. Or slimy."

"Wait, you couldn't tell what it was?" Tio found it difficult to remember Alim's blindness with how they stomped around so confident.

Alim had mentioned that ethersight outlined everything but only used a description like glob for Tio and Hali—though with more pleasant phrasing.

"Maybe it's the ambient ether overwhelming my senses."

It was faint, but there was a swirl of the usual colorful haze in the air. Did such little ether really overwhelm Alim? Tio had expected barrierless surges to be denser. Was there even enough ether here to open a starportal?

Tio stepped over a pool of bubbling mud to a small, grassy blue mound and watched Hali and Alim finish setting up.

Hali forced Alim's arms and legs into different positions. "Gather the ether. When enough converges, the energy will collapse in on itself and explode, spreading back out. You have to catch it when it's collapsed and create a doorway before the ether disperses."

"A doorway?" Alim's bushy brows shot up in confusion.

"In both a visual and functional sense. It's like shaping a big rectangular tunnel to the Arboreal Path. Empyrea's roots are all connected, so once inside, follow them and you'll find your way to the other surges easily. Haze barriers have the brightest trails."

"And I can take you two with me?" Alim asked.

Hali poked Alim in the forehead. "Not unless you want us to come out the other side in noodly strands. Let's wait until you have your final attunement and a lot more experience before attempting that, you know?"

Chapter 32 Tio

"So, Alim is on their own? We just got the gang back together…" Tio twirled a finger in the air, wrapping it in the wispy ether. "How will they get back to us?"

"Etheric signatures," Alim said under their breath. "Your distinct energy will lead the way no matter where you go."

Hali punched Alim's shoulder. "Well done."

Tio retrieved one of Empyrea's remaining seeds. "Take this. Just in case."

"Seriously? I don't have your gift. How am I supposed to grow it?"

"If Orbi was right, there's no surge there and no eidolon to bury with the seed. Don't worry about rushing its growth. This seed… this is an experiment. To see if we can replace a destroyed surge. We can do the same at Overlook Plateau if this works."

"That won't help us heal Empyrea in the here and now," Alim said.

"I'm working on that," Hali said. "Remember the runes I was developing to free my family? One is meant for short-range teleportation. With some tweaks, it may be able to reach the Ethereal Realm from inside Arboreal Path."

"No special blood required?" Alim asked.

Special blood?

Hali gave Tio a gloomy glance. "I hope not."

"Am I missing something?" Tio asked.

"Tio, I owe you an explanation about my runes after Alim's training."

"Okay, way to make it sound ominous." Tio scratched his mud-encrusted beard. "I need to study everything we've found and prepare for my meeting with the Conclave." Belsa was safe with Geno gone, but Tio wanted to give Orbi's ashes to the Conclave before leaving for the Ethereal Realm.

Alim laughed. "Gonna look over your well-documented notes?"

"Not a fan of cat drawings?"

Hali motioned for Tio to give Alim space. "Ready to give starportals a shot?"

"Before you go, let's complete your new look." Tio tied one of Alim's cleaned-up yellow cloths around their bandaged eye. "Now you're stylish."

"Yours is the last word I trust on style. Is this my Dreamer cloth?"

"What else would it be? Don't worry, between the bandages and the cloth, nobody can see your pretty face."

"Good. Mangled as it is, people might projectile vomit on sight."

Mangled or not, Alim had no reason to hide their face. It was androgynous, but tough. Tio only wished he'd been able to see Alim's eyes unobstructed by their visor before. But that didn't stop him from poking fun. "People didn't before?"

Alim forced Tio out of the practice area. "I'm going to enjoy my Tio-free East Peaks vacation."

Three spiraling pillars of ether surrounded Alim—one of each ethereal color, alternating in time with Alim's dance-like stomps and square arm movements. The tops of each pillar simultaneously assaulted the pool of mud with sparkling energy, erupting into an intricate translucent gate. At moments, the gate appeared solid. Tangible. At others, it flickered, barely distinguishable from the swamp behind it. It reminded Tio of the Lunar Vault.

Birds with glinting metal wings soared through the fading gate and over Alim's head, unfazed by the phenomenon.

Fiery veins snaked up from Alim's neck to their face as ether wrapped their hand, touching the misty gate. A shockwave repelled Alim and the gate imploded.

Hali caught Alim and set them down. "See, you're not so heavy without all that armor."

"I might as well be naked. As soon as we get to a blacksmith, I'll be even more armored than before." Alim straightened their shirt and squished a boot into damp grass. "Sorry to be a disappointment. Hali, you weren't wrong about the blood toll. I can't try that again…"

Maybe this was too much to ask of them, but what do we do if Alim can't open a starportal?

CHAPTER 33

Another shockwave rippled the etheric clouds of Iron Swamp as the starportal exploded. Half a day of attempts had left Alim sprawled in the mud, trounced by endless recharging and expensive blood tolls. No subsequent starportal had come as close to opening as the first.

"This is impossible. Sorry I'm such a disappointment," Alim said.

Hali winced like Alim's words stung her. "Don't be so hard on yourself. Couldn't have asked for a more marvelous first day. We'll make a celestial of you yet! Tomorrow, I'll try supplementing your power with runes."

Undine's chilling waters surged through Alim and soothed the aching.

"Right." Tremors bounced throughout Alim as their body melted into a cloud of ether, funneling into the indent left behind by the gate's shockwave.

The Path's constellations appeared, coating the milky coffee swirls of its sky as winding roots grew underneath Alim.

Come with me, Undine said.

A little warning next time? What did you do?

We're walking the Path, together. Well, I'm walking it and you're tagging along. Think of it as a reverse of our normal flesh-spirit relationship.

Watery hands waved at Alim, and they realized they were seeing through Undine's eyes. Disembodied and without control like in a dream. *Does this mean I can take a nap?*

You've earned one.

Down the Path's last dimmed road, the earthen spirit crouched and stared into the darkness. Nomine lived! Hali had mentioned Orbi's link had been cut. Did that mean spirits didn't share their eidolon's fate if there was no link? Nomine's outer rocks looked to be shaved down, revealing coppery and pearlescent layers.

Undine sat next to Nomine. "You mapped the way to Sylphine, right? Can you take us?"

Spirit names never failed to entertain Alim. *Lung spirit? Pebble spirit? Who came up with that naming convention?*

Ine doesn't mean spirit, Undine told them. *Not in our language. It's closer to "celestial child" to denote our birthtree, Empyrea.*

It's a family name then? One day you have to tell me more about the other spirit trees.

Nomine grumbled like rocks rubbing together.

"Stop apologizing for that. I didn't think the poison in your tea would be so strong either. Or that Alim wouldn't be able to detect it."

He continued grumbling and tiny landslides leaked from his eyes.

Nomine wants you to know he's sorry. We went into the Path to look for you, but you were already gone by the time we got here.

Apology accepted, though I'm holding out hope this last fruit will take it easy on me. If there is another fruit.

Nomine raised a hand to a set of unlit stars, and roots sprouted, twisting themselves into a new road to a shadowed section of the Path. A gloom radiated from it like the Path's blocked road to the Ethereal Realm.

Not bright like Hali had said. Did that mean the surge really was gone? Even the roots were dim by comparison. Undine walked for what seemed like no time at all before Nomine halted and pulled a thread of ether, ripping open a rectangular doorway of glittering stars.

This is a starportal?

"Thank you, Nomine," Undine said. *He can't join us. There's no surge, no eidolon. Nothing to sustain him. And if Sylphine is still alive somehow, we don't need the two of them competing for what little ether is left in there.*

The earth spirit returned to his somber crouching at the gateway to East Peaks. Alim convulsed within Undine as she stepped through the starportal and their shared body became etheric mist once again.

CHAPTER 34

The scent of freshly baked pita bread drifted across town. Alim would kill Hali if they found out how many sweets she'd declined. Especially the layered pastries filled with nuts, drizzled with sugar syrup. An Ahsiem staple. No doubt Alim loved the stuff… best not to mention it. Tio had wanted to keep some for Alim, but there was no way the dessert would last.

Alim had already been gone for days. Spirits didn't have the same instantaneous teleportation as a celestial's starportal, but this was taking longer than Hali had expected. *Stay safe, Alim.*

Tio pulled out a sealed letter and whistled to the two metal-winged birds slinging mud to search for dinner. One of them craned its long neck, staring at Tio with the front half of a toad dangling from its hooked beak. Unkempt, bristly silver eyebrows of metal twitched as it gaped its beak open and let the toad free.

It waddled over to Tio, chattering.

"Please fly this letter to Belsa." Tio threw down seeds he'd been collecting from the swamp as if in payment.

Pecking at the bounty, the stymphal gave a noisy reply.

"The green ribbon on your leg says otherwise." Tio pointed above its talon. Hali had seen it before. Rev had said it was a symbol of druidic friendship.

The stymphal squawked, pelting Tio in the face with his own seeds.

With flecks of gold in its head feathers, almost like a crown, the second bird hopped over with tame chirps.

Tio bowed. "Thank you!" He tied the letter around the stymphal's leg with stringy grass. As it soared north, its friend scooped up the last of the seeds and hopped back to its mud pile.

"Stymphals," Tio sighed. "First animals I ever tried to talk to when I was growing up here. Always irritable about something."

"Was that necessary?" Hali asked. "Belsa is only a week or so away."

"I wanted to let my familiar know I'm coming home."

"Seriously? You truly are a druid."

"Is that bad?"

"Not bad. Nostalgic…" Rev had been similarly attached to her giant eagle. She'd spent a week chasing after it through the South's mesas along the Great Haze. Just to say hello. Ever since, the two had been inseparable.

Hali and Tio continued through cracked brown streets lined with towering structures of dried, pale mud bricks. The same blazing-sun imagery from Alim's breastplate was plastered everywhere alongside diminutive approximations of sunbathing basilisks. Being adopted into Wolloisha after Thauma fell, people were far more accepting of Solstoran beliefs here. They weren't as widespread as in the desert but still quite popular. The only clue to Ahsiem's Thaumic history at this point was the symbols carved into their doors to ward off evil. It was a tradition going back to the Old Faith, and they weren't too far off since they were actually runes capable of creating thresholds phantoms couldn't pass. At least, not in small volumes. Hali's phantasmal storm stunt in Strago had proved there was a limit to what warding runes could handle.

Every twenty paces or so a sun marked resting areas along a glittering gold wall where people mingled, had picnics, and worshiped. Ahsiem's prayer wall was quaint compared to the ten-story glory of Pinpin's, but it had its own charm. Would Alim pray if they were here? As unreligious as Alim seemed, they struck Hali as the type to get a decade's worth of prayer in all at once just in case.

Tio ran ahead from vendor to vendor and purchased more food than he could carry. This was the most enthusiastic Hali had ever seen him, though he would act like he wasn't having a good time if she brought it up, so she kept it to herself.

"Slow down!" A cool breeze sent a shiver up Hali's arms as she caught up to the energetic druid. A new jacket would be nice—she'd have to keep an eye out while in town.

"Sorry. It's been a while since I've had Wolloishan food. I'm stocking up on the best stuff, so Alim can try too!" Tio's bushy beard almost hid his smile.

"Somebody's homesick."

Homesick. Take me home. The whispers were louder than Tio now. Ikazu's presence was still non-existent after protecting Hali from the phantasmal storm. She was alone with Kthon now.

"Belsa is my home. There's nothing to miss about Ahsiem," Tio said.

"Besides the food apparently. It's okay to be nostalgic for your birthplace, you know? Don't you have family here?"

"No. My family ditched after I left." Tio ripped a small piece of pita, dipped it into a pile of hummus, and devoured it with the same audible chomp Alim always did. He closed his eyes and rubbed his belly like them too, completing the Alim-like eating experience.

"Why's that?" Hali asked.

"Mom became a Solstoran priest around the time I left for Belsa. Dad moved with her. He was always disappointed I wasn't born a water mage anyway."

Chapter 34 Hali

In Wolloisha's desert, having a water spark was like being born strapped with gold bars. Even when Ahsiem was Thaumic territory, water mages would seek riches in Wolloisha's desert by helping the oasis grow. But druids could help an oasis just the same, so why would he be disappointed with Tio?

"Surely nature is more valuable than water," Hali said.

Tio dismissed her with a shrug. "My flourish didn't manifest until much later. Probably thought I was a dud. I wouldn't have been happy at an oasis anyway. No more than I would have been hacking away at iron."

"Did you not have friends here?"

"Have you met me? Of course not."

Fair.

"How about you? Do you ever miss Thauma?" Tio asked.

"Every day. But it's my family I miss the most. I'll never forget them."

"Sorry, I should have thought—" Tio pinched his wrist and squinted at Hali's rune. "We'll defeat Kthon and set them free."

Shadows erratically bent around Hali as if the sun were doing laps around the world. "If you knew half of what I've done for them, you would hate me."

"Hali, don't be silly." Tio stroked his green beard. "I hate all people."

"Didn't that line get you in trouble the last time you used it?" Hali squeezed the pierced sun of the Lux rune on her arm as its splatters of purple ink lost ground to green. "This rune. And the other two. They're made with eidolon blood."

"Then you"—Tio inhaled slowly—"you killed Sulin and Anemo?"

"And Zergi. There's no excuse. There's nothing I can do to make things right. I did it for my family, but all I accomplished is adding to Kthon's collection. Anemo is trapped with my family and thousands of phantoms from the storm at Strago."

"I understand." Tio shrugged. "I took a life for Alim. I've disregarded laws for Empyrea."

Nonchalant as always. "That's not the same scale, Tio, and I'm not sure you comprehend. Empyrea is dying because of me. Your whole journey is only necessary because I brought Kthon into Zergi's surge, and I've done nothing but hinder you."

"Am I supposed to treat you differently because you made mistakes? You're back. That's enough, right?"

"Does anything worry you? Besides people."

"Healing Empyrea. And Alim's been gone so long. What if they can't get another fruit and can't learn to open starportals before the solstice?"

"I'm sure Alim found something and is only taking time to recharge their ether," Hali said. "But if Alim comes back unable to make starportals, using my teleportation rune to bypass the Path's blockage is still our backup plan. The redesign is trickier than expected though." *The original requires eidolon blood—I have to adapt it to accept ether provided by Alim.*

Tio looked away. "Wait. Let's check out that shop." He pointed at a wagon with an odd, but familiar, carving on it. It looked like bunny ears swirling with ether. *Have I seen that logo before?*

A hulking old logu with tall ears and a rain-catching hat hauled a large crate of ore into the back of the wagon. Was he the same merchant Hali had put to sleep at Tovaloreande Sanctuary? Must be. How many traveling logu merchants existed outside Diya?

"Tio? It's good to see you, kid!" the logu said. His wagon nearly lifted off the ground when he sprang down.

"You recognized me, Barbaroli?"

"What, thought a beard and antlers would throw me off?"

Tio's cloak had seen better days, but between it and his green hair, nobody could mistake him. His eidolon-gifted gray freckles, vines, and antlers only made him stick out more. He probably hated how recognizable he was.

"Say, could you take us to Belsa? The Conclave will compensate you."

Barbaroli glanced at Hali with recognition before returning his gaze to Tio. "Not a problem at all! I was about ready to head in that direction.

Chapter 34 Hali

Wilton should be bursting at the seams with potential customers at this point. Put up your things. We can leave before noon. Is it just the two of you? Where's Alim?"

"Just us. This is Hali." Tio set his grass satchel into the back of the wagon. "Alim is investigating the last surge on their own. It's a lot to explain." Tio hopped onto the front with a book in hand.

Barbaroli waved at Hali. "Mighty coincidence seeing you again. And with my good friend Tio to boot!"

Hali played with her ring. "Thank you for giving us a ride." Rest sounded nice after traveling on foot for so long.

"It's like I was telling you before, Hali. The Pensa family always helps those in need. Even when it's not appreciated."

"I never thanked you..." Hali had been much too thorough considering how nicely Barbaroli was treating her. *Using both Sapper and nightmare runes was overkill.*

"No need. The deed is its own reward, is it not? The refreshing two-minute nap you gave me was thanks enough."

How did he know I cast a spell on him? And two minutes? Do logu have resistance to magic?

Barbaroli let out a bellowing laugh and climbed onto the wagon next to Tio. "Now, Tio, tell me all about your adventure! I need to know how lucrative this book deal is going to be."

Resurrect! Us! Kthon shouted in Hali's ear with thousands of voices.

Hali's runes burned black as she pushed against the shadow spirit's creeping thoughts. *I can't contain Kthon through to the solstice. Not without Ikazu. And Alim's not ready to face Kthon. I need...* The tattoos pulsed north to Spirit Arboretum. *I need Vinn's eidolon blood.*

CHAPTER 35

The earth shifted, splitting into a small geyser, and spouted a dense fog of Alim-Undine essence skyward. The fog mingled with falling snow as the last of it spewed out. A resting anzu lifted its lionesque head and yawned, spreading out its eagle wings. Several more ether geysers formed and whistled as they released more colorful fog. The anzu yawned and summoned two miniature tornados with its breath. Wind churned from the beating of its wings as it lifted off and soared away. Alim's head pounded as their ether turned to flesh.

Let's not make a trip like that ever again, Alim said as they patted themself everywhere and cherished having a body.

It worked, didn't it? Undine swished in their head with bubbling heat, warding off the mountain's freezing air.

Debatable. How can I be sure you put all my parts back where you found them?

You'll forget any of those parts existed before you know it.

Comforting.

Snow up to their thighs, Alim shivered, their teeth chattering despite Undine's effort to keep them warm. Aches ran through their wounded eye with each touch of the chilly breeze. It made them desperate to peel their cloth and bandage back and itch to their heart's content.

Surrounded by innumerable white-crowned mountains, Alim knew Yinsen caverns must be underneath them. Weren't they supposed to be inside the cave? Had Undine missed the mark?

I never miss my mark.

Please don't read my thoughts. I'd prefer to judge you in peace.

This flesh should learn to control thoughts better.

For the record, I didn't miss you.

Liar.

Ahead, a large hole in the mountain path led into the caverns, with singed tree roots running over the lip. Alim shuffled snow aside to reveal a patch of dirt, molded their etherite into a shovel, and dug. Empyrea's flickering seed in hand, they felt the crushing responsibility it represented. Without the seeds, there were no surges. Without surges, there were no gifts. A headache developed just thinking about it.

A stiff breeze flaked ether from the seed, drifting into the caves. Alim gently set it onto the soil. The seed's dimming ether became blinding for a single moment then crumbled as wind stole its remains, scattering them into the depths. *What made it rot? Was I too slow? The world is going to be magicless…*

The last trail of light twirled in front of Alim. It drew a symbol in the air before whistling towards the caverns.

Undine's comforting sauna turned to boiling soup. *It says follow.*

Alim secured a length of rope and lowered themself to the melted rock floor. A rune was carved near exploded stone. *Hali really was here. But if the eidolon survived its encounter with her, what happened?*

At the colorful light's end, a cracked sphere awaited, oozing with black pus. *Sylphine! It's her core. Please help her,* Undine said.

Alim's blood swished as they grabbed the seed's ethereal light and guided it into the sphere's cracks. The secreting black energy dispersed, and the light disappeared. The image of a root-entwined owl filled Alim's mind as the ground rumbled and a gale pushed against Alim. A little girl composed of raging typhoons appeared before them, missing both legs and with one of her arms mangled.

"What happened to you?" Alim asked.

The wind spirit held her head with her good arm while her other limbs expelled turbulent energy. "Can't remember… broken."

Just like Vulkine. "Undine is with me. We'll help you."

"Who's Undine?" Sylphine asked as the core sucked her back in, cracks spreading.

Undine chilled Alim's blood. *She's worse than Vulkine. Sylphine doesn't have long.*

Can't we do something?

Yes. Undine deconstructed Alim into ether and brought them into the Path.

Nomine stared at the core in Undine's grasp and his rocky jaw creaked.

"Please, do for Sylphine what I did for Dryadine. We must keep Empyrea whole so Alim can open the way to the Ethereal Realm."

Thundering bellows reverberated across the Path. Nomine held Sylphine's core and crushed it against his chest. Ether seeped into him and formed a beating, pink sphere that shone through the cracks of his craggy body. Nomine walked into the unlit road and raised his arms wide in the air as Alim did when recharging. Brilliance and glitter returned as Nomine broke apart, dissolving into the Path's roots.

Undine, explain.

You're witness to the linking of spirit and eidolon.

Another deconstruction and reconstruction, and musky, metallic gasses nipped at Alim's lungs. Iron Swamp? A mountainous pile of pink hopped around Nomine. Focusing their ethersight, Alim saw details

Chapter 35 Alim

carved into the light. It was the eidolon—an absolute behemoth of a frog. Little trees dotted its back with a deceptively strong, sweet mango aroma.

"We've met before. You were... smaller." *Tio held this eidolon in his hands and thought nothing of it. Unlinked eidolons just wander around on their own as normal animals?* Alim extended a hand as if frogs gave handshakes. "I'm Alim."

A sticky, slimy tongue slapped Alim's hand. "Prithvi. A pleasure to meet a celestial for once. I'm the only eidolon to never see one of the prior two!"

Nomine rumbled and pointed to Alim's sheathed etherite.

Jingling like ice, Undine said, *Nomine is asking you to create etherite.*

"A trial?" Alim asked. "Do we really have time for that?"

The earth spirit denied Alim with a shake and gestured a weird figure with his hands. An axe?

Undine said, *You've more than proven yourself as a celestial. This is to replace your weapon.*

"A new axe? Yeah, this chunk is too small to make a weapon big enough for my tastes. Let's fix that," Alim said. *Now how do I do this?*

Hali had given them some pointers on the trip to Iron Swamp. Something about layers, but that only made them think of cake. Alim's veins twitched as ether piled in front of them. Instead of growing taller or wider, the haze remained in the same spot as more ether was added. As if it had endless capacity. Sweat dripped onto the mist and bounced off as if it were water repellant.

Did I create a haze barrier? Alim gave the pile a couple of smacks. Rock solid. *Do I just.... keep going?*

Blood sloshed in Alim's shoulders as if Undine had shrugged from within.

I wasn't asking you.

Ether thickened. Took on a metallic sheen. The pressure felt like their arms might blow off as they smashed the concoction into a condensed

Arboreal Path

block. Alim stuck their hand against it and loosened the etherite. Metal coiled around their forearm like a color-shifting spiral bangle with five loops.

Prithvi's tongue shot up to a tree on its back and shook a mango free. Nomine handed the fruit to Alim and nodded.

"Eat," Prithvi said.

"Thank you." Alim bowed their head.

Wood creaked as Prithvi griped. "We do this for our own preservation. Our greed requires no thanks."

Ornery, eh? "Doing something for yourself isn't automatically a greedy choice." *Right, Tio?* "I'm eating this fruit to give myself the ultimate magic after all."

Legs crossed, Alim hyped themself up by patting their cheeks. *I made it. This is happening. Somehow, I'm holding the last spirit fruit. Will unlocking all this celestial magic change me? I hope I change for the better.*

One bite was enough. Before Alim even had a chance to notice the hurricane raging in their blood, they found themself standing in an unending darkness—back in the Path, but in their own body, with no Undine coursing through their veins.

A twisting set of pink stars blazed in tornado arrangement among the white-stained brown sky among the other elements, and more stars than ever snaked up the green constellation's cloudy top—it looked like an upside-down tree now.

The Path completed, all roads shimmered with the three ethereal colors. All except one—the road to the abyss blocking the Ethereal Realm. With the Path complete, the abyssal road now ended in a door of wavering black ether.

I did it. I really did it.

Alim walked slowly to the door. *No more pallids. Druids will return. Mages won't die out. Hali's family will be free.*

Alim reached out, but the door's ether did nothing. *I can't control it? Maybe with direct contact…*

Chapter 35 Alim

Ether refused Alim's call again as they pressed both hands against the door. They sat and ran fingers through the unbraided side of their hair. *I'm missing something, but what?*

A wobbly voice called out from the other side. "My celestial."

I'm not alone? I didn't recognize the voice. Is another spirit here? "Who's there?"

No response. Alim tapped their braids. *Oh! I can't manipulate ether that's been controlled by another. Did somebody else put this here? The mystery spirit, maybe. If adding my own ether makes etherite more malleable, could I repeat that process here?*

Alim raised both arms high, gathering ether from each of the constellations. Blue whirlpool. Orange flame. Amber mountain. Pink tornado. Green tree. As the five colors of mist cycloned around Alim, purple ether leaked through the doorway and joined the party. Alim planted five fingers on the door and funneled the whirlpool's ether, adding a splotch of blue to the blackened door. With each successive color, the splotch grew brighter, until it was a gleaming star. Grasping the star, Alim twisted it like a doorknob, and the door swung open. Lavender fog flooded the Arboreal Path, obscuring the elemental constellations.

Inside, Alim saw the mystery spirit. Or half its core, at least. Remnants of purple ether clung to the halved sphere. The etheric signature… Hali had the same one. *No, it's the hole in Hali's signature. Wait, Kthon? Is this Kthon's core?* Alim reached out to grab it, but the door slammed shut as a stinging, icy pressure whacked their cheeks.

"Wake up!"

Who?

The Path's road cracked. A flash of blue, and Undine stood over Alim, repeatedly slapping them and splashing droplets of blue light.

"Stop. Stop! What's going on?" Alim shoved Undine off. "I was about to unblock the Path."

"The Keeper is in danger!"

Empyrea and the Path will have to wait then. "Take us to him!"

"I can't—he's not in a surge. You have to use a starportal."

Alim gave Undine their hand and absorbed her. *Time for teleportation attempt number two. No messing up this time.*

Alim's arm veins bulged as they gathered the Path's abundant ether. Their face flushed red, the colorful haze building until the air itself became scarred. Tearing the scar open, a jagged gateway to emptiness awaited. Alim focused on Tio's chaotic aura, stepped through, and the scar closed behind them.

CHAPTER 36

None of the Conclave elders had ever been so quiet. All three hung on Tio's every word. Pai kept stroking his teal-speckled white beard, making Tio miss his own—scratching a bare chin wasn't nearly as satisfying, while Ren repeatedly jumped out of her chair, almost ripping out her green fishtail braid in frustration. Bel only muttered to herself and wrote into an organized notebook.

At the end of it all, Tio placed two ornate golden urns on the square meeting table alongside the jewelry box with Empyrea's seeds. Opening the box to reveal the dimming seeds, Tio slid one to Bel. "Orbi should be buried at its home under Overlook Plateau. Allister gave permission to enter Refulgent Wastes to do so."

Tio dug through his satchel, pulling out a letter with Allister's cloud-and-crescent seal.

Ren bowed. "I'll perform the burial ceremony personally." Her volunteering was expected since she managed New Fion—Belsa's animal conservatory in Spirit Arboretum.

Arboreal Path

"So, the final piece. When my friend returns, we're going to find Empyrea and heal it. One way or another. I don't plan on returning until—"

Tio fell out of his chair and his coffee spilled as the Conclave's redwood meeting tree shook. Creaked. Tilted. Grabbing on to the leg of one of the attached seats, Tio swung between chairs as if they were monkey bars while the elders created and landed on ledges in the tree's inner walls. His flourish connected to the tree, asking for a bridge to the room's exit. Bark stretched under Tio and he fell onto it and bolted through the leaning door, finding the redwood had been cut at its base. Tiny druids halted the lean with their flourishes as Tio stretched his shoulder vines down his arm and slung them across a branch, lowering himself to ground level.

"Tio? What's happening?" Marshmallow asked as she worked with the other druids to pull the redwood upright, sweat dripping from purple hair.

"I don't know yet. Hold on to the Conclave tree."

A human-sized golem skidded across the grass with unusual speed for a hunk of metal dragged along by a puppeteer. Its beady eyes shone pink as its circular head twisted around as if it was looking for something.

Is it moving on its own? Sipherra is automating golems now?

Spindly legs squeaked as it leaped forward, latching a pincer hand around Tio's neck. Flowering vines crept up the golem, holding the pincers back. Shoulder skin yanked—it felt as if it would tear right off if Tio pulled his vines any tighter. After the vines loosened, the pincers clamped down on his throat. A second pincer grabbed at his antlers, twisting against them. Tio jerked back, ripping another antler tine, and rammed his head into the golem. Velvet tore from his antler as it scraped across steadfast steel. Unfazed, the golem slammed Tio into the ground by his neck and squeezed ever tighter. Pressure ramped in Tio's head until it felt ready to burst.

An ethereal flash. The sound of crumpling paper. Dismembered steel pincers fell with clinging glitter. Rippling air folded, tore open, and Alim jumped through, bashing the golem with their shield. Tio coughed as Alim gave him a hand. Etherite axe ready and shield raised, Alim clashed with

Chapter 36 Tio

the golem faster than Tio could keep up with. Tio scurried along the border of their battle until the golem was within reach.

His vines wrapped around the golem's legs, and steel squeaked as vines snuck inside the golem through joints, gaps, and creases. Green leaked through bulging metal plates until the golem fell apart, flowers and vines pouring from within. The golem's head rolled into Tio's leg and tipped upside down, revealing an odd symbol carved on the inside.

Vines retracted, Tio lifted the golem head. *This looks like a rune?* After sketching the symbol into his notebook, Tio kicked the head away as Alim approached. *I'll show Hali this rune later.* "You learned starportals!"

"And you shaved." Alim tapped their braids.

"Yes, and what an achievement that was," Tio said as he rubbed his cheeks, missing his abrasive whiskers. "I assumed you'd come back to a surge with Undine since starportals gave you so much trouble. Does this mean you attuned to air? How?"

Cheers reminded Tio where he was. "Actually, hold on." He ran to an applauding crowd of druids, who had... sort of fixed the Conclave tree? It was still leaning but stable with the trunk having been morphed by druids to sprout new supporting roots. "Good job, Marsh... uhh."

I really need to make time to learn the other druids' names. Every druid was part of a different generation and Tio had been too focused on his own studies to ever get to know them. This one always had marshmallows in her pocket for some reason.

"Mona," Marshmallow said as she nervously munched on marshmallow puffs like they would pay her blood toll.

At least my nickname started with the right letter. "Mona, please let the Conclave know I'm going to Spirit Arboretum. If Sipherra is here, that's their real target." *With Geno gone, who's calling the shots at Sipherra now? Is this Allister, somebody else, or did Geno send these things before she died?*

Alim waved a hand in front of Tio's face. "Sorry, I think I have the wrong antlered green light. My Tio doesn't have that sort of confidence."

Arboreal Path

"Shut up or I'll confidently headbutt you." Tio shook his antlers about, flinching as cool air brushed against the peeled velvet.

"Wait, does your antler have like a shiny, white gash in it? Did something happen?"

Tio rubbed the exposed antler, finding ridged wood rather than bone. "I guess my antlers are… wooden? Not very stag-like."

"Maybe they're not antlers but tree branches?"

Tio shrugged. "We have more important things to worry about." He stripped the loose velvet. "Come on, we need to get Hali. She's at my place."

On the way, Alim explained how Nomine had taken on Sylphine's air ether and linked with the frog eidolon of Iron Swamp's surge, Prithvi. The only remaining task was for Alim to open the door to the Ethereal Realm in the Arboreal Path. With only a couple weeks until the solstice, time was short. But first, they had to make sure Sipherra didn't destroy Vinn's surge.

"How did you know Belsa was under attack?" Tio asked Alim.

"Undine and Prithvi. Remember how you feel sick when eidolons are in danger? Guess it goes both ways, since Prithvi knew you were in trouble."

Arriving at his home with a setting sun in a dim purple sky, Tio noticed his doorway's drapes had been pulled wide open. Peering inside, he saw a lazy Sir Fluffyboi asleep in the middle of a pile of cat toys. Tio petted the cat's head.

"Kitten, you're home!" Sir Fluffyboi purred and stretched like she'd been asleep during Tio's entire journey. "Your friend was nice."

Alim examined the shelves, picking up games and books as if admiring the art. *Can Alim even see the art?* Tio realized which books Alim had found and blushed. *I really hope not…*

"Where's Hali?" Tio asked as he shuffled Alim away from his not-so-hidden stash of romance novels and all the embarrassing covers of beautiful people.

"Gone. It's too bad. I hadn't gotten my fill of playing yet." Sir Fluffyboi started to groom herself with no shame.

Chapter 36 Tio

"If she's not here…"

Undine burst from Alim's forehead, splashing against Tio's bookshelves. Her face had a hole where one of her eyes should be and her arm had a gash in it. The water warbled as if maintaining her form was straining her.

Alim ran to Undine. "What's going on?"

Undine gurgled and her face looked to be ready to slide off her head. "Vinn."

Sipherra had already got to the stag eidolon?

"One thing after another, isn't it?" Alim gawked at the westward wall. "I see more silver lights like the golem had. They're gathering at Spirit Arboretum, but Hali is there too. She's fighting Vinn—has to be."

"No way. Hali gave up on eidolon blood."

"It wouldn't be the first time Hali changed her mind on that subject. Look at Undine—somebody's already wounded Vinn. We might have to kill Hali."

But she's our friend… "Can you afford to make another starportal? Spirit Arboretum is more than half a day from Belsa."

"I don't think I could take you with me, and teleporting again might leave me too drained to fight. Aren't Majesty and Stripes here?"

"Of course, but they could be at risk if Sipherra is also in the arboretum."

"Shouldn't you let them decide if it's a risk?"

"Fine," Tio sighed. "But they're not getting near the surge."

At the free-roam stables, Majesty and Stripes were chasing each other, weaving between trees. Tio whistled for them. Alim almost fell as Majesty bolted over and nuzzled them. They arrived at Spirit Arboretum's Starpath by nightfall.

"If it weren't for the sky, I would think this were the Arboreal Path." Alim's head whipped around as a tired Majesty trotted.

Uncountable stars peppered the gap between the Lunar Vault's scattered green light and the twin moons' yellow and orange glows. The dirt road cutting through the arboretum emanated its own light. Tio didn't know how, but it had a hint of ether mixed in. Studying the ether-infused dirt had been a big start for his research before the Conclave had allowed him to visit the haze barrier.

Tio guided Alim through a shortcut on the border of New Fion and Bansil Way. Wispy, droopy willows on the Fion side clashed with the ashen-barked and bloodsap-leaking gorwood trees on the Bansil side.

"That creepy sap is blinding," Alim said as they shielded their already-covered eyes.

"Sorry, this is the fastest route." *Will they be able to see at all near a haze barrier or inside a surge?*

Ahead, wisps of ether led to the barrier and clanging metal. Sipherra was here, but there was no sign of people. Enough tracks for five monstrous golems snaked through bent trees.

"Five? Tio, I can't beat that many. We need to go around."

"And waste more time?" Tio knew they needed help to take on so many golems at once. Automated or not, Alim was right that fighting head-on was the wrong choice.

"No phantasmal storm to save us this time. Maybe if we had some basilisks—that was my plan to get you out of Strago."

Wait…

New Fion had rare animals with all sorts of flourishes—basilisks included. Ren had warned him to steer clear of a nearby basilisk nest when first researching the barrier. Striped and spotted orange lizards the size of wolves with puffy, portly cheeks and dangly flaps were piled on top of one another in the willow branches. The biggest among them carried several eggs in a pool of water on its back.

If Ren can have cordial conversation with basilisks, then so can I. At the base of one of the willows, Tio said, "Please help. Our forest is being attacked by machines and we need your might." But it must've come out all wrong like "I like your muscles—please flex on the metal," because every basilisk laughed and ignored him.

Chapter 36 Tio

With a slosh and a splash, Undine stepped in front of Tio. "Let me handle this. I've got a bit of nature magic in me."

"Talking water?" one of the basilisks said with a flicking tongue.

Green bubbles rose in Undine as she shouted with half her words garbled. "Hey!—*splash*—your—*splash*—family—*splash*—right in the—*splash*—or I'll smash your—*splash*—eggs with—*splash*—metal."

Popping sounds littered the air.

"What did you say? My flourish had trouble translating you." It felt strange being on the other side of a magical translation issue. *Maybe animals hear something similar when I speak?*

"Can she say that?" Stripes asked.

"I can appreciate a bit of saucy vulgarity," Majesty said.

"It's probably better you don't understand—"

Water splashed Tio in the face as a hole blew open in Undine's chest. "It worked," Undine said as her liquid reconstituted.

"Okay, that's your cue to leave, Stripes and Majesty." Tio ran towards the barrier as basilisks rained from the branches and crackled the air around him.

"Great plan, Undine," Alim said as they caught up to Tio. "Don't worry, I'll block their air blasts."

Ether rushed past Tio's face, and he felt waves of immense heat accompanying the thundering booms behind him. A tree crashed in front of him as metallic buzzing filled his ears. Tio leaped over the trunk and skidded to a stop as a golem appeared from nowhere.

With loud sizzling, the golem's head vaporized, and several molten holes materialized as dozens of basilisks crawled over the tree and skittered past Tio yelling, "Melt the metal!"

Alim grabbed Tio by the arm. "Come on—let's go."

Shield raised against the onslaught of liquefied steel, wooden splinters, and lifted earth, Alim pushed to the barrier with Tio close behind.

The purple and green mist funneled into a nearby ether reactor. A perfect rectangular tunnel sliced through the barrier to the surge with one hulking construction golem holding it open as somebody in lavender robes ran through and memories crashed over him. The weight of Alim's axe in his hands. The relief and satisfaction wrought by taking the swing. A flash of Osanshia's shocked face, her ruined braids falling like the wilted tree they'd been based on.

The haze-barrier tunnel crashed closed at Alim's command and the resulting tremor brought Tio back to the present. Alim slashed through the golem's skinny legs and kicked it over as easily as they would a tower of stacked blocks. Tio forced his vines into the reactor and tore it apart until its humming engines ceased.

Was that really Osanshia? Did she steal these golems or was Sipherra still working with her? Is she helping Hali, or is it a coincidence that they're both here? *Could we even beat Hali if we had to?* Tio steeled himself to the best of his ability. *Deep breaths.*

CHAPTER 37

At last Hali's collection of eidolon runes was complete. Eidolon-blood tattoos glistened with shifting ethereal colors against her brown skin as Hali knelt in stained-red grass, focusing on taming her rampant blood toll.

Each rune activated in sequence. Sapper's claw and orb on her right arm. Control's leaf helix and snakes on her left calf. Lux's scythe and sun on her left arm. The first of her new additions, the teleportation rune Egress, burned with vines and leaves with unblinking eyes on her right calf. And finally, Meld. Stacked triangles interconnected with spirals on her right wrist. Meaning "eternal phantom tree," the Meld rune had been the only rune to bypass Kthon and Ikazu to interact with Rev and Rasal directly. Where once she had hoped Alim would power the rune to release her family from Kthon, now it would work in conjunction with the other four eidolon runes to kill Kthon.

But first Hali had to prevent the binding rune from activating. Its circle and incomplete triangle burned brightest of all. The stinging, putrid scent of oranges overwhelmed her cardamom candles. Ragged breaths and distorted, meaningless whispers invaded her thoughts, and Hali contorted as if her runes were breaking her bones, stretching and reconstructing her in Kthon's unnerving image.

Grass grew over Hali, strapping her to the ground. Cooling water splashed her face. Vinn's soaring fig tree came into view as the stag lay next to her. "Control over five eidolon runes when you are no longer a celestial seems an impossible task even for you, Sereiamina."

Everything in Hali throbbed erratically and her stretched proportions snapped back. "Then why'd you let me take your blood?"

Vinn's wounded eye and shoulder had already healed, but it took labored breaths from the process. "For Zergi's sake. It is not safe to keep Kthon in your body forever. He will escape. My blood will help you avenge Zergi and keep Empyrea safe from the false spirit."

Only if I can contain Kthon. My new runes may be meant to help strengthen the binding rune's hold, but the added eidolon blood also empowered Kthon...

Vinn cried out as a stone cracked against its face. Hali pulled herself out of the grassy restraints and unsheathed the dagger from her boot. Another stone smashed her wrist, knocking the weapon aside. Through Kthon's raging blood toll, Hali couldn't feel anything. Only by the shadow spirit's obsessive healing tendrils did Hali know her hand had been broken.

Spotting her assailant, Hali thought the earth mage looked familiar. Frayed orange hair. Battered lavender robes. *Isn't she the one Tio killed—Osanshia? She captured and tormented Tio and Orbi. Wounded Alim...*

Hali's Egress rune tingled. The world flashed white, and Hali appeared next to her rune book across the grove and retrieved her broken dagger from its spine. Another white blink and Hali was behind an audibly confused Osanshia. Hali thrust her jagged rainbow blade through Osanshia's swinging amethyst-coated arm, shattering gemstone and bone. Screaming, Osanshia smashed a flanged mace into Hali's shoulder and forced her to stop twisting the blade.

Chapter 37 Hali

Meld rune burning, Hali felt her celestial powers return. Colorful haze folded into small chunks of etherite. Stretched into needles.

One by one, Hali dodged attacks and countered by sending needles flying into key points of Osanshia's neck, arms, and legs.

Osanshia stomped the ground, but the earth did not mold to her wishes. "My gift won't—"

Ears rang. Vision darkened.

When senses returned, a swollen-faced, bloody Osanshia lay below. Hali's knuckles ached, and blood boiled as her senses faded again. Blackened mist crept from Hali's binding rune and coated Osanshia. Soaked into her.

Osanshia's memories swam by. Graduation. Becoming headmaster of Wilton's academy. Joining Gren Consortium. Hunting Tio.

Shadows sculpted into gangly limbs and grabbed onto Osanshia as if to pull itself out from the gloom. Boney fingers closed on Osanshia's jaw to stop her screaming as another hand pinched into her skull. Kthon tugged, and her body unraveled to trails of gray dust. Her existence erased, Osanshia was no more.

Kthon's head flopped out of the gloom, taking on Osanshia's rugged silhouette. *Good riddance.*

"Hali?" somebody called out.

Kthon and Hali turned as one to see Tio, Alim, and Undine leaving a breached haze barrier with lingering specks of Osanshia wafting by them.

Roots wrapped around Hali's legs and flipped her upside down as Tio ran to a bloodied, unconscious Vinn and ignited his hands in green healing light. Kthon skittered after Vinn on all fours with spideresque energy. Tugging on the cord of shadow linking Kthon to her binding rune, Hali reeled him in as he flailed and clung to the earth.

Tio collapsed against Vinn as Alim and Undine stood between him and the shadow.

Now's not the time for a communion, Tio…

347

Dragging himself to Vinn with stretched arms, tendrils exploded from Kthon's back. Wild swings of a glittery multicolored axe cleaved the wriggly limbs, leaving behind steaming stumps, and moisture built in the air like a storm was brewing, freezing one snowflake at a time into an icy maul. Undine snatched the maul and smashed Kthon into the air as Alim gracefully transitioned to celestial magic, detonating the surrounding fog-like fireworks and blasting mist-leaking holes throughout Kthon.

Hali struggled against the roots, trying to use any of her magic for herself. The blood toll intensified. All six of Hali's runes masked the surge with ethereal light, but Kthon diverted their power to fuel himself.

A tendril exploded from each of Kthon's holes, and Alim crafted a haze barrier, trembling with each movement. Tendrils rampaged against the barrier, cracking it with each collision.

Alim raised their arms up, letting the surge's ether entangle them.

Recharging mid-combat? You really are a celestial now.

Undine smashed Kthon's Osanshia-shaped head right as two tendrils erupted through her and she burst into a series of puddles.

Smashing through the small haze barrier to Alim's upraised shield, Kthon hurled them against a fig free.

Kthon then crouched over Tio as he returned to the waking world.

Stop! Hali pushed all her power into her binding rune.

Spindly fingers pinched into Tio's head for mere moments before Vinn swiped Kthon with its tree antlers and the roots retreated, dropping Hali.

Two of her runes activated. Tio's hands touched the grass as if he was trying to use his spark, but nothing happened. Two more runes activated as Hali ran between Kthon and Tio.

"Who are you?" Tio asked Hali, wobbling.

The last two runes activated, and white flames engulfed Kthon's shadowy cord, returning him to his tattoo prison.

Chapter 37 Hali

Did Kthon get to Tio's memories? "I—I'm sorry, Tio. This was the only way I could think of to kill Kthon, but I failed to control him." *Like I always do.*

With exhausted breaths, Tio said, "Woah, did you just apologize? Since when do you apologize?"

"Wait, you remember me?"

"Of course I do. Why wouldn't I?" Tio scratched his chin. "Vinn said it gave you blood willingly, but why? I thought you were done with eidolon blood."

"I should've told you. Kthon was breaking his bonds. Eidolon runes let me contain him longer, and… kill him when the time comes."

"Killing Kthon may be necessary," Alim said as Undine's water seeped into them. "I found a spirit's core in the Arboreal Path. The shadows leaking from it have been blocking the way to the Ethereal Realm."

"Whose core?" Hali asked. *I don't recall any spirits dying in the Path.*

"Seeing Kthon in person has confirmed my suspicions. The core and Kthon have matching etheric signatures."

"Impossible. If Kthon has a core, it's in me."

"I guess it'd be more accurate to say half a core. Some sorta purple haze barrier kept the remaining ether inside. Maybe you have the other half?"

Half. Half…

Alim checked Tio for wounds. "That's the third time you've had weird memory problems. First when your antlers appeared. Again after healing Hali in Oressa. And now."

"Tio, you still don't remember how you got your antlers?" Hali asked as she noticed pale bark peeking through a tear in his antler velvet. "It could be important."

"No. Only that I was on top of Empyrea's branches when it happened. Or at least, I had a vision I was on Empyrea."

Malakine. Originally two separate spirits, Malakine was a shadow spirit before merging with the first celestial spirit. Would the merger have changed Malakine's etheric signature? When Hali split them apart, the shadow spirit half of Malakine must've escaped to the Path before dying.

The celestial spirit half must be inside Kthon now, absorbed when Malakine's white ether splashed me.

"The core belongs to the previous celestial spirit, Malakine. Not Kthon," Hali said.

"Okay, then why does the etheric signature match with Kthon?" Alim asked.

Could it be... "Malakine was with me when I cured the ethereal plague. I had thought a stray spirit got caught in my celestial magic and fused with the plague. I thought that's how Kthon was created—a mixture of plague and spirit."

Alim tapped their braids. "Are you saying Kthon is the celestial spirit?"

"Malakine wasn't a celestial spirit. Not really. Instead of linking with Empyrea directly, Malakine fused themself with the corpse of the first celestial spirit. Kthon must be the ethereal plague controlling a portion of Malakine's ether. Or perhaps Malakine's ether gives them control over the plague?"

"Why wouldn't Malakine just link directly to Empyrea?" Alim asked.

Vinn's voice echoed. "Because it wasn't Malakine's decision to make, and the spirits would never have allowed Empyrea's youngest and most reckless child to become a celestial spirit."

Hali said, "Fusing also allowed them to gain celestial magic without sacrificing their original element to Empyrea."

"What does any of this have to do with my antlers?" Tio asked.

"The wood on your antlers is the same as the Arboreal Path. Malakine's other half was the first celestial spirit. She gave you those antlers. Through me..." *Ikazu is the first celestial spirit. Has to be. Ikazu could've communed with Tio when I pulled him out of the first haze barrier.*

"So you're saying Malakine created Kthon on purpose," Alim said. "To what end?"

Chapter 37 Hali

"Kthon can absorb ether faster than any of Sipherra's reactors. Malakine's goal has always been to take back Empyrea's stolen ether from mortals. I never followed along… until Kthon held my family hostage." *I was a fool.* "We have to destroy the core to unblock the Path and use Kthon's stolen ether to restore Empyrea."

Vinn rumbled. "And risk Kthon linking with Empyrea? He would be worse than Malakine."

"If I communed with the first celestial spirit once, I can do it again. Together we can keep Kthon suppressed."

Hali nodded. "My new runes will let me isolate Kthon's ether and release it in small quantities."

Alim pounded their chest. "And I'll redirect the ether into Empyrea."

"Once the ether is gone, Kthon should be weak enough for me to overwhelm with my eidolon runes. Then we can set the phantoms free from my binding rune." *At long last, my family will be at peace.*

"My pack has enough supplies for a couple of elixirs," Tio said. "Alim, can you take us to the Ethereal Realm now?"

"No, the last starportal and Kthon have done a number on me. I'll need to recharge for days."

"The Ethereal Realm is physically closest under the Lunar Vault during winter solstice. If we wait until the ethereal lights, your blood toll for starportals should be dirt cheap." *Rasal, Rev, we're so close. Hold on a little longer.*

CHAPTER 38

Wilton's streets were somehow brighter at night than day, with decorative lights along its buildings and a towering festival wheel bouncing off the Lunar Vault's green aura. In front of the wheel, a stone fountain shot color-shifting water skyward. Even the town's namesake wilted purple tree acted as a beacon signaling for the Vault to open.

Shouts of glee came from all directions. Except from Tio. When he wasn't grumbling, Tio felt like he might jump out of his skin as everything from the blaring music to the greasy odor grated on his nerves. Most irritating was Alim's enthusiastic smile, which hadn't gone away since the group had entered the land of endless food vendors.

Hali's curls bounced into view. "Hey, Tio, come on. We have a few days before the ethereal lights may appear. You don't have to be Alim, but try to have some fun, okay?" She handed him a green puff of sugar.

The new flowy knee-length dress Hali wore was predictably black, but the pink metallic sheen of its cherry blossom pattern was less expected. Insisting on forgetting the mission for a day, Hali had forced the three to buy new clothes.

"It's not about the ethereal lights," Tio mumbled as he pulled down on his shirt's sleeves. It was sort of about that. How could anybody have fun when the very thing they were celebrating represented the beginning of the end. The mission's deadline and their one chance to get things right.

"Stop doing that. You're going to stretch it."

That's the point.

Wearing properly fitted clothing made Tio sympathize with the time he'd convinced Sir Fluffyboi to wear a sweater. Hali had needed to correct him on the shirt's color—periwinkle. Though that did sound more interesting than somewhere-between-blue-and-purple.

Even the pale green pants constricted him with their stupid ironed crease. The boots though—those Tio had come to appreciate after trudging through mangroves and swamps. Wool? Not meant to get wet. Water flourishes were great at wringing the muck out, but the stench never left.

"Do you need a distraction from the crowds?" Alim said as they inhaled wispy pink sugar, ensuring the world knew how good it was too with loud, uncomfortable noises. That they were caressing the Solstoran sun embroidery on their padded yellow vest didn't help either.

"A distraction?" Hali plucked purple puffs of her sugary treat and nibbled carefully as if avoiding getting her new dress sticky. "What about a card game? *Volatile Lemurs?*"

"Sounds great!" Alim's black-and-yellow plaid skirt billowed over thick white pants as they hopped through the blurring mass of people. Hali had spent half of yesterday trying to convince Alim the skirt would be a good look for them, and Tio had agreed. Alim only gave in when Hali brought up how Diyan warriors of all genders wore skirts to battle. But there was no way Alim wasn't itching to put armor over the whole ensemble.

Tio let small pieces of sugar melt on his tongue, squashing any hint of a smile before Alim could pounce on it as a sign of solstice joy. "I guess we can play, if you want to." He adjusted the flowering vines wrapped around his shoulder.

Alim's sigh ejected with all their built-up complaints. "Can you lay off the grumpy persona and at least admit the ethereal floss tastes good?"

"Leave him alone, Alim." Hali's eyes burned holes in Tio. "It'll be fun to play a game again, even if I have no clue what's going on." She pulled Tio towards the festival wheel. "Let's talk books on the way. Did you read the one I lent you?"

"*Ferocious*? Kind of ridiculous with the immortality and lightning powers. The things people think druids can do," Tio said. "And why do the druids have to be evil?"

"It's fiction."

"Even fiction should make sense—they didn't have to call them druids. Still, would've been more fun if the main characters had got together at the end."

"The whole point is they want to kill each other and… you're messing with me. Put away that stupid smile."

The weight of Empyrea lifted as Tio laughed.

"About time, Tio. Can we please have fun now? It's solstice!" Alim blew glittering etheric dust at Tio's face. "Solstice joy!"

Tio coughed, waving the glitter away. "That's abuse of your celestial powers."

"What do you think Barbaroli's book is going to be like?" Alim asked. "Is he going to turn our journey into a novel? It'd be fun to read back."

"Guarantee he puts all three of us in a romance." Hali pretended to retch.

"Dibs on Tio," Alim said, lightning fast.

Tio joined in on the retching.

"What? You're looking spiffy in your new outfit, and who wouldn't love those little eidolon freckles?" Alim's hand grew dangerously close to squeezing Tio's cheeks.

Tio swatted Alim away. "I wouldn't date either of you in a thousand years."

Chapter 38 Tio

"You might want a longer time stipulation there. If we get trapped in the Ethereal Realm, it's possible a thousand years could pass for us," Hali said with a half chuckle.

That's a scary thought. Tio hadn't considered what the Ethereal Realm's time dilation effect might be, or the possibility of getting stuck there.

"It won't come to that. I'll get us back here in no time!" Alim bumped into a small girl. "Sorry... Charlie?"

"How can you see with your eyes all wrapped up?" Charlie adjusted her lopsided antler headband in her fancy blonde bun and dusted off her pink-and-green dress.

"Magic," Alim said with wiggling fingers.

Charlie looked at everybody with frantic energy. "Tio, look—we match!" She pointed at her headband before running over to prod at Hali's ring. "You kept it!"

Hugging Hali's legs, she asked, "Are you here for the light show?"

I don't want to be here.

"What do you mean? It's too early for the ethereal lights," Alim said.

A cane smacked the ground as Allister hobbled over with metal braces on his legs. "Sipherra's etherite golem will kick off the solstice with ethereal fireworks."

Deep breaths. Too many people. Too much excitement. *I need to leave.*

"I'm going to smack the gray right out of your hair, Allister! Is this golem going to hunt us down too?"

"Hunt you? If it did, you wouldn't be in any danger. All it can do is put on a light show."

"Automated golems attacked Belsa with Osanshia. When are you going to reign in Sipherra?"

Tio wandered away from their argument, clasping his wrist and wishing he'd invested in a new bracelet. Mind turned off, he found himself under the festival wheel, behind the solstice-decorated etherite golem and the ocean of people waiting for the show.

Arboreal Path

The golem's railed arms rotated backward with a *thunk* and loud bangs resonated as it shook and ejected cannisters upward. Popping fireworks and cheering were drowned out by a green light bathing the sky with a thundering boom. A shockwave ran through the fairgrounds, setting off a chain reaction as neon signs and street lanterns across the square exploded. Waves of people screamed and scattered.

Long, bright streaks of pink, green, and purple stained the sky. *The ethereal lights? Did the golem trigger them?* The light rained down and flowed through the streets, evaporating any person caught in the way. *No! Why are the lights coming to ground level?*

A familiar whirring hum came from the golem as passing ether was diverted into its etherite arms like they were magnetic. *The golem is a reactor? It must be automated too. Hali mentioned the runes inside the last golem converted phantoms into ether. Is this golem also running on phantoms?*

Its head twisted around, its beady eyes glistening pink with absorbed energy. A hand raised, pointed at Tio, and buzzed, teeming with ether. Tio ducked behind one of the wheel's carriages as a bolt of ethereal lightning shot out, threatening to burst his eardrums. The carriage rattled as it melted, and the bolt struck Tio and threw him into a stone fountain, knocking over its decorative dead-tree top.

Aching all over, Tio swore he heard his bones crunch as he splashed his way out of the fountain. His skin flaked off in thick chunks, revealing a second layer of skin underneath. Tio picked one up, examining what appeared to be bark matching Tio's golden-brown complexion.

Did I grow this to protect myself? When did I— My second communion with Vinn? I felt another presence then. A wolf. This must be another eidolon trait.

"Tio!" Charlie called out as she opened her locket and tossed each of the different gemstones within at the golem, lodging them into a panel on its leg and spinning them like drills.

"Charlie, what are you doing?" Tio yelled.

Chapter 38 Tio

"We're doing our part," Allister said, pulling Tio to his feet. "Seems I've yet again underestimated Geno Sipherra. She's haunting us from beyond the grave with these golems of hers."

Using the ethereal lights as yet another source of ether. Geno thought of everything.

Little hands tossed a storm of wires aside and flipped a switch as if Charlie knew exactly what she was looking for. A wisp of gray ether leaked from the golem's eyes. Ethereal lights continued to surge through the streets, intensifying as the golem no longer redirected it.

"Where're Alim and Hali?" Tio asked.

"Follow the lights. Alim is protecting Hali as we speak," Allister said.

Protecting her from what, the ethereal lights? Why—Kthon. The ethereal lights are trying to destroy Kthon just as the haze barrier did back at Spirit Arboretum and the phantoms at Strago. Alim will be eradicated on the spot if Kthon doesn't absorb the ethereal lights first. If Kthon gets any of that ether, our whole mission may fail.

Charlie shouted, "I can reprogram it to create a barrier around the library."

"Good, head that way and I'll round up survivors," Allister shouted back.

"We'll meet you there." Tio ran alongside rushing light rivers, careful not to let them touch him. Though he could hear distant cries, Tio saw no people on the way. *Has everybody on this road already been killed?*

At the end of the street, purple and pink lights crashed against Alim's outstretched arms as if they were projecting an invisible wall with their mind. Each collision between the two etheric forces generated tremors, shattering windows, and littering the road with glass. Shadows leaked from Hali's wrist, twisted into a claw, and latched onto Alim, tossing them away. Then Hali's runes encased her in a white light, and she vanished as ethereal lights crashed.

"Alim, can't you get rid of these ethereal lights?" Tio asked as ether whisked by.

"Don't think that'll be necessary. The lights were after Kthon... look."

Ether rushed back into the sky, blasting southeast as it did every year. *Then we brought the lights down by coming here? I should've predicted this...*

"We have to go after Hali. Kthon's going to hijack the eidolon blood in her runes like back in Spirit Arboretum." *What atrocities could Kthon commit with five eidolon runes?* "Alim? What are you looking at?" Tio couldn't see anything unusual with the Lunar Vault. Why was Alim staring at it?

"I'm seeing colors I've never seen before. With my ethersight at least. Orange and yellow. And—" Alim projected a haze barrier right as a wave of blue light erupted from the Vault and bathed the town's streets. "I can't open a starportal and keep these lights at bay."

Outside the barrier, Tio heard people screaming, and bits of etheric dust puffed skyward as the screams stopped.

"Can you take us to the library? Charlie and Allister are setting up a safe zone there." Tio hoped Charlie's plan would work. At least then Sipherra's inventions could make a positive difference.

Alim took Tio by the arm. "Don't stray far. My barrier's going to fluctuate in size every time it gets hit."

The barrage of blue lights was soon joined by distorted coils of orange and yellow. The lights sparked like fireworks as they collided against Alim's barrier and were repelled into the surroundings. Complete erasure was the only way Tio could describe what happened to the buildings caught in the crossfire. *Is this what ether is capable of? This will never be safe to harness. We have to abandon the idea of ether tech entirely.*

Seven stragglers ran by, screaming as a yellow stream chased them.

"Over here!" Tio shouted, beckoning the people inside Alim's barrier.

The last person stepped through just as a yellow explosion erased two buildings ahead of Alim, opening a shortcut to the library. Alim's arms wobbled as they guided everybody through.

"You need an elixir." Tio uncorked a blue bottle.

Chapter 38 Tio

"No, save it. I can make it." A small rash formed on Alim's neck.

"I can't heal etheric drought. Drink it."

"No, I can recharge my ether in the Path. You and Hali can't." Alim's barrier shrank. Blood leaked from their nose and blotchy bruises appeared on their arms.

The disabled golem sat outside the library's glass walls with Charlie and another engineer tinkering on it furiously. Charlie looked over as she bopped the golem's head and it whirred with angry clanking gears. Its arms absorbed inordinate amounts of ethereal light and erected a large haze barrier of the new trio of colors.

Tio caught a collapsing Alim as the smaller barrier they were maintaining dissolved. Electrical crackling and thundering booms signaled ether clashing with ether.

"Allow me to help!" one of the stragglers said. "I'm a Sipherra engineer."

"Knock yourself out." Charlie hopped off the golem and opened the door for everybody. "Where's Hali?"

Good question. Could Kthon also want to go to the Ethereal Realm? "She's safe from the lights. A rune teleported her away."

"I can sense Hali and Kthon in the Path," Alim whispered as Tio set them against a bookshelf.

Staring out the glass walls, Charlie said, "The second solstice's lights are so pretty. Do you think they'll calm down like the first did?"

A splotchy, stained blue hand offered a tiny bottle to Tio. "Your friend could use this." It reeked of fish oil and grapes.

Elixir? Who could have found the ingredients in Wilton?

"Thanks," Tio said as he saw the fake druid he'd met before—Druid Trainer. Dark blue hair mismatched his brown stubble, and the golden beak on his purple feather hat sat agape in permanent surprise. "Sorry, what is this? Is it real?"

"Of course it's real! Old druid recipe, passed down from my family for generations. Got the list right here from my great-great-grandpappy."

Druid Trainer closed the beak on his hat before yelling at it. "Quit your yammering—these fine folk need peace."

Elixir is Thaumic… But the list of ingredients is right. "It's such a small dose."

"If it's enough to open a starportal to the Path, then that's all we need." Alim stole the tiny bottle and downed it.

The glass walls rumbled, and Tio turned to find a crack forming in the haze barrier. A wisp of orange snaked through and pierced through the Sipherra engineer, evaporating them. The other scrambled to the golem's control panel and mashed on buttons. A yellow torrent engulfed the second engineer as the golem absorbed the invading ether, but not in time to save them.

How many people have died due to this second solstice? The library was packed, but there was no way it would hold the entire town and its festival visitors.

"The golem's not at full output yet," Charlie said. "We need to control it manually."

"I'll do it." Allister dropped his cane and approached the library's glass doors.

"What do you know of golems?" Druid Trainer stopped Allister. "As our resident golem thrasher, I believe I am best suited to make repairs."

Allister sighed. "You're a con artist. The only reason you haven't been arrested is because of how much money you make the Consortium in Gren City's arenas."

Druid Trainer held out a small two-pronged blade with a little ball of electricity hovering between the prongs.

"A Sipherra universal key?" Charlie asked as if she wished she had one.

"This." Druid Trainer waved the blade about. "This is Wrathbolt, Divine Blade of the Breezechaser."

That name started out as the angsty musings of a teenager and nosedived straight into comedic parody. Is this guy okay?

Chapter 38 Tio

"Watch." Druid Trainer sauntered outside like he was in a dramatic play and pressed Wrathbolt against the golem's eyes. A small hatch flew open on its chest.

"That's the override panel. He really has a universal key," Charlie said.

Blue lights wriggled through the cracks of the golem's haze barrier and darted at Druid Trainer. He blocked the assault with Wrathbolt, but the impact threw him through the glass ceiling onto the library's third floor.

Charlie ran to the door. "I'll fix this!"

Allister blocked her way. "No, we can find another engineer."

The air folded into a jagged black gateway of stars.

"Alim, what are you doing? We can't leave yet!"

"That's not me," Alim said as they grabbed Tio's wrist.

Twisting roots of light wrapped around Tio and Alim, dragging both through the starportal.

CHAPTER 39

Crushing anxiety flooded into Alim. It was nostalgic, in a way. Something they had experienced before when proving themself to the Dreamers. Spending every waking moment upkeeping the mask of competence so they would be accepted as a peer. But this wasn't their anxiety—it felt foreign. Borrowed. Alim sat in an empty void. Dark as the Path's abyssal road in every direction. An overwhelming desire to fidget skulked within them, and Alim resorted to twiddling their fingers to sate it.

A small boy with grassy hair appeared in the void, running with a group of other children.

Tio?

Shouts of "you're it" accompanied gentle tagging and laughing, but Little Tio stopped and crouched while the others continued running after each other. Alim looked down at Little Tio and he jerked his head away.

Alim tried to speak, but words refused to form. Instead, their thoughts projected outward as if slung by a trebuchet. *Are you okay?*

Little Tio's response inserted itself into Alim's mind. *I don't know.*

Chapter 39 Alim

Why don't you play with your friends?
I don't know.
Did they upset you?
I don't know.

A sense of alienation permeated Alim, joining the borrowed anxiety. It pained Alim to hear a kid sound so defeated and lost. They wanted to help. To tell him that he wasn't broken. *It's okay to not understand why you feel this way. Take a break and play with your friends later.*

Alim fell through the floor, landing on the shining roots of the Arboreal Path, their hand still gripping Tio's.

"What did I just see? Tio, was that you?"

Tio didn't look like he knew. "It wasn't just me then. Druids call that a communion. An exchange of emotions. Another old nature flourish power I guess."

The Keeper was a cute fleshling, Undine said.

Ew, even your word for kids is skin-crawly.

"Is this Arboreal Path?" Tio asked as he looked around at the lavender fog-covered roots.

"Yes, though it's not always so gloomy here. You'd like the sky here when it clears up. It's like coffee with splashes of cream and elemental constellation sprinkles."

"I don't usually take sprinkles in my coffee."

"Whatever." Alim pointed towards the shadowy door. "Hali's etheric signature is on the other side, with Malakine's core." Alim maintained their grip as Tio pulled away. "I know, no touching, but you're not a celestial. What'll happen if I let go?"

"You going to be this clingy in the Ethereal Realm too?" Tio ripped his hand back. "Look, I'm fine."

"Sorry. Our plan has already gone so awry, I don't know what to do."

"Well, I know exactly what to do. Open that door." Tio reached for the star-like doorknob and his hand passed right through. "Or you can.

That works too."

Alim wiped slick palms against their skirt. *Kthon won't beat me twice. I can do this.*

Gathering ether around their boot, Alim kicked the door open. A shadow tendril barged past Alim and grabbed Tio. Rainbow loops vibrated on Alim's arm, turning to spinning buzzsaws and eviscerating the tendril as they punched through it. With a tap, the etherite shield expanded and Alim slammed a second tendril with it, pushing to the other side of the doorway.

"Where's Hali? And Kthon?"

Ethersight didn't reveal anything except for Malakine's bright purple half-core with its protective haze barrier. "I don't know, but we can destroy the core before Kthon gets his hands on it." As Alim picked up the core, they heard a voice.

"My celestial."

"Did you hear that too?" Worry creased Tio's brow.

The core flickered. "You're not Sereiamina."

"I am a celestial," Alim said. "But not your celestial, Malakine."

Alim slammed a fist into the core, and the haze barrier cracked. Again. And again. By the sixth time, the core itself burst and the ether within whirled to the glittering roots below, bubbling into the right half of a human-sized, withered, black porcelain doll.

The doll jittered. "I mustn't be here. Return me to my core at once, my celestial. I await Sereiamina to make me whole again."

Malakine's been waiting for Hali to bring Kthon here? This is a trap! Alim bolted to the abyssal door to shut it, but a gaunt-faced, shadowy owl peered through and swiped them with a wing. Piercing silver eyes locked onto Malakine's core as Kthon skittered inside, dragging an unconscious Hali by a taut cord of shadow.

Tio helped Alim up. "Think you can buy me time to get to Hali? I might be able to commune and suppress Kthon."

Chapter 39 Alim

Communing was meant to prevent Kthon's release, not push him back into the rune, but... "It's worth a shot."

"Kthon!" Malakine dragged themself across the ground with their one arm. "Make me whole again! Let the surges Quake once more and fill you with Empyrea's ether."

Not only did Malakine create Kthon on purpose, but the Quake?

Alim transformed their bangle into an axe as they leaped forward and cleaved across Kthon's frail torso. Upper body flopping backward against its single wing, arms clinging by a thread of shadow, Kthon oozed orange-scented black goop. Resounding snaps bounced around the Path from Kthon's bending and rebending limbs. Alim slashed again, but Kthon disappeared as the axe made contact.

Reappearing behind Alim, Kthon smashed their head against the hard, wooden road. Every muscle and bone in Alim ached in unison. Undine dripped out from under their face-covering and seeped into the Path's roots.

Kthon is using Hali's Egress rune to teleport. Must be why I couldn't see him when I opened the doorway.

Tio grasped Hali's forearm. His chaotic green aura blazed until Kthon's wing wrapped Tio up, obscuring him from Alim's ethersight. Kthon clambered off Alim and scooped up Malakine, cradling them as one would a newborn child.

"Return my ether to me. Together, Empyrea's ether will be restored." Malakine caressed Kthon's shadowy beak as his face spun, morphing between hundreds if not thousands of distinct features. Soft. Rugged. Old. Androgynous. Young. Logu. Masculine. Animal. Human. None. All.

Kthon held Malakine aloft and cracked the former celestial spirit open, lapping up the ether within before crunching down on the corpse. Joining the ever-changing faces, Kthon's limbs contorted as Hali's six runes overwhelmed Alim's ethersight. A baby's cry perforated the air, lingering until Alim regained control over their ethersight and found themself alone.

CHAPTER 40

Stomach flipping and the urge to vomit rising, Hali blinked as tall blades of yellow grass slapped her face. Blood pulsed through every tattoo, feeding her captor via the shadow cord dragging Hali and coating her dress's metallic cherry blossoms in dirt. Kthon gurgled out orange-scented puffs of black smog and grasped at the phantoms swimming over the meadow to the crest of a distant hill, climbing the enormous trunk of a tree.

Empyrea? Brown bark shimmered with ethereal colors, and gray mist swirled around expansive branches. So tall it pierced endless clouds of ether, revealing the sky's green hue. A set of pink and purple moons shone alongside a scar splitting the sky apart to reveal a blue interior. Ether drifted from wounds throughout Empyrea's wilting roots into the blue scar. Was that the other side of the Lunar Vault? *This is what causes the ethereal lights? If Rev had let me come to the Ethereal Realm, I could have closed this side too.*

Kthon leaped onto Empyrea's trunk, yanking Hali into one of its ether-leaking wounded roots. He raked with flailing limbs, peeling away

Chapter 40 Hali

bark to reveal a pulsating, fleshy orange interior. A shadowy tendril pierced the orange flesh, releasing a flood of black-and-white ether unto itself. Hali's runes burst off her skin into clouds of orange, yellow, and blue ether.

Drinking it, Kthon undulated. Grew. Morphed. His features became indistinguishable, like an amalgamation of many disparate human, animal, and plant parts. Intense citrus assaulted Hali and her blood cooked her insides until she blacked out.

Deep breaths, a green-haired teenage boy chanted in Hali's head. He held a thread and needle in unsteady hands.

An injured rabbit squirmed and squealed, pinned under the boy's legs as he stuck the needle through wounded flesh. "Get offa me, ya clumsy kit." Hali felt a tingle as her mind translated its words.

"Kit? Who helped convince that wolf to let you go? You're lucky to have a leg." The boy sounded caring even in his confused agitation. Hali had forgotten what Tio looked like without antlers, lynx freckles, and vines.

The situation reminded Hali of when she was younger and a baby leviathan had snatched a dog at Sky Tower. Hali had fended it off with her air spark and taken care of the dog, removing the water from its lungs with careful puffs of air and keeping it warm until a traveling healer could arrive—that was when she'd met Rev.

"I had that whole situation handled. Let me go!" The rabbit kicked against Tio's legs.

"Like it or not, I'm here to help." Finishing the suture, Tio tied a knot and bit the thread off. "But you're free to go when I'm done."

The rabbit bounced into Hali and burst into green stars, obscuring her vision. When the stars faded, Tio was over her, emitting healing magic.

"Was that... a memory?"

"Sort of. I don't think I've ever sewed up a rabbit, but I'm sure I've done so to a couple other animals before. Sorry, communions with people seem to be a thing now." Tio tipped Hali's head back and poured a blue elixir of fishy grapes down her throat.

Blech. Should've given him a better-tasting recipe. "No, I'm sorry for messing up. I never should have created those last eidolon runes. Kthon wouldn't have been able to bring himself here otherwise."

Tio laughed. "I liked you better when you didn't apologize so much."

"Where's Alim?" Hali heard pulsating, like a heartbeat in absolute darkness. "Where are we?"

Two glowing seeds illuminated the area. They sprouted little white tendrils as ether wafted at them.

The runes on Hali's arms and legs had faded, appearing no more than scars. All except the circular binding rune, which had become an ordinary, unmoving tattoo in silver ink. Overhead, a hanging orange sac throbbed through a jagged bark cleft. Clumps of dirt rained as everything rumbled.

"We're under Empyrea. I don't know how long these roots will keep Kthon out, but Alim should be right behind us. We got separated in the Path when Kthon grabbed me."

"Kthon didn't absorb you?"

"What's the point with Empyrea right there? Though Kthon doesn't seem to be following Malakine's orders. He was supposed to be a plague bomb. Instead, he's out there shredding Empyrea."

Shadows squeezed through the cracking roots and Hali slashed through each with a dagger, evaporating them. A roar rattled her brain, sounding like a mixture of a lion's roar, a wolf's howl, an owl's screech, and a baby's cry. *Rasal. Kthon completed the resurrection to create a body and free himself.*

"You can't make contact with the first celestial spirit through my binding rune anymore. Kthon has all the world's ether at his disposal."

He stroked his chin and tied Empyrea's seeds to his shoulder vines. "This thing is absorbing ether, and Kthon is made from ether right? Could it absorb Kthon?"

Chapter 40 Hali

"It would never store enough, but it may be able to extract Rasal and Rev!"

Tio gave her a confused look.

"When I saw Empyrea, it was attracting phantoms. 'Returning to Empyrea' is literal. Maybe the seed will do the same."

"It's worth a shot if I can get close enough."

"I can make a rune to immobilize Kthon for you, but I may need another elixir, and Alim will have to feed it ether." Hali offered her dagger to Tio. "You'll need to defend yourself."

"This is the last elixir." Tio gave her a blue bottle in exchange, looking nervous at having a blade in his hands.

Creaking roots spread apart, and a shadowy claw darted inside. Rainbow light flashed forth, and the claw wriggled on the ground as it evaporated. Alim jumped through a starportal, hacking away at the invading tendrils.

"There's our muscle," Tio said. "And our distraction."

A shield spilled out from the metal dome on Alim's arm. "Yeah, sure, I can distract."

Alim led the way out with their shield raised against the incoming shadows. As soon as they were out from under Empyrea, the three dispersed. Hali had a rune in mind, but it would need to be massive. Larger than Hali's library back home.

Imagining the shape in her head, she shoved her broken dagger in the dirt and ran.

CHAPTER 41

An etheric blast rushed from Alim's extended hand, holding Kthon at bay in the sea of tall yellow grass as Hali and Tio took off. Black mist rippled off the hulking mass, with an orange shine underneath it like holding a light behind skin. Small hands wriggled out from the sides, gripping the meadow. Allowing it to push forward against Alim's celestial power.

Insides churning with the force of a hurricane, Alim used their free hand to shift their bangle into an axe and swipe at varying animal limbs attempting to grasp past them. Each burst into orange dust and trailed off in the wind. Pulse pounding and drenched in sweat, the etheric blast dwindled with the last of Alim's endurance.

A barrage of talons. Too many to deal with. Alim bashed the leading talon with their shield at the last moment, and ether exploded underneath them, assisting with their leap and carrying them far above the barrage and Kthon. On the descent, their axe bit into the neck of a goat-human hybrid head—Kthon grew more difficult to discern as time went on.

Chapter 41 Alim

Instead of severing it, the axe got stuck halfway through as Alim landed on its back. Same as in the Path, Kthon's sobbing stopped Alim in their tracks. All other sound faded, leaving only their own breathing and the crying.

I can't do this. A sharp spider-like leg pierced through Alim's side and raised them into the sky. Inside their mind, Alim heard a child's voice. *Forget me.*

An immense, crushing stress flooded Alim and, for a moment, memories overwhelmed them. Except not their own. None stayed long enough for Alim to tell what was happening.

Alim struggled not to black out. Empyrea's warmth embraced them like a miniature sun, bright enough to see vague fuzziness through their face-covering. It had been a while since Alim had felt a summer sun on their bare face, and it was a welcome distraction from becoming an Alim-kebab. Food. Now there was a real distraction.

Thoughts shifted to a world of kebabs, cakes, and brownies. Before they could drift into this edible realm, Alim's own face greeted them as a blob of light instead as Tio sat them down in a patch of mirror grass. *At least I don't have to see myself anymore.*

A soothing sensation accompanied mending flesh. Tio stopped the rejuvenation process without finishing, having only stopped the bleeding.

"You should be more careful, Alim," Tio said.

"Careful isn't in my repertoire these days."

"Hali is a bad influence on you." Tio had one of her etherite daggers. Evaporating black-and-white mist flowed off its orange-dust-stained blade. Had he cut them free? His skin appeared wooden, with claw marks where Kthon had raked his arm. Another nature gift power, or an eidolon trait?

"Hope you two are taking advantage of my distraction," Alim said.

"No such luck yet. Maybe you should work on your distracting skills?"

In the distance, Hali swiped at the ground with a shattered dagger using large, sweeping motions, running after each swing. The battlefield was slowly turning into one giant rune.

Rumbling. The meadow's yellow and mirrored grass became as blades and pierced through Kthon's four main legs as if made of steel, bending back through the dirt. Roots wrapped around its five heads—because of course it had five now—and wrestled it into submission.

A shadow crept up behind Tio and attacked, but Alim intercepted the blow. Colliding against Alim's shield, the shadowy snake bisected itself, allowing the other half to bite into Tio's wooden shoulder. It reeled Tio in, bringing him close to its ever-changing set of visages. Alim recalled their axe, dislodging it from one of Kthon's necks and brought it down upon the snake. As it chopped through, the snake became incorporeal, dropping Tio. Alim seized their axe from the air and transformed it into a spear. A second snake caught Tio by the wrist and Alim took aim. Blood churning, cramps froze Alim's arm before the throw, and they leaned against their spear, wheezing.

A flurry of human hands manifested from Kthon's wounds, tugging on loose flaps of shadow-skin. Each hand tore pieces of skin into thin strands and began to wrap Tio up in a cocoon of flesh.

Hali sprinted by Alim, deflecting several cat claws extending from one of many torsos. Kthon squealed as Hali thrust her broken dagger into an eye and used it to climb up and reach for Tio. A new head sprouted out and pushed Hali down. Right under a bear claw. Alim knocked Hali out the way, and the claw crushed them into the ground.

Someone called out. *New family.* A different voice this time—a woman's.

Alim's brain felt like cracked glass as they pushed against the bear claw with their back. They clumsily shoved the claw away, whirled around, and jabbed their spear into it. Only for a dangling extremity jutting from the bear limb's elbow to wrench the weapon from Alim.

A new bombardment of darkness sailed towards Alim then from Kthon's back. Lightheadedness set in as their blood consumed itself as fuel for the creation of two etheric tornados. The wrathful haze deflected most

Chapter 41 Alim

of the shadows, but a couple made it through and broke themselves against Alim's shield. The darkness exploded into a swarm of miniature pitch-black daggers, bouncing off the shield and arcing around it to embed into Alim. Breathing slowed. They desperately needed to return to the Path and recharge. *Wait. This is the Ethereal Realm… can I recharge here?*

Human faces molded in Kthon's shoulder and exhaled shadow snakes. Fangs sank into Alim's arm. Burning… it felt as if they were disintegrating from the inside. Rainbow steel carved the human faces off Kthon in a flash as Hali vaulted from the amalgamation and landed next to Alim. Grasping their arm, Hali hauled Alim away from Kthon.

"Get Tio out of there…" Alim mumbled as glowing white roots blocked the ethereal clouds and throbbing headaches coaxed consciousness away.

CHAPTER 42

Endless darkness in every direction, only interrupted by white ripples accompanying Tio's steps. Green light emanated as Tio held his hand out like a torch. The light only got lost in the void, not helping him see anything. All he could do was wander without direction.

Communing worked, but where's Kthon? There's nothing here. Immense pressure crawled into Tio with ease. Nothing like the catoblepas or the eidolons, Tio felt his own emotions, the fragmented emotions of Kthon's amalgamation, and great emptiness simultaneously. Beyond overwhelming, Tio had no defense here. Without proper care, he might become another part of Kthon.

Tio's aura danced in the dark as his arms and legs trembled so badly he couldn't walk. *Deep breaths. Hali and Alim are depending on you. Find the first celestial spirit. They'll know what to do, I hope.*

Hundreds of faces appeared. Laughing faces. Crying faces. Furious faces. A loud hum droned as they faded in and out. Unable to focus and trying to look everywhere at once, Tio closed his eyes and covered his ears.

Chapter 42 Tio

Shallow breaths. Aura weakening, it gave way to the shadow. Something thin and sharp grazed Tio's skull and bile burned his throat.

A woman with long, silky black hair kneeled in front of Tio, making sure they were eye to eye. Her yellow veil and fiery orange-and-red Solstoran dress stung to look at.

"Mom? Why are you leaving?" Tio asked, avoiding her eyes by finding every stain in their run-down concrete floors. "Can't I go with you?"

"Didn't you tell me you wanted to become a druid? That can't happen unless you go to Belsa."

"I don't know."

"That can't be your answer to everything, Tio. Changing your mind is okay. You're still young and there's plenty of time to decide." A murky gloom obscured his mom's face.

"I do want to be a druid," Tio said. "Animals will be better friends than people."

"Promise me you'll be friends with people too." Subtle static coated her words.

"People are the worst. All I need is a cat."

She twitched as black-and-white cracks distorted her skin. "Promise—" The strange woman's fingers grew into black tendrils and grazed Tio's cheek, scooping up his tears.

Tio bolted backward, crashing into a cabinet he hadn't realized was there. His brain rattled as a woman with familiar features approached him with a concerned frown. Black hair. Yellow veil. Orange-and-red dress. Who was she?

The strange woman tousled Tio's hair. "Are you nervous? You have a big future ahead. Grow. Make your own path in life."

Stop touching me—I don't know you. Tio scratched his wrist, searching for a non-existent bracelet to sate a habit he had yet to form.

"And please make some friends. For me," the strange woman said, evaporating into dust.

The house crumbled, and Tio returned to the dark with tear-stained cheeks. Wiping his face clean of tears—unsure how they'd appeared there to begin with—a crippling headache threatened to split Tio's head open. His aura hugged his skin, offering only scant protection against the encroaching dark. Tio didn't want to be here anymore. Regret. He regretted everything. *What made me think I could restore Empyrea? I'm not special.* This whole journey had been a waste of time. Worse, he'd wasted Hal… he'd wasted Ali… Who had helped him? *Did I come all this way on my own?*

Deep breaths. Tio stood on wobbly legs and held out his arm, bathing everything in a blinding emerald glow.

A corridor illuminated. With each painful step, it was as if he was relearning to walk. Shadows pounded against his aura, and although he flinched with each assault, Tio persevered.

The luminescent corridor led to ruined gemstone buildings. It reminded Tio of Strago and Stoneport, where he'd… done something? With his usual level of athleticism and finesse—none—Tio heaved himself over a short wall.

Collapsing on the other side, Tio gawked at fleshy orange tendrils with bark glued in patches, with purple slime wrapped around the walls. They encased a giant barn owl and held it against the ruins' decrepit ceiling. Tio yanked at the tendrils, but his hands only slipped on oozing slime. A strike with the rainbow dagger of mysterious origins didn't serve any better, bouncing off without a scratch. Sitting down and crossing his legs, Tio meditated. His aura breathed and expanded until it touched the owl.

"Get out of my head, druid."

"What's your name? I'm here to help."

"My name? I don't remember. It doesn't matter. Soon you'll forget too."

Forget? Tio's head felt like it might rupture when he heard the word.

Chapter 42 Tio

"I don't plan to be here long enough to forget anything. You're an eidolon. One of the living embodiments of Empyrea's roots. Your name…" He searched within the depths of the owl's mind. It was lined with holes. Gaps in knowledge, trying to drag him in to fill them.

"Your name is…" Tio inhaled, steadying his quivering body, and maintaining his meditation stance. "Anemo," he said while exhaling.

The owl's eyes flew open. Its screech bounced off the ruin walls and the slimy tendrils wilted, receding into the stone floor. Anemo's feathers ignited with a fiery blue aura. "Druid. I know whom you seek. Their connection to Kthon is what holds us together."

"What do you mean? Am I… seeking someone?" Tio asked.

"Kthon has already found your memories. You'll be one with us soon." Anemo tapped him closer with its blazing wing. "Stay near me—I'll lead the way."

Tio moved in lockstep with Anemo, leaving the ruins behind and entering another swathe of emptiness—this time pure white as far as he could see. Green and blue auras mixed while batting away innumerable shadows creeping from every direction.

One shadow broke through, its head twisting around as it ducked under Anemo's swiping wing. Tio stabbed a shadow with his dagger, but it was unaffected despite orange guts pouring from its wound. Lips formed in the shadow, making a moist clicking sound as they pulled back to reveal a bright orange smile that went from ear to ear. The head turned upside down and stretched at Tio as dozens of eyes opened one by one with the same unsettlingly moist clicks. Tio tripped, falling against Anemo.

Gusts of wind brushed against Tio's hair as Anemo snatched him in its talons and took off into the sky. Far below, creeping shadows chased, turning to small black dots as Anemo soared higher and higher. A repetitive thumping grew in volume as they approached an orange light, overtaking the flapping of Anemo's wings. The closer they drew, the dimmer the light grew and the louder the thumps.

Once through the light, a throbbing sack of flesh awaited. White veins stretched across thin purple skin, an orange glow shining through. It was shaped like a pulsating, beating heart and attached to squirming floors and walls composed of the same fleshy material. Two spirits were strapped to the walls with tendrils as Anemo had been. One looked to be constructed of white wood; the other black porcelain.

"Who are they?" Tio asked.

"Malakine," Anemo said. "Or what's left of them."

Tio scratched his hair, trying to place where he'd heard the name before. "Is that who I'm here to rescue?"

"No, you're looking for Kthon's first victim, in the heart—" Anemo rolled out of the way as fleshy limbs appeared from every direction, but two grabbed its wings and yanked it onto its back.

Tio fell from the owl's grip and crashed in front of the translucent heart. *Who's inside?*

Aura clashing against the orange glow of the heart, neither gained nor lost any territory. Static engulfed the unrelenting heartbeats, and tendrils slammed against Tio's aura, knocking him over. Orange began to overtake green.

Reaching up, Tio grazed the heart with a finger. Two auras within responded to his own. Tio attempted to commune only to be dragged away by a tendril and slung into sticky, ethereal sinew stretched between two lifeless dolls. One black porcelain and the other white wood crowned with branches. Somehow, Tio knew them. Spirits?

A message vibrated through the sinews, raking every bone. "Welcome back."

Have we met before?

"You don't remember me? A shame. I so enjoyed our meeting on Empyrea's branches."

A second vibration rocketed to Tio's antlers. Specks of green light shed from them, replaced by bright white light. Sticky sinew writhed as

Chapter 42 Tio

the light singed it. Eyes closed, images of a white-and-black spirit talking to Tio atop Empyrea flashed. "You're the first celestial spirit. Hali named you Ikazu and... you gave me my ethereal blood."

Burned sinew released one arm. Then the next. "I can free you, like I did with Anemo." Tio's skin turned to bark as he climbed across to Ikazu and reached for their hand.

"Detach me from Malakine's stitching. Remove me from Kthon's embrace. It is by their leeched sustenance I survive at all. Without Malakine or Kthon, there is no me."

"But you fought back against Kthon, right?" Tio asked.

"Perhaps I misrepresented my level of autonomy. This form you see." One branch at a time, Ikazu's crown wilted. "I am nothing more than a puppet. A tool for another to speak and interact where they cannot."

Tio racked his brain, trying to figure out what Ikazu meant. "But... you gave me ethereal blood. You speak as a celestial spirit."

"My memories, powers, and knowledge are locked within my ether. Free for use to those who know how."

"Who?"

"Look to the heart," Ikazu said as the ethereal sinews snapped.

Tio crashed against the damp, warm floor as flesh walls consumed Ikazu and Malakine.

Somebody new entered Tio's mind. *Leave this communion. Kthon has engorged on centuries' worth of Empyrea's ether. It is too late for the spirit tree to recover. Forget the Ethereal Realm and magic. Please take Sereia home.*

Who's Sereia? As if his brain were expanding, Tio's skull strained to remain intact against a surge of realization. This voice belonged to one of the auras inside the heart.

The second aura didn't speak. Only injected the image of an auburn-haired woman and the word *mom*.

Rasal? You're Rasal. And I'm... I'm here to free you. For Hali. Tio pushed his aura, feeling his blood vaporize as the tendril dangled him upside down.

Arboreal Path

No additional emotions, images, or thoughts came as Tio's aura intermingled with Rasal's.

"Wake up," Tio said as his green light overtook orange and consciousness waned. "Your mom needs you."

The beating heart quickened in response.

Something—everything was watching Tio. Cracks snaked across the white void. Thousands of drippy eyes set their gaze upon him.

"Let me in, Rasal."

Rashes snaked across Tio's arms. *Etheric drought?* Tio was numb. All pain faded. His aura connected to Rasal's as Kthon's unbearable presence coated Tio's eyes black.

Rasal made his only desire known. To be forgotten. The white void swirled together with darkness, creeping towards Tio and quashing his aura. The void congealed into a sludge, rising and overtaking him. Unable to move his limbs, Tio stretched his neck to keep himself above the flood as his flourish sputtered and the void snuffed out his light.

Tio awoke screaming. At least, he thought he was. No sound came despite the stinging in his throat.

Besides a tenfold-worse headache than Tio had ever experienced, he couldn't feel anything below his neck. Viscous goop spilled as sunlight poured in.

"Hold on, Tio!" Hali yelled as she swiped through the shadows puncturing Tio and connecting him to a throbbing cocoon.

Dust trailed behind Tio as Hali dragged him away from the flailing amalgamation Kthon had become. Pained wails pulsed waves of energy through the field and scraped bits of yellow grass into the air.

After making it to Empyrea's roots, Tio's wits returned. Reaching for his wrist to pinch the skin, Tio's hand came away dusty. *Oh no. This is me.* Tio craned his neck to find the left side of his body was flaking off.

Chapter 42 Tio

Disintegrating. Most of his left arm and leg were already gone. Hali was covered in it as she forced a blue elixir down his throat.

I doubt an elixir's going to do much now. Tio coughed up the gross-tasting liquid.

Hali set Tio next to Alim, who had fang marks on their arm with severe rot. From Empyrea's hill, it was clear to see how Hali had turned the meadow around Empyrea into a large rune with the spirit tree at its center. The symbol reminded him of a melting castle.

Alim gasped and bent Empyrea's leaking ether into Tio's crumbling body to no avail. "Hali, what can I do? Celestial magic has to be able to fix this, right? Or is there a rune?"

"You can't fight etheric death," Tio said with another cough. "I overused my flourish during my communion…"

"Etheric death? This isn't the plague?" Hali asked. "You can't die. Our Stranded Lands needs you."

Alim grimaced, pointing at Kthon. "What's happening?"

Tio smiled through the pain. "Your family is free."

Various limbs sprouted and fought each other on Kthon's body. An owl screeched. A baby's wailing followed, aging rapidly until an adult's battle shout replaced it.

"Tio, this is your doing?" Hali asked, grabbing his hand.

Emotions sank into Tio. Her self-blame. Self-hatred. No, those were miniscule. In this moment, worry for her friends and family overrode it all. Friends—the word retriggered his headache.

"I'm sorry. For everything I messed up. For you both. There's no fixing this. Nothing I can say or do to possibly atone." Hali's speech was slow and labored as if mid-marathon. "Yet you did this… why?"

Again with the sorry. "You're not as bad as you think."

"I don't deserve forgiveness."

"Everything happens regardless of deservedness." Tio's voice grew hoarse and bubbled as the disintegration spread.

Hali plucked a seed from his shoulder and took her dagger back, wrapping the seed around its hilt. "Well, you're getting my apology whether you deserve it or not. I'll set things right."

Alim said, "We'll see your mission through to the end, Tio. Empyrea will be restored."

Hali and Alim hugged Tio without so much as a complaint from him. In a way, it was comforting.

Returning memories inundated him, filling the remaining gaps left by Kthon's touch. *I kept my promise, Mom.*

CHAPTER 43

Diving between slamming tendrils and raking claws, Hali slashed through anything impeding her progress as Alim erected haze barriers to thwart errant assaults. Kthon, countless phantoms, the eidolons, Ikazu, Rev, and Rasal waged war within their shared writhing body. Tio had done that. Without him, Kthon would still have full control and success would be nigh impossible. With each moment Hali lingered around Kthon, dodging its attacks, the seed attached to her dagger sapped the shadow's ether and revealed a pale orange, fleshy underbelly with dozens of grasping red hand silhouettes bulging against a translucent membrane.

Hali slid across the field to the southern end of her enormous rune. "Did you charge up enough celestial energy, Alim? Channel ether into my rune. As much as you can."

Alim rubbed the rotting fang marks on their arm. "Not even close."

"Well, recharge and charge my rune at the same time. As soon as you feel etheric drought approaching, let me take over." *I can't lose you too.* "Let me handle Kthon."

Alim funneled multicolored ether into the rune's trenches, feeding its insatiable blood toll with one hand while the other was raised to keep themself energized. Broken dagger trembling in her off hand, Hali wiped orange muck from her intact blade onto her dress as she stood between Alim and Kthon.

A small bump tracked Hali along an exposed shoulder and down a black ethereal arm. Inverting in on itself, Kthon's original hollow-eyed face sprouted out and lunged at Hali with a stretching neck. Hali sidestepped and plunged her dagger under Kthon's chin. Black ether crept into the seed, leaving behind a husk of rotted wood. The left side of the wooden jaw clacked open and discharged blackened branches with a tremor-inducing shriek. Each branch sprouted a new shadow-infused wooden head, mouth agape and releasing more branches past Hali and at Alim. Wood cracked under Hali's dagger, but for every neck she sliced, three more sets appeared.

Dozens of wooden skulls cracked themselves upon Alim's haze barrier and exploded with black ether, disintegrating the barrier.

"I can't afford another barrier, Hali," Alim shouted, clouds of purple and pink tracing down their arms.

I'm well aware.

Carving a shrapnel rune into the dirt, Hali pressed her hand into it. With a tingle in her blood, chunks of strengthened dirt and stone shattered countless Kthon heads. "How're your ether reserves? Do I need to step in?"

"Please." Alim raised both hands. Wisps of color coated them.

Spikes of white wood erupted from Kthon's back, impaling the remaining Kthon heads before any reached Alim or Hali. *Thanks, Ikazu.*

Placing both hands down, Hali activated the colossal rune and set the blood within her veins ablaze. Ethereal light gushed across Empyrea's meadow and Kthon flopped onto his side, contorting. Animal and human limbs alike faded, leaving behind only the monstrous, faceless shadow of Kthon. *Goodbye, Rev… Rasal… you're free.*

Chapter 43 Hali

Eyes sprung open with an unsettling squish throughout shadow and flesh, all focusing their gaze on Hali. Shadows darted and clipped her legs. Alim intercepted one lunging flesh tendril with their shield as Hali tumbled under another. Catching herself, Hali threw her seeded dagger through one of Kthon's eyes. Incoherent convulsions ripped up swathes of yellow and mirrored grass, and glowing roots coursed through Kthon, bursting out in every direction. The remaining shadowy mist encasing Kthon disappeared as the seed absorbed the outer layer of ether. Sinewy, pulpy tissue was all that remained.

Phantoms leaked from Kthon's cavernous pores in droves, and a terrifying screech burst Hali's left ear as gray phantasmal fog enveloped the meadow. Kthon leaped onto Empyrea, scraping its bark and scooping out the orange innards. Ether pulled back into Kthon with every screech he unleashed, but not enough to ward himself from the phantoms tearing at his flesh. Orange, blue, and yellow ether intermingled and shot into the sky like a new set of ethereal lights, getting caught in the Lunar Vault's pull. Flesh ruptured and ether drained until nothing was left except for an emaciated black-and-white spirit glued together by dim tree roots. Malakine.

Two voices spoke as one. "My celestials. Why do you betray Empyrea?" Malakine's connective roots began to unravel.

Alim approached with careful steps, etherite bangle gyrating and reshaping into an axe.

"Stop." Hali clasped Alim's shoulder. "We can't kill the celestial spirit." *What might happen to Empyrea if we were to do that?*

"After everything Malakine has done?" Alim snatched their completed axe out of the air.

"Malakine wants what we want." Hali blocked Alim. "This is a time for a second compromise between mortals and spirits." *Rev would've wanted as much.*

"You can't be serious. The ethereal plague and Kthon were both Malakine. They killed Tio!"

I've done so much wrong for my family. Would I have done any different if I were Malakine?

"Mortals steal our power when left unchecked. Is Empyrea's current state not proof enough that the Corporeal Realm needs to be purged?" Malakine's head fractured down the middle, tearing further apart with every word. "Link with me and open the Lunar Vault. Empyrea will be healed."

"At the cost of turning Our Stranded Lands into Refulgent Wastes!" Alim's axe glowed orange before melding into yellow and blue, matching the three new ethereal colors.

"We can cut the Ethereal Realm off." *Would Tio be satisfied with a magicless world in exchange for Empyrea's survival?* "Give us time to figure out a way."

Split faces twitched until completely horizontal. "To separate the realms is to kill Empyrea. The phantasmal cycle must be preserved. My celestials, this is your burden. Link with me."

Alim looked back at Hali. "Phantasmal cycle?"

Empyrea gathers phantoms. Its roots expel ether. Sparks are… "Our magic is sourced from the dead?" *Empyrea created spirits too. Were they also made from phantoms?*

"Link. With. Me!" Electricity darted between Malakine's halves.

Sorry, Tio. Hali held out her broken dagger. "We're not dooming our realm for the sake of magic."

"My Vault. My plague. My Kthon." Bolts of ethereal lightning struck Malakine, melting their halves into each other and spiraling them together. "My celestials. My Empyrea."

Malakine created the Vault? The ethereal plague? This has never been about ether for them. Wiping out the Corporeal Realm was Malakine's intention from day one.

"Killing you and keeping Kthon locked away is the one good thing I've done in the past five hundred years. Mortals don't need magic. Not if it means keeping you linked to Empyrea."

Chapter 43 Hali

"Hali—" Ethereal currents jolted through Alim and they buckled to the patchy dirt.

"Useless. Purge. Cleanse." Malakine channeled another bolt, but a wave of water splashed into existence and redirected it back at the celestial spirit, dissolving their white half.

Undine conjured her ice maul and slammed Malakine into Empyrea's trunk.

Hali dug through her rune book, searching for anything to help while longing for the power of her tattoos. Alim groaned as Undine doused their wounds in restorative green water. Another bolt arced from Malakine's stable half, but Alim caught it with their celestial magic just before it struck Hali.

Veins swelled in Alim's arms as they contained the shuddering ether into a ball. Haze leaked from Alim's pores like sweat.

No, you can't leave me alone. Hali threw her book aside, grabbed the nearly emptied elixir and poured its last drops into Alim's mouth.

Alim hurled the lightning ball into Malakine with a deafening boom. The celestial spirit's remains dripped from Empyrea, their two mouths mumbling incoherent words.

Enough spirits and eidolons had died already. If Malakine died, it would be catastrophic for both realms. "Let me bind Malakine."

"And have another Kthon inside you? We'd be back where we started, and Tio would have died for nothing."

"Tio didn't die for my freedom. He died for my family's freedom. For the continuation of magic." Hali removed her binding-rune ring. "And although Malakine will become my 'burden,' they will be bound in this ring. My body will be a prison no more."

Hali pressed her ring into Malakine's molten puddle and ignited her blood, activating the ring's rune. Black-and-white ether gurgled as it soaked into the ring, sealing shut with scattered bands of mist.

"I'll find a safe place to keep the ring. Away from Empyrea and people alike." *Maybe my home? Its ether surge has no connection to the Ethereal*

Arboreal Path

Realm and Sipherra couldn't get in either. "Once more, Empyrea is without a celestial spirit."

"The spirits will convene soon. Empyrea's future must be discussed," Undine said.

Rising to her feet, Hali looked to Empyrea. The phantoms swimming amongst its tall branches absorbed into the tree and gray billows escaped the bark. Hali followed behind Alim to where they'd left Tio and helped Alim wrap him in his green Conclave cloak.

It should be me in this bundle, not you.

Undine bubbled and plucked the last seed from the cloak. "Empyrea will remember your efforts, Keeper."

Alim kneeled. "When we get back, we'll make sure Belsa celebrates your life." They blubbered out a chuckle. "It's your fault I can't look at mosquitos the same way anymore and have to think twice when I'm tempted to pick a flower. But I failed you as a bulwark and a friend. My time will be spent observing the world through your lens, so I can better appreciate living things as you did."

Hali crouched next to Alim. "Your sacrifice may go unnoticed by the people of Our Stranded Lands—and I'm sure you prefer it that way—but the effects will be known to all." *If only you were here to see it.* "For a self-proclaimed people hater, you forgave too easily. Cared too much. Forgot to think of yourself." *What you did for my family is a debt of immeasurable magnitude.* "There will be no rest in my future until Empyrea, the spirits, and the eidolons are all restored."

The three bathed in silence, lost in time, as phantoms swam between them and climbed to Empyrea's great heights.

"Death brings life. Return to Empyrea and be reborn in the joining." Opening her rune book to the flame-tooth rune, Hali's blood tingled as she leaned close and breathed a puff of blue flame onto the cloak's fig leaf.

CHAPTER 44

Intermixing blue, orange, and yellow ethereal energy swirled around Alim's hands before they guided it onto Empyrea's mangled root. Shimmering wood grew layers of bark over exposed orange flesh.

Stepping back, Alim scanned for the next wound and spotted a trail of green ether flowing up through the jungle of tree-height iridescent blue mushrooms. This gash was much smaller. With a slight twinge in their blood, it was sealed.

The last one. Time to turn back.

With Empyrea's wounds patched up, pressure cascaded off Alim's shoulders. Even the ether-hungry Lunar Vault had shrunk to half its original size. So miniscule was the amount of ether drifting to the Vault, only ethersight could detect it. Closing the Vault was their next task, as Hali had done once before on the Corporeal Realm side when she first became a celestial.

Crossing a mushroom-top bridge to Empyrea's meadow, Alim found Undine gathering soil into a wooden pail.

"Was that the last of the wounds?" Undine asked.

"Yes, we're finally done."

"Can we visit him?"

Alim tapped their braids in anticipation. "That's the plan of course!"

They walked in silence into the dandelion forest. A constant flow of large seeds floated down from the canopy on purple parachutes, like a giant had blown on the trees to make a wish come true. Seeing how far they could go without stepping on dandelion fuzz made for a peaceful distraction. Anything to distract from the task at hand, made all the easier by the thick, fluffy canopy blocking Empyrea and the Lunar Vault from view. The deeper they got, the more coated the floor was, increasing the difficulty. Alim hopped between the purple patches with increasing pace, until they tripped and fell, rolling into one of the thick flower stems.

"You done?" Hali closed her book with care. "Tio's waiting for us."

Hali led Alim to an ashen mound of dirt.

"Undine, do you have it?" Alim asked.

Dumping her pail of soil onto the mound, Undine handed Empyrea's sprouting seed to Alim.

Alim wanted to give Tio a proper druid burial, and he had earned the same important trees he'd given to the eidolons. Would it even grow? Tio had said there was no shame in a burial tree that didn't grow, but nothing would frustrate Alim more.

Tio, our work is complete! Empyrea is healed. Today we close the Lunar Vault and go home. Our visits will be less frequent, but don't worry. Hali and I will come back and let you know how things are going.

Alim pushed the seed into the soil and Undine stuck a finger in, soaking it in her nature-infused water. A little glowy green twig greeted the Ethereal Realm. One day, it may rival Empyrea. At least Alim could dream.

Hali placed the book she was reading on the mound. "Absolute romantic garbage. Just how you liked it. Don't worry, there's more where that came from."

Chapter 44 Alim

"You had a romance book lying around? Here? I thought you hated that genre."

Hali gave a Tio-style shrug. "A book's a book. Sometimes you'll read anything when your options are exhausted." She pointed to the jagged blue scar in the sky. "Now you need to deal with that. And yes, before you ask, that means no more ethereal lights."

Solstice will be a less beautiful time without it, but I've had my fill of ethereal lights.

Hopefully this will allow Refulgent Wastes to recover. Thauma will be Thauma again. Or at least prevent future wayward spirits from repeating Malakine's fanatical plans.

"I get how closing the Vault will stop Empyrea's bleeding, but is that enough? Doesn't Empyrea need a celestial spirit? What happens with Malakine locked up?"

"Too many questions. Too few answers." Hali shook her head. "I don't know. We have to wait for the spirits."

"I volunteer Undine." A small flaming child emerged from Empyrea's dandelion-coated root.

Undine took her focus off Tio's tree. "Vulkine?"

Nomine slid in next to Vulkine, rumbling affectionately.

"Me? Celestial spirit?" Undine asked.

"Who better? You were there when the first celestial spirit was lost just as Malakine was. Yet you didn't come to hate as they did."

"Excuse me, you're older than me. You were there too," Undine said, bubbling.

Vulkine's flames brightened. "Kthon has rendered me rather useless for the job."

Nomine beckoned to Undine.

"Fine, if you both agree." Undine turned to Alim. "Our link is finished. I will become trapped in Empyrea while my celestial powers grow, but you can always see me in the Path."

"You're not going to start calling me 'my celestial' are you? I think I preferred 'this flesh.'"

Undine flicked water into Alim's face. "'My friend' works as well." She bowed as she placed a hand on Empyrea's root. "Goodbye, Alim." Undine vanished alongside Vulkine and Nomine.

Hali grasped Alim's shoulder. "You okay?"

Sniffling, Alim followed Tio's mantra, exhaling the biggest breath they'd ever taken. "No. A lot has happened. Can't even process it all—I'm sure this is going to hit me like a ton of bricks in a couple of days." Alim tapped their braids. "How do I close the Vault?"

"When it does hit, talk to me. A good cry would do us both good." Hali's eyes glistened as she scratched her head like she was also channeling Tio's unconfident energy. "Create a haze barrier over the Vault, as you've done before but on a much larger scale."

"How do we know somebody else won't open it back up?"

"Celestial-controlled ether holds up better than natural ether. We'll revisit periodically to refresh your connection to it just in case."

"Sipherra won't be able to use a reactor to absorb it either?" Alim asked.

"If they could, the etherite golem at Wilton would have broken my seal on the Vault. And mine is five hundred years old at this point. Same deal with my haze barrier at Und dal Sylph manor."

At least there was comfort in that. If Allister couldn't prevent Sipherra from continuing down the course set before it by Geno, then at least they wouldn't be able to doom Our Stranded Lands.

Grasping the last cloud of blue ether, Alim piled it into the Lunar Vault. As if part of a puzzle, they had to twist the haze into the exact shape of the scar. Every jag. Every crevice. Every splotch. Once it was adjusted, Alim was able to push it forward and lock it in place. A cyclone plowed inside Alim's blood as the haze hardened and a barrier sealed the Vault.

Burning veins cooled, and Alim amped themself up to open a starportal by slapping their cheeks.

Chapter 44 Alim

"What are you doing? Rest." Worry wrinkled Hali's brow.

"I'm tired of eating bizarre, bland plants. And... I need to get away from here. No more celestial stuff. At least for a while. Maybe say hi to my folks in the Mudplains or something." Alim pulled the threads of reality apart until a perfectly rectangular doorway of stars materialized. Extending a hand to Hali, Alim said, "Let's go home."

Hali grabbed hold. "Let's."

The Ethereal Realm dissolved, making way for the Arboreal Path's elemental-constellation-filled milky-coffee sky. The blinding root-road seemed wider than last time. Orange, yellow, and blue lights snaked around them, constructing a pathway before disappearing through a starportal.

"There's one last thing I wanted to try." Stars were ether, same as the moons and the Lunar Vault. If Alim could affect the Vault, maybe they could affect the stars.

Milky swirls above parted with Alim's swinging hands. Bright green lights streaked together. Split apart. Until a five-pronged fig leaf lit the sky alongside the whirlpool, tree, flame, mountain, and tornado.

"That's sweet," Hali said. "Clever use of celestial magic. Tio would have loved it, you know?"

"Think so?"

"Hold on, are you seeing this?" Hali asked, pointing at the darkness off the side of Empyrea's trailing roots.

"No..." Alim channeled a ball of ether and detonated it over the edge, sprinkling harmless glitter across the darkness. Still nothing.

Hali walked out without falling, gasping as if gawking at marvelous sights. "Come on!" She dragged Alim off the road.

Alim stumbled, but an unseen floor caught them. "Can you describe it to me?" they asked while readjusting their blindfold.

"It's... a jungle? Never seen anything like it. Not in Spirit Arboretum, surges, or the Ethereal Realm. Everything is soaked in ether. How can you not see it? This—I don't think the Path is a mere road in-between realms anymore. The Arboreal Path is an Arboreal Realm." Hali pulled Alim forward and placed their hand against something scaly.

A wet hand grabbed Alim's. Orange light filled their left eye, and yellow filled their right. From above, blue pierced the veil of darkness and Alim saw. Saw everything. Detail returned to the world. Undine's root-entangled face looked back at them from a mountain of fish-like rainbow scales as she released Alim's hand.

The world dimmed, but a blue light continued shining from Alim's forehead.

"Being a celestial spirit has taught me a lot," Undine said. Floating stars sparkled inside her face. "Our link transcends stars. So long as you are within my realm, my eye is yours."

"It's beautiful." Hali poked Alim's forehead. "Like a lotus blossom."

"You weren't gone long. How did you have time to learn anything?" Alim asked Undine.

"Time within Empyrea is… more unusual even than the Ethereal Realm itself. The ether you restored has gone to good use. New spirits and seeds within decades, maybe even years, instead of centuries! I'm still stuck here… there's much more to learn. I wish I could go with you to explore this new realm our efforts created."

As Hali had stated, verdant jungle expanded in all directions, painted in the six ethereal colors.

Taking a step back, Alim realized the scaly mountain of shimmering rainbows was not a mountain at all. It was a tree, taller than any they'd seen other than Empyrea itself, jutting from the earth and splitting at the top like a whale's tail.

Rings of ethereal haze pulsed off the trunk, wafting through branches covered in white leaves fluffier than a lion's mane. Thorns the size and shape of antlers snaked across the branches alongside large, ethereal-colored pods thumping with chaotic green light.

"Undine, what is this tree?" Alim asked.

Chapter 44 Alim

"The culmination of this new realm. Kthon's unleashed ether expanded our surges to the point where complete consumption was inevitable for the Corporeal Realm."

"You created this tree to stop the surges?" Between the foliage, Alim recognized familiar domed formations with the slight glint of steel underneath. Further in the distance, a wheel of flowers rotated and flickered with dim lights. *We're in Wilton!*

"No. Vulkine, Nomine, and I agreed to remove the wall between your realm and the Arboreal Path. This was the best compromise."

"Compromise? Like the one that gave us our sparks?" Hali asked.

"Yes. By doing so, we merged the surges with the Path and rerouted the rampaging ether to Empyrea's roots. Such was not enough to contain it... but this tree grew in the aftermath and absorbed what Empyrea could not."

"Is this another spirit tree?" Alim asked.

"No. Whatever this tree is, it's new to us. It exists in the Corporeal Realm, where spirit trees cannot grow, but its roots are tangled with Empyrea's and cross between realms—linking them together not unlike how we were once linked."

"Then... the Arboreal Realm has taken over a portion of the Corporeal Realm?" Alim's thoughts turned to Charlie, Allister, and Wilton's many residents. "Did anybody survive?" *If this realm has haze barriers or requires starportals to get in or out, people would have no way to escape. How quickly did this spread?*

"No mortals have been within this realm since Empyrea brought me here." Undine bubbled with ethereal foam. "I don't know." Her face began to sink into the tree.

"Wait!" Alim called out as they grasped for Undine's disappearing hand.

"We can check for survivors," Hali said. "Perhaps Undine's senses aren't as strong as eidolons. Or the size makes it impossible."

"Allister and Charlie were holed up in the library—we should go there first," Alim said.

"That's close by." Hali hiked in the opposite direction of the distant wheel.

Everybody better be safe. Alim chased after her through impossibly thick undergrowth.

A massive block of flowers—each bigger than Alim's head—and grass crawled across glass. It reminded them of a three-story greenchurch, but without a lick of green. Tangled in vines on the steps leading to Wilton's old library was the etherite golem. The same one responsible for triggering an early solstice.

Wiping a layer of dusty moss from its head, a dim light emitted from beady eyes and bounced off text etched into its arm.

> *A second solstice, new colors bright and fun.*
> *Sky vault split with brilliant light, blonde as my bun.*
> *Hail falls and glimmers like pumpkin-dyed treasure.*
> *With warm embrace, my solstice ends in azure.*

"Second solstice?" Hali ripped a hidden flyer from under a layer of thorny vines on the library's glass door. "This says the same thing. Has to be the ether Undine mentioned, you know?"

"There was a second wave of ethereal lights after you were taken to the Ethereal Realm. Same colors as the ether Kthon unleashed. What else does it say?"

Hali handed it over.

> *I hereby order Wilton's evacuation. Follow the routes as marked. Nobody is to deviate, not even to your homes, lest you throw away the efforts of the two engineers whose lives were lost maintaining our barrier against the overwhelming Second Solstice. Leave behind anything except food. When this is over, valuables and keepsakes will be retrieved by Dreamers, including our golem protector as a monument to all those lost to the ethereal lights.*
> *Allister Wyn of Gren Consortium*

Chapter 44 Alim

An attached note included a map of Grenvel drawn on it. Red arrows weaved from Oressa and Wilton to Gren City. Did the Arboreal Realm extend all the way to East Peaks? *If it extends to all the surges, does that include the ones that didn't have barriers?*

"They survived then." Hali fiddled with her ring.

The gemstones from Charlie's locket were embedded into the golem's joints, keeping them from falling apart. "Charlie kept the golem going after two other engineers died trying. She performed a miracle."

"Yeah. More than one." Hali squeezed her ring and slipped it into her dress pocket. "Could you... open a starportal to Thauma? Und dal Sylph Manor." Her words were brittle, as if a gentle nudge might destroy her.

Right. Go say goodbye to your family. "Sure. Flare up your etheric signature using a big blood toll if you need me. If not... meet me back at Gren City." Alim hugged Hali like they'd never see each other again.

"Now I know how Tio felt. Calm down and quit your blubbering."

Hali returned the hug with surprising strength. Alim's spine gave a satisfying pop as if their stress was locked between the bones.

"But in case I don't see you for some time, I'm proud of you." She spun, gesturing with wide arms. "The abundant new life around us. This was you and Tio. All I did was get in the way."

Alim found a finger pressing their mouth shut before they could retort.

"Don't try to give me any credit. I don't want it. Let yourself feel a sense of pride for once." Hali forced Alim to nod in agreement.

"Thanks," Alim sighed. Blood churned as they chiseled a starportal into existence, focusing its tunneling power to the surge around Hali's home.

Hali looked back, said, "Sorry," and disappeared through the gateway.

Had to sneak one of those in, eh?

Alim weaved a tall basket-backpack from etherite and filled it with golem pieces. With each part, their mind wandered, concern growing thick as Empyrea's roots. Would the Arboreal Realm truly be a place where spirits and mortals coexisted in peace? Where nature and civilization thrived together? Or was this merely one of Undine's fanciful dreams? Alim tapped their celestial eye, hitched the basket onto their back and began the trek to Gren City.

CHAPTER 45

Crystalline teal water reflected a bedazzling sunset from far below the cliff as Hali's feet dangled over the edge of her family manor's roof. Hali lifted the carved copper lion, complete with raspberry hanging from its mouth, and set it in her lap, turning it to face the shimmering Lungs. The binding rune throbbed, still sore from where an "R" had been carved through the bottom of its silver circle. With this addition, Hali's only remaining runic tattoo had been rendered inert.

It was an empty feeling. Life without Ikazu's ever-present protection. Knowing she could never again relive moments with Rev. Never feel Rasal's joy at experiencing those memories alongside her. For some seventy years, Hali had known but one ambition—to release her family's phantoms from Kthon, one way or another. An eternity of peace within Empyrea awaited Rev and Rasal, but how long would Hali have to wait until she could join them? Without them, what else mattered? The weight of their torment had been lifted, only for the loss of a new friend to linger in its place.

Give me one more day with my family, Alim. I have a lifetime of apologizing to catch up on for Rev and Rasal both.

Hali slipped the binding-rune ring from her pocket and admired Charlie's craftsmanship. The gemstones sparkled as if coated by celestial magic. Brighter even than Tio's contagious giggle. Hali took a green cloak-scrap—her only reminder of Tio—and used it to tie the ring to the lion statuette's tail. Sorrow dripped onto the lion's mane as Hali clung to it and lay back against the roof. Distant wavering lake water and dancing ethereal haze lulled Hali to the first peaceful sleep she'd had since the shadow had donned Rasal's face.

Glossary

Arboreal Path, the: Existing between the Corporeal Realm and the Ethereal Realm, this connective world allows celestials to recharge their power and connect to each of the elements.

Celestial: A mortal with the power to control ether itself. Celestials of the past were thought of as heroes, having defeated the Old Faith, sealed the Lunar Vault, and cured the ethereal plague.

Conclave, the: A council of three druid leaders. Currently they have no power outside the city of Belsa.

Corporeal Realm, the: A word used by scholars to describe the world in which mortals reside as opposed to the Ethereal Realm's world of gods, spirits, and mystical beasts.

Coveted South, the: Everything southeast of Phantasmal Reef. The countries of the Coveted South are thought to be centuries ahead of Our Stranded Lands in technology and quality of life.

Diya: An island off the shore of Thauma and the homeland of the Iogu. Known for magical artifacts, basic machines, and its many freedoms due to a lack of government.

Dreamers, the: A company of mercenaries. They're well known for repelling a Diyan invasion of Grenvel and for sending explorers deep into Refulgent Wastes.

Druid: A human born with the nature gift. Rare and weak in modern times, they can speak to animals and plants.

Eidolon: An animal-tree hybrid borne from the linking of a special type of immortal animal and a spirit. Thought to be an extension of the spirit tree in the Corporeal Realm.

Ether: The source of magic.

Ether Surge: These ether-dense regions form due to the presence of an eidolon. When the eidolon is not linked to a spirit, the surge will have no barrier and the eidolon may wander, which gradually shifts the surge's location. Sometimes shortened to "surge."

Ethereal Realm, the: A word used by scholars to describe the world of gods, spirits, and mystical beasts.

Etherite: A rainbow metal first found in East Peaks by Sipherra. It is the metal of choice for any celestial or spirit and is stronger than anything mortals can currently manufacture due to a shortage of enchanted artifacts.

Empyrea: The name druids gave to the spirit tree. Though some have started to worship it like a deity, most only liken Empyrea to a story about the origin of ether and magic.

Familiar: An animal with which a druid has a strong bond of friendship.

Flourish: Formerly used throughout *Our Stranded Lands*, this term is used in the city of Belsa to refer to the type of magic a human was born with.

Gift: The most popular term in Our Stranded Lands for referring to the type of magic a human was born with.

Golem: A lifeless puppet constructed from an element to allow a mage to control it. Modern designs improved the concept by encasing the element in durable metals.

Gren Consortium: The leadership council of Grenvel with representation from the libraries, mage academies, merchants, and mercenaries.

Grenvel: Due to the devastation experienced by the rest of Our Stranded Lands, Grenvel became the largest and most influential country. It's most known for being the largest supplier of food and its rising technology.

Haze Barrier: A wall of fog created by ether surges when a spirit links with an eidolon, which keeps any mortal from getting inside. Eidolons are connected to their barrier and can sense when anybody interferes with it.

Logu: A species of mortal known for their ability to enchant objects with various magical augmentations.

Lunar Vault, the: Formerly Nihali, one of the three ethereal moons. Its destruction nearly caused a catastrophic event and now is left as a lingering green scar in the sky. Sometimes shortened to "the Vault."

Mage: A human born with the air, water, earth, or fire gifts. They can telekinetically control their gifted element.

Old Faith: An old religion which betrayed the people of Grenvel, triggering a rise in atheism and a distrust of runic magic.

Glossary

Our Stranded Lands: Everything north of Phantasmal Reef, including Grenvel, Wolloisha, Diya, and Refulgent Wastes.

Phantasmal Reef: Blackened waters filled with the gray clouds of phantoms and streaks of silver lightning. Formed after the Quake tore the land between Wolloisha and the South asunder. The Reef stretches across the continent and circles Our Stranded Lands, preventing any ship from crossing.

Phantom: The ghost-like remains of dead mortals. Though a rare occurrence, phantoms were thought to roam the Corporeal Realm if the deceased were to die without spilling their blood on solid ground. Once Phantasmal Reef formed, no sightings of phantoms were reported elsewhere.

Quake, the: A world-altering event which sunk a significant portion of Wolloisha and Diya and separated the north from the south by creating Phantasmal Reef.

Rune: A word from the language of the spirits. When written, the word siphons blood in exchange for a powerful spell in any variety of elements or effects. Due to an association with the Old Faith and the rise of natural-borne magical gifts, runes fell out of use.

Sipherra: A mining company which grew rapidly after discovering etherite. Their expansion into experimental technologies gained the company influence throughout Grenvel.

Solstora: The sun worshipping religion of Wolloisha.

Spark: A term used in *Thauma* to reference the type of magic a human was born with.

Spirit: Beings composed of magic, thought to live in the Ethereal Realm.

Thauma (Refulgent Wastes): A country once ravaged by a magic-eating plague. The attempt to cure the plague left the land blighted, forcing its people to evacuate to the Coveted South.

Tovaloreande Sanctuary: Created by a rebellious Old Faith priest, whose death was thought to be the origin of natural-borne magic and sparked a rebellion against the Old Faith. Sometimes shortened as "the Sanctuary."

Wolloisha: The southern-most country of Our Stranded Lands, Wolloisha is home to mountains, deserts, and the Solstoran religion.

Acknowledgements

Arboreal Path is my first novel, and I couldn't have done it alone.

To YOU, for taking the time to read Arboreal Path. Yes, even you, the one who flipped straight to the back for some reason. If you enjoyed the experience don't forget to like, comment, and subscribe… oops, wrong platform. Just leave an honest review on Amazon, Goodreads, or your preferred social media! Or go oldschool and share your copy with a friend.

To my mom and sister, for being my first beta readers and number one fans! Your encouragement and feedback went a long way to making this possible. Arboreal Path is a success so long as you two enjoy the read, even if I did cheat by making it about druids.

To Fenril, Ekirei, Seph, Sylex, Neosis, Drei, Chris, and Telos for being part of my crazy chatroom RPG antics in the early 2000's. Who knew all that writing would come in handy? Those adventures we had were a big inspiration for Arboreal Path's world and characters.

To Starfyre for getting me back into reading. I wouldn't have decided to try my hand at writing otherwise.

To Erin Young, for collaborating on this project with me. And by collaboration, I mean doing all the work while I fumbled with my keyboard until something resembling a story came out. You identified themes and areas of intrigue I didn't even know were there. Without your diligent assistance, this story would not be what it is—a book I'm proud of.

To Casey Gerber, for creating three wonderful book covers and adding a touch of professional beauty to the book's interior with great character illustrations, a detailed map, and fancy lil' flourishes.

To Laura Kinkaid, for helping put the final touches on the novel!

About the Author

Jason M. Vallery, Lover of Cats, Demolisher of Snacks, Video Game Encyclopedia.

Creating characters, worlds, and stories has always been a favorite pastime of mine, from text-based role-playing games, multi-user dungeons (MUDs), multiplayer role-playing games, to short stories. Learning to apply those experiences towards writing was a fun and exciting challenge which has resulted in my first novel, *Arboreal Path*.

Now, if you'll excuse me… I need to go play with my cats, delve into some video games, and catch up on books!

CPSIA information can be obtained
at www.ICGtesting.com
Printed in the USA
LVHW090308201021
700928LV00011B/525/J